S0-AGX-929

THE SPELL'S THE THING—

to conjure wealth, defeat enemies, entrap demons, or grant a noble lord or lady all the power he or she could desire—for good or ill. So join those who have mastered the arcane arts as they work their magic in such tales of enchantment as:

"The Bane of Trigeminy"—He was the finest student at the Wizards' Academy with a brilliant future ahead of him—if he could just pass one *final* test. . . .

"The Dead That Sow"—She was a healer but she was still an outsider and, despite the many services she'd done them, the villagers would rather see her sent to the Wizard's castle than sacrifice one of their own. . . .

"Frog Magic"—He'd fallen for one of the oldest tricks in a wizard's repertoire, and if he'd didn't find a way to break the transformation spell soon, he'd probably spend the rest of his life eating flies—and enjoying it, too!

WIZARD FANTASTIC

More Spellbinding Anthologies Brought to You by DAW:

ELF FANTASTIC *Edited by Martin H. Greenberg.* They are beings of legend from a realm just beyond our own, a kingdom where time holds little power, where beauty casts its aura over the natural world, and where magic can transform anything—or anyone. So let such spellcasters as Jane Yolen, Andre Norton, Dennis McKiernan, and Elizabeth Ann Scarborough reveal the perils and promises of elvish magic in stories that may lead the unsuspecting into the fairy hills only to emerge into a world far different from the one they left behind.

TAROT FANTASTIC *Edited by Martin H. Greenberg and Lawrence Schimel.* Some of today's most imaginative writers—such as Charles de Lint, Tanya Huff, Rosemary Edghill, Nancy Springer, Kate Elliott, Teresa Edgerton, and Michelle West—cast fortunes for the unsuspecting in sixteen unforgettable tales ranging from chilling to whimsical, from provocative to ominous.

CASTLE FANTASTIC *Edited by John DeChancie and Martin H. Greenberg.* Here are sixteen original stories created especially for this volume, from the final tale set in Roger Zelazny's unforgettable *Amber,* to the adventure of a floating castle in search of a kingdom, to the legendary citadel of King Arthur. Join such master architects of enchantment as Roger Zelazny, George Zebrowski, Jane Yolen, David Bischoff, and Nancy Springer on a series of castle adventures that will have fantasy lovers, and D&D players begging for the keys to the next keep on the tour.

WIZARD
FANTASTIC

EDITED BY Martin H. Greenberg

DAW BOOKS, INC.
DONALD A. WOLLHEIM, FOUNDER
375 Hudson Street, New York, NY 10014

ELIZABETH R. WOLLHEIM
SHEILA E. GILBERT
PUBLISHERS

Copyright © 1997 by Tekno Books.

All Rights Reserved.

Cover art by John Howe.

DAW Book Collectors No. 1072.

All characters and events in this book are fictitious.
Any resemblance to persons living or dead is strictly coincidental.

If you purchase this book without a cover you should be aware that this book
may have been stolen property and reported as "unsold and destroyed" to
the publisher. In such case neither the author nor the publisher has received
any payment for this "stripped book."

First Printing, November 1997
1 2 3 4 5 6 7 8 9

DAW TRADEMARK REGISTERED
U.S. PAT. OFF. AND FOREIGN COUNTRIES
—MARCA REGISTRADA
HECHO EN U.S.A.

PRINTED IN THE U.S.A.

ACKNOWLEDGMENTS

Introduction © 1997 by Martin H. Greenberg.

In the Service of Mages © 1997 by Dennis L. McKiernan.

Ilian © 1997 by Josepha Sherman.

Hell's Mark © 1997 by Jane M. Lindskold.

The Bane of Trigeminy © 1997 by Mickey Zucker Reichert.

A Thing or Two About Love © 1997 by Richard Parks.

The Dead That Sow © 1997 by Michelle West.

Frog Magic © 1997 by Andre Norton.

How the Wild Hunt Came to Trygvadal © 1997 by Diana L. Paxson.

The Yellow of the Flickering Past © 1997 by Dean Wesley Smith.

Soul Catcher © 1997 by Linda P. Baker.

Wizard's Choice © 1997 by Janet Pack.

Mastery © 1997 by Sherwood Smith.

Bird Bones © 1997 by Jody Lynn Nye.

Willy Wizard's Magicland © 1997 by Connie Hirsch.

Visible Breath © 1997 by Nina Kiriki Hoffman.

Familiar Territory © 1997 by Kristine Kathryn Rusch.

Spellchucker © 1997 by John DeChancie.

Proving Ground © 1997 by M. Turville Heitz.

The Wizard of the Birds © 1997 by Jane Yolen and Adam Stemple.

Mirror, Mirror, on the Lam © 1997 by Tanya Huff.

Of Tides and Time © 1997 by Dennis L. McKiernan.

CONTENTS

INTRODUCTION

When the word wizard is mentioned, what do you think of? The flowing robes of Merlin as he practices his sorcery? The painted face and gourd rattle of a Native American shaman? The intricate rituals and spells of an Oriental geomancer, or perhaps the wild ceremonial mask and frenzied dancing of an African witch doctor?

Different cultures all over the world have always been fascinated by things or events they cannot explain. When people in these societies claim to do what is commonly held to be unexplainable, often they are called magicians, or, in times gone by, wizards.

Even those who would not consider themselves to be unearthly or arcane in any way fall under this rule. When the Spanish first came to Mexico, many of the native races fled in fear when the conquistadors came riding along on their horses, which didn't exist in Central America. Now keep in mind that the Incas and Aztecs both controlled powerful, advanced empires in their own right, claiming such innovations as their own calendar and the cultivation of corn. But when the Europeans came with their metal armor and matchlock rifles, these mighty empires proved helpless against the "powerful magic" of the foreigners.

As Arthur C. Clarke postulated, "Any sufficiently advanced technology is indistinguishable from magic." After all, to a sixteenth century Native American, what's the difference between a metal-clad man who kills by pointing a stick at someone, and a scaly green

9

alien who kills just by looking at someone? Anyone or anything with sufficient power to back him (or it) up would be viewed as a wizard or, in some cases, like the supposed "ancient astronauts," as gods.

Of course, there were also charlatans throughout history, those who said they could do magic and couldn't, disguising their false claims with slick talk and various potions and devices that they claimed would "do just the trick." Unlike the genuine wizards of legend, these tricksters and con men rarely survived for long.

Magicians became even more common in the Middle Ages with the advent of alchemy, a "scientific" way of doing magic. As laughable as alchemy is today, its practitioners were on the right track. The track that led to science, that is. When the Renaissance occurred in the thirteenth through the fifteenth centuries, it pretty much wiped out most traces of magic that had existed up to then, removing it under the inexorable advance of science and technology.

Nowadays, science is the rule, not the exception. Magic today is practiced only by those who work their spells within the confines of a laboratory, such as quantum physicists and others who work in worlds invisible to the naked eye. Their wizard's tower has been replaced by a laboratory, the magic tome supplanted by the computer, arcane words of power discarded for complex chemical equations.

And yet, there are still true sorcerers in existence today, even as you read this. Men and women able to bring entire worlds into existence with a wave of their pen. Well, nowadays it's usually a mouse or a keyboard, but the adage still applies. Of course, we're referring to authors, who are the only people left in the world who can literally create something out of nothing. But what if . . .

Those three words, combined with a dash of imagination and some of the greatest wizards of today, the authors in this book, are about to take you on a journey through magical realms where wizards hold vast power in the palm of their hand. Where a power-hungry priest learns that you can get too much of a good thing. Where a wizard learns what it's like to be on the lower end of the food chain. Where flowing robes and mystic incantations are the rule, not the exception, and mighty mages fight demons, monsters, and, of course, each other, for power unlike any other . . . the power of magic.

IN THE SERVICE
OF MAGES

❖❖❖

by Dennis L. McKiernan

Dennis McKiernan is the best-selling fantasy author of *The Dragonstone, The Voyage of the Fox Rider, Eye of the Hunter,* and *Caverns of Socrates.* His latest novel, *Into the Forge,* was published in September 1997. His short fantasy fiction has been collected in *Tales of Mithgar,* with other fiction of his appearing in *Weird Tales from Shakespeare* and *Dragon Fantastic.*

In a world ruled by magic, what chance does science have?

When the summons came for Naxianpheria, she was deeply involved in creating a geysering fountain of erupting lava in the very center of her deep, fiery caldera. This feat had taken no small effort on her part—oh, not that the fountain of fire was difficult; on the contrary, the spew of molten stone was trivial. The truly difficult part was locating the very center of her ever-changing, evolving, devolving, expanding, contacting, rising, collapsing, growing, shrinking, amorphous, demonic caldera. But at last she had devised what she believed was an unfailing method for doing so, and just as she had put it to the test, just as the searing lava had begun to explode upward from the heaving, bubbling molten floor, just as she had settled back on her fiery ledge to drink in the sight, *that* was the moment the summons came.

12

"*RRRAAAAWWW!*" she bellowed in fury and fought against the spell, raging and lashing out with her power. But even though she was a greater demon, in the end she had to obey . . . for someone knew her true name, Naxianpheria, and she could do naught but answer.

She found herself trapped in the web of a spell, and she dashed her considerable will against it, seeking a weakness where the invisible tracery might break . . . to no effect, for whoever had cast this spell was someone of great power.

"Naxianpheria," intoned a voice, and in the dark of night beyond the web of arcane energy stood a slight-figured man, weary, stooped with fatigue.

Probably a cursed Mastermage. Still Naxianpheria battered at the spell holding her, for if he was weary, perhaps he had overlooked some small, insignificant element. But the intangible tracery held fast.

"Naxianpheria, answer me. I *command* it!"

Grimly, Naxianpheria turned her baleful yellow gaze upon the weary wizard. "I hear, O man."

"I have a task for you, Naxianpheria."

Naxianpheria did not respond, but waited in silence, her baneful stare not leaving his face.

"I am exhausted from battle"—he gestured at the debris of magical combat scattered across the night-time 'scape—"and my enemies pursue."

"May they arrive swiftly," growled Naxianpheria.

Ignoring her words, the mage continued: "I would go where they think not to look, a place where I can rest."

A gleam lighted Naxianpheria's baleful eye. "My caldera?"

The wizard smiled. "No, my demon friend. Your caldera would be too, ah, inhospitable for the likes of me. Instead I would go"—he pointed into the star-spangled sky—"to Shirene."

Naxianpheria raised her hands in puzzlement. "Shirene?"

"The greater moon," explained the wizard.

"Oh," said Naxianpheria, "Ruxula."

The wizard shrugged. "Shirene, Ruxula: by any name it is the greater moon." He gazed up at the mist-shrouded orb, ghostly in the night. To one side, glittering and sparkling, rode a twinkling, bright point of light: It was the smaller of Argalia's two moons, in its closer orbit now overtaking the larger satellite.

"Naxianpheria, I have summoned you to step across space and bear me thence to Shirene, to Ruxula, for I know your true name and you must obey."

Naxianpheria raged and battered at the spell, but in the end the wizard was right: She had to bend to his will.

"Hear me and swear to my oath, demon: That you will do naught but my bidding, and when the task is done you shall leave and do me no harm, nor shall you return to harm me afterward."

Sighing, Naxianpheria so swore, and with a simple gesture, the mage dispelled the cage.

Carefully, gently, almost lovingly, Naxianpheria took him up in her arms and sighted on the greater moon. Then she softly said, "O master, this journey will weary me much. It would ease my labors somewhat if you would allow me to step first to the surface of Arn and thence on to Ruxula."

The mage looked up at her. "Arn?"

"The lesser moon," she explained.

"Ah, Jong, you mean," he replied, pointing at the scintillant mote of light.

"Arn, Jong: By any name it is the lesser moon. And two small steps with a pause in between are more readily accomplished than one giant leap."

The mage sighed. "Oh, well and good, if it will ease your way."

"You so bid, master?"

"I do so bid."

Naxianpheria grinned widely, her fangs and tusks glistening, and she stepped to the gleaming crystalline surface of Arn, the minuscule moon less than a mile in diameter, with its facets and angles and points and planes and other such, all of which caused it to wink and glitter as it tumbled along its orbit. And Naxianpheria watched as the air exploded from the wizard's lungs into the vacuum of space. And she watched as he gestured feebly and tried to speak a spell, but of course failed. And she watched as his eyes bulged and he tried to scream, but only demons can shriek in space.

And after long moments and long moments more, bearing the wizard's corpse, Naxianpheria stepped onward to Ruxula, into the mists of the greater moon.

She buried him there among the graves of the other Mastermages she had just as faithfully served. Now there were but four of these science-ignorant *fools* left who knew her true name.

She hoped to serve them soon.

ILIAN

❖❖❖

by Josepha Sherman

Josepha Sherman is a fantasy writer and folk-
lorist whose latest novels are the historical
fantasies *The Shattered Oath* and *Forging the
Runes*. Her latest folklore book is entitled
Trickster Tales.

Now, you are to picture Toledo in the days of
knights and honor, Church and darkness: the
narrow streets, the houses pressed close together. Picture one man in a hooded cloak making his way along
those dusty streets, looking for one particular house.
Call him Rodrigo; though that was his birth name, it
is not the name he uses now. For Rodrigo, a young
man and quite ambitious, has taken holy orders.

Not by choice. It was the custom in that time for
the second son of a noble house to be given to the
Church. Rodrigo had already accepted his fate, knowing that a clever man, a learned man, could rise high
in his profession, become as powerful, perhaps, as the
king himself.

But how he could do that . . . ah, that was a subject that
nipped and nagged at him! How could a man achieve the
power for which he hungered?

That question was the reason why Rodrigo wandered the streets alone, hood pulled far forward so
none could recognize him as a deacon in the Church.
For the man he sought might—hopefully would—help
his career, but was not, to understate it most delicately, one who would help Rodrigo's reputation if
word got out.

That one was known by only one name: Ilian. He was, the rumors whispered, a wise man—a wizard, some said—who lived quietly there in Toledo, where, if the rumors were true, he studied all manner of strange Arts. It is a fact that whenever a man becomes wise in arcane ways, there will be others wishing to gain his wisdom, even if it means danger, even if it means the loss of everything.

There will be no danger, Rodrigo thought. *I will be careful. No one will know.* He discarded all thoughts of danger to his soul; such worries were for the superstitious. *Magic is but a tool. A tool to help me advance, make me powerful.*

At first no one seemed to know the house he sought. But after slipping coins to this street musician and that beggar, Rodrigo finally found himself facing a house no different from the others on the street, one built about a central courtyard and presenting nothing to passersby but a blank, whitewashed wall set with high windows and one wooden door.

Can this really be a wizard's home? It looks so . . . bland.

But then, he told himself, witches were burned these days, sorcery was forbidden by Church and State, and a true wizard would be wise enough not to advertise too blatantly. So Rodrigo took a deep breath and knocked.

To his surprise, the door swung soundlessly open, revealing no one. "Enter," called a voice. "You are expected."

Expected? Nervous despite his best efforts at self-control, Rodrigo stole inside, standing in sudden cool darkness, not certain where to turn.

"This way," directed the voice. "In the courtyard."

Rodrigo followed his unseen guide, then stopped short, blinking as his vision readjusted to the sudden blaze of daylight. *Was* this a wizard's home? Nothing at all here seemed sorcerous, or even unusual! The courtyard was cheerful with sunlight and cool with the plashing of a fountain. Shaded by a luxuriant fig tree, a plump, gray-haired woman, presumably the housekeeper in her plain, neat gown, stood talking deferentially to a man in a bright blue robe—costly velvet, Rodrigo noted. This, then, could only be the master of the house.

This? This was Ilian? A little chill of disappointment settled in the pit of Rodrigo's stomach. The man looked just like any other comfortably settled man, a reasonably successful merchant, perhaps, a round-faced fellow of uncertain age, caught in nothing more dramatic than telling his housekeeper what to prepare for dinner.

"Wait a moment, good Anna, if you would," the man—Ilian?—added. He turned to Rodrigo with a courteous little wave of the hand. "Please, enter. Be seated. And yes, before you ask, I am Ilian. And you are the one who is known as—"

"Rodrigo. Call me Rodrigo."

Ilian beamed at him. "Of course. What may I do for you . . . Rodrigo?"

Boldly, now, Rodrigo told himself. *Just because he looks so plain doesn't mean he does not wield great power.* "There are rumors about you, my, ah, lord."

"Oh, I'm sure there are. Some of them may even be true. Continue, please."

This was not going as well as it might. "The rumors name you a wizard," Rodrigo said bluntly.

"Indeed they do. And quite rightly."

Ah! "Then I—"

"Your pardon, my lord Rodrigo. Do you understand what wizardry means? No darkness here, my friend, no devils. I do not slay for hire, nor play games with souls. If you want poisons or succubi, seek elsewhere."

"You misunderstand me. I'm not interested in such . . . tawdry matters. I wish to study with you, wizard. I wish to learn not some marketplace tricks but the true wisdoms."

"Do you, now?" Ilian's smile was amiable. Almost, Rodrigo thought, condescending. "And do you realize what that entails?" the wizard asked. "Magic is no easy course of study."

"I'm not afraid of hard work."

The amiable smile faded slightly. "There is far more to magic than mere work. Power, my friend, is a dangerous burden, dangerous both to you and those around you. A wizard must be totally, utterly trustworthy, utterly honest. He must never break a vow nor forget those who helped him. Can you be such a totally trustworthy man?"

Rodrigo bit back an impatient hiss. "I can be trusted, I swear it. I will not forget those who helped me."

"I wonder. You have already failed to be utterly honest, deacon. Tsk, don't look so shocked; a poor wizard I'd be if I failed to know so much about my visitor. You are the Deacon of Santiago."

"And you are not afraid to name yourself wizard to my face?"

"I have no need for fear."

It was said quite calmly. But just for an instant, cold, sharp power blazed from that mundane, pleasant face. It was gone as swiftly as it had appeared, leaving Rodrigo shaken.

And Ilian continued to smile his amiable smile, nothing more now than an ordinary man. "But you, good Rodrigo, are *you* not afraid? The Church warns that those who deal with wizards imperil their immortal souls."

Rodrigo wordlessly waved that away. "Smaller minds are always going to fear those with learning."

"True enough. But," Ilian added slowly, "there is another matter we must consider. Deacons, unless they are truly dullards, which, I might add, I know you are not, do tend to be promoted by Mother Church. And in the process, they gain much fame and influence without ever needing to resort to magic."

"I'm not interested in mere advancement. It's wisdom I seek."

"Indeed? How noble of you. Come now, friend Rodrigo, tell me this: If your Church does, indeed, advance you, would you, so elevated, still remember old . . . acquaintances? Would you still honor your . . . tutor?"

"How shallow do you think me?" Rodrigo snapped. "Of course I would!"

The wizard studied him for an intent, alarming moment, seeming, Rodrigo thought uneasily, to look into his very soul. *He will never accept me. He must know I'm not here for abstract learning.*

But, unexpectedly, Ilian nodded. "So be it." Over his shoulder, he called to his housekeeper, "Partridges, I think, Anna. Purchase two nice, fat partridges for dinner. But we may be working late. Do not begin cooking them until I give the order. You, Rodrigo, follow me."

The housekeeper curtsied and scurried out, and Ilian led Rodrigo out of the courtyard and into a large, dim, slightly musty room. Books crowded the shelves and shared floor and table space with scrolls and strange, intricately worked . . . instruments that glinted with bronze or silver.

Magical devices, Rodrigo thought, when he could not puzzle out their purpose by any other explanation, and felt a shiver race up his spine. *It cannot be too late to turn and leave—no. Not without the power I seek.* "What now?" he asked uneasily.

"Now," Ilian said brightly, lighting a lamp with a casual glance and seating himself on a heavily cushioned chair, "we begin. Come, sit. First we shall discuss theory."

But they hadn't gone very far into what Rodrigo found an all but impenetrable tangle of obscure words and concepts before a knock sounded on the study door. "Master?" a servant called. "There is a messenger come to the house, seeking your visitor."

Ilian raised an eyebrow. "Is there? Are you expecting anyone, Rodrigo? No? Let us see what urgent news drives a man to a wizard's home. Bid the messenger enter."

A plain-faced, plainly clad man came rushing in, eyeing Ilian apologetically. "Your pardon for the intrusion, m-my lord, but I must speak with the Deacon of Santiago, and quickly!"

With a wary glance at Ilian, who shrugged and waved an expansive hand, Rodrigo nodded. "I am he."

"Deacon, hear me: Your uncle the archbishop is very ill. Indeed, he—he lies upon his deathbed even now, and has called for you."

Ilian said nothing, watching Rodrigo warily. *A test,* Rodrigo thought. *If I do not go, I am branded heartless. But if I do go, I am abandoning my studies. Which image would the wizard prefer?*

But Ilian gave no clue. And after a moment, the deacon said, "I'm sorry. I am in the middle of important affairs. I cannot leave just now."

The messenger left, and Ilian nodded as though Rodrigo had, indeed, answered some unvoiced question. "Come," was all that the wizard said, "let us return to our work."

Four days passed, four days in which Rodrigo heard much about the theories of magic but little about the substance of the art.

"Don't be so impatient," Ilian scolded mildly. "Without a good foundation, no house may stand. And so it is with the house of wizardry. There must be a good theoretical foundation. Now, in the words of Pythagoras—"

But all at once, a servant announced that another messenger had arrived for the Deacon of Santiago.

"My, you *are* a popular fellow," Ilian said. "Shall we hear what this one has to say?"

The messenger rushed in, bowing hastily to both men, then blurting out, "Deacon, hear me: Your uncle the archbishop has died."

Rodrigo piously crossed himself. "God's mercy on his soul."

"Wait, I beg you. There is more. I—I have come with glad tidings as well. For word has come that you are to be appointed archbishop in his place!"

Rodrigo sat back in his chair, stunned. It was Ilian

who waved the messenger away. "So, now, Rodrigo, fascinating news!"

"Archbishop," Rodrigo gasped at last. "I never thought . . . I never dreamed . . . archbishop." *Such a mighty jump—I am not ready, I cannot—* Gathering his senses, he said in a rush, "Ilian, good wizard, you surely must see that I can no longer stay here and study magic."

"Indeed you cannot!" Was that a sarcastic glint in the wizard's eyes. "It would be most . . . unfitting. Go, good Rodrigo, and serve the Church well."

But just before Rodrigo left the wizard's house, Ilian called after him, "Ah, a favor, if you would."

"As you will it."

"I have a son. He is a good, holy young man who knows nothing of what I am. Will you not appoint him deacon in your place?"

Well now, look at this! The wizard fears for the safety of his soul! He wants a son in holy orders to pray for him.

"Never fear," Rodrigo said smoothly. "I will look into it."

But, settling into his new life as archbishop, Rodrigo thought, *I am too new to this post, too young. I must have those I can trust about me, those who will look to me with proper gratitude.*

The last one I want in such a post is a wizard's son!

Would that mean Ilian's enmity? No, surely not. The wizard would realize Rodrigo's situation. And if he did not, well now, Ilian would never dare draw unwanted clerical attention to himself!

So Rodrigo appointed to the deaconry none other than his maternal uncle, a clever old priest who knew how to remember his kinsman. After making the decision, Rodrigo spent some time in prayer and some more in fear, just in case Ilian did seek revenge on him.

But . . . nothing sorcerous happened. Time passed, and Rodrigo relaxed. Surely common sense had prevailed and Ilian had realized the hopelessness of his request. The subject of wizardry was too perilous to ever be considered again.

But Rodrigo's uncle, old as he was, died not long after, leaving the deaconry vacant once more. Unwelcome thoughts of Ilian slid back into Rodrigo's mind. Uneasy, he entered his private quarters, then stopped with a gasp as a parchment slowly formed itself into reality on his desk. Warily opening it, Rodrigo found a message from Ilian. But there was nothing at all menacing about the contents:

"I understand how busy and complex your life has become. And so I will not add to the complexity save to ask this one small favor: pray appoint my son as deacon."

No, Rodrigo thought. Quickly, he set fire to the parchment, to his relief seeing it burn to harmless ash. *I will have nothing to do with wizardry.*

And he sent a polite, carefully worded message to Ilian, saying only, "I will look into it."

But—after placing holy relics about every corner of his quarters—Rodrigo appointed his own brother, a wary and grateful young man, deacon instead.

A year stole by, another, yet another. Not one word was heard from Ilian, not one more mysterious message appeared on Rodrigo's desk. And at last the archbishop decided with great relief that the wizard must have forgotten all about him. He settled with great enthusiasm to make a name for himself as a pious clergyman, and all the while concentrated on building as strong a foundation of allies as he could.

And one day Rodrigo received a message not from some perilous wizard but from the Vatican itself. Word of him had reached even there, and now, the message told him, the good archbishop was to be raised to cardinal and was summoned to Rome.

I didn't need magic. I didn't need it at all. No one knows I ever consulted a wizard. None save Ilian—and he is too wise to ever open his mouth about it.

There, among the solemn gold and marble splendor of the Vatican, still so breathless from excitement he could hardly speak or examine his fine suite of rooms,

Rodrigo was granted yet another honor. He was informed that he could appoint his own successor. Alone in his quarters, too overwhelmed to allow even the most courteous of underlings, he pondered the matter.

Who did he dare appoint. Who would be the safest? Most useful?

God, to have this authority! No one shall ever know I was once weak enough to be tempted by magic!

"Your Grace," a respectful voice murmured. A servant? Rodrigo glanced up, frowning. Who had dared enter without his leave?

A figure in a plain brown hooded robe such as a common priest might wear faced him.

"Who are you?" Rodrigo snapped.

The figure threw back its hood—and Rodrigo nearly choked on his horror:

Ilian! This was the wizard Ilian!

But the wizard showed no anger, no flash of sorcery. Instead, he knelt most humbly and said, "I know so powerful a potentate's life is full of weighty matters. I will not keep you long. But . . . my son truly is a most worthy young man, and because of me, he has not been advanced. Will you not grant him a post? Will you not grant him your vacant post?"

A wizard's son not as deacon but as archbishop? Impossible! Oh, the young man might, indeed, be every bit as holy as a saint. But what if he let slip something about his father? What if he mentioned that Ilian had once tutored Rodrigo in the forbidden arts of—no, no, it was not to be considered!

But: "I will consider it," Rodrigo said courteously, and had Ilian ushered out.

As soon as the wizard was gone, Rodrigo barred all the doors and windows and sat clutching a golden crucifix, sure sorcery would be attempted even in this most holy place. But nothing untoward happened. The days passed, and still nothing untoward happened. And at last Rodrigo roused himself and appointed a well-born bishop, a distant kinsman who would remember him with gratitude.

Years stole by with no more alarms save for merely

political ones. Rodrigo ingratiated himself here, bullied just a touch there. And when the old pope died—ah, he was properly humble when he was named to the papacy himself. Never a thought of Ilian bothered him now, never a worry about the past.

And then, right in the middle of a papal audience, a figure in plain brown robes appeared before him.

"Ilian!"

"Indeed," the wizard said, pushing back the hood of his cloak. "Oh, don't be so alarmed," he snapped at the papal guards. "You can see I am unarmed. Save, of course," Ilian added wryly to Rodrigo, "for my arts."

"You would not dare—"

"Please. You told me, back when you first came to study magic with me—"

"No, no, I never did such a thing!"

"Indeed. You told me then that you would never forget your old tutor."

God! This was worse than ever he'd feared! How could the pope be involved with sorcery? How could he be accused, here, before everyone, that he had ever been the student of a thrice-damned wizard?

"Liar!" Rodrigo snapped."Heretic! I swear before God that I never had anything to do with you. Guards! Seize this heretic! Throw him into prison till we can burn him at the stake as a sorcerer!"

"Ungrateful man!" Ilian said in indignation. "You would burn me, would you? Then you shall not share my partridge dinner!"

And suddenly the pope found himself back in Ilian's home, there in the wizard's study.

"What in the name of—where—how—" Rodrigo glanced down at himself. No elegant robes, no seals of office—God, he was nothing but a—a lowly deacon once more! "What have you done to me? *What have you done?*"

"Very little, really," Ilian said modestly. "But it was a pretty thing, wasn't it? What, were you really vain enough to believe in such a meteoric rise to power?"

For all that, the wild, soaring climb to archbishop,

to cardinal, to pope, all that whole, grand, detailed progression to glory had been nothing but—illusion. It was still the day it had been when Rodrigo, humble deacon, had first sought out the wizard.

"I warned you," Ilian said mildly as Rodrigo stared, openmouthed and dazed, "that magic is a dangerous burden, that a wizard must be utterly trustworthy. What, would you put a drawn and ready crossbow in the hands of a child? You, alas, have failed the test. Good day to you, good deacon."

"What's that, Anna? Oh yes, he's gone. No, he will not return. No, he will not dare bring the law down on our heads, either, not unless he wants to be revealed for what he is. Anna, my dear, there will be only *one* partridge for dinner!"

NOTE: This story was inspired by the folkloric theme of the illusion-beguiled man, often a cleric, who believes that years have passed and that he has risen to fame and fortune; in this theme, which is found throughout the world, the man, who has been untrue to his word, is taught a good lesson in honesty and humility when the illusion breaks.

HELL'S MARK

❖❖❖

by Jane M. Lindskold

Jane Lindskold has made a career of proving that one can do the impossible (such as making a living with a major in English or gardening on a sand dune). Currently, she lives in Albuquerque, New Mexico with her husband, Jim Moore, and assorted small animals. A full-time writer, she has published over twenty short stories, seven novels, and various bits of non-fiction. Her two most recent novels are *When the Gods Are Silent* and *Donnerjack* (in collaboration with Roger Zelazny).

In the southeastern section of the city where I live there is a nightclub whose bottom level is a direct annex of Hell.

I don't mean this in any allegorical sense. I mean it exactly and literally. I've been there and I bear its mark. I always will.

The club is there for anyone to enter. The real trick is getting out with your soul your own. Most do leave intact, not because they have any particular power or virtue but . . . Can you follow this? . . . precisely because they do not.

Okay, more slowly. Would Hell knock itself out to grab the type of person who will pass into its infernal grasp anyhow? No. Simple. Hell wants those marginal cases, the ones who are teetering on the edge. Oh, Hell wants the saints, too, but saints aren't going to be attracted to a nightclub. There are other traps for them. They don't figure in this story—or maybe they do. I can't quite make up my mind.

The club is called the Double Decker. I first learned
of it a few months after I had been informed that I
possessed the power of six Chinese wizards.

Chinese wizards are the best of the best. The reason
is that Chinese civilization is so old that every type of
magical ritual has already been developed. New initiates simply need to match their particular gifts to the
appropriate format and "Poof" they're in business.
There's nothing left but getting better and better—
with none of the mismatching that happens so often
in other cultures.

I once knew a Finnish initiate who was tone deaf.
Now, all Finnish wizardry is structured around songs.
So here is this guy just fountaining raw power, but
with no way to direct it. He spent *years* looking for a
style that would suit his talents. (He eventually settled
on Pacific Northwestern shamanism.)

A Chinese initiate in a similar situation would go
to one of their conveniently located centers of magical
learning and, after a few simple tests, be matched to
the format best suited to his talents. The teachers
often assign secondary rituals, too, sort of like majors
and minors in college.

So you can see why the Chinese wizards are considered the Whiz Kids of the magically adept. And, when
I sauntered into the Double Decker, I'd only had a
couple of months to adjust to the idea that I had the
power of *six* Chinese wizards—fully-trained ones, too,
not just initiates.

Now, learning that I had some wizardly power had
not been a complete surprise. My mother is a *curandera*. That's the polite term for a witch. The nasty one
is *bruja*.

Curandera do things like roll an egg over your forehead to cure a headache or boil a pig's brain to make
love potions. They can cure the evil eye, too.

My mom was really good at what she did, so good
that she'd about given up on love potions, since she
didn't want to force anyone into a relationship with
anybody else. She figured that was verging on black
magic. Mom's very ethical.

My father doesn't practice the Craft in any form; he's a bread maker for Rainbow Bakeries. On *his* father's side, though, he's descended from a Hopi kachina dancer, a fellow who was head of all sorts of medicine societies. Probably a gonzo wizard, too, but I really wouldn't know. The Pueblo people have gotten a bit sour about telling their secrets to outsiders and that includes granddaughters raised Catholic by *curandera* mothers. Anyhow, Grandpa Hopi died when I was just a squirt, so I don't really know what he would or wouldn't have told me.

So I grew up, went from gangling, to presentable, to just maybe pretty—dark-haired, doe-eyed, and clearly Spanish. I attended Mass with Mom and Dad, and wondered in the back of my mind, just like you wonder what job you might have when you grow up, if I would develop any magical power.

By the time I was thirteen, it was pretty clear that I would. By the time I was sixteen, Mom arranged for me to get some elementary training in the *curandera* arts. By the time I was eighteen, Madre Flora Negra had told Mom to have me tested.

Tests aren't quickly arranged, so I was a freshman at UNM before the High and Mighty assembled. I can't tell the details of the Test. That's a Craft secret, but I will tell you that by the time it was over I had the Examiners leaping after me, just struggling to keep up. It was a second test at the start of my sophomore year that gave me my beginner's rating: CW6—the highest rating anyone had ever been given since that system had been established.

So there I was, nineteen turning twenty, the most rawly talented wizard of my generation, worrying about what classes to take, what homework to slough off, and whether my team would win Homecoming. Except that I wasn't doing any of that. That's what I let Mom and Dad believe. What I was doing was venturing out and getting a taste of what Power can give you.

Now, there are a lot of the Talented in New Mexico. I think it has something to do with the blend of cultures: Hispanic (Mexican and Spanish), Anglo (all varieties), Pueblo (all varieties), Navajo, Apache, and Hippie. So when I got comfortable at UNM, I associated for the first time in my life with my peers in the Art. Except that they weren't my peers, not really. I had less training, but more potential. I knew it, they knew it, but they liked me anyhow.

The leader of our little band was a perpetual senior named Danny. Right up there with Danny was Vanessa, another senior (but only for the first time). Then there were the rest: Madeleine, Pedro, Cindy, William, and me. We were a fractious group, drawn together by a sense of our difference from the rest of our classmates rather than by any similarity to each other.

Despite our differences, we hung out together, cut classes together, and even *went* to class together. With our knowledge of various arcane traditions, we were a nightmare to our instructors in Comparative Religions and Introductory Anthropology. Our love for the horizons beyond those most see made us God's gift to our instructors in Philosophy and Literature. We didn't do as well in the nuts and bolts classes like Math and Biology, though Vanessa nearly gave an elderly Astronomy professor a heart attack (figuratively speaking) by casting frighteningly accurate horoscopes in class.

I think she nearly converted him to believing in magic.

Life breezed on through the Fall term and into the Spring. That's when we learned about the Double Decker Club. Pedro told us about it. He'd been taken there by his brother, a ganger with a taste for rough places.

"It's the coolest place," he enthused. "Down in the War Zone, you know. When I went there with Juan, I could just *taste* the sulfur wafting up."

Well, of course, then the rest of us had to go and take a look. In preparation I went browsing at a thrift store where I found one of those Chinese jacket dresses with a high collar and a short skirt. Mine was green watered satin. To complement it I found black fishnet stockings and a pair of glittering green pumps. With my hair swept back in a lacquered butterfly barrette I thought that I looked like something out of a James Bond movie.

I rode down to the club with Danny, Madeleine, and William in Will's old cherry-red Camero. We were all keyed up and slightly nervous. Most of our gang was only initiate-rated; Will and Madeleine hadn't even been tested. Only Vanessa and I had real wizard ratings and my training hadn't gone much beyond Madre Flora Negra's *curandera* stuff.

In the parking lot we met up with the others. Pedro was feeling real pleased with himself, eating up his role as native guide. He may be a little guy, but his gang tattoos are the real thing and his leather jacket isn't just a fashion statement—it's armor.

"Now listen up," he said, strutting around us like bantam rooster, "the club's called the Double Decker for a reason. Up top is a fancy restaurant. Below is a dance floor. What we're here to get a glance at is below that."

He wouldn't say anything else, just grinned and tweaked Cindy's nose ring when she whined that it wasn't *right* for him to hold out on us.

As for me, I couldn't wait to see for myself.

"C'mon," I said, grabbing Danny by the arm, "you want to get old hanging in this parking lot?"

The foyer we walked into was shaped like a wedge of pie with the door we'd come in at the tip. The entire room was made out of glass blocks lit from behind by pulsing, multicolored strobe lights. You could feel the floor shaking slightly from the bass beat of some powerful speakers down below. At the back of the pie wedge was a wide, triangular door.

At the center of the room was a doughnut-shaped counter and in the doughnut's hole stood an absolutely gorgeous woman. Tall and voluptuous, she was dressed in something like you'd see on Academy Award's Night, but on her the sequins and satin and rhinestones looked *good*. I could hear the fellows drawing their breath in really hard and knew that the other girls' eyes were probably as full of envy as my own.

"Restaurant or dance hall?" the spangled vision asked in a tone of voice that made it seem like she was asking something far more intimate.

"Dance hall," Pedro said immediately, his teeth glinting white within his Vandyke beard. He'd known about this woman, of course, and was enjoying our reactions.

"Creep," Cindy muttered.

Pedro paid the cover charge for the lot of us. We'd given him the money earlier, not wanting to look uncool by digging through our pockets and getting change. The vision in the Bob Mackie gown handed him a bunch of bracelets made out of hologram plastic.

"These must be worn at all times within the club. If you leave and want to come back, just show them at the club door."

We strapped our bracelets on and headed for the door she indicated. Watching Pedro hang back, I judged that something else startling or unusual awaited us and resolved to hide my reaction.

I managed, but just barely. We had emerged onto a five foot wide catwalk with a floor of scarlet lucite. Four staircases constructed from slabs of opaque, multicolored plastic were staggered evenly around the circumference. Two led up, presumably to the restaurant level. Two led down to the dance floor. The pink ceiling above us was translucent, presumably so that the diners could look down and be tempted to dance off their repasts.

After letting us stare for a moment, Pedro led the way to where the nearest staircase corkscrewed down.

"When it gets crowded, people come up here to cool off and watch the dancing," he explained. "You can also go up to the restaurant, but people from the restaurant gotta get a bracelet before they can come down here."

"How's the food?" Cindy asked, trying to seem nonchalant.

"*Bueno*," Pedro said. "Maybe we can get a late dinner."

Danny and Vanessa had already started down the stairs and the rest of us hurried to catch up.

Vanessa was wearing a white sequined mini-dress, long white gloves, and matching heels. With her dark red hair swept up and held by pearl pins, she looked like a very fashionable bride.

Danny wore his usual black leather jacket and black jeans, but in honor of our night out he had found a bright red tuxedo shirt somewhere. The dance floor was pretty warm and when he unbuttoned his jacket the effect was like flame blossoming out of his chest.

The rest of us were dressed somewhere in between. In this place, my James Bond look was just right and the lot of us caused a little ripple of interest as we descended to the dance floor, selected partners from our own numbers and started dancing.

This left one person out, but Vanessa has never had to wait long for someone to notice her. By the third number we were mingling freely with the clientele.

The Double Decker was turning out pretty promising and I would have been completely content except that I hadn't yet seen Hell. I worked my way through partners so that by the fourth dance I was paired up with Pedro.

"So, I don't get it," I said. "Where is it?"

"Patience, *querida*" he answered enigmatically. "The hour is early yet. However, given *your* gifts you may be able to see what is still hidden from others."

He swept me into his arms (not at all an unpleasant feeling) and toward the center of the dance floor.

"Trust yourself to me and unfocus your sight."

I drooped against him, glad that the song currently playing was one of those slow ones where couples hang around each other's necks and make out. For the first dozen measures, I didn't sense anything much, then I caught a faint odor of sulfur.

Although my first impulse was to glare at Pedro for teasing me, I remained relaxed. That's when I realized that there was an opening in the floor, similar to the one in the catwalk above but only about twelve feet in diameter.

It gave me a real start to see couples drifting across the opening, dancing as if there was a solid floor beneath their feet. Of course, there was, for *them*.

Now that I'd found the opening, I located the stairways down in a jiffy. There were three of them, the treads broken from chunks of jagged obsidian, the rails gouts of fire. At the head of each stair sat a lean black dog with outswept ears, sort of like what you'd get if you crossed Anubis with a bat. Each dog's nostrils were flared as if taking a scent and with a shiver I realized that their ruddy gazes were tracking *me*.

"The song's ending, *amiga*," Pedro whispered in my ear. "Better come around."

I did, shaking slightly and rewarding him with a kiss on the mouth. Then I dragged him toward the bar.

"I saw it!" I said softly, although the noise from the next number would have covered me shouting. "The hole, the stairs, the hell-hounds!"

I bought us both rum and cokes and with my first sip discovered that the Double Decker didn't believe in watering its drinks.

Pedro glanced at his watch and shook his head in admiration. "You *are* something, Lucia. The hour is just rising eleven. I saw nothing until the witching hour."

Dragging scrawny, bespectacled William in her wake, Cindy came over to our table. Her blonde hair was woven with beads that sparkled in the lights and she wore a lycra-spandex bodysuit with cutouts designed to show off her various tattoos and body piercings. Despite her avant-garde exterior, I knew her to be the product of a politely suburban family.

Her Power had first manifested as poltergeist activity, but an adept counselor at the therapy camp where her parents had sent her had recognized Cindy's real trouble as magic with no outlet.

Although she hadn't been initiated yet, Cindy was already talented at various forms of conjuration and, until my arrival, had been Vanessa's obvious heir. That she resented me not a little, I already knew, but I pitied her, too. I had always had my family's support. Cindy couldn't even tell them what she could do without risking being locked up as a mental case.

So I grinned at the two of them, gestured toward a couple of vacant chairs and offered to buy them drinks. They accepted and, as I was coming back with a dry martini and a dark beer, I realized that Pedro was boasting about what I'd seen.

Pedro's family is dirt poor. Only the fact that he's brilliant got him a scholarship for college. Well-off Anglos like Cindy and Will (and Danny, Vanessa, and Madeleine) can punch his buttons. Far from resenting my Power, he reveled in it, Hispanic to Hispanic. When I returned, he was doing some not so subtle rubbing their noses in what I had done.

Cindy grabbed the martini I slid over to her and, for a moment, I thought she was going to smash the glass against the wall. She controlled herself, though, and downed the stiff drink with what I would have thought impossible speed.

"So Lucia has seen the gateway to Hell," she snarled. "I don't doubt it. She's probably been there, too, and impressed all the devils and demons with her wit and power."

Will's gray eyes widened and he made a shushing gesture but Cindy was too mad, or too drunk, to care. Fortunately, no one outside of our table could hear what she had said.

"It wasn't easy," I started, but Cindy wasn't in the mood to be placated.

"Of course it wasn't," she sneered. "If you say it was easy, then you're diminishing how wonderful you are."

"Shit," I sighed.

Fortunately, at that moment, Danny came over. He may not be able to finish all his required courses and graduate, but he has a calm wisdom that blends our tempestuous lot into something like a second family. Maybe it's a part of his magic, but all I know is that as soon as he pulled a chair over and draped an arm around Cindy the anger started ebbing from her.

"What's wrong, Cinders?"

"Pedro was just bragging that Lucia's seen the gateway," she sobbed.

"So what bothers you more, the bragging or the seeing?" he said reasonably. "Because if it's the seeing, you should take a look for yourself. It's starting to manifest and even the Mundanes are feeling its presence."

Danny was right. In the minutes since I had my initial glimpse, the gateway had become clearly visible to any who had the eyes to see. Unmagical dancers were drifting away from the center of the dance floor, feeling an abyss their eyes told them was not there.

"Sheesh," Will hissed, tugging at his collar as if it were suddenly too tight.

Cindy's eyes widened, but she didn't say anything. As if in response to some silent signal, Vanessa and Madeleine came over to join us.

"Did you see . . . ?" Vanessa asked, sliding in to perch on Pedro's lap.

We nodded. Madeleine nervously stroked the white ferret she wore like a collar around her slender neck. Its pink eyes shone like jewels in the club's dim light. Idly, I wondered how many of her dance partners tonight had realized that her collar—and her rattlesnake-skin belt—were alive.

"Those dogs aren't dogs," she said. "By reflex, I reached to touch their minds, and what I met was so full of hate and fury I nearly passed out."

She looked pale beneath her rouge and lipstick, and no wonder given what she'd just felt. Although plump and brown-haired, Madeleine reminds me of Cinderella in the Disney film. Birds flutter out of trees to sit on her hands, rabbits hop out of their burrows, even goldfish goggle at her. The trip I made with her to the Rio Grande Zoo will stay with me for a long time. For her to touch an animal's mind and find it full of hate rather than welcome must have been shocking.

"Well," Cindy said, her question for the group but her gaze on me, "what do we do now?"

"Now?" Pedro echoed, puzzled. "We dance, we drink, and maybe we go and get some dinner. Then tomorrow we wake up and try to decide how much homework to do with a hangover."

"That's all?" Cindy shook back her hair haughtily. "We've got adventure and challenge literally at our feet and all you want to do is dance?"

"What else?" Pedro said reasonably. "I'll go to Hell in my own time."

A few of us grinned at his joke, but Danny, ever sensitive, stroked Cindy on her arm. "What did you think we should do, Cinders?"

"It's there!" she cried. "It's a challenge bigger than anything I've ever imagined. Don't you think we should check it out, find out why it's there, maybe earn some brownie points with the High and Mighty? Not all of us excite them as much as Santa Lucia."

I started to answer, but Vanessa placed a warning hand on mine, and I settled for a swallow of rum and coke. Cindy wasn't done yet.

"Maybe Luce isn't as great as she's told us. I mean, what good is having the power of six Chinese wizards if you're scared to use it?"

Will rolled his eyes. "That's really dumb, Cindy. I think you've had too much to drink."

"Oh, yeah!" she retorted.

"The mixed drinks *are* strong," Madeleine said, putting hers on the table. "I'm going to stick to beer."

Still stroking Cindy's arm, Danny cocked his head

toward the music. "David Bowie. Let's stop bickering and go dance."

Cindy allowed herself to be led. I grabbed William, intending to apologize for Pedro. Pedro lifted Vanessa from his lap and took her hand. Madeleine started dancing with a guy who looked remarkably like her ferret except that his hair was brown, not white.

Since the center of the dance floor was less densely packed than elsewhere, we soon found ourselves at the border of Hell's opening into the club. The odor of sulfur was strong enough here to cover the more usual scents of sweat, cigarette smoke, and booze. The hell-hounds' eyes were no longer dimly ruddy but glowed like coals. Seeking to avoid their disconcerting gazes, I glanced down. What I saw made me stumble.

"Will, look!"

He did and it was my turn to catch him as he saw that the floor beneath us had become nearly transparent. It was as if we danced on a thinning fog, our shoes just a couple of yards above the heads of the mob that gyrated beneath us. And what a mob it was!

Everyone was vaguely human, but that apparent humanity was no comfort for it served to emphasize the distortions and mutilations that marred each figure. Some merely lacked limbs, other bore extra limbs. Not a few were clawed or taloned, pig-snouted or cat-eyed.

Just as the dancers were parodies of normality, so their dance was a parody of all dances. Even those who eschew dancing as a thinly veiled version of sex would have preferred the most obvious bump and grind to what was going on in that pit. The dancers tore at each other with claw, blade, or fang. Blood spurted and dappled the throng.

"Swing your partner" here was transformed into draw and quarter. Evisceration seemed the fashion of the moment and more than one dancer triumphantly twined a length of intestine (their own or another's I

never knew) about their necks as a vaudeville dancer
might a feather boa.

I retched as I saw a long-taloned, pig-faced demon
rip the heart from the chest of a flailing woman and
saw her in turn gouge the eyes from a long-faced croc-
odilian beast whose own jaws ran with fresh gore.
When Will steered me from the floor, I went with him
as limply as a string-cut puppet.

We were almost off the floor when Danny's cry of,
"Cindy, no!" cut above the music. As one, we swung
back in time to see Cindy, the beads in her hair
streaming behind her like a comet's tail, running for
the nearest stairway.

The hell-hound leaped for her, but it seemed to me
that he sought to push her rather than prevent her.
Rushing to Danny's side, we saw Cindy running down
the obsidian stairs, the jagged stone's razor-sharp
edges drawing blood from her ballet-slippered feet.
Then she vanished into the throng, and we could only
stare in shock and dismay.

Around us the mundane dancers continued to ca-
vort, but from a bartender here or a bouncer there, I
glimpsed a knowing nod or unkind smile. We were
not alone in knowing of the Double Decker's secret
level, but clearly there were none here who would
help us.

The six of us clustered up on the catwalk for a
private conference. An odd silence surrounded us,
muting the music.

Vanessa stilled our nervous babbling with a
regal gesture. "I want to hear what Danny has
to say."

"I thought I had Cindy calmed down," Danny
began, "especially when she shrank back from what
was going on down there. Then she stiffened and
started giggling like she'd been sniffing ether—all high
and shrill."

He took a gulp from the beer Madeleine handed to
him and continued. "Then she ripped herself away
from me and dove for the nearest stairs. She must

have waited until we were near one, because I didn't have a chance to grab her."

"We saw," William said comfortingly. "Just like we saw how the dog was perfectly willing to let her through."

"What do we do now?" Madeleine asked, her own voice rather shrill, the ferret and the snake both undulating restlessly about her body. "Surely she isn't gone forever. We'll get home and tomorrow morning it'll all be back to normal."

"I wish I believed that," Vanessa answered calmly, "but there are too many legends of people taken away by fairies and devils for me to feel confident."

"But how would the club explain!" Madeleine protested.

"They'll deny that anything happened," I replied, remembering the expressions I had glimpsed. "They'll say she must have left with a pickup. What are we going to say to counter that?"

"True." Danny looked somber. "We can't exactly say she dove into the Pit."

"Though that's what she did," Pedro agreed. "When Juan took me here, he saw nothing of the strangeness, just a very good club. I think that we will not be believed."

"Then we should appeal to the High and Mighty!" Madeleine suggested anxiously.

"That will take too long," Vanessa said, "and who is to say they will help us? They might take action against the Double Decker, but Cindy is nothing to them. She's not even been formally initiated."

"You're not saying . . ." Will began.

"That we go after her?" Vanessa nodded. "What else can we do?"

"I can't!" Madeleine wailed, clearly terrified. "You didn't touch that dog-thing's mind! You can't know how horrid they are!"

"And those are just the *perros*," Pedro added somberly. "My Power is small, only a gift for divination. I have nothing to offer a rescue. I might just give you another person to save."

Will was nodding agreement. Like Pedro, he had a small gift—his was for past-life regressions—but he was no wizard.

Vanessa shook her head in dismay, but said nothing. Danny looked at me.

"Lucia?"

"I'll go," I gulped. Then I tried to grin, "After all, what good is having the power of six Chinese wizards if you're scared to use it?"

"And I'll go," Danny said, "though my gifts are mostly for healing."

Vanessa fixed a firm gaze on the others. "Benjamin Franklin said to the signers of the Declaration of Independence, 'We must all hang together, or assuredly we shall all hang separately.' "

"Huh?" Will said, Madeleine echoing him a beat behind.

"What she means," Pedro explained, "is that what we don't do together will certainly destroy us as individuals."

"Hang together," Will said. "Hang separately. I get it, but what does that have to do with this—with Cindy?"

Vanessa leaned forward across the table. "Don't you understand? If we go and fail, you three will blame yourselves for whatever happens to us, as well as what happened to Cindy. If we go and somehow make it back, the knowledge that in a pinch we couldn't all count on each other will also destroy us."

Madeleine bit her lip. "But, Vanessa, we're not all like you and Lucy. I have a gift for animals. That's it. You're a third generation Wiccan. You've got spells and training and all that."

"My powers work best with a full coven. I don't know if they'll be any help with this," Vanessa answered firmly. "There, I've had my say. The decision is up to you."

Pedro had been staring at the gang tattoos on the back of his hands. "If I hadn't needled her, Cindy might not have been so dumb. All right, I'm with you."

Madeleine frowned. "I don't want to go, but Vanessa's right. I'd always blame myself for not trying."

Will, always the least talkative, just nodded.

"Then we're off to find the wizard," I quipped, trying to sound brave.

The others grinned or groaned, but as one we marched toward the nearest hell-hound guarded stairs. As we crossed the crowded dance floor, it was as if the silence that had surrounded our conference now continued to separate us from the mob.

"We are moving on another plane of existence," Vanessa said softly. "The journey began with the resolution."

When we reached the nearest stairway, the hell-hound rose and bared its teeth. Somehow, I hadn't realized how large it was, but when it was standing, its eyes were level with my own.

"It doesn't seem to want to let us through," Vanessa said briskly. "Madeleine, you deal with this."

Conditioned to obey the senior, Madeleine had stepped forward before she realized what Vanessa was saying.

"What? I can't . . ."

"You're the one with a gift for animals," Vanessa interrupted. "Can you only deal with bunnies and birdies?"

The rattlesnake around Madeleine's waist hissed affront and she stiffened.

"That's *not* an animal," she corrected, but she stepped forward and met those burning eyes.

I saw her wince as if from a blow and, stepping beside her, impulsively set my hands on her right wrist. My mother's teaching says that the pulse points are where the soul is closest to the surface. Holding her wrist, I concentrated on making her brave.

Madeleine hadn't looked away from the hell-hound's eyes and now, slowly, deliberately, she raised one hand, palm up, so that the creature's flared nostrils could get her scent.

"Bad doggy," she muttered. "You're so horrid, so terrible. What do you have to fear from us? Why not let us by?"

The outswept ears perked, following the soft flow of her words with what I figured was amazement. Madeleine continued murmuring in the same vein and, at last, its jaws opening in a doggy grin, the hell-hound sank down onto its haunches.

"We can go by," Madeleine said. "Quickly!"

We scurried. My calves ached in anticipation of the bite that never came.

The obsidian steps were less merciful. Slick as glass and far sharper, they made the three of us girls in our high-heeled pumps slip and slide.

Danny frowned. "Can't have you fall, you'll be cut to ribbons. Will, take Lucia. Pedro, take Maddie. I'll get Van. Walk slowly and carefully and remember, if you fall, *don't* grab the steps to catch yourself. You'd be better off falling."

"Into *that*?" Pedro marveled, looking down into the reeking pit beneath us. "I don't think so, *compadre*."

"Obsidian is sharper than steel," Danny said. "This stuff will take fingers off."

"So will *los diablos*," Pedro said, but he picked up Madeleine.

Stepping carefully, ignoring the hoots and chortles from the fiendish assembly, we made our way to the floor of the pit. When Will set me down, I nearly leaped into his arms again for blood and gore oozed into my green-spangled pumps, mostly cold and clammy, sometimes, horribly, warm as life.

Glancing at the others, I could see that they, too, were just barely holding their ground.

Vanessa, her white dress now grotesquely polka-dot, looked around as briskly as if she were investigating a new shopping mall.

"There's where we want to go," she said, indicating a curved archway across the room. A bulbous form, like an octopus with spines, sat beneath it, clearly on watch.

"How do you know?" Danny asked.

"See what's written over it?" she answered. "Remember our World Lit seminar sophomore year?"

"Vaguely," he said, glaring at a three-armed demon who was trying to cut in, rather literally, with a large cleaver. "Find your own date, bud."

"Abandon all hope," I said. "We did selections from the *Inferno* last term. Cheery."

"That's where we need to go," Vanessa said firmly, "and Danny and Lucia, you're the ones who are going to get us there."

"Us?" Danny said.

"Look at this place," Vanessa said, "mutilation and destruction. You two are trained healers—your power is in opposition to what is going on here. Heal!"

"Arf," I said weakly, but I could see what she was getting at. "Come along, Danny-boy."

Joining hands, we walked out into the dance pit. As if we were the prow of a ship in a very rough sea, the other four walked close behind us.

Remembering Madre Flora Negra's teachings, I reached for the wrist of the nearest mutilated form— a man who had been rudely castrated. Trying to touch his soul, I sent a surge of power.

"Be whole," I said, hoping I wasn't being blasphemous.

The Power's surge through me was like stepping on a poorly grounded electric cord, but the man was entire again. Only then did I notice that he had the head of a water buffalo. The demon glowered at me, backing away as if I had burned him.

"Sorry. I don't do plastic surgery," I managed, grabbing for the next monstrosity.

Beside me, Danny made a "V" with his fingers at an irate goat-horned demon who was charging him, pitchfork raised.

"Peace."

I was busy with a patient of my own (a woman with three legs and no arms) but from the corner of my eye I glimpsed a pale rainbow-hued aura extending from Danny's hand. When it touched the devil, the

creature lowered its pitchfork, suddenly too weak to
hold it. Eyes filled with a dreamy terror of the peace
that filled its evil soul, it lurched to one side, knocking
away a creature with the lower torso of a snake who
was preparing to strike at Will.

"It's working," Vanessa encouraged us. "They're
beginning to fall back. Walk briskly."

That was easier said than done. Some of the devil-
kin did cringe from our healing touch; others, perhaps
the damned themselves, were lurching toward us. Only
the fact that these often lacked legs or feet kept us
from being swamped.

When we made our way to the arched doorway,
Vanessa ordered Danny and me to continue facing the
dance floor.

"Keep them back just a little longer," she urged.
"I've the password for this problem."

Reaching for the closest victim, aware of a dangerous weariness stealing over me, I listened as Vanessa
addressed the overweight octopus.

"Let us through, please," she said politely. "We've
come to get a friend who entered here mistakenly."

"How do you know she was here?" the thing said,
spitting at the floor near her feet. I felt gooey drops
spatter my legs and nearly lost my concentration.

"Those are her footprints on the stone."

A pause.

"So they are," the thing agreed. "Why should I let
you through."

"Because this has been willed where what is willed
must be," Vanessa said without hesitation.

There was a sound like a steam engine, then a dull
explosion. Spots of something wet and smelling like
spoiled milk mixed with cat food rained down
around us.

"It blew up!" Will said, amazed.

"I knew majoring in English would come in handy,"
Vanessa said a bit smugly. "Come on!"

Danny and I each dealt with a final mutilation case
and backed through the arch. As soon as we were

through, Will and Pedro closed the door and Madeleine dropped a bar into place to hold it.

As we wiped bits of exploded Thing off our once elaborate evening clothes, we surveyed the flat gray plain in front of us. A river ran in the distance, mobs of people roughly jostling each other on the shores.

"What next?" Madeleine asked. She looked almost eager.

"Does anyone see Cindy over there?" Danny said, gesturing toward the riverside group.

"We're too far to see clearly," Pedro said. "Let's walk over. At least no one is trying to make us into *chorizo* here."

"If we avoid the mob," Vanessa said, "we should be safe enough. We might even let Danny and Lucia rest."

"I am beat," Danny admitted.

"Me, too," I said, ashamed that my much-vaunted Power hadn't given me more endurance.

"Then rest here," Vanessa said. "The rest of us will look for Cindy."

When they returned, their discouraged attitudes told us all we needed to know.

"No luck?" Danny asked.

"No luck," Vanessa answered. "She's either gone across or we've missed her completely."

"I don't think we missed her," Madeleine reminded. "You saw those footprints. I think she's gone ahead. If I remember my World Lit, the damned are judged and then the judges punt them directly to wherever they're supposed to go."

Vanessa grinned a bit at the irreverent image. "That's about what I recall, too."

"I sure wish I'd paid more attention to World Lit," Will admitted. "Can you guess where she'd end up?"

Eager to help, I piped up, "She was pretty angry when she left. Weren't the Wrathful dumped in the mud?"

"That's right," Vanessa nodded, chewing on her lip as she tried to remember. "There's a bog formed by the River Styx."

She looked as if she might add something more, but decided that it might not be a good idea.

"I dropped World Lit three times," Danny admitted, "but the *Inferno*'s coming back to me. I don't know if we'd be really smart to follow the usual route. Dante had Virgil to guide him."

"And Aeneas had a Golden Bough," Madeleine added, "to give *him* safe passage."

"There might be a way," Vanessa said. "According to what Dante says, all the waters of Hell originate from a single source on the Isle of Crete and drip down here where they separate into rivers. If we can find the source of the Styx, then we can follow it back to the bog."

"Good idea," Pedro said. "What river is that one?"

"Acheron," I said promptly.

"I suggest we go to its banks and see which way the current is flowing," Pedro continued. "If all the rivers have a single source, we can back track there."

"Brilliant!" Vanessa exclaimed. "Are you two rested enough?"

"Rested," Danny said, pushing himself to his feet, "if not enough."

Pedro's solution was neat, but not exactly easy. We walked for what had to be miles along Acheron's banks. Once the crowds behind us dwindled in the distance, we had no way of judging our progress.

Without food, not trusting the water, the sandy gravel slipping under our feet so that each step took double effort, we hiked on through empty gray. No sun, no stars gave us direction. The only sense of time we had came from our aching muscles. Needless to say, our watches didn't work.

None of us dared mention what all of us were remembering—how vast Dante's Inferno was, how vicious some of the inhabitants, how creatively cruel the torments. Sometimes having a background in the Humanities is not conducive to an easy mind.

Is Cindy really worth this? I was thinking when Madeleine gave a glad-voiced cry.

"See that! It's water falling from the sky!"

I raised my eyes from my tired feet (the glittering green pumps had been discarded long ago) to the sky. Madeleine was right. Like a tornado stuck in one place, an enormous torrent of water was tumbling from the undifferentiated gray above.

The sight lightened our feet and before long we could hear the torrent. It grew louder and louder until the once welcome break in the monotony became a new torture that made our heads scream as if they were being drummed upon.

We had given up on conversation long before. When at last we reached the source of the rivers, Danny wrote in the sand: "How do we know which one is Styx?"

Frowns all around, then Will, smiling as if he couldn't believe himself, wrote: "Achilles' heel."

From the looks on the others' faces, I could see that at least some of them recalled the story of how Achilles' mother had dipped her son in the River Styx to make him invulnerable.

"And Phlegethon burns," Vanessa scribbled.

"Not here," Pedro wrote, gesturing widely.

What he said was true. The column of water fell from the grayness above to end in a vast, roiling cauldron that overflowed into three rivers. One was Acheron, which we had followed to this point. We walked to the next river.

Pedro, who hadn't quite given up smoking, dug a book of matches from his pocket. He lit one and dropped it into the water. It fizzled out.

"Styx?" he wrote.

"Don't want to be wrong," Vanessa wrote, "or to use Will's test unless we must. Let's try the other."

Fortunately, someone had set stepping stones (really boulders) in the beds of all three rivers. We crossed this second river and trudged to the third. This one also failed to ignite when presented with a match.

Will rolled up his sleeve and, before Vanessa could protest, plunged his arm in to the elbow. He held it there, his lips slowly counting sixty. Fishing his pocket knife out with his dry arm, he poked himself. At the first attempt, nothing happened and I felt a flash of hope. But on his second try, he drew blood.

Shrugging, Will rolled down his sleeve and we tramped back to the second river. As we walked, I wondered what we'd do if this one also didn't make Will invulnerable. Maybe the charm didn't work with a mortal. Hadn't Achilles' mother been a goddess? And why had Vanessa looked so strange when I had suggested that we would find Cindy with the Wrathful? Was there something I was missing?

Although Pedro mimed volunteering, Will plunged his other arm into the waters of this river. This time, although Danny tried with a surgeon's determination, Will's flesh could not be cut.

"Styx!" Pedro wrote.

Again we began trudging, this time along the banks of the Styx. Though we looked for something—anything—to serve as a boat, there was nothing to be found. Hunger grew slowly. Thirst was a constant. Vanessa assured us, once the drone of the falling water was far enough behind that we could talk, that the Wrathful were comparatively high in the Circles of the Inferno.

"Minor sinners, really," she said.

Again I saw that watchful look in her eyes. Did she dwell for a moment on Pedro?

We walked for hours, seeing little of interest. It was as if the Inferno was attempting to bore us into submission. Still, we must have had a magic of some sort with us because we *were* able to continue. No one collapsed from exhaustion. As long as we were willing to push ourselves, apparently we could.

At long last, the Styx began to narrow, becoming a dirty gray stream. The mass of its bulk was absorbed into a slimy marsh where the air reeked. Strange, almost-human forms moved beneath the muddy surface.

"Reminds me of the *Creature from the Black Lagoon*," Danny said nervously. "Stay close, Madeleine. We may need you to talk to the natives."

There was a narrow path around the marsh and along this we made our way. From time to time, we passed clusters of mud-streaked humans shouting at each other, throwing gobs of filth, and shoving each other into the slime.

After a try or two, we learned that it was not worth trying to talk with them. All we gained for our troubles were insults and shouts of derision.

"How will we know Cindy if we see her?" Madeleine worried aloud.

"I don't know," Vanessa admitted. "She may not even be here. There is another . . ."

Her supposition was interrupted by a cry from Pedro. He was looking at something he held cupped in the palm of his hand. When I drew closer, I saw that it was a couple of the beads from Cindy's hair.

"They must have fallen free when she was hiked here," he said, "and look!"

Pedro's art, as I may have mentioned, is that of a diviner. Normally his favorite tools are cards, but now, as he concentrated on the round pieces of glass, they swirled in his hand.

"Deasil if I draw close," he said to them, "and widdershins if I do not, eh?"

The beads swirled rapidly as if agreeing, then settled into a steady deasil spin. Pedro walked to the edge of the marsh and turned right. The clockwise swirling continued. Along the marsh's uneven shore he went, rejecting false alleys, his face whitening with the strain of maintaining the spell.

As I had with Madeleine, I went and took his wrist, placing my hand on the pulse points and willing my strength to him. He steadied then, and at last we came to seven squabbling figures. I could see no difference among them, but Pedro stopped.

"The beads go widdershins no matter which way I go," he said. "Therefore, one of them must be Cindy."

We stared. None of the squabbling, mud-coated figures resembled in any way the sleek Anglo girl we had last seen in lycra-spandex and tattoos. Even their

hair was matted, so that there was no hope of identification there.

"If Lucia can support me," Danny said. "I believe
I can calm the lot. Then the rest of you can try to
figure out which one is Cindy and pull her out."

Wrinkling her nose at the prospect of going into the
mud, Madeleine answered for the rest. "Okay. Danny,
hold my ferret and snake, would you?"

Wreathed in wildlife, my hands lightly but steadily
grasping the pulse points on his throat, Danny extended both hands toward the infuriated group. To
our surprise, he began to sing the "Prayer of Saint
Francis," the one that begins "Make me a shadow of
your peace. . . ."

Feeling his voice vibrate against my fingers, I concentrated on intensifying his wish. Gradually, as if
peace were overshadowing them, the quarreling
slowed, then stopped. When the transfixed Wrathful
fastened their gaze on Danny, Vanessa was ready.

"Go!" she said, leading the way into the slime.

I watched in increasing shock as my four friends
sloshed the Wrathful with gentle handfuls of gray Styx
water. One by one, the faces that emerged were familiar, though distorted with filth: Pedro, Vanessa, Will,
Madeleine, Danny . . . me. Last of all, they uncovered
Cindy and as they carried her to more solid ground
the others congealed into pillars of mud that collapsed
slowly into the marsh.

"What the . . . heck?" Danny said, his voice hoarse
from singing.

"Those were us, weren't they?" I asked.

Vanessa looked up from where she was mopping the
worst of the mud off of Cindy's face. "Yes. She left
angry with us and she continued fighting with us
even here."

"I wonder," Madeleine said, nervously reclaiming
her familiars from Danny, "if she's still angry with us."

Cindy smiled tentatively. "I'm not. Thanks, guys."

"It wasn't easy," Danny said, "but you're
welcome."

Vanessa flecked mud from her once white dress. "It could have been worse."

We stared at her in shock.

"This is the Fifth Circle," she explained, "the Eighth is for Frauds—among which Dante counted soothsayers and sorcerers. I've been worrying that we'd have to go there."

"Good thing," Cindy said faintly, "I haven't been initiated yet, huh?"

Vanessa sighed and suddenly we saw the tension she had been under. "I guess so. I was really worried."

"I'm not done worrying," Pedro said, glancing around. "How do we get out of here?"

Vanessa looked at Will. "That's going to be your department, Will."

"Me?"

"Dante got out of here by going all the way to the center and climbing up across Satan's imprisoned body and into Purgatory and then to Heaven. I don't think we're welcome there. One of us, however, has an interesting connection to this epic we're in."

We looked at Vanessa as if the strain of organizing our troop had finally been too much for her.

"What?" Will said.

"Does anyone," Vanessa asked, "remember who sent Virgil to help Dante when he was trapped in the Dark Wood?"

"No," Pedro and Danny said simultaneously.

"Beatrice, wasn't it?" I said.

"Yes, but someone sent Beatrice," Vanessa replied. Then, taking mercy on us, she continued, "The Virgin Mary asked a saint to intercede for Dante—Saint Lucia, the saint of light. Lucia then sought Beatrice, who got Virgil, since a blessed soul couldn't very well tour Hell."

"Lucia," Will said, staring at me. "You don't mean?"

"Our Lucia?" Vanessa answered. "Why not? She's terribly powerful. Maybe this is the reason for it. Try regressing her, Will. See if one of her past lives knows how to get us out of here."

"Wait, I can't be . . ." I protested. "Me? Here? Even if I was a saint, how could I be in Hell when Beatrice couldn't?"

Vanessa shrugged. "In Canto IX an Angel comes to open the gates to the City of Dis so that Virgil and Dante can pass through. The rules on who can and cannot tour Hell are apparently pretty flexible."

Still protesting, I lay down on the wet ground. Will knelt beside me and began talking softly, moving his finger back and forth in what I recognized as a hypnotist's technique. I was certain it was all hopeless, then I stopped being aware of the dampness, and soon after of everything else.

I don't remember much of what happened next. All I know is we got out of Hell, emerging in the park in Old Town across from the Church of San Felipe de Neri. The rest of the gang treats me differently now—even Cindy.

Vanessa took us back to her apartment and those of us who lived at home called and said that we were going to crash with her.

It was a good idea. Apparently, I glowed with this pale, golden light for the next twelve hours. When it wore off, I was back to normal except for this hole in my memory.

Cindy was changed, too. Having experienced how her envy and anger is her own most dangerous enemy, she's in counseling to come to terms with it. The rest of the gang has bragging rights for having come through Hell and enough wisdom to keep them from getting too full of themselves.

And me? I wasn't precisely accurate when I said I had a hole in my memory. Sure, I don't remember how we got out of Hell or any of the amazing things the others told me that I did. The space where that should be is filled with a host of images I can't account for: pure light, incredible serenity, white-feathered wings, and absolute trust.

As I said at the start of this, there's a club in my town that has a direct annex to Hell. We've told the

High and Mighty about it, and they plan to shut it down some time next year.

Whether they do or not, it has left its mark on me. I now know why I have the power of six Chinese wizards . . . or one Saint.

It's on loan—from God.

THE BANE OF TRIGEMINY

❖ ❖ ❖

by Mickey Zucker Reichert

Mickey Zucker Reichert is a pediatrician whose twelve science fiction and fantasy novels include *The Legend of Nightfall, The Unknown Soldier,* and *The Renshai Trilogy.* Her most recent release from DAW Books is *Prince of Demons,* the second in *The Renshai Chronicles* trilogy. Her short fiction has appeared in numerous anthologies. Her claims to fame: she *has* performed brain surgery, and her parents *really are* rocket scientists.

The familiar aromas of ozone, smoke, and chalk dust wafted through the wizards' teaching room, now mingled with the anxious sweat of twenty students. Seion sat up straight in his chair, softening the air at his back with a finger-gesture and a spare thought. Folding his arms across his chest, he watched the mentors parade across the front of the classroom, each choosing a student. One more test remained before graduation, tailored to the individual and implemented by each mentor. If the student passed, he or she became that wizard's apprentice. If not, he repeated the ten years of schoolwork or dumped a dream that had claimed at least the last decade of his life.

Seion maintained a politely attentive position, resisting the urge to slump. Brown hair fell straight to his broad shoulders. A well-formed but generous nose perched amid gaunt cheeks and above broad lips. The piercing gray eyes that commoners expected from a wizard, and a sharp, clean-shaven chin completed his features. He did not share the anxiety of his twenty classmates. He knew that, for the first time in forty years, the most powerful of the wizards, Calarob Whitehand, had expressed interest in taking a student as his apprentice. Seion was the top of his class in every category from memory to mastery and harbored no doubts that the Great One would choose him.

Neither, apparently, did his classmates, the last five of whom squirmed like children. Only four mentors had not yet picked their trainees. One of the students would definitely have to leave the academy or repeat ten years of training, without even a chance to prove himself to a mentor. Most likely, that would be Laren, who had already struggled through the program twice. His skinny features remained blanched to a corpselike pallor.

Calarob stood quietly in the right front corner of the classroom, robes hiding his tall, narrow frame, his dark eyes nearly hidden amid a tidy mane of gray hair. His stance exuded a confidence and power belied by his frail-appearing build. He wore his symbol, a white hand enclosed in a green circle, tastefully small on the left breast of his cloak. To his right, centered at the front of the room, the chalkboard contained messages from various instructors, some of whom now chose students to mentor. In the middle, the headmaster had written every word and gesture of a luck spell before selecting a high level student to test. The Focus instructor's illegible scrawl slanted across the lower left corner. Upper right, the Ethics professor had written shorthand that they all understood: the squiggly red box that indicated danger surrounding a circle within a triangle. It reminded them to avoid the pathway of the wizard Trigeminy, whose ruined tower still stood like a dark and broken sentinel on a near-distant hill. Adventurers believing themselves more competent than those who came before regularly suicided on defenses even the Wizards' Council could not fully neutralize, convinced a vast treasure lay abandoned inside.

Though the events had happened longer than a century ago, rumors claimed Calarob Whitehand had played a role. It had taken at least a dozen wizards to destroy Trigeminy and the demons he had called to his aid. His grasp for power had resulted in hundreds of deaths, including those of several promising wizards. Since that time, ethics had become a part of the curriculum, focused on the need to use only for good the vast resources that naturally accompanied magic. Trigeminy, as well as his sapphire-filled triangle, had become the symbol for ultimate evil. The desperate battle that had claimed the lives of five wizards, including himself, had gained the label "the Great Carnage."

Other messages filled the board: Ethina had left her students a poetic riddle, Margon had chalked a luck icon, Barnabray had seized a spot near the headmaster's for a paragraph spattered with inside jokes that made even Laren laugh aloud, and Territhrin had written out the complete formula for a courage potion.

Seion glanced at his remaining colleagues. Two more had trotted off with their mentors, leaving only himself, Laren, and a shy awkward woman named Mythrana. She sat with her head bowed over hands clasped to white fists, long black hair like ink across the knuckles. Laren seemed incapable of dragging his eyes from the chalkboard. Every muscle formed a tight ball beneath the thin fabric of his brown apprentice's robes.

Seion knew his demeanor little resembled his companions'. No nervousness touched him. He never doubted his disposition, his worthiness to serve the Master.

Territhrin stepped to the front, the least powerful of the established wizards who had consented to taking apprentices this year. His lesser ability stemmed partially from being only two years out from his own training, but teaching also tended to draw the weaker wizards. The stronger ones had larger, or too many, matters to attend or had garnered enough fame and money to concentrate on their own hobbies and inventions.

Territhrin did not hesitate, understanding how much excitement and misery lay upon his decision. "Mythrana," he said carefully, as Laren collapsed in his chair. Pain filled the professor's pale eyes. "And Laren," he finally added, looking askance at the headmaster.

From the doorway, the headmaster hesitated, then nodded, the understanding clear. At least one of the students would probably not pass whatever test Territhrin presented. Even if both managed, Territhrin could handle two since he had no other apprentices. Next year, however, he could not present himself for another.

Seion considered all of this in the abstract, pitying those without his natural and studied skills. Laren remained still several moments, frozen beyond movement. Then, he practically launched himself from his chair, galloping toward Territhrin like an eager puppy. Mythrana managed to retain a bit more decorum, probably as much attributable to the realization that the worst had yet to come as to breeding, training, or trust in her own competence.

As the others shuffled from the room, the choosing finished for all intents and purposes, Calarob finally stepped to the front of the room. He studied Seion through brown eyes that held the wisdom of the ages. Without a word, he turned, sending a nonverbal request for the academy's best student to follow. Though Seion could neither duplicate, nor even fathom, the nature of the inducement, he followed. Calarob had not sent him a direct mental message or a physical gesture, simply made his intentions clear through no method the student could fathom. Seion marveled at the old wizard's repertoire, desperately eager. He knew Calarob's test would strain even his abilities. Yet master it he would, and become the envy of every classmate as he learned the secrets of the Whitehand.

Still without speaking, Calarob led Seion from the room, down the long hallway, and outside the main door. From the safety of the Wizards' Academy that had served as Seion's home for a decade, they stepped out into late fall air filled with the icy promise of winter. Wind whipped Seion's hair, but it barely ruffled Calarob's thick, gray locks, as if even the elements shied from his power. A week-old memory dragged itself to the fore. When the headmaster had first announced the honor of Calarob presenting himself as a mentor, several of the top students had stiffened, nostrils flaring, until the realization that Seion would draw him surfaced. They held the old wizard in an awe that more closely favored fear than most realized. Seion did not share their concerns, though he wondered whether his composure resembled the fatal attraction of a moth for a flame, or if a decade of accomplishment had simply inured him to success. No academy project had ever proved too difficult for him; his spells, potions, and recitations always earned him the best grades in the class. All of this had simply culminated in the obvious. His selection by the most powerful had surprised no one, not even himself.

For half an hour, wizard and student walked in a silence filled with thought. Seion scarcely noticed the scenery floating past as they traveled from the school grounds, across the soft grass of the Magic Meadow. They wound between the tended gardens and sculpted trees of an area that served alternately as quiet place of contemplation, practice ground, and a playground for the wizards' children. At length, they reached a well-traveled road pounded by the hooves of caravans and the booted feet of travelers. Calarob magically smoothed a few wheel ruts from the surface with level motions of his hands.

Seion waited patiently, torn between assisting and the realization that the great wizard might as easily resent as appreciate his contribution. Though he knew himself capable of helping without intruding, Seion chose not to do so. No matter how competent, his actions might offend his mentor.

A moment later, Calarob continued down the roadway, Seion mimicking the auspicious strides of the elder wizard and attempting to emulate his manner. Calarob still had not spoken a word as the spires of his mansion came into view over a hillock. Many of the wizards had claimed weakening baronies or had drawn enough followers for villages to form around them. But Calarob had deliberately chosen a barren area devoid of the lakes or rivers necessary for trade and to water a populace. He kept his grounds by magic and the area beyond his influence collapsed into a sandy ruin. He could have ruled one of the large cities but chose instead to live a solitary and quiet life in a manufactured hamlet between the Wizards' Academy and the ruins of Trigeminy's tower.

To Seion's surprise, Calarob did not stop at his mansion, continuing past the dense carpet of grassland, into the desolation behind his home. They left the road, breaking trail through twisted weeds and brambles. Long, black seeds and sand burrs clung to the hem of Calarob's robes, the only indication that the plants did not spare him in the manner of the wind. Seion idly wondered if he had discovered his mentor's weakness; at least one of the elements did not bow to his whim. Seion grinned at the thought. His own mastery neither favored nor faulted any of the twenty-three disciplines, any of the seven elements, any of the three devenities. Someday, far in the future, his power would surpass even that of his teacher.

Calarob stopped.

Seion did the same, crafting a spell that sent bits of foliage springing from his robe. He mouthed words of warmth, and the breezes tugging at his clothing no longer knifed through the thin fabric like ice. Only then he realized they stood in front of a listing shack, its boards sagging and cracks at its seams admitting the chill.

Still spotted with brown bits of flora, Calarob finally spoke. "Your test: You will go inside. You will summon a demon. You will ask it for the bane of Trigeminy in a single word. You will bring that answer to me." He raised a robed arm, the sleeve flopping back to reveal a weathered wrist. "You will find me at my home." Without another word or even a pause for questions, Calarob strode back across the field.

Seion did not bother to watch his mentor leave. He headed for the shack, a smile creasing his lips. *A demon summoning. The most difficult task learned at the academy.* The test seemed almost too predictable, a disappointment. Remarkably difficult and desperately dangerous, the summoning of the most terrifying and hideous creatures in existence had become a mission cliché for its use as the ultimate example. Whenever anyone wished to demonstrate a wizard's prowess, they claimed his final exam consisted of summoning a demon.

And now they'll talk about me that way. Seion's grin broadened as he realized future wizards would claim such a thing anyway, regardless of the truth. Yet, he had somehow expected something different, something unpredictable and special, from Calarob Whitehand. *Human,* he reminded himself. *Like the rest of us.* The thought seemed sacrilege, even for its truth. The idea of dragging an icon to the level of ordinary mortals tightened his chest to a horrified knot. Yet he had to admit, though magic might keep him alive past a normal life span, even the greatest of wizards fell prey to his own foibles, injuries, accidents, and, eventually, to death.

Bothered by this train of thought, Seion abandoned it. He shoved aside the excitement of his new pairing, the realization of the vast knowledge his future held, for the task at hand. If he failed his test, he would not survive to repeat the decade of teaching. The demon would likely see to that.

Concentrate. Seion entered the shack. Its inside looked little more secure than its outside, the walls heeling leftward and wide gaps between the boards admitting freezing wind. The water-damaged floor warped toward the center, little flatter than the ground. He frowned, a frigid gust slapping his back from behind and mingling with the breezes fluttering through myriad cracks. Closing the door, he lowered his head. Emptying his mind of all other thought, he brought forth syllables of warding. Punctuated by the appropriate gestures, he spoke the words of the spell, suffused with the familiar warm tingle of dredged magic. As he cast, he paused repeatedly to scrawl portions of a pentagram in black chalk across the floorboards.

At length, Seion rose, the enchantment finished, the last line drawn to perfectly join the first. He studied his handiwork, lips twitching downward. He had drawn the shape meticulously, and sprinkles of color glowed amidst the black lines. Yet, the natural spaces between panels on the floor left tiny breaks he dared not ignore. Though too small to allow a demon to escape, the imperfections stabbed at his sensibilities, begging closure. Worried for his concentration, he started a new spell. Containing and directing a demon would require more strength, focus, and ability than all his previous projects together. He could not afford such a trifling particular to seize his attention at an inopportune moment.

The second spell flowed through Seion's fingers, strengthened by the movements and words he used to direct it. Gradually, the lines solidified, the multihued sparkles growing brighter, the board gaps fully bridged by hovering chalk. Only then, Seion dropped to his haunches, admiring his handiwork with a relief that brought a new rush of magical power. Still, he waited several moments longer, drawing strength through his contacts with wood, air, cold, and earth, funneling back the energy lost to the spell of warding. The elements answered his summons, rapidly dragging him back to the fullness of his power.

Seion rose, stepping back, judging every movement. He returned the chalk to his pocket as he measured his location, comparing it to the center of the pentagram. The proper arrangement would keep him beyond reach of the trapped creature yet maintain his contact with as many elements and devenities as possible, to maximize his power and minimize his danger. He took a half step forward, shuffled right, then farther right, then retreated that same half step. Finally happy with his position, he rooted the summoning sequence from memory. He had watched Margon call a demon less than a month previously, focusing fanatically on every word and gesture, even as most of the other students stood locked in awe or scrambled to take notes.

Again, Seion lowered his head, hair falling like a curtain across his face. Closing his eyes, he entered a darkness devoid of idea, drove everything extraneous from his mind, and forced an inner calm tinged with anticipation. Panic had no place in the mind-set of a wizard, yet neither did unpreparedness. If anything untoward happened, he would need to face it with cool-headed dispatch. *I can handle anything,* Seion told himself. And believed it.

From that point, Seion leaped, like a diver from a cliff plunging into icy water three stories below. Three words, gruff as curses, brought him to the unformed, colorless world of the demons. He claimed the first his consciousness touched, binding it with loops of magic powered by the disciplines, the elements, and the devenities together. The creature howled, a sound rich with an evil so ancient it defined the word. Then it damned him with sounds that, though not-quite-words, fell on his ears like hammer blows.

The shock of those noises jerked Seion deeper into the swirling thickness of chaos. He backpedaled with a wild jerk, hauling the flailing and pitching demon toward his own world. A powerful spell-word flashed through the soup. Abruptly, the resistance disappeared, and they both boiled into the world of wizards and law. Seion spasmed back into his own body while the demon raged against the confines of the pentagram, an inky blur of anger that barely resembled a grotesquely distorted human. A bulbous, hairless head swarmed with warty extrusions towered on shoulders as blocky as boulders, with no neck between them. Eyes like hot coals burned beneath fleshy folds that took the place of lids. A hole tunneled into either side of its head, replacing human ears. Its chest seemed to fill the room. Its fists pounded the ceiling, and legs thick as tree trunks ended in bare, toeless feet.

Trusting his wards, Seion froze in place, surprised

to find dizziness swirling through his head. He had tapped more energy then he realized, yet it did not matter. His studies told him that the creature would rage for hours before surrendering to his bindings and five-sided ward. That would give him plenty of time to replenish his exhausted stores of magic.

The demon froze in mid-roar. The eyes leaped like flames, and its long, lipless mouth broadened into a warped parody of a human smile. The noise that thundered from its throat no longer mingled wrath with horrible frustration. It sounded more like laughter.

Sudden alarm shot through Seion. Swallowing bile, he mustered his ragged forces to his bindings.

The maneuver served only to rescue Seion. Ignoring the wizard, the demon raised fists like sledgehammers, slamming them against the ceiling. Wood shattered, hurling shards. One fragment carved a gash across Seion's cheek, and warm blood trickled along his throat. The cabin shuddered, then collapsed, boards tumbling like paper. The demon howled in wicked triumph.

NO! Seion did not waste breath shouting aloud nor moments contemplating an error that seemed nonsensical, impossible. As the demon blustered toward him, he flinched reflexively, hurling a weak stream of remaining power into the bindings. He sought the pentagonal ward, finding only bits of magic-infused chalk flung randomly through the wreckage. Then, his vision filled with teeth as long as his forearm and sharp as daggers. Foam dripped from the demon's dark mouth, and its breath reeked of things long dead.

Panic exploded through Seion's mind. Ducking behind an out-thrust arm, he screamed like a townswoman, eyes closed, awaiting the inevitable. Logic fought for control of scattered thought. He grasped at a thread of reason. *If you don't act, innocents will die for your mistake.* He forced his lids apart, seeing the warty back fleeing toward the roadway. The bindings had held. It could not harm him, but others would not prove so lucky.

Seion staggered after the demon, a clump of hair clotted with blood flopping against his ear. His first

thought, to magically transport himself between creature and road passed quickly. Even if he could muster
the power to perform such a thing now, he would
arrive with no strength left to banish or battle the
thing. Biting his lip, he marshaled his confidence. *You
can handle this.* His hands winched to quaking fists.
You can handle anything. The internal fortitude
helped him mobilize, allowing him to siphon discrete
energy from the contact of each boot with the ground,
from the dribble of blood, and from the air that
screamed around him as he ran. Even the splinters of
the wood that had cut him assisted.

With barely enough power for the most minor of
spells, Seion blundered over the hill. Fresh as a new
summoning, the demon stormed toward the roadway,
its body like a hole in the scenery, as if it sucked in
shadows and repelled the light. Beyond it, Seion saw
a caravan of three horse-drawn, covered carts snaking
along the roadway, accompanied by several riders.
"No," he whispered.

The demon's laughter transformed to high-pitched
squeals of evil pleasure. It doubled its pace, fairly flying toward the unsuspecting caravan.

Seion quickened his own run. Cold air burned his
lungs, and his feet pounded faster than he could control them. The downside of the hill proved his undo-
ing. Unable to shorten his strides, he found his upper
balance thrown too far forward to check. He tumbled,
head over feet. Weeds crumbled beneath him. Thistle
stabbed through his robes. Rocks stamped bruises
across his head and torso. Pain wrestled with training.
Seion forced himself to suck energy from every contact, whether with air, ground, or plant life. The
scramble to his feet at the bottom dragged pain
through every part of him, and clinging burrs stabbed
him with every movement.

Seion's bleary gaze turned road and demon to blurry
streaks of gray and black. He started sprinting again
before his vision cleared, gathering power as he moved
and hardly daring to believe how little he had managed to muster. A horse screamed, its rider echoing

it a moment later. Seion waited only until he could differentiate demon from caravan, then hurled all his energy into a shield between them.

The sudden spell drained the last dregs of Seion's strength. He collapsed, limbs weak as rags, head buzzing. He watched the demon slam against the barrier hard enough to bounce backward. A fang snapped, sending a hunk of dark tooth spinning. The horse fled in terror, the unseated man curling into a fetal position on the road.

The cart horses went crazy, rearing and bucking in foaming frenzies. The first cart toppled, spilling silks across the muddy road. A man and a woman rolled from the wreckage. He flopped to the roadway, ominously still. She flailed amid the cloth, her screams muffled by the shield. The second cart remained upright, though the horses spun it in wild circles. The last cart was kicked to splinters. The horses bolted back the way they had come, trailing scraps of harness. Two women and a man lay amid shattered planks and dresses.

The world gained a dreamlike quality. Seion frantically gathered scraps of energy as the demon hurled itself repeatedly against his barrier. The last of the horses fled, trampling wares and humans in blind, panicked haste. Pain screams wafted from the wreckage, different from the shrill shrieks of terror that seemed endless. Every sound tore at Seion's sensibilities. *What have I done?* He discarded the thought from necessity. If he survived, he would have another decade of schooling to contemplate his errors and attempt to live with the guilt of the carnage his own incompetence had wrought. For now, such focus could only hamper his mustering.

A sharp, sickening tinkle, like breaking glass, filled his hearing. Agony stabbed him as his barrier surrendered before the beast's attack, and the demon raged through the new opening he had created.

"No!" Seion screamed. Never in his entire life had he felt so helpless and small. He attempted a spell but found his coffers empty, tapped out. He did manage to stand, limping and stumbling to the road as the demon seized the woman from the first cart. "No!" he managed again, hurling himself physically at the creature even as the woman's wail of agony cut him to the bone. He heard the tear of flesh. Hot blood sprayed him like a fountain. Then, he thudded against the dark mass of its bulk.

The demon roared, flinging aside the shredded corpse to claw at Seion. It spun, the force tearing at Seion's hold. The student wizard clung, digging his nails deep into the slimy flesh, anchoring his knees against irregular protrusions, fumbling for the utility knife beneath the thin folds of his apprentice's robes. He shouted words of banishment, though he had no power to enforce them. The demon bucked and snorted, every movement tearing at Seion's hold. *Delay, only delay.* Seion realized that his maneuver gained nothing but a few moments for the humans to run. Yet, injuries and fear paralyzed most in place. Just one man dashed for the forest, assisting a limping woman.

Clinging with one arm, Seion groped through fabric with the other hand, foiled by the demon's spirals. A claw slashed his leg, carving off a line of fabric and flesh. *Binding's dead.* Pain lanced through Seion, galvanizing him. His hand closed around the hilt of the dagger. He dragged it free in triumph, just as the demon lurched leftward. Forced to use both hands, he clamped his fingers around the hilt and the demon's upper arm at the same time. Then, an abrupt jerk in the opposite direction unseated him. He flew through the air, dagger jarred from his fist. He slammed into a tree, breath knocked from his lungs, mind swimming.

The demon closed its claws around a man.

Tears filled Seion's eyes. He raised a shaky hand to wipe them away. That simple movement incited a wave of pain that sent curtains of spots weaving across his vision. He dropped the arm, fighting for consciousness.

Then, a firm voice rolled across the plain, speaking the same magical syllables Seion had. He quelled the instinct to find the speaker; movement would send him to oblivion. It could only be Calarob Whitehand.

The demon whirled toward the sound, mouth open in a tremendous roar of rage. It charged Seion in a wild rush that brought it barely to him before its form faded, returning to the world from which it came.

Only then, Seion surrendered to the darkness.

Seion awakened in an unfamiliar bed, a bandage enwrapping his leg and another stuck to his cheek. He tried to sit. Dizziness dropped him back to the bed, and a rush of pain accompanied the movement. He groaned.

Calarob appeared at his bedside, the brown eyes inscrutable, expression lost in the mane of gray hair.

Seion looked away. "I'm sorry, Master," he said, the words woefully inadequate. "I'll head back to the academy as soon as I'm able to—"

"You can't," the elder interrupted. "Have you forgotten?"

Believing he must have, Seion shook his head. "Forgotten what, Master?"

"You're my apprentice."

No words could have surprised Seion more. "But I failed the test. I lost control of the demon."

"The test was summoning it, not controlling it."

Those words made even less sense. "But people died because of me. I made an unforgivable mistake."

Calarob made a gesture, then took a seated position, floating in the air as if perched on a chair. "You could have run. The bindings would have kept the demon from harming you. I can work with an apprentice who takes responsibility for his mistakes." He added softly, "Even when they aren't his."

Seion fought the exhaustion and pain that numbed his thoughts, certain he had misunderstood. "Excuse me, Master?" he prompted.

Calarob looked away. "I went to school with a wizard once. The most powerful in my class. Perhaps the most powerful ever." He met Seion's gray glance. "Everything he did, he did with great strength and precision."

Seion swallowed. Aside from the years of schooling, the description fit himself.

"As all of us, he gained confidence with power. Too much confidence, perhaps. He never understood the consequences of his actions. Believed himself the best, which he was, but he came to mistake lack of error with perfection." Calarob's brows rose. "Do you know who I'm speaking of?"

Seion thought he did. "Trigeminy."

Calarob smiled, a bittersweet grimace; and his eyes turned moist and distant. "You will never forget what happened here today. It will temper everything you do." He turned, rose, and paced toward the door. His last question barely reached Seion. "In a word, do you know his bane?"

Seion lowered his head. "No," he admitted.

Calarob shook his head sadly. "If only 'Gem' had had the same opportunity."

A week passed before Seion had the chance to return to the road and the shack, to review his mistake. Heart pounding in his chest, eyes burning with tears, he went first to the shack's remains. Little had changed. Wind had scattered the splinters, but the shattered planks still lay strewn across the field. He would clean the mess, but first he needed to find the error that had stolen his assurance and resulted in innocent deaths.

With magical sight, Seion found the scraps of his chalk pentagram, the flecks of magic flickering toward death. He worked swiftly, calling energy to reconstruct the floor and its drawing, worried that to tarry too long would mean losing any chance to find the error. The pentagram re-formed, its black outline crisp and careful except for a single flaw. At the farthest point from where Seion had stood, an entire point was missing. *What the . . . ?* He walked to the spot, studying it in fascination. An irregular smudge marred the ward, speckles of magic dead amid a black smear of chalk. Seion wiped tears from his eyes, yet the marks still remained, blurry and indistinct, except now he could also make out the tread of a boot. It looked suspiciously like his master's footsteps. *Sabotage!* Seion dropped to his haunches, aghast at the finding. *Master Whitehand deliberately sabotaged my ward?*

Another thought filled Seion's mind, sending him running to the roadway. As he now expected, he found nothing out of place. Not a scrap of wood, cloth, or harness. Not a single drop of blood. No one had died by his mistake. The wizards had conspired to trick him and the demon together. The caravan on the road had been an illusion. *No one died.* Joy suffused him, and a smile eased onto his face.

Seion rose, reveling in wind that ruffled his hair like a brother and brought words in the voice of Calarob Whitehand. "I'm sorry," it whispered. "I hope you understand."

Seion turned toward the ruined tower of Trigeminy. On clear days, southern breezes still carried the scent of ozone and the carrion smell of overconfident adventurers who fancied themselves heroes. "I understand," he said back to the wind. The summoning of the demon had brought the requested answer after all. "The bane of Trigeminy, and nearly of myself, was pride."

Seion hoped his Master heard.

A THING OR TWO
ABOUT LOVE

❖❖❖

by *Richard Parks*

Richard Parks lives in Mississippi, works with computers, and writes. He has a wife named Carol, whose first date with him was a campus screening of *Psycho*. As for other details of his personal existence, well, the less said the better. He firmly believes that his stories are much more interesting than he is. Humor him.

In a cave deep in the Northern Mountains there lived a Dragon and a Princess. Dragon played host to all visiting heroes; later he left their bones in neat little piles by the door and promptly forgot the names of all but the very few who tasted particularly good. The Princess slept an enchanted sleep and didn't do much of anything except lie in the claw-carved bed Dragon had made for her and look ravishing. She being a True Princess and he being a True Dragon this was all they expected of each other.

One fine spring afternoon, when Dragon and the Princess happened to be asleep at the same time, there came a knock on the door. Dragon opened one eye and considered the matter. His appetite wasn't exactly keen—he had already left one exceptionally tough hero half-chewed that month. The knocking persisted, and he opened another eye as a faint voice came wafting through the cracks.

"On guard, Fiend! I am Prince Eric of Sturga come to rescue the Princess Allison!"

Dragon opened his third and final eye and made a mental note of the name. He wasn't optimistic, knights-errant as a group weren't very tasty, but princes were worse. Fed on weird delicacies from birth, they tended to lie like stones in his stomach.

"I suppose you have your heart set on this?" asked Dragon.

"Open this door, or I'll break it down!"

There wasn't much chance of that, so to spare the newcomer embarrassment, Dragon gave the door a nudge with his forepaw. The prince, standing too close, was knocked sprawling partway down the rocky slope.

His armor made a gratifying clatter.

Dragon bared his long teeth in a grin. *A bag of gold to the harper who sings this part of the story honestly.* The chance of losing part of his hoard didn't worry him; Dragon considered himself a student of the possible and let the saints worry about miracles.

Dragon studied his opponent with professional detachment as Prince Eric hauled himself upright using his sword as a crutch. He was larger than most, with long fair hair, blue eyes, and a face that wasn't so much merely handsome as a sculptor's masterpiece waiting to happen.

Everything a hero should be, Dragon thought. It depressed him a little.

While Dragon looked at Eric, Eric shielded his eyes against the glare and got his first good look at Dragon.

"Gods . . ."

"Don't tell me," sighed Dragon. "I'm bigger than you expected, yes?"

"By a few hundred stone," Prince Eric admitted, "but I've sworn to rescue the Princess Allison, and rescue her I shall. Prepare yourself!"

Sometime later, with his armor shredded and most of his hair singed, Prince Eric leaned on his sword again and tried to catch his runaway breath.

"Well fought, Dragon," he managed.

"Thank you," Dragon replied courteously. "Well fought, yourself." Which wasn't just manners—Eric *had* scratched one of Dragon's scales. He rarely took so much damage.

Several times during the fight Dragon had found himself trying to think of an excuse not to kill Eric. He couldn't find one, but the trying allowed the fight to drag on. Then he tried to think why he was trying to think of an excuse in the first place, which of course let the fight go on even longer. It was during one of these distracted periods that Eric had landed his scale-marring blow.

When Eric recovered enough to lift his sword, the whole thing began again. And again. The shadows lengthened.

"Prince Eric," Dragon said finally, "should a gentleman such as yourself be fighting so late in the day?"

From his present position—flat on his back—Eric considered the matter. "Well, I seem to recall some reference to it in the Code of Chivalry, but I'm not sure."

"I wouldn't want you to compromise your principles for me," Dragon said, "We can pick this up later, if you don't mind. I'm a little tired."

"It would certainly be chivalrous to allow you some rest," said Eric, "Perhaps tomorrow . . . ?"

Dragon shook his head, causing a minor rockslide. "Tomorrow's a holy day," he pointed out. "The Feast of Saint St. John the Persistent. It'll have to be later."

"Later is fine," said Eric. "Good night, Dragon."

"Good night, Highness," said Dragon, going back into the cave and closing the door.

Now why did I do that? Dragon wondered. It wasn't because he liked Eric—which he did, but that was beside the point. Dragon had been on good terms with several heroes before devouring them. He shrugged, and several small stalactites shattered. Dragon crawled deeper into the cave to where Princess Allison lay sleeping, her long golden hair lovingly arranged on the pillow. He drank in her beauty like a familiar vintage, resting his three eyes on the curve of her dainty breasts, the roses of her cheeks, the line of her dear little nose.

"Do you know why I let him live, Dearest?"

It wasn't exactly an answer, but, deep in dream, the Princess smiled.

Later that evening, Prince Eric of Sturga, the third son of Konrad II of Sturga and heir to not very much, slept the sleep of the totally exhausted next to the cold ashes of his campfire. He shivered occasionally through the thin blanket, but not quite hard enough to wake himself. Somewhere in the depths of sleep Eric's situation was a lot better. Somewhere there was a quiet stream, and soft grass, and a soft lap to lie his head in. Princess Allison tended his wounds in regal silence.

"I failed you," said Eric, close to tears.

Allison daintily dabbed blood from a long scratch on his cheek. "You're the first to even survive the attempt," she said. "Surely the fates spared you for a reason." Allison dampened her kerchief in the stream, watching blood drift away in little red puffs. "Will you try again?" she asked.

"If it means my death," he said, knowing that it probably would. "If I have your promise . . . ?"

"Slay him, and I will be yours for as long as you want me," she replied, turning her eyes away with becoming modesty.

Eric lay enraptured by the thought, just as he had the first time Princess Allison had appeared to him in his dreams, the most beautiful vision he had ever seen. The fleeting dreams were no longer enough; he had to make them real.

Somewhere near Eric's camp a meadowlark began to sing, and within the dream the grass grew colder, Allison's touch more distant.

"There's little time," she said, "but now that you've proved your courage, I am free to tell you—there's another way. Seek the mage Amadon at Crumbling Tower due east of here. He can help you. . . ."

Allison disappeared, and Prince Eric awoke stiff, sore, and chilled. He regarded the pitiful remnants of his armor a little wistfully, and finally left them where they lay. He buckled on his sword and dagger, unhobbled his gray stallion, and rode toward the rising sun.

Crumbling Tower was hard to miss. It was intricately cracked from base to crenelations, and bits of it pelted down all the while Prince Eric approached. Oddly, the tower never seemed to get any shorter or the piles of debris any taller. Eric turned his mount loose to graze at a safe distance, stepped carefully over the rubble-filled moat and—with many nervous glances upward—made a dash for the door. He made it and rapped the lion-headed knocker once. The lion spat a stream of stale-smelling fluid into his face.

"Poison!" shrieked Eric, dabbing frantically at his cheek.

A voice from within the tower demurred. "Hardly the Nectar of the Gods, but not as bad as that."

Amadon stood in the open doorway, a wide grin on his face. He wasn't what Eric expected: he was little more than a boy, with a wisp of fine yellow hair on his chin pretending to be a beard. The rest of his hair was short, ill-cut, and unruly, and he had watery blue eyes that seemed a little too large for his face. It gave him a look of constant amazement.

"Sorry about the knocker," he said, "but I get so few visitors I couldn't resist trying it out. Not very subtle, but effective, don't you think?"

Eric bit his lip and nodded, already starting to question Allison's judgment, if not her intentions. "You *are* Amadon, aren't you?" He hesitated, then added, "the Wizard?"

Amadon sighed deeply. "It's that hateful Meralna's fault. The witch in the next valley. She put an 'Illusion of Youth' spell on me, and just because I grew a wart on the end of her nose. It's not as if it was the only one *there*, heaven knows. Still, it was clever trick; I confess it. Who expects an almost-beardless boy to know anything about the Mystic Arts?"

"I imagine it's a problem," Eric said, trying not to sound too abrupt, "but I've got one of my own."

Amadon looked him up and down. "Your youth isn't an illusion, so let me guess—love."

"Partly," admitted Eric, "but mostly it's the dragon."

Amadon's eyes narrowed. It made his pointed hat fall over his face. He paused to adjust it. "That wouldn't be the one guarding Allison of Adriatica?"

Eric frowned. "There's another?"

"More than you can shake a sword at," said Amadon, "but he's closest. Come in and we'll discuss it." Eric hesitated and Amadon grinned. "The tower is perfectly safe—another of Meralna's illusions. I'll pay her back when I get around to it."

The inside of Crumbling Tower wasn't crumbling at all. It was a simple round tower with a spiral staircase. The walls were lined with tapestries that changed scenes while you watched, and the main room was packed full of some of the oddest bric-a-brac Eric had ever seen: grotesque glassware, statues of green marble and lead, metal popinjays that sang the time and hour in tinny voices, and several spring-cog objects that didn't seem to do anything but hum together in harmony. Eric was a bit overwhelmed.

Amadon watched his reaction carefully, then he smiled. "Nine parts of wizardry is the accumulation of trivia, Prince Eric. You gather and consider until the patterns are clear, then tap their power. My old master learned his most powerful spell by studying all the synonyms of 'salubrity.' "

Amadon kept up a stream of such trivial chatter as he seated Eric at a round table and poured him a goblet of rich red wine.

"How do you know about Princess Allison?" Eric asked between sips. "Or me, for that matter?"

"The necessity of trivia, dear boy. Let's see . . . Allison of Adriatica. Quite a little hellion if the stories are true: self-centered, vain to the point of obsession, even dabbled in Black Magic, not to mention politics—"

Eric stiffened. "I'll thank you not to slander the woman I love, Wizard!"

Amadon smiled a disarming smile. "Your pardon, Highness, but I can't help but glory in the details: kidnapped by a dragon under mysterious circumstances, kept in an enchanted sleep for four hundred years, heroes slain left and right trying to rescue her . . . the first one of your ancestral kinsmen, I believe. Prince Alexander of Sturga. Did you know about him?"

"Of course!" snapped Eric, "but this is hardly—"

"Relevant?" Amadon sighed. "My boy, *everything* is relevant. But I can see you're not interested. Your main concern is to slay the beastly beast and claim the lovely lady, yes?"

"I mean to rescue her," said Eric. "I'll marry her if she'll have me."

"Oh, I'm sure she will."

There was an undercurrent of cynicism in Amadon's voice that irritated Eric. He rose, finishing his wine in one long gulp. "I can see this is a waste of time. Allison was mistaken—"

"Sit down, Prince."

Eric sat down. He didn't want to. He didn't have any choice. The compulsion was overwhelming. "What have you done to me?"

"A minor enchantment—in the wine, of course. I've not lived so long by allowing armed men near me without some precautions."

The effects of the potion, triggered by Amadon's voice, left Eric's vision a little fuzzy except when he looked at the wizard. Now he could see through the illusion: Amadon was a wizened old man with face and head totally shaven. His eyes held little of the aimless humor in those of the illusory boy—it had been replaced with an odd, unsettling intensity.

"I mean you no harm, Prince, but it seemed as if you were going to leave without asking for my assistance. Since I've decided to give it, that would not do at all."

Eric was still angry, but pragmatic enough to realize the matter was out of his hands. "Very well. What do you want in return?"

Amadon shrugged. "The only thing of real worth in this world—trivia. *Knowledge*, to the high-minded. If you rescue Allison, I may be able to add the missing pieces of her story, and frankly I'm interested."

"How can you help me?"

"Well, surely when you fought the dragon, you noticed he was awfully hard to hurt?"

Eric, not for the first time, got the distinct feeling that the fates had written down the story beforehand and given the scroll to Amadon for safekeeping. "I never said I fought the dragon."

Amadon laughed. "You didn't have to; it's in the pattern. I know you, Prince. Or rather, I know what you are: a hero, down to your toenails. You wouldn't come to someone like me except in utter desperation. Now, to business. That dragon is harder than Sturgan steel. The only way you're going to defeat him is with something harder. Come with me."

Amadon led Eric up the spiraling stairs like a bald vulture, circling. He stopped at a door that looked like all the other doors along the way and opened it with a key that looked like all the other keys on his belt. Eric stepped inside and gasped.

The room was large, and every few feet along the walls there hung a suit of armor of exceedingly fine make. Racks of weapons stood about full of swords and axes and war hammers and some things Eric didn't recognize at all. The far wall was empty, but large chests were lined along its entire length.

"Pick a suit that fits," Amadon said. "The straps may need a little grease."

Prince Eric picked a suit of delicately fluted Milthan workmanship and set to with a rag and a cake of lard while the wizard fiddled with one of the chests.

"—know I left it here somewhere . . . ah!"

Amadon pulled a long bundle from the chest and handed it carefully to the prince. Eric unwrapped a longsword edged with a blue-white crystalline material that turned the light from the small window into rainbows.

Eric's eyes widened. "Is this . . . ?"

"Yes," said Amadon wearily, "but don't get any delusions of invincibility. It cuts well enough, but it's not much for parrying. Too brittle. In fact, it's fair to say you'll only get one stab at the beast . . . so to speak."

Eric couldn't hide his disappointment. "It was hard enough to ask for help in the first place. And now you tell me there's no certainty? What if I fail?"

"Then Allison will have to wait for another hero. I doubt if she'll wait long; something's kept that dragon fed over the years."

'But it has to be *me*," Eric insisted. "I love her."

Amadon shrugged. "You're in love with an idea. You don't even know her."

"That's where you're wrong, Wizard. I've met her, spoken to her."

"In your dreams?" asked Amadon, mildly.

"Yes!" It came out like a snarl. "It's the truth; do you doubt me?"

Amadon shook his head slowly. "Not at all, but old men were young men once upon a time, and that's just as true for wizards. I seem to recall a thing or two about love. Have a care, Prince. That sword won't help you there."

Dragon heard the old familiar knocking and opened an eye.

Already?

He opened the rest of his eyes and looked sadly at the princess. She lay, demure and silent, as always.

"I'll have to kill him this time, My Love," he said. "He's determined to take you from me."

Allison smiled.

Eric hid the sword behind his shield as Dragon peered out the door.

"Hello, Your Highness. Are you ready now?"

Eric nodded. He held the sword at the ready, but hesitated. "Dragon, before we meet again, there's something I must know."

Dragon's eyes—all of them—narrowed. "What is it?"

"Why did you kidnap Allison?"

"I didn't. She came willingly."

Eric shook his head. "That can't be."

Dragon shrugged, and the earth trembled a bit. "As you will. Be ready, Prince Eric—I really must kill you now."

Eric gripped the diamond-edged sword tighter as Dragon inched forward. *One thrust* . . . Eric tensed.

"Prince Alexander!"

Amadon . . . ? For one silly instant Eric wanted to stop, but his reflexes had taken over. Just as Dragon turned, distracted, Eric sprang forward and drove the blade with all his strength into Dragon's massive chest. The beast screamed, spitting fire. A claw from a convulsing leg grazed Eric's shoulder and sent him spinning down the slope again. This time his head met something harder than it was, and night fell a little early that day.

When Eric opened his eyes again, he was immediately aware of something very large.

Himself.

"Amadon, what have you done to me?"

"Nothing, dear boy. But I can't say I'm surprised."

Amadon perched on a jutting shard of mountain, just out of easy reach. Eric looked down at his dragon's body. The sword lay several yards away—unbroken—and the wound in his dragon chest had closed as if it had never been.

"Wizard, change me back this instant!"

"Highness, your ability to ignore the obvious astounds me." Amadon sighed. "I didn't change you in the first place, and if you'd been listening—"

Eric still wasn't listening. "Change me back or—" He breathed fire a full second before he realized he knew how, but by the time the fire reached Amadon, there was nothing left of him to burn except his voice. It wasn't particularly flammable.

"Go greet your lady love, Eric."

Eric glared at the spot where Amadon wasn't. "This wasn't how I planned to greet her." But, because he didn't know what else to do, Eric crawled into the cave.

Princess Allison lay asleep in her bed, radiating serene beauty.

"Quite striking for a woman of four hundred and twenty." A stalactite with Amadon's face was smiling. "As I suspected, it was Allison who set up this little love nest. She kept it going. How better to keep the dragon fed than to make each hero think he was the chosen one? Yet as you've discovered, the beast can't be killed—not really."

Eric glared at him. "You knew!"

Amadon appeared in human form at the bedside and shook his head. "I suspected; not the same thing. The evidence suggested that Allison was an adept; your transformation was the final proof of that. Still, I admit none of the hints really conveyed the genius of her concept." Amadon bowed his head in respect. "To cast a would-be lover as the dragon? To enchant *herself?* That was a master stroke."

Eric-dragon looked at his love woefully. "But *why*?"

"Because it fits the pattern: Allison was—is—vain. Obsessively so. This way she can remain young and beautiful forever."

"It's not true," Eric insisted. "She *promised.*"

Amadon shrugged. "And she meant it. Slay the dragon and she is yours forever. Or at least until time and the burdens of being her watchdog wear you down. Like Prince Alexander. I rather thought he was the one."

"Damn you! Never mind how I got this way! Change me back!"

Amadon shook his head. "Don't be deceived by her seemingly dormant state, Prince Eric—Allison makes the rules here, but there *is* a way. I believe it just arrived."

Eric-dragon turned at the faint scrape of metal on stone, and his dragon's blood burned a few degrees colder. Someone with Eric's body and Dragon's eyes stood in the doorway holding the diamond sword. A trail of red from a scalp wound marred his face.

"I believe you've met Prince Alexander," Amadon said.

Eric's soul was at war with itself as the changeling limped closer. "Alexander . . ."

The former dragon looked right through him, his eyes fixed on the sleeping princess. The point of his sword made little chopping motions in the air.

"What are you doing?" Eric demanded. Amadon removed himself to a stalactite's eye view from the ceiling.

"She betrayed me," Alexander hissed. "After four hundred years!"

Alexander's threat marked a clear path for any hero to follow. Eric was almost grateful. "I can't let you harm her," he said, moving between them. It wasn't just instinct; part of him wanted to kill Allison himself. None of him could do it. Student of the possible . . . Where had Eric heard that before?"

"Don't be a fool!" Alexander snapped. "Let me attend to her and I'll make the exchange with you willingly. I've rather grown accustomed to being a dragon."

I do believe that's true, Eric thought. "Then make the change *now*!"

Alexander's eagerness, so brightly mirrored in his eyes, betrayed him. Eric turned his frenzied lunge with one flick of a talon. "You were after me all along, weren't you?"

Alexander's pretense fled. "Allison is mine!"

"She betrayed you," Eric reminded him.

Alexander smiled a bitter smile. "Do you really think I didn't know she might? Or that it makes a bit of difference?"

Eric shook his head. "You've loved her for four hundred years. You had to know what she was."

Amadon's laughter rang through the cave. "Trivial paradox!" he chortled. "Love can die, but it can't be killed. Not even by the truth."

Eric looked at the beautiful devil on the bed. *Quite true. Unfortunately.* "Be silent, Wizard," was all he said.

Eric's new body tensed for combat as Alexander took a swordsman's stance. Now Alexander hesitated. "She'll betray you, too," he said. "Sooner or later."

Eric could do no better than to turn Alexander's knowledge back on him. "Do you really think that makes a difference?"

Alexander smiled again, but there was no bitterness now. It was the smile of one comrade-in-arms to another. "Not in the least."

Dragon licked the last scrap of flesh from Eric's right femur and dropped the bone into the pile with the others. Something glittery on the floor caught his attention. The sword. Dragon paused in thought for a moment, then smashed the blade into dust with one blow of his paw.

"I gather your decision is final, then?" Amadon was speaking from the ceiling again. The sight of him was beginning to annoy Dragon.

"Did you get what you wanted?" Dragon asked.

The stalactite nodded, creaking. "Powerful, vintage trivia of the first order. Meralna will be so jealous! To celebrate, I'll add a bit of advice, gratis—kill all the heroes the first time they appear, Prince Eric. Don't let Allison think your love is fading."

It was good advice, but Eric didn't really need it. Already he gazed at the lovely fiend in the bed with a dragon's true pride of possession, and with delicious anticipation of the dreams to come.

"My name," he corrected firmly, "is Dragon."

THE DEAD THAT SOW

❖ ❖ ❖

by Michelle West

Michelle West has written three novels for DAW, *Hunter's Oath*, *Hunter's Death*, and *The Broken Crown* (Book One of *The Sun Sword*). Her short fiction has appeared in many anthologies, including: *Tarot Fantastic*, *Sword of Ice And Other Tales of Valdemar*, and *Phantoms of the Night*. She lives in Ontario, Canada, with her husband and son.

She woke to the night with a cry, the haunt of a memory that could not and would never be escaped, no matter how years and wisdom might soften it. Men with torches, pitchforks, daggers. Dogs, long-toothed and near-feral with the passing winter.

No, she thought, as she grabbed her shawl and listened a moment. *This is not that place. I am not that woman.* It was peaceful as she lay awake, thinking of the long road between that night and this one. Knowing, suddenly, that it would happen again, here, even if there was nothing left to take—nothing left to cull. She was not a young woman anymore, and her heart was not so fond of fear and life as it had been.

They came to her home past sundown, in the dark of the Lady's night, when they should have been sleeping in their beds, with their husbands and wives wrapped round them, the evenness of familiar breath a counterpoint to the beating of heart. Instead, they stood beneath the flickering glow of torches and a single lit lamp, and they trod across the herb beds and gardens that she had so carefully laid out in the fall and the spring.

Summer now, and she knew it would be a good harvest.

Or it would have been, had anyone been there to care for her garden.

She'd been in this town two years and three months; she'd arrived at the beginning of the thaw, found a patch of land that would take a small cottage, and had offered her services to the villagers in return for their help in building that small home. She grew her healing herbs and played midwife for the village births, and in return they brought her the food that they labored over.

It had been a good life; the lord who owned the village did not deign to greet her, and when he sent his men out to collect their tithe, they came and went without incident; the villagers gave what was asked for.

They had always seemed so friendly, and so accepting.

She did not see them at once; it was the old dog that woke her, his voice much like a bear's rumble of anger and anxiety, his muzzle a trembling wetness of nose and tongue against her sleeping cheek. She would have let him out, and quickly, but by the time she'd pulled her coats and shift on, they were already rapping at her door.

Too many of them, she thought, *to be here asking for help.* She took a deep breath and opened the door.

She was wrong, although she didn't know it then.

"Seamus," she said to the man with the lamp. "What are you doing here, at this time of night, with so many angry torches and angry men? You didn't come this way three weeks ago, when your daughter was caught in the grip of the summer sickness."

He had the grace to blush and look at his feet.

"And you, Freda, why are you here with these men? You've a son to look after, and he's not yet finished the course I set him when I gave you the cured *verrenne.*"

"We like it no better than you," Freda said, speaking where Seamus had suddenly lost the ability. "But *he's* sent us, Maggie, and he's sent us for you."

She looked up then, to the castle that crested the hill, and saw in the light of the full, bright moon that the bridge had indeed been lowered. "And the last girl?" she said, her voice low.

From somewhere in the back of the group, a torch wavered and fell, to be caught by another hand. She heard a dry sob, a terrible noise of loss just beginning to be felt. Answer enough.

"Are you come to drag me off without even a change of clothing, then?"

"If we have to, yes," Freda said. "Because if it's not you, Maggie, it'll be Seamus' girl, or mine—and they don't have what you have."

She felt her heart sink.

"You're not a weak thing, not a child," Seamus said, holding the lamp aloft. "We'll take you any way we have to. But—"

"But you'd rather I choose it."

"Yes."

"And what's in the castle, then?" she said, more to herself than to the villagers who waited in such a terrible shadow of red and black and moonlit sky.

"The lord," Seamus said in a hushed tone.

"The Wizard," Freda said.

"You've seen him, then?"

"No. None of us have ever seen him."

"What does he say that he wants with me?"

"Do we know the affairs of lords? He wants what he wants, and there's no point denyin' him; he gets it one way or the other."

"But if you haven't—"

"He doesn't have to be seen to be felt. Maggie, please. I'm asking you."

"Let me get my things," she said softly. "It'll take an hour at most—I want my seeds and I want my clothing, and I want my lute."

*　　*　　*

The old dog followed her, trotting at her side like an anxious escort. She hadn't the heart to send him away, and when Seamus lifted a hand to swat him, she stepped between his fist and the mongrel. "You'll leave him be," she said, with what dignity she could muster, and he did.

She had dignity, and she had strength; she had a certain confidence in her skill as an herbalist. They failed her only once, as she approached the castle itself.

For there, at the cross formed of the road that escaped the castle's bridge and continued through the town, and the rough road that circled the town itself, a body was nailed to a post; a young body, a girl, she thought, even in the darkness.

"She was there," Freda said, her voice so quiet it could barely be heard over the sound of crickets and the rush of the river, "four years. We thought—" And then she looked away.

"You can't leave her here!"

"Does it matter?" the older woman asked. "She's dead; she doesn't notice."

"And her father?"

"Aye, he notices. We'll take her down, Maggie— but after you've been safely brought, and not before— or there'll be more than just her up at the crossroads."

"I've never—"

"Aye. Two years, you've been here. For four years we've had peace. There aren't no bandits, Maggie; they don't dare. Even when the harvest is good."

"And it's worth—worth *this*?"

"No. But when we don't have a choice, we'll take what we can get." Bitter words. Terrified words. Relieved words.

Maggie knew that she was an outsider, then. But she'd always been that, a bit. There were times when it was safe to be just that, and times when it cost; she paid the price now. Curling her fingers into her palms, she took a breath. Thinking, wondering, what it would have cost her parents to give her up to the death that waited in the castle. If they would have done it at all. Wondering how the man whose daughter now hung at the crossroads could bear to take her down. The guilt could destroy a life, and yet leave it living. She'd seen it, once or twice, and it still shadowed her memory.

The dog pushed his nose into her hand, seeking either food or reassurance; she didn't have food, so she patted him on the side for a moment. Then she took the path, willing the villagers to leave, willing—in spite of her own fear, to leave the villagers with their dead. Glad, for just that moment, that she did not belong to them, with them, that the blood for a girl who seemed far too young in the shallows of the night was not on her hands.

The bridge was down.

She knew what it was, how it worked; she'd crossed over deeper moats in her time, and into keeps far more elaborate than this. A healer's art was a healer's art, after all, and the sick and the needy weren't in a position to be all that choosy when the practitioners that they would otherwise rely on had failed. Many a noble had found relief at her hands. Even a Queen, although she did not speak openly of it, for it was the only healing that she had attended under threat of death.

But she had thought that here, she might find peace to practice the small crafts she loved.

Well, enough of it. She squared her shoulders and bent down to give the dog a quick hug and a shove. Then she passed beneath the portcullis and into the torchlit courtyard. At her back, the bridge, pulled by no hands that she could see, began to rise. She wondered what would have to be paid, and to whom, to lower it again.

The courtyard was empty, and the hall, although the doors did roll back to reveal the vastness of height and the emptiness within that seemed to go on and on. She did not call out, because she did not want her voice to seem as weak and thin as she thought it might; instead she followed the swing of doors inward, as if there were, indeed, some guide.

And so at last she came to the room that would have, in another place, been a throne room, a gathering of supplicants and courtiers and their finely dressed guards. There were no men and women, no political speeches prettified by manners and custom, no jockeying for favor; there was just a man, standing, his back to the great fireplace that seemed to absorb the light.

She found her voice then, and a little of the anger that she'd kept from the villagers. "You summoned me?" she demanded, walking toward him, chin slightly tilted, eyes unblinking.

He stared down at her, and as she approached him, she realized there was over a foot between their heights. But he did not answer the question. Instead, he said, "You are an outsider in the village. A stranger. I thought perhaps you would understand what it is like to be . . . different."

"Pretty words," she replied, thinking of the girl who hung at the crossroads. "And prettily asked, now that I've no choice but to answer them."

"Choice is overrated," he said. "Come. Let me show you to your rooms."

She raised a brow. "Just like that?"

"Isn't that how it always happens?"

"Yes and no. First, I believe," she said, with gravity, "you tell me exactly what it is that you require of me. If you are indeed a bespelled King, a trapped Knight, some forlorn hero, you tell me what I must do to earn my freedom—and what price I pay if I fail."

"Freedom?" He laughed, bitterly. "There is no such thing. And failure? I believe that you have already seen the price. And there will be days when it will not seem so horrible as all that, I assure you."

Her quarters were not old and dusty, as most of the castle was; they were fine, but not the fine of old stories. Rather, they were fine in the way that lived-in things are fine. There was an old spindle, an old loom, needles that shone with newness, sharpness; there was thread, carded wool, and beyond that, in windows that were low and wide, boxes of dirt into which seeds might be planted.

The windows looked out, but not onto the village alone, for the rooms were rounded, with windows that followed much of the curve of the wall; they looked out upon the forests to either side of Clearbrook's flats, and gave a clear glimpse of the river out of which the moat seem to have been carved: magic there, a great work in her opinion.

There was a bed, one neither too wide nor too narrow, and an armoire; a chest of sturdy drawers older, she was certain, than her grandmother. There was a mirror that was beveled, cut by the hand of a master, but it was yellowed beneath the glass, and in need of silvering—so it seemed the wizard was either not so gifted or not so rich as all that.

Dinner came to her room, left on a tray at the foot of her door; she ate, and then started a fire in the grate, and then let sleep take her.

As she drifted closer to dream, she thought that she could like these rooms, if she knew what the price of her stay in them was. They had the feel of home about them.

Of course, home or no, they became a bit much once she'd had the time to unpack and sit in them for three hours, and at length—Maggie had never been a timid woman, nor one particularly well brought up— she left the rooms and set about exploring. She'd been into castles and manors, it was true, but never one so deserted that she'd been left for hours on end with curiosity as her only companion.

So she began to satisfy that curiosity, and because of it, she met the boy.

Had it been evening, or even night—and she had seen many, for fevers tended to burn highest when the moon was at her peak—she would not have been surprised, but he came to her in the bright fullness of day. She thought him a wisp of smoke, drifting up from the edges of a fire—but there was no fire, no wood-smell, no acrid burning. There was just the twisting of smoke, a pale thin thing that hung in the air like a child's tale.

She was in the courtyard, then, and in the courtyard, he was at his weakest, as she would come to know later. But it was in the courtyard, at his weakest, that she first saw him, and it was glimmering, like the hint of a promise, like the fleck of sunlight upon water that is not quite still, that she best remembered him.

He was not a babe, not a young child, and yet, not an old one; he stood on the threshold between a mother's care and a young man's over-proud sense of duty and accomplishment. He was neither too pretty nor too homely, but his cheeks were gaunt, and his eyes, and he had about him the look of a child poorly cared for.

He caught at strands of her hair, and they fell through his fingers. She did not speak, but let him play around her skirts as if he were a chance accident that always happened in her life. As if he were a wild thing that would be driven away by attention.

But later that evening, she received a summons to join the wizard in his rooms, and there, she ate the first real meal she'd yet had in his company. He did not speak much, except in idle pleasantries of little note: He asked her how she found her rooms, and how she found the castle, and what, if anything, she might desire to change in it.

And she answered idly, or she intended to, but the ghostly face of the young boy disturbed her meal, rising from the smoke of colored wax when the breeze in the room changed the lap of the flame.

"The boy," she said softly, "is he . . . trapped here?"

"What boy?"

Something about the way he said those two words made her fall silent, and Maggie rarely fell silent in the face of anyone's tone, especially if it was not one to her particular liking. She turned her hand to the fine, if discolored, linen that was draped across her lap—quite needlessly, as in a situation as uncomfortable as this, she was prone to eat neatly and perfectly.

He chose to ignore her question entirely, but he did not speak again, and when at last she rose, begging tiredness and a need to tend to her night seedlings before she slept, he let her go.

"Stay to the paths that you know," he cautioned her coldly. "And the rooms that you have been granted. I see that you did not bring a lamp; do so, in future. For this eve, I will make certain that you will not be lost."

The torches in the hall showed her the way to her rooms, and the way seemed thinner, darker—a place where shadows had eaten away what was solid and steady from the lay of stone and beam. Even her breath came out unnaturally loud as she took the steps that led to her rooms.

They were comfortingly free of ghosts and night fears, and a fire was burning in the grate. But as she crossed to the windows to look at her seed beds, small though they were, her eyes were caught by moon upon the water.

And the moon wore the boy's face, in cool silver.

She rose before dawn from a troubled sleep, and she dressed for dew and chill. A momentary frown sculpted deep lines into her forehead, and just as quickly let them go; there was, of course, no lamp in either this room, or the other. Still, if the sun had not crested the horizon, its light was already thinning the night, and Maggie felt a wild impatience to be gone from the room itself.

She drew a shawl round her shoulders, more for

comfort than for need, and stepped out of the safety of her rooms and into the long hall.

The torches were flickering dimly between the heights of thin, narrow windows. They cast few shadows, and made no menace of those they did cast, but as she approached one, it would gutter, and another, just out of reach, would catch its spark. Curious, she began to follow the torches for a second time.

They led her, just as surely as the first set had, but to a different place. Maggie Averro walked across the threshold of a room that was heavy with cobwebs and dust and dry, dry air. She heard the wooden slats of the floor creak beneath her feet as she made her mark through the perfectly undisturbed layers of dust.

And there, for the first time since the day before, she saw the boy. He stood, his feet disturbing nothing, his back to her. His head, white hair falling down the nape of his neck, was angled up toward one wall. She walked gently toward him, but stopped some ten feet away. Because he was a wild thing, and she did not wish to startle him.

As if he could hear the hesitation that he could not see, he turned then, and smiled; it was a fleeting expression, one that could easily be a trick of the light that shone through him. He lifted a spindly arm, pointing straight up from the round curve of his shoulder to the tip of his finger.

She saw that he chose to show her a painting—or at least she thought it must be—it was as web-covered as the walls, protected from her humble vision by airborne dust and other things that these empty webs might once have caught. It was also high enough off the ground that she could not begin to reach it; until she spoke to the master of the castle, it would remain obscured from sight.

The wild child rose then, and she felt a cool, cool breeze in the room—a gallery, she saw, as she finally looked away from his suddenly shifting form. She looked back as the breeze grew louder, and she saw that the boy's cheeks were puffed up in a child's exaggerated expression as he blew away the webs that hid the painting from her sight.

He stopped almost in mid-breath; there was sound and then silence as she stood, half-gaping, at what his tiny breath had revealed: A portrait. A man, a woman, and a child.

The man was tall, and dark-eyed, of proud bearing. Even, she thought, because there was no reason not to think it, of cruel bearing. The line of his lip was a little too thin, the line of his eyes a little too narrowed. But he was handsome. Maggie wondered whether or not the portrait painter would have survived had he not been.

In the curve of his arm was a woman, and she was lovely in a radiant way; where the man was hard-edged and cool, she was soft lines and warmth, and her eyes had the shape and the lines of someone who laughs often. Her hair was a deep, deep brown that is not quite black, and her eyes brown as well. Her lips were turned up in a smile that was affectionate, and it was clear that the object of that particular smile was the young boy who stood in front of her. One of her hands was upon his shoulders, and one of the man's as well; they were joined by the child.

And there was no question at all that the dark-haired, serious child caught between this man and this woman was the ghost child. She lifted a hand, as if she could reach his painted face.

"I see," a voice behind her said, "that you are not even as obedient as the last . . . visitor. It does not bode well."

She turned slowly, refusing to start or jump, until she faced both the doors to the gallery and the master of the castle. "I'm not prone to obedience as a whole," she said softly. "Although I will often offer a willingness to listen to reasoned discourse in its place."

He smiled, and she thought she saw the lines of the hardness of the portrait in his face, but she couldn't be certain—she wasn't foolish enough to turn around and check. Defiance was one thing—but Magdala Averro had survived this far by knowing how to walk the edge of defiance without being cut by it.

"Very well," the wizard said, his voice completely icy. "If you will hear it, I will tell you the tale of the boy you find so fascinating. And when I am finished, perhaps you will understand my reluctance to have him discussed or acknowledged."

She bowed and nodded politely, making her way out of the gallery at his unspoken command.

It was breakfast that morning; she would remember it later as dinner because the light of day never quite seemed to penetrate the hall. There were eggs on her plate, remembered more clearly than the time of day because they were fried and soft, and when she cut them, they were an astonishing yellow inside—bright and vivid and new. Or if not that, more safe and familiar to look at than the man whose home she now shared.

He did not eat.

But he spoke, taking his time, measuring his words as if they were too precious to him to part with. As if, she thought, he wasn't certain that what he chose to buy with them would be worth the price.

"The picture," he said, "in the gallery is old. You are the first visitor who's seen it in years."

She said nothing, but set her plate aside; the moment he began to speak in earnest, she had no need of it. Maggie Averro was a healer; she had spent her time by the beds of the dying, at all ages, any age. She knew how to listen to rage and pain and fear when it came from certain knowledge—what was often harder was to disengage herself from those who knew their death, and turn to face those who they would leave behind, for *those* people often demanded miracles that no healer alive had ever worked. Nor could.

And this man spoke with the voice of the dying.

She wondered if he knew it.

"Years ago."

She waited.

"That man was a wizard. I don't know if you can see it in his eyes, but it's there if you know how to look. This castle belonged to him, as did the lands the village occupies now. He took a wife, and she was as different from the wizard as night from day. You can see that as well."

"Yes."

"What isn't well known is that she was also a wizard."

She had no reason to question his story except knowledge, and in a conversation of this nature, knowledge was not reason enough. But she thought as a wizard he must know that women could not bear children who could also stand above nature. They couldn't.

Memory.

He stopped speaking a moment as he waited for her objection; when it didn't come, he seemed to relax. To become, she thought, oddly deflated—as if the argument, the defense of facts, was the only thing he understood well enough to hold onto.

"He loved that in her. The power, that she was an equal, his equal. He did not so much love the child that came of their union, for he thought that child impossible. And it should have been." He looked down at his hands as they lay, palms flat, against the table. "I do not believe that he desired children, that he would have ever had them. He was a responsible man, if a cold one.

"But the child came.

"A boy, a son; she thought the wizard would have been happy, to have everything that most men desire: Power and legacy. For she had everything that most women desire: Power and legacy. But he was not happy.

"He did what he could by the boy, and she as well. But they were not anchored to this world; they lived in the heights of their towers, by the lights of the glyphs in their books, by the song of words that human voices could not utter. They forgot to eat for days, and they would forget to feed him. That is the nature of wizards. And yet he thrived and survived."

"He did not die an adult," she said.

"No. But he did not die of their neglect." He lifted his chin. "I killed him."

She nodded quietly.

"You are not like many women."

"I expected you would say something of that nature," was her quiet reply.

"And you weren't afraid of hearing it."

"I was." It was true; she had been. Anticipation of a thing was often far worse than the thing itself; she learned this time and again. But she had grown no better over time at judging which fear was anticipation and which was wisdom, and so she lived with fear, here and there, as all men must. "Why did you kill him?"

"There are reasons why a child born to a wizard woman does not survive. Neglect is the most common, and it comes in many forms: benign, foolish, a lack of understanding about what harms a child when a wizard has grown so used to being above all hurt."

"If you say that to impress me, it doesn't. Wizards die just like any other man if they're careless."

"Do they?"

"Yes. I've attended one such death."

"Later, you will have to tell me of it."

She nodded. It was better that than refuse, although she had no intention of speaking of that particular death to anyone.

"As I said, there are reasons why no children should be born to a wizard woman, but chief among them is this: The child is not .. contained."

"Wizards have had children," she said softly. "For the wizard lines continue to this day."

"Yes," he said distantly. "But the women—they are no longer wizard by the end of their pregnancy, by the birth of their child. That's why there are so very, very few."

She knew the truth of the words, and nodded. "They have many," she said softly.

"What?"

"The not-quite-wizard women. They have many children."

He shrugged, as if this were not his concern, and indeed it was not. Not his. He continued. "This boy—he was born of two such parents.

"When he was two, he destroyed half the castle—and the servants—in a blaze of child's temper. There was no will behind the action that no other child does not have—but the power behind it was more natural than speech.

"Ten minutes later, he was weeping in his mother's arms. He destroyed the castle because he wanted her attention, and she was elsewhere, in her meditations, with his father. Ten minutes after that, he was happy, smiling brightly.

"But the dead took days to bury, and after that, the wizards knew that they could not in good conscience take in other servants who might meet the same fate. For they, as wizards, had been proof against his rage. Others were not so lucky."

Her eyes widened then, and he saw this and smiled. "You see where this is going, don't you? He was a child, but he was no child at all—and as he grew, it became clear that he *could not* be contained. Yet he was sweet natured in his way, and she—his mother—loved him in her fashion; she could not be swayed to do what was necessary, or right.

"His father was not so foolish a man—as I said, he was a man who understood his responsibility. Yet he waited until the day that a messenger arrived from the village, and the young boy found the messenger before either of his parents.

"The boy was curious, because he saw no others, and because he did not understand the difference between himself and them. He did not intend harm—

but harm was done, and that night, the boy's father came to his chambers while he slept, to do what had to be done.

"But he discovered that he had waited far too long; the boy could be harmed—could be physically hurt— but not killed by a man whose power had become so insignificant in comparison. He did his damage, and he paid for it most terribly, and as he died, his wife felt the strains of his muted, voiceless screaming, and she came at once to his side, to see that her child was killing him.

"She meant to save her husband's life. She failed, and she lost hers as well." His hands curved slowly into fists, fingers inching up the smooth wood and then turning in. "I arrived as they struggled, the boy and his mother. I was not fond of the wizard, but I loved his wife, although in the end she chose him over me, a thing I've never understood." His smile was crooked, a broken thing. "Although she tried to keep it from me, I understood her fear, and I knew that it was growing almost daily. I had hoped—

"Did I say there was nothing he could not do? I was wrong. Having destroyed the fires of two wizards— destroyed them completely, leaving no hint of smoke or charred bone in the tower room—he was almost spent, and spent, he was not a match for me. It was a near thing, and it cost me much.

"I bound my life to this castle, to the earth, and the earth's roots *here*. To gain what I needed to defeat him. And I have never left. I cannot leave." He pushed himself out of his chair, levering white knuckles against wood grain to do so. "And the boy's spirit is likewise bound; I would have set it free if I knew how, for I hate it more with each passing season."

"I have only one question," she said, as he gained the door.

"Yes?" He did not turn to face her.

"Who killed the girl whose body adorns the cross-roads?"

"Not I," he said softly. He left.

* * *

In the afternoon, she sprinkled seeds into a flat, thin dish of water; later, she would transfer them into the window boxes that spent so much time in the clear air and sunlight. It eased her, these seeds, this planting. It was a part of life she understood, and if it bothered her to lose a seedling or two to blight or unexpected frost or hail, it did not break her heart the way other losses would. Even cats or dogs. She'd learned over time that gardening was one of the few things that she did that brought forth a life which did not then control hers in some way.

And she was a healer by trade and inclination; she needed that sense of life and growth.

The little boy came partway through her closed door, and stood there, as if he were carved from smoke and air, a relief that jutted out of the flat, old wood. He lifted his hand, balled it into a fist, and passed it in and out of the wood until she realized that he was knocking.

"Come in," she said softly, as she turned back to her work, feeling the air's chill as if it were already late autumn.

He cast no shadow, but he was one; he came and sat in a crouch by the thin, liquid-filled dish. Rocking back and forth on the balls of his heels, his hands wrapped round his legs, his chin on his knees, he looked almost solid, a study of a pensive child.

"I don't even know your name," she told him as she laid the seedlings down. It hadn't seemed important in the morning.

He shrugged, as if it didn't matter.

She was a healer, and a woman used to speaking with the dying. But she was not used to speaking with the dead, and she found it awkward: Do the dead need comfort? Do the dead need rest? Do the dead need to know that it is rest they are going to?

No. She rose, feeling the movement in the small of her back. "I'm not a young girl anymore," she said to the boy. The shadow at the crossroads fell over her expression. He winced, as if the words were plain on her face, as if he expected them.

"Did you kill that girl?"

He was silent for a long time, and then, as she opened her mouth to ask the question again, he turned and fled.

Why, Maggie thought, as the sun set on a room that was empty and still, *am I here*?

She did not mean the rooms, of course, although she'd pretty much figured out whose rooms she'd been given: The wizard woman's. The woman who had somehow made no choice between the power that she used and the power that she could not use: wizardry and life. How old had she been? Wizards, it was said, could live forever if the strangeness of their life did not consume them.

And it was true, in its fashion, but to live forever they had to step out of the realm of the things that changed: the living.

It was hard to step that far away. In the evening hours, the night returned to her, and she saw men with torches. Just men, that night: no women, no half-guilty villagers come to apologize while they forced her from her home. And dogs. Wolves were never so savage as the dogs that ran wild.

Oh, she'd attended the death of a wizard once. Once.

Three weeks passed; she marked them by the growth of the seedlings in the boxes, the slow trickle of days, one after the other, in a season that was growing warmer. She was left alone by both wizard and ghost, as if neither the man nor the boy could face the words she might have offered. There was nothing at all to threaten her. Nothing at all to alarm her.

But she woke one night at the beginning of the fourth week, to the light of the moon's unsheathed edge. Glimmering with knowledge, her eyes shining in the near dark, she rose; she found her clothing, mended many times but still sturdy enough for her daily needs, and dressed. It took longer to light the lamp, for her hands were shaking. But she lit it, and then she went out of the tower rooms.

The torches did not light for her, and in truth she did not need them. There were these, her rooms, in this tower. The wizard's rooms were in the other, nearer the cistern. She went not to his rooms, but to the rooms that lay closed between them. To the door that stood, fine and sturdy, closed against intruders. The gallery.

She thought the door might be magicked, but it was only jammed, as if it had been closed with great force. During this humid season doors were often harder to move from frames; she set the lamp down and put her shoulder into the task until she succeeded; Maggie Averro was stubborn when she knew it would do some good. What had taken time was *learning* when it would do some good.

The picture was where it had been, but robed in night; she brought her lamp as high as she dared to alleviate the darkness. But it was not to gaze upon painterly strokes that she had come; it was to gaze upon the names that were etched in fine hand into the golden plate on the frame.

She read them quietly, neither speaking them nor moving her lips over their syllables. For these names, she was certain, still had power, for all that they belonged to the dead. Mortals gave the dead so much weight, so much terrible power. It was only mortals, after all, who understood death well.

She thought of her son. Her son.

Swallowing, Maggie Averro rose, walking into a night that she had never left.

She found his rooms, taking the steps and the turns that the torches would not touch with the radiance of the light they shed. She had thought he might live in the other tower, for there were two, but she was not so very surprised when she found herself by steps that led into a darkness that the open sky never touched. Wind wafted up those stairs as if it had a voice; she shielded the lantern from what it might say as she began her descent.

Thinking about wizards.

About wizards who chose to bear children. And it was a choice, where so little birth in this world was; a wizard knew her body and her body's season as well as she knew the external world she sought control over.

We are defined by our power, she thought, as she lifted the lamp high. *We choose it, we wrap ourselves in it, and we let it go only when we are faced with a greater power.* Words of war. She could well understand why a wizard would struggle to hold on to the power that had defined her life: to give it up, for the uncertainty of a future and a future life over which, in the end, a wizard would have no control.

But understanding it did not make that woman less of a fool. The epiphany of the loss and the gain, and the reason for either, was not one that could be easily explained, perhaps because each wizard came to it on a different road, under different moons.

The darkness was oppressive. Hidden by it, exposed by the lamp she wielded, she felt her vision waver as the tears pricked her eyes. She refused to shed them, because the shedding of them had never given her much in the way of peace for what it exposed—and she could not be seen as weak, not now.

The stairs opened into a long hall. The hall led into a cavern. She knew, as she followed the rough stone walls what she would find, although she wasn't certain what it would look like.

As she stepped into the cavern, lights flashed and flared, things come to life with a will of their own. They were harsh in the darkness; they did not illuminate so much as expose.

Ah.

In the center of the room, the tableau. A flat, wide bed, appropriate for a lord's manor—or a castle—crimson sheets, gold edges worn with dust and time, charred by the lapping edge of an old fire. High above it, swirling like wind-beaten smoke, the form of a thin, spindly child, face moving too quickly for Maggie to see its expression.

To either side of the bed, a figure.

Bloodstained limbs, charred and blackened skin, lidless eyes, thatches of hair where the scalp and face had not been deformed by fire. She knew death when she saw it; these two were dead. But not long dead, she thought. Or rather, frozen in the moment *after* death, some grisly reminder, a warning.

A burden. She did not even blanch at what she saw; did not scream, did not lift hand to mouth in the horror that would have—that had—gripped any other prisoner who had come this distance. Because Magdala Averro was a healer, and she had come to heal the sick and the damaged, and she had come to a place that had seen death, half-expecting to see more of it. A doctor did not faint or cringe in the sight of her patient.

And her patient slowly rose from his place in the long bed, as if pulled by strings, by her presence.

"A wizard does not have the power to bring the dead to life. Flesh cannot hold a spirit beyond its time, or beyond its ability," she told him gravely.

"You!" His face fell into lines of fear and fury, and this, too, she expected. "How *dare* you come here?"

"Carrelo d'Andressa di'Connait, I have come because you summoned me, and you have business with a healer."

"I did not summon you *here*!"

"But you did," she said, and she looked up to where the ghostly boy now stood, midair, above the bed, watching her with an expression of fear—an expression that mirrored the man's.

He looked up, looked up to see what she saw, and cried out in rage and denial. Wordless, as any child might be when caught in a lie that they no longer understood to be a lie, not completely.

"You killed your parents," she said softly, her tone

making the words a gentle statement of fact, not an accusation.

"I? I did nothing! *He* killed them!"

She set down the lamp by the cavern's mouth, as far away from her as possible. Then she brushed her hands off on her skirts, and took a firm step toward him. Seeing in his face the boy's face, as she saw in the crown of a tree the sapling it might once have been.

"You are the boy," she told him. *"Carrelo d'Andressa di'Connait, I summon you and call you to witness."*

And they both turned as if slapped, boy and man, as if one.

"It is time," she said softly, "to leave this place."

"I didn't kill them!"

"There is nothing left here for you."

"He killed them! I killed him!"

"You sundered yourself from yourself, your power from the vessel that gives it life, so that you might forget what you *cannot* forget. He is not dead, Carrelo. He is you. He is the you that killed the wizard Andressa, and the wizard Connait, your parents. If you have chosen to—"

He attacked then. She had not expected it at that moment; it was sudden. He looked up in an anguish of rage and hatred, and the mist-wraith boy was pulled down and down again, to be consumed by the man's body. She saw the light, the eerie coupling of the physical and the unnatural, the signature of a power so great she was momentarily at a loss for words. And then, in the bed's center, a boy—but a boy with an ancient hatred, a terrible, terrible pain—a loss so profound that only absolution might save him. The absolution of the dead.

She could not give him that.

But she could give him something else.

As the boy-man, the boy-wizard, the boy-killer, turned the force of that anger outward, Maggie Averro folded her arms across her chest.

"This doesn't impress me, you know," she said softly.

His eyes grew round, wide with shock and outrage, wide with childhood's sudden temper and rawness. He threw his thin arms wide, and the bodies that had stood as pillars went flying to either side.

"Don't you know what I can do?" he shouted. "Haven't you seen it for yourself?"

"Oh, yes," she answered, letting some of the sadness and anger she felt show. "I saw the girl at the crossroads. Did she come here, Carrelo? Is that why you killed her?"

He roared in a rage and fury, and the fires came and spoke with his young boy's voice. Lapped up, melting rock, cracking the ground to either side of its heart. And she did not so much as brace herself.

The fires passed through her as if she were air, or less, a thing that their heat could not touch. The ground splintered then, at a force not fire but subtler, older; she stood her ground, and beneath her feet, there *was* ground. Not even the cavern's ceiling fell upon her when it fell; it fell to either side.

"I tell you," she said again, "that I am not impressed. Come, Carrelo. I have called you, I have named you, and it is time to leave."

Lightning. A rush of water from the ancient depths below. She wondered, idly, if the castle itself still stood above them, or if it had been reduced to blocks of dusty rubble and old wood. And she waited, knowing that he would spend his power—all of it—in an attempt to kill her that was as premeditated, as thoughtful, as adult, as his parents' deaths had been. Which was to say, not at all.

She heard the howl of guilt and the agony of it; the loss of love, the certainty that it was gone forever. And she had never heard such a cry, and yet she had.

She waited, because she could wait. And when he was spent and exhausted—as even the most powerful of all wizards in the world must become who must *also* live—she made her way over the piles of debris to where he sat, little chest heaving, face awash with the sweat of labor, and she took him into her arms

as if he weighed nothing, and in truth, he weighed
very little.

He did not even strike her, but instead threw his
arms around her neck and began to sob, and the sobbing held questions, and the questions were about his
mother, his much loved mother, about her terrible,
terrible death, about *why* she had tried to kill him,
had tried to help his father. What had he done? Why?
Why? Why?

And she smoothed his knotted hair and murmured
words that meant comfort, and only comfort, as she
carried him from the room, stopping only to hook the
battered lantern by the crook of her thumb.

Because it was natural to her, as natural as breathing. Because a wizard who chose to bear life, to create
it, to nurture it, bore a life of Power. Because to bear
such a life, to withstand its storms and its growing
pain, such a woman had to step *outside* of the stream
of power and life that moved such a child, that moved
all things. For wizard children were children, and they
had tempers and tantrums, and they learned from
them just as others did. And only a wizard woman—
or a man, though she'd never heard of one—had the
power necessary to step outside the bounds of power
itself; only a wizard woman who stepped completely
out of that life and that focus, could glide above those
tantrums, could raise a wizard as if he *were* just a
child.

A loved child.

A cherished child.

And such a wizard woman as that, a mother, didn't
have the power it took to protect such a child, a grown
boy, from the whims of other fates.

She was crying, because the boy in her arms was
not her son, and because he would become so in time.
She wept because this was the first time, since the
death of her only child, that she had not cursed the
choice, the terrible, necessary choice, she'd made to
bear that boy. Why bear him to bring him to death?
Why create life in a world where life is always uncertain? She knew, that night, in the terrible, terrible

darkness, that had she kept her power, she could have killed the villagers easily. Horribly. And her son would have lived. And she had always wondered.

Until tonight.

Andressa, she thought, *thank you. I could not protect my son from death, and you could not protect your son from* your *death. Perhaps this time.*

There was no answer except the wuffling snore of a child.

And it was enough.

FROG MAGIC

❖ ❖ ❖

by Andre Norton

Andre Norton has written and collaborated on
over one hundred novels in her sixty years as
a writer, working with such authors as Robert
Bloch, Marion Zimmer Bradley, Mercedes
Lackey and Julian May. Her best known creation is the Witch World, which has been the
subject of a number of novels and anthologies.
She has received the Nebula Grand Master
Award, The Fritz Leiber Award, and the Dae-
dalus Award, and lives in Monterey, Tennes-
see, where she oversees a writer's retreat.

The puffy green-skinned body on the water-washed
rock opened his large eyes. To have one's life so
quickly changed could not help but disorient one for
at least a short period of time. The trick was to remember who he was and what he had been, not the
he of here and now.

A fly buzzed by, and his mouth snapped open; a
loop of sticky tongue gathered in that brash intruder.
The frog gulped, and then he shivered. What had happened was an act of this alien body, not by conscious
thought of his own. He must be on guard.

"How did you do that?" The sharp croak sounded
hardly more than adolescent peeping. He stared down
at the speaker who clearly WAS a frog.

"As you do also," he croaked, forgetting his resolution of moments earlier to gather in a tempting offer
of larger prey, a dragonfly.

"No—I mean how did you get here?" The small
frog hoisted himself up on a lower river stone and

109

raised a forefoot to point. "You appeared, just out of the air."

The large frog sensed more than passing curiosity—there was awe in that question. Another of those too bright youngsters who were more curious than was good for their own good. Anyway, there was no time to be wasted with this insignificant youngling, but it seemed now that the small frog had lost his proper awe. Not stricken abashed by his elder's offended silence, he continued. "How do you do that—poof out of the air? One minute nothing—then you?"

"It is a long tale and one difficult to explain," the big frog was badgered into replying with almost a turtle's snappishness. "It does not matter," now he was thinking aloud, "how I got here. The question is how do I return?"

Return—how long would it take the present frog's personality to absorb Hyarmon, Wizard, Second Class, who had certainly been fatally careless today? Wizards removed enemies in this manner; they did not fall victim themselves to such snide tricks. In spite of his attempt at control, he mouthed another fly. Yes, this body would certainly, sooner or later, abort the persona of a man—unless he moved swiftly.

"Get back where?" persisted the younger frog.

Such a change included an element of time, but there was always a key. He need only discover the lock into which his fitted to be at once surrounded by familiar walls. He hoped he could deal with the problem—and later, with more fineness, with Witchita who was responsible for his present plight. His pop eyes now focused with some force on the younger frog.

"You know the river well, youngling?" he demanded.

"Sure. I've gone as far as the mill," the creature was plainly boasting, "and as far up as to where the stink water comes out by the falls."

Falls! Hyarmon had his checkpoint. Fortune was beginning to favor him now.

"A long way indeed." He tried to tame his croak with a touch of pleasantry.

"Dangerous, too!" The small frog was puffing himself up. "The stink water hole can make one sick."

Holding the frog part of him firmly under control, Hyarmon readied his body for a leap into the water. Only those four strong legs refused to obey him.

Of course. How could he have been fool enough to believe it would be that easy? It required some concentration to be able to inspect carefully the rock on which he had come into being. Frog sight might distort those lines but not enough that Hyarmon did not recognize the carvings. He hunched around to learn that he was completely netted.

The Arcs of Arbuycus. Hmmm, he might have known she would not settle for such a single step as transformation. Back again in his first position he glanced down to discover that his audience of one had expanded and was continuing to expand, as other frogs swam in to join his interrogator. The latest comer was as large if not larger than himself—and the crowd parted respectfully to let this one through.

Pop eyes centered on pop eyes. The newcomer gave a croak as loud as a shout, and the rest were instantly silent.

Hyarmon dared a probe. He encountered nothing but frog thoughts. No, this one was not to be touched by spells—but there was always the power of thought. He possessed and used that out of memory.

The large frog turned as if to take himself as far as possible from this potential rival. But Hyarmon's thought power held. The object of his intense gaze hastily submerged, but he was not going to escape so easily.

Holding onto his catch with determination, Hyarmon now tried to turn part of his attention to the frog who had first discovered him. The frog jerked, its four legs twitching, then sprang for the same rock as Hyarmon occupied. The wet green body landed with a plop on the horn of one of the inscribed Arcs. So! It could be done—now was the time to reel in his prisoner.

Sullenly fighting against the power which was drawing him, the large frog rose into sight. For a long moment the silent battle of wills continued, and then the frog came out of the water to stretch its own body over that already laid there.

Hyarmon observed the result with care. His hind limbs stiffened then he leaped, to stand for an instant on the quivering green bodies before the water enfolded him.

Upstream the younger frog had said, so upstream it would be. Paying no attention to the rest of the company Hyarmon exerted himself and then relaxed. Yes, he could depend upon the natural instinct and the rythym of this body to serve him. He kept an eye on the nearest bank. Witchita had sprung one trap; he could well believe it was not the only one—she would not want to confront him after this trial.

The hole spoken of did stink. He was not sure of the strength of frog sense of smell, but this was bad enough. It was undoubtedly a drain and surely the door he sought.

He continued to fight his way through water which was soupy with slime. The drain slanted upward, but he could find holds for his four feet. What he feared most did not happen until he was well up the shoot when a wave of dirty water suddenly showered and battered him, but he held on with desperate determination.

Though he had never explored such inner ways within the walls of his tower Hyarmon was sure he was drawing near to his goal. A dim light flittered into the way ahead, and he resumed his efforts so that fortune favored him as the scullery maid was not at work at the sink into which he crawled. He lay exhausted and panting on the hard slate of the tub unaware of voices until a name and some words made sense.

"He didn't never ride outside th' gate, I tells you. Young Master Brame said that it was all fast locked. Certain th' Noble Lord could've gone that way, but don't we all know what we hear when the gate spell is loosed?"

"Well, he ain't here, an' that one queens it in th' Great Hall as if she sits on the High Seat by rights. Gives orders right an' left this mornin'. I seed her put somethin' in th' drink she gave to Master Brame an' the guard sergeant. Now they trails behind her like they was pups and she their dam. I tell you that this here is no place to be, with that fine madam ruling it."

The voices were fading as the speakers moved away. But Hyarmon had heard enough. So Witchita was playing with potions now? His determination to deal with her was more than part anger. Such herbs could be used too often or in too great quantities.

It took him several desperate leaps to clear the high wall of the sink. Hyarmon could now hear movement and talking in the kitchen beyond the scullery. So he sought passage from shadow to shadow, his sleek, damp hide gathering a fur of lint and dust.

Hyarmon was near winded when he finally won to the top of the stairs and dragged himself into the Great Hall. The gleam of witch lights was plain, marking this a night hour. He searched by thought for guards—luckily in this his human persona was still serving him.

The hall was oddly quiet; no coming and going of spell-constructed serving goblins. In fact there was no table in evidence, but the High Seat stood there and toward that he made his way in weak hope.

There was no use in trying to reach his laboratory. The very devices he himself had set up for security would betray him now that he wore this alien guise. But determination won over fatigue, and he made it not only up the step of the dais but, in one last exhausting leap, to the High Seat, where he subsided, puffing.

Witchita might have changed his proper outward body, but once he was here the numbing caused by his strange form wore off and he grew fiercely alert. Wizards had tools, yes. But behind those there was always a mind which controlled such and Hyarmon now drew upon the powers of his.

After a short rest, his mind began to work furiously. He lifted one foot and then another alternately to scrape from his moist skin all he could of the debris he had gathered during his journey, wadding it down on one of the wide chair arms.

"Now!"

Hyarmon could not make the proper passes cleanly and accurately while he was in this body, but he could visualize and that was useful now. The soggy mound arose sluggishly, thinning out into a dank mist. Two of the energy globes swooped, answering his unspoken orders, while the rest fanned out as if driven to some task.

The doubled lights swirled around Hyarmon. He could feel no change in his body—no—what he wove now was an envelope.

To all purposes a man sat in the High Chair—materialized out of that dream visitor Witchita doted on. The figure solidified into seemingly complete life and Hyarmon dispatched one globe to summon. He must concentrate on holding this shadow self together long enough to serve his plan. If Witchita were entirely alert, she might have sensed the spell in formation. She had triumphed before on her own. Perhaps she was just vain enough to believe as she was now so bedazzled by dreaming that she did not sense danger—for her.

There was the sound of a protesting hinge, and the door opened. One of the globes appeared to light the one who entered. So—it was night. He had chosen the proper time for, as she swept forward, he could see her lithesome body more revealed than concealed by a spider silk night shift, though she had bundled a shawl about her shoulders.

Hyarmon might have smacked his lips at the appearance of a very large and succulent fly. Dream drawn she was! She had in a way ensorcelled herself and needed only a slight touch from him to seek certain pleasures.

The young man, pale of countenance but handsome of feature, did not rise from the High Seat but held out both hands in welcome, his eyes alive with passionate promise.

"Cevin!" she breathed, and her own arms came up to welcome his promised embrace. Hyarmon poised beneath the shadow he had built.

She was bending forward, having already taken the dais step, apparently not finding it strange that her phantom lover did not rise to greet her.

Still bemused as one caught in the web of sleep she leaned forward, her lips slightly parted to welcome his kiss. Lips indeed met lips but not as Witchita had expected. Her eyes widened, and she stared in terrified horror at what she had so spontaneously kissed. Yet even as her dream snapped into nothingness so did the one she had come to meet change again. The frog had vanished as had the lover. Hyarmon sat firmly on the High Seat of the Great Hall.

"You—!" She cowered, as well she might. Not only cowered, but her body was twitching wildly. The silken shift puddled as a frog, half hidden within its folds, stared at Hyarmon.

He surveyed her critically. Then, to make sure the transformation was complete, he made a quick pounce and lifted the wildly kicking frog to the level of his eyes.

"You undoubtedly make a beautiful frog, Witchita," he observed. "But I fear you shall never know the freedom of the river in which to plan a revenge."

He snapped his fingers and his wand materialized. Apparently she had foolishly neglected to break it. Still holding the frantically squirming frog in one hand, Hyarmon sketched out an oblong line on the floor. With the proper words he created a crystal aquarium. Into this he dropped the frog, who was struggling to bite with toothless jaws.

"Water—" Another pass of the wand and the aquarium was filled. "A rock for a High Seat, dear Witchita," he ordered, "and, of course, I shall see that each day you shall have the best flies to be found."

The frog had climbed to the top of the rock and now was making an attempt to leap out. However, there seemed to have also come into existence an invisible cover which kept her prisoner.

Hyarmon chuckled. "Remember your history, my dear. Frogs, kisses, and beautiful young women have met before. You thought to match lips with your desired one, but there is a different ending to this tale."

He clapped his hands and a goblin flashed into their presence.

"Smurch," Hyarman bade him, "take this aquarium to the bower of the lady Witchita. See her carefully settled and catch some flies, come morning, for her delectation. My dear, I trust you will meditate on past foolish acts. You shall be, I assure you, kept safe and secure."

If a frog could glare, the captive achieved that now. Hyarmon laughed and waved the goblin and his burden away. Now, he arose from the High Seat and stretched luxuriously, then decided to go up to the laboratory and see what mischief there had entertained Witchita during his involuntary absence.

HOW THE WILD HUNT CAME TO TRYGVADAL

❖❖❖

by Diana L. Paxson

Diana L. Paxson's novels include her *Chronicles of Westria* series, and her more recent *Wodan's Children* series. Her short fiction can be found in such anthologies as *Ancient Enchantresses, Grails: Quests of the Dawn, Return to Avalon,* and *The Book of Kings.*

T*he hanged man twists in the wind, limbs jerking in a dreadful parody of the struggle in which his life fled. But the ravens pecked out his eyes weeks ago. Clouds are scudding up from the southwest, glimmering in the moonlight as the storm wind rips at them, then curdling together and sending down a few flurries of snow. But the man who swings from the gibbet pays it no mind.*

Erlend Bjornsson struggled toward consciousness, knowing this was a dream, the same that had come to him every night in the month just past. Distantly he could hear the wind howling around the eaves of the old farmhouse as if the Wild Hunt were ranging the skies. But that awareness only plunged him deeper into the dream.

Along the road a man comes walking, aided by a staff. He is wrapped in a tattered cloak, with an old, high-crowned hat pulled down over his eyes. When he comes to the crossroads he pauses, looking up at the gibbet. The wind drops, and the corpse stops swinging as if the wayfarer had commanded its attention. For a

*long moment the two appear to be engaged in some
unearthly conversation. Then the wind picks up again,
whipping at branches, scattering the last of the summer's leaves. The hanged man twists in his bonds, and
the wanderer turns away and continues on.*

At least that part was different. At the thought, the
dream images broke up into a tumult of impressions,
and Erlend passed into a restless slumber, some part
of his awareness still attending to the uneasy rise and
fall of the wind. A sudden sound brought him upright,
blinking. It had been a branch or a loose board, he
told himself, flung against the side of the house by the
storm. Then the sound came once more.

Erlend frowned. On such a night as this, honest folk
shut the doors of their closet beds tight and pulled the
blankets over their ears. On a night of storm at Yuletide, only the Wild Hunt rode abroad, or else Jarl
Ivor and his houseguard. Not that there was much
difference between them these days.

A gust of wind whistled through the thatching. In
the lull that followed, he heard the noise a third time,
and recognized it as a knock at the door. Erlend grimaced at the touch of the cold air as he eased out
from beneath the covers. The jarl's men wouldn't have
bothered to knock before kicking in the door, and a
thief would be silent, if indeed the jarl's taxmen had
left anything to steal!

The door of the closet bed creaked as he opened
it. Limping, for these days his joints gave him trouble
when it was cold, he padded across the scrubbed wood
of the floor.

In the room he could hear the wind more clearly.
He paused, remembering tales of other things, not
human, who must be invited to cross one's threshold
before they could enter in. A faint light edged the ill-
fitting door. What was out there, in the light of the
full moon and the storm?

He should turn around and climb back into bed,
Erlend told himself. If he needed help, no one would
come to his call. The farmfolk had all run off, as if

Jarl Ivor's disfavor would curse them, too. But it seemed to Erlend that if there were some wight in this world less fortunate even than he was, he ought to show him hospitality.

It was no troll that stood there, or if it was, it was an old and battered troll, leaning on a staff with a hat pulled down over its eyes. Erlend squinted into the moonlight, certain he had seen that figure somewhere before.

" 'Tis a cold night, and I have wandered far," said the stranger. "Will you give me a night's shelter within?"

"So that you be no unholy wight," Erlend answered him.

"Unholy?" The bowed shoulders shook with what might have been laughter. "That am I not. And I mean no ill to you or yours."

"Then you are welcome," said Erlend, his tone gentling in spite of his unease.

He stepped aside, startled by the hollow thunk of the staff on the floorboards as the stranger came in. His guest sat down on a three-legged stool by the hearth, and Erlend took the poker and stirred up the coals. A flicker of flame scattered light and shadow across the big table and benches, the stones of the hearth, and the seamed features of the man who huddled beside it. As the flame grew, he straightened, sighing in appreciation of the warmth, and Erlend could see that he had lost an eye.

That was not unusual. There were many old soldiers roaming the land. The great lords ate men in their quarrels, and those who were injured but did not die were cast adrift to fend for themselves. And yet, as the old man unwrapped his cloak, Erlend could see that the tunic beneath it was of good cloth, of some dark color, perhaps black or blue. Neck brooch and belt buckle glinted silver. The fellow might be a wanderer, but he was well to do, or at least he had been.

Erlend set a pannikin of ale to warm above the fire,

wondering what the old man had been doing out on the moor.

"You called me here—"

Erlend whirled. Surely he had not spoken aloud!

"Your anger called me," the stranger added, stroking his grizzled beard. "From afar I could smell it on the wind. I have wandered through many lands, and learned the scent of terror. What is it that has you at once so wrathful and so afraid?"

Erlend felt the fine hairs prickle on his neck. "At the crossroads stands a gibbet," he said slowly. "If you could talk to the man who hangs there, he would tell you. Jarl Ivor goes too far, but who is there to stop him? Not King Magnus—his crimes set the example for such men as these."

The stranger gave a grunt of laughter. *"A spell I know, if on tree I see a hanged one hoisted on high: Thus I write and the runes I stain, that down he drops and tells me his tale,"* he quoted softly.

The fire flared up and Erlend realized that what he had taken for rough wood on the old man's staff was twisting lines of deep-carved runes. The *Visenda-madhrs* used such, he had heard, but there had not been a Man of Knowledge who knew *fiolkyngi,* the great magic, in the district for a very long time.

"Who are you?" he whispered, staring.

"I have been called by many names. For now, Harbard will do," the stranger replied.

"What are you?"

Harbard laughed. "I am your answer."

Erlend coughed. He had not been aware of having asked a question. But in another sense, for the past month all his waking consciousness had rung with one desperate cry—*"Where shall I find justice and recompense for the death of my boy?"* And his sleep as well, he thought, for now he remembered his dream.

He shook his head. "Something tells me that your help is not such as should be sought by a Christian man."

"That may be true, but how much help have the priests of the White Christ been to you?"

"They take my tithe, but the tithe Jarl Ivor takes is greater, though he never enters a church from one Yule to the next," Erlend said slowly. "It is my son Sigurd that swings from Ivor's gibbet. The Jarl wanted his wife Thora for a concubine, and she would not go with him. So he charged Sigurd with the theft of a cow and killed him and took the girl. I tried to fight, but they were too many. Jarl Ivor has killed the son I loved, and ended my line, for Sigurd had not yet begotten a child. I would make a bargain with the Devil himself to be avenged on him."

"I am no devil, though some have called me so," Harbard said grimly. "I will help you, if you will give me what I ask when the deed is done."

"I swear it," said Erlend. "In blood, if need be—"

"I've no need for your blood, only your trust," came the answer. "Listen carefully. This is what you must do—"

The tardy Midwinter sun was just rising when Erlend got on the road the following day. Harbard's instructions had been quite clear. Less clear was what had become of the old man himself. When Erlend rose, a little later than he had intended, for they had talked long into the night, Harbard was nowhere to be found. And then Erlend had to milk the one cow that was left to him, and gather the things the *Visendamadhr* had told him they would need. The fields lay undisturbed beneath their blanket of new-fallen snow. The road was a ribbon of white between the fences, on which no foot had trod.

Trust—thought Erlend, *is what I pledged. And if the old man was only a dream, whence comes this knowledge of* fiolkyngi, *this plan that is beating in my brain?*

When Erlend reached the crossroads, he paused for a long time, looking at what remained of his son.

"Farewell, my Sigurd. If I succeed," he whispered finally, "I will lay your bones in the churchyard. If I fail, no doubt I will be dancing in the wind beside you before many days have passed."

After that he went on. All the district knew that

Jarl Ivor was keeping the feast of Yule at Trygvadal.
The whole week long they would be at their drinking,
with scarcely a pause for Christ's mass. In the old days
men had honored the gods with their feasting; now
they just got drunk and stayed that way until the
feast was done. They did not, unfortunately, drink
themselves quite insensible, Erlend thought as he
turned off the path into the forest, or he could simply have walked in and struck off the Jarl's head
where he lay.

"We must ring them round with runes," Harbard
had told him. *"Then Ivor will be in your power."*

But what runes? he wondered as he stared about
him. He had counted on the *Visenda-madhr* to instruct
him when the time came.

Before him was a birch tree, bent to the eastward
by the winds. Something about it drew him, and as
he reached it, runes shaped themselves in his mind.
Unwilled, his hand gripped his knife and he began to
scratch the first stave into the bark of the tree, a *Hagal*
rune, bound together with *Tyr*, for justice.

What am I doing? Words gibbered in his mind. *Is
this the right rune? Where are you, Old Man?*

As he watched his hand carve the runes, more
words came into his awareness, in a voice that was
not his own.

"Do you not yet understand? I am here. . . ."

Starting, Erlend stared around him, but not a leaf
stirred. *He has cast a spell of invisibility,* he told himself. But that voice had been dreadfully intimate, like
some hidden part of his soul. If what he heard was
his own *hug,* it had a wisdom he had never suspected, but if this was madness, it was better than
the grief that had nearly driven him insane. And he
would have to hurry, for the few hours of light were
nearly done.

Letting that inner voice direct him, Erlend moved
from one tree to another, scoring their bark with
runes, drawing a circle of power around Jarl Ivor's
hall. Awareness narrowed to the puffed vapor of his

breath and the power that flowed through his hand to take shape in the stave he was scratching on the tree. Lost in the rune trance, he did not hear the crunch of booted feet in the snow.

A hand closed on his shoulder and spun him around, and his knife went flying. For what seemed a long time Erlend blinked stupidly at his captors. But when they bound him, he understood at last that he had been taken, and then it was not Jarl Ivor he cursed, but Harbard.

Jarl Ivor's men dragged Erlend into the hall. The warriors had found him during a lull in the drinking, when the men headed for the outhouses, or into the woods to clear their heads before returning to the beer vats once more.

The Jarl's hall was large, but ill-kept, as if whatever women Ivor abducted were not given the authority, or perhaps did not last long enough, to keep it in order. As the men dragged him along Erlend glimpsed long tables and benches, some of them broken, and the man-sized ale-vats standing by the wall. Jarl Ivor himself was a big man, sprawled in his high seat with a drinking horn in his hand. Erlend, listening to the edge of anxiety in the ribald words with which his captors told their tale, thought Ivor looked bored, and all the more dangerous because of it.

"What's your name, fellow?"

With mingled astonishment and anger, Erlend realized the lord had not recognized him. Had Ivor wronged so many that he no longer remembered their faces? Erlend stared around him and saw his son's wife, Thora, clutching a beer jug and watching with a kind of weary curiosity. *She* did not appear to know him either, and though she looked unhappy, she did not seem to have been so ill-used as to have lost her senses.

If some wizardry of Harbard's had disguised him he must not waste it. At least he could deny Ivor the satisfaction of knowing he had destroyed Sigurd's family entirely.

"Ye may call me Grimnir, a *Visenda-madhr* am I, a man of power!" The word meant one who was hidden, a good name for a Wise Man. It came to him he had heard some story about a man of that name, but he could not remember it.

"A *seidh-skratt* more likely," answered the Jarl, using the old word for sorcerer. "And what ill-wishing were you after, out there in the woods today?"

" 'Tis a powerful moment, now when the dark is at its strongest—" Erlend said in a voice he did not recognize as his own. "I did but scratch a few luck runes to bring you fortune."

"I make my own fortune!" growled the Jarl. "And I know a spell or two to wring truth from a trickster! You, Tore, and Olvir—" he gestured to his men. "Stand that cracked table on end next to the fire and tie this wastrel to it. Then build up the fire. We'll see if a little roasting will loosen his tongue!"

In his prime Erlend might have done some damage to Tore and Olvir as they tied him, but as it was, his struggles did no more than amuse them. The table was too heavy for him to shift; by the time he had got his breath again, sweat was already beading up on his brow. Abruptly he remembered what the tale about Grimnir had been. It was a name the god Odin had called himself once when he was captured and tied between two fires. Unfortunately Jarl Ivor knew the story, too.

"Tell me about the runes, old man," said Ivor. "Whatever spell you intended has come to naught. I've given orders for my men to cut down every tree on which you carved a rune. Their wood will serve to fuel your fire!"

Erlend shook his head, and sweat flew from his brow and hissed on the fire. *Harbard,* he thought, *you deceived me! You refused my blood—will my roasted flesh please you better?*

Immediate and unexpected, the answer came. *"Praise a sword when tried and the day when 'tis ended, and do not curse me until you know what the outcome will be. . . ."*

My death will be the outcome! thought Erlend, but for a moment something, perhaps hope, flared as if in response to the flames. But even to think about the fire increased his discomfort. The layers of clothing closest to his skin were soaked with sweat already. A man could die of overheating, whether the fever came from without or within.

Jarl Ivor held out his drinking horn to Thora to be refilled, then took a long, ostentatiously appreciative swallow.

"Ah, well." He lowered the horn and wiped foam from his lips with the back of his hand, "I was wondering what we should do for amusement now that we have heard all Olvir's songs!" The note of anticipation in the men's laughter made Erlend shudder.

He should be grateful, he thought, that it was only Jarl Ivor who was tormenting him. He had heard that King Olaf, whom some now called a saint, had had some truly inventive ways of persuading men to abandon the old gods when he imposed the faith of the White Christ on the land.

"Pile the wood high, lads," cried the one called Tore. "This *seidh-skratt* will be singing for us soon!"

Erlend licked lips already dry and closed his eyes. *My Sigurd, you made no sound when they tightened the noose around your neck. I will not cry out now.*

"What, no songs or spells?" came a voice in his ear.

Erlend gasped as a knife pricked his throat, but it was withdrawn before he could push his neck against the blade hard enough to sever something vital and deprive them of their fun. In the next moment he felt the sting of the cut and wondered if he would have had the courage.

Ivor did not hold me worth slaying when he took my son, he thought despairingly, *and he had the right of it. What evil wight deluded me into thinking I could get the price of my Sigurd's blood from this man?*

Time passed. Olvir cast another log on the fire, and sparks swirled up, stinging Erlend's skin like blackflies and bearing with them a blast of heat that made him writhe in his bonds. This was not the swift agony that carried consciousness away, but a constant discomfort that gradually stressed the body until the heart began to pound and the lungs to fight for each breath.

At least Sigurd's death was quick. In another moment I will scream, and Ivor will have won. Who could endure this?

From within, the answer came, *"I did. . . ."*

Was that supposed to be some consolation? Somehow more time had passed. Erlend smelled food, and the sour reek of spilled beer.

You are not Harbard, but Odin, the fickle and untrue, he told that inner voice. Now, when it was too late, Erlend realized who, and what, the stranger at his door had been.

"I never promised you comfort, only vengeance. Endure, and you will serve both my purposes and your own," said the god.

Your purposes! The anger that had been smoldering within Erlend's breast caught fire from the heat that surrounded him and burst into flame. *Then come here yourself and suffer with me!*

There was a moment of stillness. Then he realized that the top of his head was tingling. The feeling spread; now he felt dizzy, and wondered if he were going to faint. Too much heat could do that to a man. He twitched, and fine tremors began to roll through his body. One of the men pointed and laughed, but it was not fear that shook him, it was power.

When Erlend was carving the runes, the god had eased in like the soft wind that gently stirs the leaves. But this was a storm of the spirit that would carry him away. Inner senses told him he was falling, though he could still feel his feet on the floor. And then, abruptly, though the heat of the fire was still a torment, it was no longer *his* torment. He had become a passenger in his own body, observing in wonder the actions of that Other who had entered in.

Olvir, sensing some change, came toward him, steadying his wavering steps by leaning on a spear.

"Speak, *seidh-skratt!* Your magic burns before you. What did you mean by those runes?" The spear jabbed through cloak and tunic and shirt; Erlend noted the prick as it pierced the skin of his breast with detached interest. But the god within him laughed.

"The skalds will sing sad tales of your Jarl when they learn how he offers Yuletide hospitality. You have made me warm at your fire, but I have been offered neither bread nor ale. When I have refreshed myself, perhaps I will tell you what you wish to know. . . ."

For a moment Olvir's face showed only amazement. Then it darkened, and he began to throw wood onto the hearth. The fire blazed up in an explosion of sparks, and Erlend smelled scorching wool. Now there were only sticks left in the pile, and Olvir, swearing, stumbled off to bully the thralls into bringing more.

It must be late. Most of the Jarl's men slept at the tables, heads pillowed on their arms, while others sprawled on the floor, for the night was far past. In the momentary silence, Erlend could hear the timbers of the hall creaking. The wind was rising outside.

"Quickly, drink this before he returns—" Thora pressed a drinking horn against Erlend's lips, and he shared the god's pleasure as the cool, bitter, liquid went down. In one long swallow he drained the horn.

"Thank you," he said as she took the horn back. "You have offered me the hospitality of this hall, and your seed shall inherit it."

Thora stared back in blank amazement. Then she saw Olvir returning and ducked into the shadows behind the table and away.

"The heir of Trygvadal has given me good welcome. Ask, and I will answer your questions." The voice was unmistakably that of Harbard now. Olvir looked at his master uncertainly and Ivor, rousing, leaned forward in the high seat with a canine smile.

"What runes did you carve into my trees, and why?"

"Runes of weight and wyrd, that you may receive the honor you deserve. I thought that if I did you that good turn, perhaps you would welcome me—"

In just that voice, thought Erlend, *he persuaded me. . . .*

"I make my own fate," grated Ivor, "and need no help from priest or sorcerer. But foreknowledge can be a help when one is planning. Tell me what will be—"

"I see you riding in the van of a mighty host. You will serve a great king, and where you pass, folk will tremble in fear," said Harbard.

"Magnus will summon me to court, then! I knew he would see his need for me before long!"

"Indeed, before the Yules are over, he will be speaking about you to his men. Does that earn me a drink, Jarl, or relief from these bonds?"

Jarl Ivor shook his head. "When I send a sharp-eyed thrall to scout for game, do I reward him as if he had made the stag or the boar appear? Still, if you continue talking, I may relent, who knows? Tell me if my fame will live after me?"

"You will have a noble pyre, my Jarl," Harbard answered, "and in Trygvadal your name will be spoken when that of King Magnus himself is scarcely a memory."

Erlend listened to this in amazement. He knew what discomfort Harbard must be feeling. Why was he promising Jarl Ivor glory? Angered, Erlend tried to regain control of his body, but the god within him had a firm grip, and he could do nothing.

"Well, that is not so bad!" Ivor's laughter was too loud, and the way he lolled in his seat suggested that even *his* legendary capacity for beer had a limit, and he was nearing it now. For a moment his eyes closed, then he hiccuped and sat up again. "Throw a few more logs on the fire, Tore, to keep us warm through the night, but leave our prisoner where he is. Time enough to release him when his prophecies come true!"

The Jarl sank back in his high seat, and in another moment he was snoring. Erlend had expected Harbard to react with anger, but from the god he sensed something different, a watchful anticipation. Tore dropped the wood into the fire pit, then he staggered toward a sleeping bench by the wall.

Erlend listened to the chorus of snores and coughing from the sleeping men. The logs hissed and steamed in the heat and then the bark caught on one of them and he saw the rune he had carved there outlined in flame. *Thurs,* the Thorn that made men sleep, tied into a bindrune with *Iss,* for stillness. Certainly they were slumbering now.

He expected the god to release him, but Harbard still seemed to be listening. Outside, the wind had grown louder. Above the snoring of the Jarl's men, he could hear it sighing in the trees. A breath of air came in through some chink in the walls and the fire that flickered along the edge of the log flared and set the wood next to it aflame.

Erlend realized that for some time he had been hearing a whisper. It came from his own throat, but so softly that he recognized it more by sensation than sound. The god was chanting the names of men: Sigurd . . . Visbur . . . Hrolf . . . Ingjald . . . Halvdan . . . Eric . . . Ragnar . . . and many another. With each name, his voice grew a little louder, but the wind was rising also, so that the words seemed part of the storm.

The Oskerei! thought Erlend. *He is summoning the Wild Hunt to Jarl Ivor's hall!*

Now the wind was roaring, but the litany of names went on. Some of them he recognized as men whom all thought safe in Hell. Apparently they were riding with the *Oskerei,* which some might think the same thing.

Come, then! he added his own calling to that of the god, *and carry Jarl Ivor away!*

"*Kaun!*" He felt his voice rise suddenly to a shriek of command. In the blazing wood the Torch rune flared in lines of fire.

In the next moment wind howled through the hall, whirling glowing coals from the fire pit in an explosion of sparks. Erlend winced inwardly, but none touched him. The same could not be said of the rest of the hall. Tables and chairs, hangings and strewn rushes on the floor—suddenly all were starred with dancing flames. But the brightest fire blazed in the thatching, fanned by the wind.

Smoke swirled through the hall and Erlend coughed, and as he felt it rasp his throat realized that his body was once more his own. But Jarl Ivor and his men slept on. *He will have a noble pyre indeed!* thought Erlend, *With his folk to attend him, like an ancient king.* Was his own death the price of this vengeance? He found himself curiously reluctant to die in Ivor's company.

"Do not curse the day till 'tis over," said the god, only an inward presence now. *"You must live if you are to keep your promise to me."*

Something stirred in the shadows. Erlend squinted through the smoke and saw Thora, the only one beside himself whom the sleep spell had not bound. Hoarsely he called her name.

The girl turned, eyes widening as this time she recognized him. Holding her shawl over her nose to filter the smoke, she hurried toward him, her face full of questions. But there was no time to ask them. Now the timbers were burning as well. Thora snatched up a knife from one of the tables and began to saw at his bonds.

Erlend scarcely noticed the growing heat, but smoke was making it hard to breathe. It seemed an age before the tough ropes parted. He tried to follow Thora, but his legs would not bear him, and he collapsed to his knees.

Close to the floor the air was clearer. "Down!" he croaked to the girl. "Crawl—"

She reached down to help him rise, realized what he was saying and dropped to her hands and knees beside him. Together they struggled toward the doorway.

It took both of them to slide back the heavy bar. In the next moment the doors were flung open by the wind. The lesser folk of the household, whose sleeping places were farthest from the fire, began to stir. But the other end of the hall blazed with Muspel's fires. Another gust of wind set the smoke to swirling and fanned the flames still higher, shaping themselves into men and horses that galloped through the hall. Then Thora tugged at his sleeve and Erlend stumbled after her into the icy air.

A few of the thralls got out after them, but neither Jarl Ivor nor any of his sworn men were ever seen again as living men, and only Erlend saw the ghostly figures that rose up on the smoke of that burning to join the riders who rioted among the flames. Three times they circled the burning hall. At their head Erlend saw a horse with more legs than any mortal horse should have, whose rider bore the ringmail of ancient times and a spangenhelm of blackened steel. But his face was that of the *Visenda-madhr* who had come to Erlend's door.

Then, with a roar, the roof of the hall fell in.

A few weeks after they had returned to the farm Erlend was repairing a piece of harness at the big table, when Thora set down her spinning and came to stand before him.

"Father-in-law, I must leave you," she said. Her face was white and set, and he could see that she had been weeping. When they returned, Erlend had been weak from his ordeal, and she had nursed him. He had hoped that despite her grief for her husband she could be happy here.

"What do you mean, child?" he asked. "This is your home, just as if Sigurd had lived."

"I cannot stay here. I believe I am with child."

"But that is wonderful!" exclaimed Erlend. Vengeance had eased his sore heart, but it left no hope behind it. He had thought sometimes, these past days, that it might have been better for him to die in the fire than to outlive his son.

She shook her head. "You will remember that Sigurd was away for two weeks hunting before I was taken. It is Ivor's child."

Erlend stared at her. He had not spoken with Thora

about what had happened to her in Jarl Ivor's hall, knowing she had not gone with him willingly. And he had rejoiced, thinking that if his own line must perish, the Jarl also had died without begetting a child.

"Are you certain? None of the other men—"

She shook her head. "He had not yet tired of me. You need say nothing. I will go to my cousin at Setesdal."

Erlend frowned. He knew that cousin—he was a hard man, and in his household Thora's life would be little better than it had been in Ivor's hall. But how could he foster *Ivor's* child?

"Because I ask you to—" came a voice in his head that he had not expected to hear again. *"This is my price for helping you to your revenge. It is a man-child she carries. Teach him* fiolkyngi, *and when the land is free of this evil king, claim for him the Jarl's heritage."*

Teach him! thought Erlend. *I am a farmer, not a* Visenda-madhr!"

"Are you not? Think again, old man, and remember the runes. . . ."

At the words, Erlend found himself seeing in memory the runes that he had carved upon the trees outside Jarl Ivor's hall. But this time he understood all their myriad meanings, and how by burning them the Jarl had unleashed their magic inside his hall. Knowledge poured through him, borne by a wind of power.

He rubbed his eyes, realizing that the god had left in his head something more than a few chaotic memories. He felt like a man who goes through his house door one morning and discovers it has opened into the Otherworld. He looked at Thora, and saw how her body was already rejoicing in the new life it bore, despite her spirit's pain.

"Stay, Thora. Even the gods cannot restore the son I lost," he said slowly. "But to give me Jarl Ivor's son to raise seems a fair recompense. He shall bear Sigurd's name."

Inside his head he heard Harbard's laughter, but more welcome was Thora's smile.

This happened in Norway in the time of that King Magnus who was afterward blinded for his sins and deprived of his throne. But in Trygvadal the Wild Hunt rides still at Christmastide, and when it comes, folk whisper that Jarl Ivor follows in Odin's train, and hasten to bar their doors.

THE YELLOW OF THE FLICKERING PAST

❖❖❖

by Dean Wesley Smith

Dean Wesley Smith is an editor and writer whose works appear in *Journeys to the Twilight Zone*, *Phobias*, *The Book of Kings*, and *Wizard Fantastic*, among other places. He has also published several novels, including *Laying the Music to Rest*. He lives in Oregon with his wife, writer and editor Kristine Kathryn Rusch.

Act One: A Yellow Oil Mess

Sixteen days after I killed her, I took my dead wife to a movie.

She had always loved movies.

Actually I think she loved the memory of movies more than any one film. And she loved the smell of the buttered popcorn you could buy in theaters, even if the butter was actually only a melted yellow oil from big yellow cans. She said it was part of the movie-going experience and that was all that mattered.

On our first date to a movie I laughed when she asked for an "Extra large, extra butter, please."

"You know that shit will kill you?" I said as the guy with a thousand pimples pumped the handle of the butter machine like he was huddled over his first *Playboy* centerfold. Miss July.

"Sure," my date, soon-to-be wife, later-to-be-dead wife, had said. She never once offered me any of her popcorn. That was sort of how we argued from then on.

And we argued a lot.

She asked for the same "Extra large, extra butter" every time we went to a movie. She never missed a movie.

We went to a *lot* of movies.

Of course, people who saw us at the movies thought we made the perfect couple. "Fit together," they would say, but after I came out of the coma induced by new love and the first year of marriage, I just didn't see why. She was a light blonde, with a large, white-toothed smile, and wide, innocent green eyes. I actually had light brown hair, but I suppose it looked closer to her color because I kept it cut so short. I had dark brown eyes and people said I squinted a lot. I was almost five-six when I wore my good shoes, and while in heels she still wasn't as tall as I was.

Besides that, we argued all the time, *and* I hated movies and didn't eat popcorn, especially with yellow oil.

The last year of our marriage I started daydreaming about the dreaded yellow oil. I figured no human body could digest that stuff, so it must have been building up in her body over the five years and seven days we were together. Maybe even for years before, just waiting for the right circumstances to set it all off in a huge bang. I dreamed she would explode and the police would just nod and say, "Yellow oil buildup."

But I could never figure out how to set off the explosion. I watched the papers for months hoping to read about another yellow oil explosion, but never did.

I even consented to sex one night last year, thinking that might set her off. But the thought of her exploding had me so excited that she said I didn't last long enough to even get her hot. Maybe that was why it didn't work.

Sadly, she never did explode, or even melt. The yellow oil didn't kill her.

I did that. I killed her with a curse from a book of Wizard curses I bought at a used bookstore downtown. A big brown book with a guy on the cover wearing a pointed hat and a star-covered robe.

I wish the yellow oil had killed her instead, in a huge, messy wife-explosion. I wouldn't have minded cleaning up the mess.

After my now dead wife would get her "Extra large, extra butter," she used to love the walk down the carpeted halls of the multiplex theater, past the posters of the other movies showing in all the other theaters. She would stop and point out every show she wanted to see, as if I really cared. The last few years I even stopped pretending I did care, but she kept right on pointing them out.

Then, after the pointing-at-the-poster routine was done, she would go into the theater and look around in the low light to find just the right, *perfect* seat. Finding that exact right seat was always treated as one of the most important events in life. I think a good seat meant more to her than Christmas or her mother's birthday.

Once she had found that *perfect* place, she always whispered to me that she hoped no one would sit in front of her.

I always just nodded and she would settle in, happy, content, wide eyes focused on the blank screen ahead.

On the times when someone did have the nerve to take the seat in front of her, she would make a rude, almost piglike noise and make us move to new, *perfect* seats. Which, of course, again took time. And once settled, she would again whisper to me that she hoped no one would sit in front of her.

For a popular movie we moved a lot and usually ended up sitting down front. Then I would get a sore neck from looking straight up at the screen. I always felt I was looking up the actor's nose. Nose hair can really distract from the plot of a movie.

I think more than even the movie, I think my now-dead wife loved the previews of the coming attractions. Something about the possibility of a future trip to the movies held her spellbound like a deer in front of a car's headlights. We never saw a preview of a movie after which she didn't whisper to me that she wanted to see the movie. And didn't it look just wonderful?

The word wonderful was always followed by a long sigh. Just once I wish she would have sighed like that after we had sex.

Near the end of the second year of our marriage I started writing letters to the theater begging them, at first, and then demanding, that they not show previews of coming movies. A nasty phone call from the police department made me stop writing.

The theater kept playing the coming attractions.

She kept wanting to see every movie.

Of course, we went to them all.

And they all had coming attractions.

I still get dizzy just thinking about it.

That, and all that yellow oil she ate.

Act Two: The Unlawful Christmas Argument

The idea to take my dead wife to a movie was hers, of course. It seemed that my killing her, then wrapping her body in plastic and stuffing it in an old trunk in the basement didn't even slow down her love for movies. I guess I was wrong to expect that it would.

For over two weeks after I killed her, I kept saying no. No way in hell was I going to be seen in a movie theater with the ghost of my dead wife. And there were no curses or formulas in my Wizard's book for getting rid of ghosts, so I had to keep listening to her and arguing with her.

And of course, as when we were married, she ended up winning all the arguments. She finally used the old it's-almost-Christmas routine, and I caved in like a tunnel cut through mud. But I said I would do it on my conditions.

She didn't care about that. But she did say we had to follow the ghost rules. Wizard curses, ghost rules, my conditions. This was going to be a very complicated trip to the movies.

Before I bought the Wizard's book, I didn't know

Wizards even existed. And I never expected that I might be one, but since one of the Wizard curses worked for me, I suppose I am. But so far I've not been able to make another curse work. But I'm going to keep practicing, because what Wizards can do is really cool stuff.

Before she died, I didn't realize that ghosts had rules either. But they do. A lot of them. And I discovered the ghost rules are sometimes a little tricky to figure out. For example, the main rule about why she was still even around. She said she had her reasons, and they were for her to know and me to find out. She said that a lot during our marriage, and I never found out a thing.

I didn't expect that now that she was a ghost this time was going to be any different.

As far as going to a movie went, she figured that if I could get her body close enough to the theater, she, her ghost, not her body, could go inside with me and see the movie. For some ghost rule or another she had to stay fairly close to her body, which is why she had been hanging around the house.

She decided I could put her body in the car and then park the car next to the theater. A simple plan, really. Just get a two-plus-week-old dead body right up next to a public theater and then leave it for two hours. I laughed at her when she said that was what we needed to do. I flat out said, "No way."

She kept at me, kept me up all night again with the what-a-wonderful-Christmas-present it would be for her. I tried a Wizard curse on her that was supposed to have turned her into a frog, but she stayed a ghost and kept at me.

I gave in again. About sunrise. Using Christmas in arguments should be outlawed in all marriages, even after death.

We waited until after dark, which really didn't upset her because she hated the cheap early shows. She always said going to a regular show was much better. I never did figure out what was the difference between a cheap show and a regular show, except the price.

Every time I asked her about the difference, she just looked at me as if I was stupid and just couldn't see.

At least this time I would only have to buy one ticket.

As I loaded her body into the hatchback, she stood in the driveway to watch for the neighbors and cars on the street. It had only been a few weeks since she had died, and the decay and smell wasn't too bad. Or at least I tried to convince myself that it wasn't that bad.

I had her wrapped in three sheets of plastic and taped so tightly shut no air, or anything else for that matter, could get in there. Yet I was sure as I draped her over my shoulder that I could smell a rotten, nose-clogging smell of decay. Like a dead dog three days beside the road.

She laughed when I mentioned it and told me it was my guilt catching up with me. But I swore I could smell her rotting, right through the plastic bags and all the tape, guilt or no guilt.

It took what seemed like an eternity to get her body settled and the hatch closed. The backs of newer cars just weren't made for holding bodies like the trunks of the cars my parents owned. Those trunks were big. To get her in the hatchback I had to remove the spare. No telling what problems we would have if we had a flat.

She came through the door without opening it and settled into the passenger seat.

"This is going to be so much fun," she said, and I shuddered. She had said those very words before every movie we ever went to, almost like a recording.

Maybe this was my hell. No maybe about it. I was in hell. I was destined to take my dead wife to a movie three times a week for the rest of my life. Maybe I should just kill myself now and get it over with.

If I could only be certain that would end it.

Act Three: A Yellow Tinge

"You won't think it's sweet if we get caught," I said about halfway to the theater after she told me I was being sweet for taking her to a movie. "I get tossed in jail for killing you, and you end up haunting the local cemetery."

She shrugged. "Couldn't be much worse than hanging around here with you."

"Now don't start," I said. "This is how you got killed in the first place.

"Don't you dare blame me again for what happened." She had her hands on her hips, the sign she was getting mad. "I'm the one who is dead, remember."

"How can I *ever* forget?"

Actually, I had never really totally hated her. At least not enough yet to kill her. But I suppose it was building to that. I sure had wished she was dead enough times.

It was her way of arguing that got to me. One afternoon she started in on me. Or, as she tells it, I started in on her. Either way doesn't make much difference. I got so mad I yelled a Wizard curse at her that I had just read that morning. She laughed, so for a special effect, I tossed a handful of sparkle dust from the magic shop in her face. I read that Wizards were always using sparkle dust, and I guess it worked.

She backed up away from me rubbing her eyes, tripped, and hit her head hard on the edge of the counter as she went down.

I was over her immediately. I didn't like the way her head hitting that counter had sounded. A sick, deep smacking and cracking sound. Granted, I had cursed her dead, but I wasn't sure I really wanted her that way.

Too late. She was already dead. And her ghost was standing above me leaning over her own body.

"Now see what you have done," she had said. Even dead, she had started out annoying.

We rode the rest of the way in silence to the theater. I remembered we had done that a lot. Especially the year before she died. Actually, in the two weeks since she died we had gotten along better than ever before. Something about her not expecting sex, I think.

I parked as close as I could to the multiplex theater building, and suddenly she was in a good mood again. She clapped her hands together and floated out of the car before I even had it stopped.

"I'm in heaven," she said, moving toward the ticket window.

I shook my head, muttering that she was a long way from heaven, but I certainly wished she would go there soon. I locked the car and checked twice to see if the hatch was shut tight and the blanket over her body was in place.

By the time I had bought my ticket to the show she wanted to see, she was already inside, floating in front of the popcorn counter, looking sad.

I moved up beside her and as softly as I could, without moving my lips, I asked, "What's wrong?"

She pointed at the popcorn.

"You knew you wouldn't be able to eat any?" I whispered.

She shook her head. "No, it's not that. I can pick it up and put it in my mouth." To demonstrate she took a piece from the counter and popped it into her mouth and chewed with her mouth half open. Thank God no one was watching.

"So what's the problem? And since when can you pick up stuff?"

She shrugged. "I've been doing that for days now. But I can't taste the popcorn."

More stupid ghost rules.

I stared at her for a moment and then glanced around the theater lobby to see if anyone was watching. Again we were in luck.

"Maybe I can find a Wizard spell to help you," I said. "Or maybe you'll just get better with practice." I regretted saying that immediately.

"Oh, you think so? Then get an extra large, extra butter. I'll practice all the way through the movie."

I was about to object when this couple moved up behind me and I was forced to get the guy behind the counter's attention and buy an extra large, extra butter popcorn and a small drink.

By the time I found her in the sixth theater down the hall the previews were already starting. I started to say something and she shushed me, just like she used to do when she was alive.

Dead. Alive. Nothing changes.

I balanced the popcorn on the rail between us and she began to eat handfuls, dropping exactly the same amount that she used to do when she was alive, only this time the dropped popcorn went through her and gathered in a pile on the seat. I'd have to ask her later how that worked and why I couldn't see the popcorn after it was inside her. More and more strange ghost rules.

I glanced around to see if anyone was watching or sitting close. We were in luck. This movie was a real dog and there were only five other people in the theater.

After every preview she leaned over and whispered that she wanted to see that movie, just like she had always done. And, as when she was alive, the thought made me shudder, but now for different reasons.

I spent most of the movie trying to work out plans of escape. I even thought of just going out of the theater and walking away. But I didn't have the guts to do that. Besides, eventually the police would find the car and her body and I would get caught. The life of a fugitive just wasn't one for me.

When the movie ended, she sighed. "I really love movies."

"No kidding," I said under my breath, and luckily she ignored me. I sat still, watching the credits and waiting until the other people left before standing.

"Too bad you couldn't just stay here."

Again she sighed. "That would be wonderful."

We headed out the back door near the screen in silence, and it wasn't until I was at the car that I had realized what I had seen.

The multiplex theater's back door was right beside the screen. Under the screen, like in old theaters, was a stage, only this stage was fake, just used to get the screen up in the air. A maintenance man, or someone,

must have left the access door open to the area under
the stage, revealing rough planking on the floor spaced
evenly over hard-packed dirt.

There was nothing else under there, and no reason
for anyone to ever go under there.

"You really want to stay here?" I asked her as she
settled into her seat.

She looked at me with that questioning look, meaning she didn't understand. I always had liked that look
because it meant she didn't understand something
about me. She always took such pride in knowing *everything* about me, so that look had always cheered
me up; tonight was no exception.

I pointed back at the closed door. "Go back through
there and take a look under the stage."

"But—"

"Just do it." I loved having the upper hand.

She shrugged and floated/walked/moved toward the
closed metal theater door and then through it like it
was the surface of a lake.

A full minute later she was back, excited. "I see
what you are thinking. You could bury my body under
the stage, and I could see all the movies I wanted."

I nodded and she tried to hug me, which failed totally. But I suppose it was the thought that counted.

We went home, got me gloves and a shovel, and I
tossed in my Wizards book just in case I might need
it. We were back at the theater in less than an hour.
I backed the car right up to the closest place I could
get near the stage door, and we waited until the next
show ended and the people were leaving.

She went inside and stood guard. When she mo-
tioned that the coast was clear, I blocked the door
open. As the credits were playing, I got her body from
the car and under the stage.

While she watched the movie again with eight live
people, I buried her. I had to be real quiet, especially
taking out and replacing the flooring planks. But I got
it done, finishing the digging in the noisy love scene
in the middle and the putting back the flooring in the
loud chase scene at the end.

I did a quick Wizard invisibility blessing over her grave, then left the shovel in the back corner, as if it had been left by a workman. I went out behind the last movie-goer of the last show.

She met me in the car, smiling. "Thanks," she said.

I think that was the first time in years she had said that to me. I was taken aback. "My pleasure," was all I could think to say.

"Would you come tomorrow night and see a movie with me?"

"Sure," I said.

She clapped her hands together like a kid. "Great. You can buy me some popcorn."

"I'd be glad to," I said. And I really meant it. Since then I went to the movies there about once a week. No one ever talked about the ghost of the twelve-plex theater, except to complain about rude noises from empty seats behind them.

No one ever found her body.

I bought her popcorn every week and we never fought again. She seemed totally contented.

But after a few years I noticed she had this yellow tinge about her. I tried a Wizard curse to help her, but it did no good. I figured it was just too much yellow oil buildup.

SOUL CATCHER

❖ ❖ ❖

by Linda P. Baker

Linda Baker's short fiction also appears in
First Contact, New Amazons and *Dragon-
lance: The Dragons of Krynn.* She lives in Mo-
bile, Alabama.

The soul catcher was unraveled. The woolen
strands hung loose and limp on the bentwood
frame, the colored beads in a clump at the bottom.
The mountain clans who made the soul catchers believed the intricate weavings and the magic-wrought
blue beads would protect the destiny of the soul
from evil.

Lura, who had been born into a plains clan, wasn't
sure she believed in it. But her mother, who had
bought her the soul catcher, said the teachings of all
clans had truth in them. If that was so . . . Lura took
the tangled mass in her hands and sighed softly. It felt
rough and scratchy and cool, like wood and wool and
glass beads.

Wadded mass of soul catcher in hand, she wandered
across the big, second story room which was hers
alone. Her sister's was across the hall, with a view of
the garden, and her parents' was on the first floor.

Her room was the largest, and it looked out over
the rooftops of the city and down on one of the busy
streets that led to Market Square. The morning sun
shone through the rows of tall windows which lined
the south and east walls, and Lura's bare feet registered the cool . . . warm . . . cool of alternating bars
of sunlight on the polished hardwood floors.

At the open middle windows, with the early spring

breeze touching her face, without thinking, she held the soul catcher up to the sun and wove a spell. It was a variation on a mending, simple and effortless. The words came easily, her lips barely moving, and the forming of the spell felt good, the passing of the earth energy warm and familiar.

The soul catcher moved in her hands, shivered, then was still and taut. When her eyes snapped open, the tangled mass was sorted and whole again. The blue beads interspersed through it seemed to twinkle a darker blue. She caught her breath at what she had done, looking around like a guilty child to see if anyone had observed her transgression.

All she saw was movement in the windows of the house across the street. For the briefest moment, a shadow, the slow wafting of curtains which spoke of a hand abruptly drawn away.

She stepped quickly backward, out of sight. After a moment, she tilted her head until she could see around the edge of the windowsill and squinted, but she could see nothing in the bright reflection of sunlight off thick, sparkling glass.

That was all she ever saw across the way . . . slow moving curtains, flitting shadows, reflections on the blue-tinted glass. Never the man who owned the house. Never whether he was watching her, instead of the street below.

The house across the street was larger than hers, finer, with thick iron workings twined along the balconies and pink marble bricks inset at the corners of the windows and a large, shady stoop reaching out to the street.

But of the owner of the wafting curtains, she knew little. She had only seen him from across the street, leaving his house or returning to it. He was a Protector, in the pay of the Royal family—she knew that much on her own, though no one had ever said so in her presence. She knew because he had Protector eyes . . . always waiting, always watchful.

Lura leaned forward and looked down. The stoop across the street was empty except for the carved stat-

ues of lethers, their wings outstretched, but the street
was busy, as it always was this time of morning, and
it distracted her. The wide cobbled way was bustling
with early morning traffic, merchants on foot hurrying
toward the merchant district, as her father would soon
be. Peddlers with carts filled with vegetables, hurrying
toward the market. Dusty travelers on horseback, not
hurrying at all.

That, she thought, would be the best thing to be on
a busy street. A wanderer, ambling along on a tired
horse, seeing all the wonders of a city for the first
time.

An imperious knock interrupted her reverie. Before
she could answer, Crecia, her younger sister, pushed
open the door and slipped into the room. Cre grinned
impishly and swished the long skirt of her tunic across
the floor in a mock bow.

Crecia was her exact opposite. Younger and smaller
than Lura, and also prettier, in a playful, cheerful sort
of way. She was a study in the colors of the earth—
brown hair, brown eyes, dressed in brown tunic, tan
vest, brown boots.

"Father and Mother are ready to go," Crecia announced. "Father wants to see you before they leave."

Lura had forgotten that her father would not be
scurrying off to the merchant district this morning. He
was going home for a trading visit. Home . . . to Daeghra, the village where her parents and their parents
and their parents before them had been born, where
she and Andret and Crecia had been born.

For a moment, she felt such an ache for the home
she could never see again, for the brother she would
never see again, that she didn't respond to the warning
of honeyed sweetness in her sister's voice.

"Father has received a betrothal proposal."

Lura's heart gave a painful thump. The house would
not be the same without Crecia. "I'll miss you," she
said. "I hope he's . . . the one you want." The words
burned her tongue, like the venom they were.

"Just like that?" Crecia said sharply, her bright eyes
fixed on her sister's face. "Just like that! You would

send me off with 'I'll miss you' and 'I hope he's who you want,' with no effort to descry whether he's the right one for me. Or me for him.''

Shame flooded Lura, washed over her as quickly as blood suffused her veins. Her face flushed. The purple tattoo on her temple, the one which marked her as *chaudin,* a searcher of souls, throbbed. "I'm sorry," she choked, no longer able to meet her sister's gaze. "You know I cannot . . ."

"I don't know that at all," Crecia retorted sharply. "However . . ." And her voice changed, became once again sweet and impish. ". . . the proposal is not for me." She paused for effect, swishing her skirt back and forth. "It's for you."

Lura gasped. "No," she whispered to herself. Then stronger, to Crecia, "No. You must be mistaken." She could not marry!

Crecia grinned wider. "Father sent me to fetch you. He and Mother are in the library, with your suitor." Crecia started out the door, then turned back. "I'd put on shoes to meet my betrothed, were I you."

"I shan't!" Lura wheeled away as her sister closed the door, ashamed to hear the echo of her raised voice. For a moment, just a fraction of a second, she had every intention of acting like a willful, spoiled girl. Of appearing in the library just as she was, barefoot, hair streaming loose from her combs.

She stood in a beam of sunlight and wiped her sweaty palms on her tunic, leaving marks across the soft silk. "I'll go just as I am," she said defiantly. But, imagining the stricken faces of her parents, she didn't.

She put on her slippers and tucked back the strands of fine gold hair that was always escaping and slipped a vest on over her tunic. It was plain but woven of the finest linre made in Daeghra.

And so she was quite presentable when she stepped through the door of the library. Her father was standing across the room, and her mother and a man were seated in the carved wooden chairs facing him.

A fire leaped and crackled in the huge fireplace, setting highlights to dancing on the glass shelves lined with books. Her father had made the shelves himself, from a spell he learned when he was a boy. Ordinarily, Lura loved the dark, high-ceilinged library with its rich wood walls and sparkling glass and scents of new paper and spicy, exotic spell components. But today, after the cool spring breeze wafting into her room, it seemed hot and stuffy and small.

Her father saw her and beamed, his expression as bright and hot as the fire. "Lura, come and meet Miral!"

Lura's body jerked as if controlled by invisible strings. It took all her self-control to remain where she was, to keep from running from the room.

Miral was the owner of the house across the street! The owner of the worked iron and pink marble and the windows from which someone watched the street as often as she did. The owner of the Protector eyes. And she knew why he had come.

Through the thin soles of her slippers, the floor seemed to leach the warmth from her feet. From her bones.

Miral stood as her mother did and turned. Lura recognized him from seeing him across the street, but it was the first time she'd been so close. The impact of his gaze, eyes as copper as the spires on the Sol Chapel, took her breath away. The mark that was etched across his high cheekbone was a mixture of colors, not solid purple like hers, because a Protector could not see all the *chau*, the soul, as she could, only a part of it. His mark showed purple and healing blue shading into the angry red of the Protectorate.

She swayed. Tried to step back, but the floor held onto her feet, refused to allow her to flee.

He was tall and wide, his shoulders broad beneath a tunic and vest as fine as any she'd ever seen. It was covered over with embroidery even finer than the stitches in her plain vest. He had only the briefest fringe of silver-gray hair around his skull, and unlike most men his age, affected no spell to cover his baldness. The curves and planes of his bare head were unnerving, repulsive, strangely attractive, all within one breath. Touching him would be like . . . like putting her hand into something cold and oozing. Like . . . She shuddered without moving a muscle.

"Miral's brought a proposal of betrothal for you."

"So Crecia told me," Lura replied, surprised at how cool her voice sounded despite her brain's urging to her feet to run. Despite the great, thumping beats of her heart.

"Lura, I'm pleased to meet you at last." His voice was deep, gravelly like fingers rasping down her back. His smile, at least, did not beam at her and demand good cheer.

She had no wish to shame her parents in front of a stranger, but try as she might, she could not school her face into a smile in return. She supposed, from the way Miral's expression grew slowly solemn and watchful, that she had not even managed to be emotionless. The despair she felt must be tugging at her lips as strongly as it was dragging at her heart.

Miral came forward and took her hands in his. Against the warmth of his fingers, she knew hers were cold as ice, stiff as old leather.

She tried to back away and could not. Her eyes felt as if they were strung on a taut wire, bouncing back and forth, up and down. She wanted to look at him. She wanted to close her eyes from the very possibility.

Though she willed it not to happen, she felt him as only a chaudin could. The knowing was on her, as naturally as she took her next breath. She felt the strength of his essence, his soul. Some sense of purpose, of destiny so strong and determined that it burned. After all these months of self-enforced emptiness, to have it leap at her now . . . ! She clamped down on the knowing with all the strength she could muster. Shoved it away.

"I'll not keep you," he said, but he did not release her hands.

She could feel his gaze like fingers touching lightly across her skin, examining her face, scrutinizing, as if searching for something. Protector's eyes, unwavering, probing. Searching for the tiniest glimmer of evil, of badness.

Lura drew on strength she did not know she possessed simply to keep her hands from trembling.

At her lack of response, he let go and turned back to her father. "We will speak again when you return." Before her parents could protest, or her relief could show itself bluntly on her face, he was gone, bowing his way out the door.

Lura attacked the moment she heard the wide front door screech closed, before they could reprimand her. "You cannot be planning to pursue this!"

The smile dropped from her father's face. "You were rude, Lura. I will not have you behave so in front of a guest."

"A guest? If you have your way, he'll be my husband!"

"Yes, he will be. We have accepted his proposal."

Lura's heart lurched as if the floor had dropped out from under her. "Accepted? Without asking me? You cannot!" But of course, they could. Every day, parents accepted proposals of betrothal for their sons and daughters without asking for permission or acceptance.

"Lura, sweetheart," her mother said gently, "Would you have said yes if we'd asked?"

"Of course not! He's a—"

"Then why should we ask?" her father interrupted. Demanded.

"Falis . . ." Her mother touched his arm and met his irritated gaze with a conciliatory one. "Give her a moment." She came across the room, trailing the ends of her travel shawl and the woodsy scent of rainflowers. She hugged her eldest daughter gently. "You would not have said yes if it had been the Queen herself with a proposal from the Prince. But you cannot spend the rest of your life hidden away in your rooms."

"Why not?" Lura murmured sulkily, but the gentle caress of her mother drained away all her anger, leaving sorrow in its place. She could never make her mother understand that to avoid what she might see reflected in a Protector's eyes, she would spend the rest of her life in a tiny closet.

"Your father and I are not immortal, as much as we might wish it. We will not always be here. In these months . . ." Her mother paused, swallowed as if the movement gave her courage to speak. "In these months since Andret died, we've despaired. I know how hard it's been for you, and we want to know you'll be cared for."

Her father joined them and patted her shoulder clumsily. His normally cheerful eyes had the melancholy droop they always assumed when Andret's name was mentioned. She could not feel anger at him either, despite his misbegotten plans for her future.

"Father, I don't want to wed. He's a P—" She bit off her own words with a shaky sob. "I don't even know him."

"You will both learn, Lura. You will learn him, the way all mates learn each other. It is a good proposal. A good joining for our family, and for you. Miral is a wealthy man and a respected one. You will want for nothing."

Lura looked over her mother's shoulder. Crecia was standing to the side of the doorway. Lura didn't remember her entering, had no idea how long she had been there. For once, Crecia was not smiling. Her young face was solemn.

Falis' beaming smile returned when he looked at his youngest daughter. "And Miral has made a most generous proposal. He asks for only the most token dowry. Which means we will be able to increase Crecia's dowry immensely."

Cre's face brightened. Lura knew what she was thinking. She liked a boy from the Chilra family, which claimed minor Royal blood. A family Crecia would never have a chance to join without either a very strong magical talent, or a very large dowry. Lura had gotten all the magical talent in the family and half the money available for a dowry. Until now.

Lura stiffened. "I'll not agree to marry him! Not

even to give you a higher bargaining price for Crecia."
She regretted the words the moment they slithered
into the air, but there was no taking them back.

Her father and mother stepped back. Her mother
looked as if she had been slapped. Her father's face
turned red. "I will forget you said that," he said, the
fury in his voice barely contained. "And I will expect
you to be in a better frame of mind when your mother
and I return next week."

Without a word to any of them, not even a good-
bye to her parents, Lura went back to her room. She
stood at the tall windows and stared down into the
street. Through the open window, she heard the front
door open and Crecia's good-byes. She watched her
mother and father as they climbed into their cart.
Watched the cart until it disappeared out of sight.
Watched all the other carts, heading toward the west
gate of the city.

That was where she must go, as soon as the sun had
set. Down into the streets, out of the city. Away,
where no Protector would bother to look for her. No
matter how many hours and days she had spent at the
window, looking down on the street and imagining
what it would be like to be down there, it was a fright-
ening prospect for a girl who had never spent a night
away from home. Who had never spent a night without her family within calling distance.

But she could see no other alternative, for it was
no coincidence that a Protector had singled her out.
And if she could not shame her parents by walking
about barefoot, she surely could not bear to look on
their faces when she was led away by a Protector of
the Royal Court. When her crime was revealed.

She was still standing at the window when the moon
made its early rise above the rooftops. The streets had
emptied slowly, merchants hurrying home to supper
and travelers searching out a nearby inn. As soon as
the street was dark, she would leave.

The sunlight was still bright, and the crescent moon
looked eerily beautiful against the blue sky. There was
something about blue. Something so soothing. So

peaceful. She could remember lying in the linre fields, flat on her back, the top of her head touching Crecia's, staring into the blue summer sky until her eyes filled with tears at the brightness.

"Lura?"

There was a soft scratch at the door, then another. Lura could not help but smile. When they had lived in Daeghra, in their little house made of mud bricks and thatch and canvas, the signal for entry into the room she shared with Crecia had been a scratching at the door flap.

The door eased open, and the top of Cre's brown curls peeked through, followed by one half of her face. "Lura?" When nothing was launched at the door, the remainder of her face appeared. "Can I come in? Are you mad at me?"

She stepped inside and closed the door without waiting for an answer. Crecia was carrying a small lovers' lantern, so called because it was so often carried when couples went out in the evenings to meet. The sides were pierced through with varying patterns and the small flame inside, all that Cre could manage with her limited magic, cast flickering, lopsided hearts and stars onto the wood floor.

Crecia was dressed to go out, in pants and tunic so nearly the same color as her hair that she almost blended into the shadow near the door. Only her pale, heart-shaped face glowed in the darkening room.

Lura smiled. "It's not your fault."

Crecia carefully put the lantern on the floor and crossed to her rapidly. She caught Lura's hands and squeezed them. "I was afraid you'd think I had something to do with Father's decision. Because of the dowry. Truly, I have not told him about Rolan."

Lura squeezed back. "I know that. And truly," she mimicked her sister's voice, thinking how much she would miss Crecia's teasing, her horrible jokes, her laughter. "I do not begrudge you the dowry. I would give you all of it regardless. And more, if I could."

"You know that all you have to do is tell them," Crecia said softly.

Lura tried to turn away, but Crecia held onto her and would not allow it. "Tell them what?"

"Tell them you are not meant for him. If truly you are not."

For a moment, the idea caught at her, leaped like a tiny flame far away in a terrible darkness. A tiny, flickering hope. Yes, it would work, but only on her unsuspecting parents. The Protector would not be fooled.

"I can't do that, Cre." Lura tried again and this time, Crecia allowed her hands to slide free. She turned away and stared at the windows across the way, at the warm yellow light coming from them. Against the inner light and the darkening edges of the evening, the lace pattern on the curtains was delicate. "I no longer have the power," she whispered.

Crecia put her arm around Lura's shoulders and squeezed. As she often did, Lura found her sister's stillness more comforting than all the words in the world. It might not be magical, but Crecia had been gifted with the rare and comforting gift of silence.

Since they were children, it had been accepted that Lura was *chaudin,* strong in her ability to see beneath the surface, in her ability to mold the earth essence that was magic, gifted in the rare magic of soul searching. Their father was a skilled Conjurer; their mother unsurpassed among the ten tribes in forest lore and communing with animals and nature.

Crecia was weak in all the wizards' ways. She had never even been marked, as a child, with the symbol that revealed which talent was strongest. Her face was as unblemished as a new baby's.

"Come out with me tonight," Crecia said suddenly. "It's Quarter Night in the market."

A shiver, combined of equal parts sorrow and fear, coursed down her spine. Made her fingers curl. How could Cre know that she had been planning just that? "Why do you say that?" she asked sharply.

"I want you to meet Rolan." Crecia clutched at her arms, suddenly animated. "Oh, Lura, you *have* to. Because . . . Because before, without the extra dowry, there was no chance. So it didn't matter. We were never going to marry anyway. But now . . . I can ask Father to go to Rolan's father with a proposal!''

"Twice the dowry still won't be enough, Cre. Not for the Chilra."

"It will be . . ." Cre glanced sideways, not quite facing her. "If you say we're destined to be together."

"I'll never be able to say that, Cre." Now it was Lura who did not quite look at her sister. She couldn't face the innocent, eager gaze, the imploring eyes.

Crecia wheeled to her, gripping her arm. Though Lura could not see her sister's eyes, the gaze seemed to pierce, the way the Protector's had. Crecia's fingers burned through her sleeve.

"Lura, please, just this once. Come and meet Rolan. And if you can't see . . . Well, then, you must meet him anyway, if he is to be your brother."

It was this last that made Lura know she had to leave. That left her no choice. She looked at Crecia, dressed in market clothes, her brown eyes sparkling as brightly as the gold chain at her throat. Lura knew Rolan had given it to her, and that her sister never took it off.

What if, by some miracle, Crecia and Rolan did marry? The thought of seeing them together was more than she could bear.

The night air had grown cool, and Lura pulled the hood of her cloak closer about her face. The movement was as much to cover the tattoo from the view of the people around her as to protect from the cold. Her jewelry and the double handful of coins she'd been able to collect from about the house were in a bag inside her skirt.

"Lura, hurry! I promised to meet Rolan at the fountain before the fireworks begin!"

Crecia was several steps ahead of her on the cobbled sidewalk and Lura hurried to catch up, the lumpy bag bumping against her thigh. As they were swept into the market square, into an even bigger crowd than the one on the sidewalk, Lura reached out and touched her sister one last time. Her fingers lingered on the soft curls of Crecia's long hair. "If we get separated, I'll meet you there."

Crecia nodded happily, her thoughts obviously on the man waiting for her, pushing forward through a mass of dancing boys.

Lura didn't think Crecia even looked back as she allowed the group to jog between them. She pushed frantically at the broad back in front of her and when the boy stepped aside, Crecia was nowhere in sight.

It was a Quarter Night, when the market stayed open and everyone celebrated the ending of an old season and the beginning of a new one. The huge square was packed with people, buying, selling, shouting out wishes for a prosperous Spring.

The mixture of stalls and tables and marketcloth spread on the ground were all overflowing with merchandise. Vegetables and dried meat from the nearby farms. Sweet perfumes and spices from across the lake. Silks and linre from the north, including the rich, embossed linre the village of Daeghra exported, through her father.

To Lura, it seemed the whole population of the city was crammed into the square. Suddenly alone in a city she'd never before even ventured into escorted, she shrank back into a corner formed by two stalls.

So many people! They flowed past her, short and tall, clean and dirty, young and old. Apprentice mages dressed in the luminous colors of the different schools, schoolchildren in brown jumpers, priests in stiff green, royalty and peasants alike with bright colored Spring scarves wrapped around their shoulders.

So many people! How could she have been so stupid? How could she block so many? The fleeting glimpses of the souls about her, of their essences, was like being caught in a whirlwind of color and sound. Sweetness, meanness, kindness, sorrow, bubbling gaiety, all tossed at her, then snatched away as if by the wind.

And the couples—couples the age of her parents, of her own age, older ones, with little ones between that must be grandchildren, and young ones, fingers entwined, faces turned toward each other even as they walked.

As the first young couple brushed past her, Lura covered her face, pressing her back against the side of a stall as if afraid of being attacked. And the knowing buffeted her. The souls of the two glowed all the colors of the rainbow. Scented the air like a confection of yellow flowers.

Lura took in a shaky breath and felt the essence of the two enter her lungs, like the sweetest smoke. The young woman looked at her and smiled, and the warmth sank into Lura's bones.

Too quickly, the young man was tugging the woman away, saying "We have to hurry." Lura followed, fingers clutching the edges of her hood tight against her throat. A bright arc of explosions swept across the sky as the young couple disappeared in the crowd.

The fireworks! She'd only previously seen them from her window. She edged out into the crowd and allowed herself to be pushed along. The fireworks were even more wonderful up close. So bright they left afterimages of green and red and purple dots on her eyelids. Gaze turned skyward, she edged around a squealing crowd of children and aimed toward the west side of the square.

Surely on that side of the square, she'd be able to tell which was the main street leading to the gate.

A stranger thrust a cup of ale at her, and she sipped from it before passing it back and moving on. It tasted warm and foamy and as metallic as the pewter pitcher.

Another stranger danced her about in a wild circle before moving on, leaving her with a smile on her face, aware of the swirling music coming from one of the stalls. The man's aura was bright and happy, his destiny shining like a new coin. Tomorrow something wonderful would happen to him. She had known it as his hand touched hers.

It was this happy smile that was swallowed up as a couple brushed past her. A tall woman, as coldly beautiful, as elegant as a perfect icicle. Her mate was almost as beautiful as she, tall and slender, with hair as blond as ripened wheat. Her arm was linked through his, and the rich silk of their robes billowed out behind them as they strode through the crowd. Beautiful and rich and important.

But the place where their souls should have joined was as black, as empty as looking into a well. It was not even the roiling blackness of the river, swollen from melting snow. It was nothing. Empty. Bleak. Nothing. Not even cold, for even coldness had a beauty to it, in the nip of winter morning, in the puff of frosty breath seen against the orange of sunrise. It was nothing.

No blow could have hurt more. The music went out of Lura's feet. The ambrosia taste of ale soured on her tongue. She wheeled away from the sight of the couple, twisting around a table filled with little glass animals. Around a mother and daughter sharing a meat pie. And came up hard against a man standing so still, he could have been a statue.

The breath whooshed out of Lura's lungs, and she froze as her gaze scanned up and up and up, past a finely embroidered vest covering a broad chest, a chiseled cheekbone marked with a multicolored symbol, to the copper gaze of Miral.

This close, he was not as old as she'd thought. Not as old as her father though his bald head made him appear so. And his eyes were not so warm as copper. They were more like hard, cold brass.

"They told me you never leave your home," he said. His voice was like it had been before, smooth, deep, sinister. If a cat could talk, it would sound like him as it toyed with a mouse. "They told me you couldn't see anymore . . ." His fingers came toward her, big, square hand, beautifully shaped fingers, curled like a claw. His heat burned her arm as his fingers touched her forearm.

Lura cried out and ran. Pushing her way through the throng of bodies. Past surprised faces. Past elbows and broad backs and corners of stalls. She stumbled and would have fallen had a woman not caught her.

As she pulled loose, she risked a glance back. The crowd had closed behind her. There was no sight of Miral, but she didn't trust that she could escape that easily.

She ran on, past people and stalls. Zigzagging through the crowd, along the bricked front of a tavern, into the first street she came to. She ran until there were no more people, until she was in darkness. Until her footfalls on the cobblestoned streets were all she could hear.

As she slowed, she realized she was crying. The tears on her cheeks were a mixture of temperatures, warm as they slid past her lashes, colder as they slid down her face and dripped off her chin.

She turned a corner, then another, then another. Walking fast now, no longer running, gasping for breath. The night air was like sand in her throat. She stumbled on the sidewalk and almost fell.

She paused to wipe her eyes and saw the shadow of a man at the end of the street. Improbably broad shoulders and the elegant curve of a bald head silhouetted against the light from the market. She shivered, looked around to see where she was and suddenly realized she had no idea. She was lost. And the Protector had found her.

Something about the way he moved said it had been no effort at all. While she had run and run and run, he had simply walked down a street, turned a corner and there she was.

"Go away," she rasped as he came closer. "Leave me alone."

He reached out to grab her, and as he did, the wide silver band of the ring he wore flashed blue in the moonlight. "They told me you cannot see," he said. "Why have you lied?"

With a cry so full of pain it could be felt, she threw herself at him, fists flying. He towered head and shoulders over her, outweighed her twice over, but in the face of her fury, he backed away.

Her knuckles connected with skin and bone, and he

grabbed her, pinned her arms to her body, held her so that she could barely breathe.

"Do you want to know why I lied about my *gift*?" she hissed in his face, the image of the couple huge in her mind. "Because it is not a gift! It is a curse!"

Furious words boiled over before she could stop them from spilling out. "I lied to them. I told them they were soul mates and they married. And when I looked at them, their joining was just as dark. Just as empty as that couple in the square."

Where his grip on her arm had eased, she struck out, trying to yank loose and hit him again. It felt so good to scream. To hit. If she could only hit something hard enough, long enough, to never remember that emptiness. Her fist connected with his ribs. Pain spangled out from her knuckles in unison with his gasp.

He caught her hand and twisted her arm until she cried out. "Do not strike me again! Do you hear?"

She heard. Some semblance of sanity seeped back through the red haze of anger. She stilled, slowly going limp in his arms. All the emotion slowly drained out of her. "What are you going to do with me now?"

"Do with you?" He released her gradually, all but one arm, and that he held carefully, as if expecting that she would try to run away. "First finish. Tell me all of it."

She cringed away from him. No. No more. She could not tell him, not even him, a Protector. The words stuck in her throat. She opened her mouth to speak, and the muscles moved, but no sound came out. But there was no reason not to confess now. He was only asking for words to confirm what he already saw. Her guilt.

She swallowed, worked the muscles in her throat and the words came out. Flowing, faster and faster, like water released from a dam. "Daeghra, my village, we've—we'd always been at war with our neighbors. Across the river. For generations, the villages fought over the land where the linre is grown. They killed each other. They burned the fields. Whichever village lost the fighting . . . starved for a season. Until they could strike back, and burn, and kill. And then the other village starved.

"Two years ago, in a battle, a group of our warriors captured a group from another village who were working in the linre. One of the sons of the other village's mage was among them. I lied to everyone. I told them that he and Tega were destined to be together. Tega is our mage's eldest daughter."

He shook her, with just his grip on her arm, like a dog shaking a toy. "Why did you do it? Why?"

Lura's teeth clicked shut on her tongue. A tiny shard of pain lanced out. A pinpoint of salty liquid slicked her tongue. Blood. Red blood. Memories surged up. Gnawing hunger in her belly. The red-gold of burning fields of linre, the red of flowing blood. A face so like her own, her brother's face, slicked with blood. Still, so still. And bloody. She drew a ragged breath. "I thought . . . I thought I could bring the villages together. I didn't use my power. I didn't even try to see their destinies. I just saw a way to stop the fighting."

Lura stared into the darkness, not seeing the dim outline of houses around her, of the street and the distant glow of the market. She saw only what she had seen last year, during the harvesting. Brax and Tega, with their new baby. And between them was that same emptiness she had just seen in the square.

"What else?" he demanded. "There is more." He caught her chin and tilted her head back until she was forced to meet his gaze. His fingers burned.

"I can't even describe it. The emptiness between two people who aren't meant to be together. It's not cold, or black, or even ugly. It's just . . . nothing. But seeing them together, *knowing* them, that wasn't the worst of it. Last year, during the harvest, I saw what could have been. I saw Brax with the woman he was meant to be with."

At last, Lura met his gaze, steeling herself for the repulsion that would come. "It was Crecia. My sister. Brax was always meant to be the one to bring peace to our people. But not with Tega. With Crecia."

The expression which crossed his face was so dark it wasn't even readable. It was beyond disgust, more than hatred.

With a cry, she covered her face. "What will you do with me now?" Not that it mattered. There was no punishment more horrible than the loathing she had just seen in the face of a stranger.

"Can you not see for yourself?" His voice was strangely soft, again the cat voice.

And she was the mouse.

"Will you not look at yourself and see what is?"

"I cannot," she said miserably. "Never again. I lied about what I had seen. I played god. And my sister must pay the price. The destiny that was hers is lost forever. I'll never use my power again."

"Foolish child!" he hissed.

She cried out as his fingers bit into her arm. Without a word, he turned and started down the street, dragging her with him. She had to almost run to keep up. Without his grip on her arm, she would have fallen on the rough street.

"Where are you taking me?" she gasped, visions of spare cells with only a tiny, high window dancing in her head. Or dark dungeons with things in the corners which rustled and squeaked in the night. Would he torture her? Would his Protector's eyes look into her soul and burn out all her power?

"To the square. To your sister."

Lura cried out. A pain greater than could be caused by mere hot iron or sharp blade knifed through her heart. "No!" The horror in her voice should have softened the will of the coldest heart, but he walked on. Inexorable. Unyielding.

With no care for the stares that followed them, the children who hid their faces in their mother's skirts, he dragged her into the crowded square. Threaded through the people and the tents and around the clumps of dancers. Straight toward the fountain, as if he knew exactly where Crecia was.

"Stop it! Stop it!" Lura threw all of her weight backward, away from the direction in which he was headed. She was no match for his strength, but her panic gave her a force that made him pause.

"Anything!" she whispered, hiding her face against his arm, aware of the stares they were drawing. "Do anything to me. Torture me. Kill me. But don't tell Crecia what I've done."

He caught the back of her head, drew her away from him as if he couldn't stomach her touch. Large hand gripping her head, fingers threaded through her braid, he turned her, pushed her forward, through a ring of people.

Crecia was across the fountain. Laughing, dancing with a young man with hair as brown as her own. She saw Lura and waved. Pointed to her partner, mouthing his name as he whirled her in time to the music. "Rolan."

Lura tried to turn away but Miral tightened his grip on her head. "Have you learned nothing?" he hissed.

Lura closed her eyes, and as if he knew, he shook her head again.

"Look. See." His fingers dug into her skull. His body was against hers, behind her, hard and unyielding, refusing to allow her to turn away, to even shrink back.

"You will see!"

She opened her eyes and the chaudin sight shattered over her, like a sheet of ice fracturing into a thousand tiny pieces. Sharp, twinkling shards of sight, spilling from the sky. Piercing her. Blinding her.

The young man who was whirling her sister faster and faster, as if the thumping of the music no longer guided his feet, was wonderful. Happy and laughing and handsome. Exactly the sort of bright, happy, warm young man she would want for a brother. Exactly the sort of man she would want for her sister. The warm brown of his soul touched Cre's and the essence of their joining glowed like embers on a winter night. Like a river of golden honey. Warm and sweet and smooth.

Lura crumpled. Only Miral's arm, suddenly around her waist, kept her from falling. "I don't understand," she mumbled. "I don't understand." She reached out as if she could touch them, as if her fingers could entwine the golden colors and draw them to her.

Leaving her arm outstretched as if he understood, Miral guided her to the edge of the fountain, seated her.

She could feel the cold, wet stone through her dress. She dropped her hand, caressed the roughness. "I don't understand."

Miral's copper eyes glowed into hers. "Has it never occurred to you that there are many destinies? Many paths? Has it never occurred to you that it was your destiny to make that mistake? That you did it for a reason?"

Lura caught at the kind words, wanting so badly to grasp them, to claim the forgiveness in his voice. "I don't . . ." She touched her face, the smooth place on her cheek where the chaudin mark was. For the first time since Andret died, it did not throb and ache.

"I can help you, if you'll let me." He held out his hand to her. "I want to help you."

She couldn't take it. Like the morning, only hours ago, when she first met him, the ground seemed to be falling away beneath her, drifting until his big, square hand was just out of reach. "But, I don't understand . . . You're a Protector . . . Sent to punish . . ."

"I did not come to you as a Protector." He smiled and the expression was warm and gentle and kind. "But, yes, Protectors protect. If punishment is required, then we punish. But we also heal."

He reached out and brushed his thumb across the frown creasing her forehead. Stroked back and forth as if he was smearing something on her skin, or perhaps wiping a smear away. His touch was soothing, calming, as if he was stroking a balm across her spirit. "Have you learned nothing from all this? You took away a destiny because you acted without thinking. You didn't use your power. Will you do the same to me?"

"To you?" She caught at the raspy stone on which

she sat. The ground was moving again, sweeping her even farther away, so far that her vision blurred and she could no longer see him clearly. Could not see his copper eyes, his strong shoulders, his elegant, smooth head.

With an effortless step, he crossed the void and caught her fingers in his. His touch swept away her guard. The essence that was Miral washed over her. His aura was blue, the blue of the morning sky and the deepest sea.

At the place where he touched her, the gold that was Lura and the blue that was Miral mixed, became the green of the shadowed forest, the green of new grass blown by spring wind.

WIZARD'S CHOICE

❖ ❖ ❖

by Janet Pack

Janet Pack lives in Lake Geneva, Wisconsin, with felines Bastjun Amaranth and Canth Starshadow. She writes, directs, and acts in radio ads for a local game store. She gives writing seminars, and speaks to schools and groups about reading and the writing profession. When not writing short stories and books, Janet sings classical, Renaissance, and Medieval music. During leisure time she composes songs, reads, collects rocks, exercises, skis, and paddles her kayak on Lake Geneva.

"**I** will find my own familiar. And not here."

A placating smile stretched the animal dealer's pudgy face. "I'm sorry, young Sir, that just isn't done. The Schola suggested you come to us for good reason. We here at Darynthian Traders can show you so much more than just common local fauna. We have some very attractive imports for your consideration today. And remember, you must choose the correct familiar for your lifestyle as well as your magic."

The dealer's droning self-satisfied voice irritated Briastros as the wizard swept under the heavy draperies and into the small viewing room. The trader dropped the privacy curtain behind them.

"After all," he continued, "you will be together the rest of your lives. All ill-considered choice would be, ah . . . unfortunate."

"Yes, unfortunate," snarled Briastros, aware that his dark eyes appeared to smolder during high emotions. And right now he was very, very angry. "Which

one of you talked Tirshellan into buying that mute
seven-colored glob she's stuck with?"

"Oh, the Hyrcanian diropsis. She insisted it spoke
to her."

"But you didn't tell her it would communicate only
once during its life," the wizard snapped. "A familiar
like that is no help. Tirshellan was good, perhaps the
best of our class. The diropsis sliced her powers in
half. She'll be subject to a life of minor spells and
conundrums because of it."

The animal dealer spread open hands, stubby fingers spangled with stone-set rings that glinted like
stars in the soft lamplight. Such a display of wealth
irritated the wizard even more because much of it
had come from his predecessors at the Schola who,
like him, could barely rake enough nonials to clink
together.

"We did not know," the trader said. "The diropsis
are new to this dealership. Perhaps becoming attached
to it was that wizard's destiny."

"Destiny! I doubt it." Briastros threw himself into
the thronelike chair designated for the viewer. A small
curtained stage made of richly-hued wooden layers sat
a few feet away, bathed in the soft light of hidden
lamps. Falsely imposing, made for show like everything else in this business. He hated it, hated the
whole contrived idea that a wizard of the land of Illastrus must come to Darynthian Traders and lay down
hard-earned coin for a familiar.

Insulting, the whole concept. And something about
the scheme was patently wrong. Familiars and wizards
should find each other, not rely on some service who
understood little about wizardry and even less about
the animals they traded, Briastros fumed. No wizard
just starting into the fullness of his or her life should
be required to pay the exorbitant prices the Darynthian Traders demanded for even one little tochim
bird no larger than his thumb.

The Schola had sent Briastros here, and he must
honor the school and his teachers by looking at at

least a few of the offerings the Traders had spent so much time searching out for him. But he was absolutely certain there was no warm, sensitive animal mind awaiting him behind that gently illuminated curtain. No partner that could double his mental strength. These Traders were the only animal agents in Darynthia, some said in all of Illastrus. He would have to find his own.

"And what else don't you know about your wares that can hurt another one of my friends or myself?" Briastros growled.

The animal dealer curtailed a sharp answer, knowing from experience that even a medium-class wizard should not be trifled with. Certainly not one who, without a familiar, could not yet be Ranked.

"Nothing, absolutely nothing, young Sir. Shall we begin?"

"Yes," snapped Briastros, feeling trapped.

Trapped, just like the first animal haloed on that stage. The curtain parted to show a beautiful thickly-furred beast of browns and creams with a long plush tail and large dark eyes in an almost-black face. It methodically worked tiny paw-fingers set with small sable scimitars through each of the bars of its cage, testing for eccentricities or weaknesses it could use toward escape.

Briastros' heart went out to the creature as his mind lanced a thought toward it. No response. This animal's cogitations were a morass of fear and frustration, fixed only on freedom in the forests it craved.

The wizard stood, disgusted by the show and by what the beautiful, obviously intelligent beast was forced to endure for his sake. "I'll buy it," he grated through clenched teeth. "How much?"

"The Darynthian ractoin, from the deep forests north of this city," the dealer enthused. "A lovely and very wise choice. How wonderful to have found your familiar on the first try!"

Briastros rounded on him slowly. "I didn't say I'd found a familiar," he enunciated clearly and slowly as if to a recalcitrant child. "I said I'd buy it. What's the price?"

"Eighty-five nonials." The dealer rubbed his hands together, trying to keep a greedy expression from his face. The wizard saw it, and added another rung to his ladder of disgust. "Plus cleaning and delivery fees, of course."

"I'll take it the way it is." The young man tossed a purse to the pudgy man and turned toward the cage. "I want the exact change back from that amount. Withhold nothing. If you do, remember that old saying about a wizard being quick to anger and slow to forgive. We can also be very creative. How would you like a spell on your business that kept your cage locks from fastening?"

"No, that wouldn't be good, young Sir." The Trader's voice chilled. "I'll get your change right away."

Briastros didn't take note when the dealer left with his purse. He rotated the cage, sending the animal within hissing to the center of its small keep. Twisting the key of the lock, the wizard opened the door and slowly reached within.

"Quiet, little one, be quiet. I'll take you back to the forest, I promise. You can run in the shadows there, protected by a little spell I have that will hide you from a hunter's eyes. You'd like that, yes?"

The creature looked at Briastros with wide eyes. Something behind them seemed to understand the difference between this person and the ones who had handled it before. Instead of biting him with sharp ivory-colored teeth, the animal reached for the wizard's arm. Taking hold, it looked into his face again, then climbed swiftly to perch on his shoulder, pawfingers and claws clinging in the black fabric shoulder of his robe, its tail draped elegantly over the other shoulder.

"Here's your change, young Sir." The trader returned with the much-depleted coin. "I advise caution. That beast is a biter—oh!"

He stepped back in surprise as the freed animal

hissed into his face. Smiling, Briastros passed beneath the curtain of the viewing area.

"He bit your personnel because of being badly handled, incarcerated, and frustrated. I'm going to loose this creature in the forest," the wizard stated, striding down the corridor of the large shop.

The dealer shrugged. "We'll just capture it again."

"Not this one." Briastros inclined his head with only the slightest degree of courtesy as he pushed open the outside door. "It will be spelled against the eyes of your hunters. Good day."

"Good day, young Sir." Frost laced the edges of the trader's farewell.

The wizard sucked in a deep breath, cleansing his lungs of the dull unpleasant air inside the animal seller's establishment. The living collar he wore chittered softly as he headed toward the northern edge of Darynthia. He laughed.

"Fresh air and sun feel good, don't they?" His voice turned wistful as the animal nosed his shoulder-length auburn hair. "I wish you were my familiar. You're quite a charmer. And I have no more money to buy another. But perhaps something will happen. A good turn for a good turn, right? Ah, I ought to introduce you to Zudieath. Perhaps you'd favor one another."

Briastros made a sudden detour, back to the Schola and his friend. He found her, as he expected, in the great Library, her soft pale brown hair framing the scroll she read in gold. She didn't look up. He cleared his throat softly from beside her chair.

"Brias!" she exclaimed after taking a moment to surface from the text. "I just found the most fascinating . . ."

Her eyes were snagged away from his by the little sable face peering curiously into hers from beside her friend's ear. Zudie's beautiful blue-gray eyes blanked for a long moment as she reached out mentally to the creature. She gasped.

With a mew of discovery and longing, the animal

leaped from Briastros' shoulder to hers and settled there, cheek to cheek with its familiar. The place across the back of his neck where it had ridden cooled abruptly. The male wizard felt a pang of disappointment.

"That was easy," he grinned, hiding his emptiness under joy for his friend. "I was going to take it back to the forest. Now I don't have to."

"I'll put this away. Let's find somewhere we can talk, but I can only take a moment." Rolling the scroll, Zudieath rose and tucked it gently back into its niche on the shelves. The three of them exited the shadowy Library into sunlight that warmed its steep steps.

"Where did you find this wonderful creature?" she asked, exultation spilling from her voice. "He's beautiful! His name is Kuritkt."

"I've just been to the Darynthian Traders," replied Briastros. A shiver trembled his shoulders before he could stop it. "I hate that place."

The smile fled from Zudie's sweet mouth. "You went looking for your familiar this morning, and found mine instead. How much did you pay?" When he dropped his eyes, she grabbed his wide sleeve, shook it, and demanded, "How much?"

"Eighty-five nonials. He's worth it. I couldn't stand seeing him caged. And then I thought of you."

"I cannot pay so much." Even in the sunlight, Briastros could see her high cheekbones drain of color. Despair at losing Kuritkt so soon resonated between them.

"I know you just bought books for your apprenticeship with the Wizard Calter. Zudie, we're friends. I'm willing to acknowledge this debt if you are. You can pay me back how and when you can. Even in trade."

"That's very generous, Brias. But this leaves you little or no money to buy your own familiar." Her blue-gray eyes searched his smoky ones, filled with concern. "What will you do?"

"I've got a few free days. I'm going to travel

around, maybe go into the woods, and find my own. Prove to that slimy dealer at the Darynthian Traders and the nay-sayers at the Schola it *can* be done!"

She captured his hands. "Best of luck, my dear friend. I must get back now. Calter has asked me to bring with me all the references the Library has on wortis leaves affecting silver." She hugged him close. Kuritkt licked his ear. "I feel ever so much stronger than I did before. I can't ever thank you enough for finding my familiar and bringing him to me! Because of you, I can to go Wizard Calter Ranked!"

"Keep in touch, Zudie. My box at the Schola will be open for messages through the end of this moon cycle."

He sighed, watching the pair bounce back into the Library, the cream-and-brown animal wrapped securely beneath her long hair. In other circumstances, Zudie might have become his wife. Wizards, however, rarely married—who of them could find a mate who understood their fascination with the intricacies of a seven-hundred-year-old prayer to a dragon? Or seeing another part of the world clearly through a crystal? Two wizards wed was an invitation to open warfare, or a growing away from each other as each became absorbed in his or her projects.

So be it. She was not for him, and he had his own quest to begin. He needed a direction in which to turn his feet. Closing his eyes and extending his arms forward, he whirled himself around on the steps of the Library, stopping when he felt as though continuing any farther would be wrong. Opening his eyes, he looked where his fingers pointed.

"North. No, north-northwest." Hitching up his long leather belt and retying his depleted money pouch, Briastros headed down the steps and across town, his mind set on discovering his own familiar.

The austere stone buildings of the Schola ebbed into the colorful big marketplace of Darynthia, which in turn gave way to residences. Those were replaced by warehouses and the docks. As well as providing a living area for professors and support staff of the school,

Darynthia boasted a deep river access to the sea through the wide mouth of the Darynt River, which made the city a popular mooring for foreign merchants. Briastros loved the unflagging tenor of the place. There was always something new to do, something new to see.

The young man had only been outside the city gates half a dozen times in his five years at the Schola. The Wizard's curriculum demanded a great deal of time and effort, leaving only hours or half-days for travel unless a Great Personage such as one of the Governing Council demanded a specific talent to serve them for a time. With his feet his only mode of transportation, Briastros had seen little of the countryside beyond Darynthia. It called to him now.

He followed that call through the rest of the city and out the north gate, through the impromptu market that always grew around the foot of the walls on the other side, and beyond into the pastures and croplands tended by people who grew food to support the city dwellers. Briastros' expectations were high and his will indomitable as he strode through the late morning sunlight.

Three days later, footsore and weary, the young wizard wasn't feeling so confident. He'd combed the northern "woodlands," no more than well-tended tree farms, for a familiar, finding within the usual chittering birds, the large rusty-colored woolly caterpillars that scavenged bugs from beneath bark with large sharp pincers, and a few ill-humored cinarils intent only on screeching at him until Briastros stepped beyond their territories. He'd worked small magicks and spells for farmers and herdspeople in return for meals and information about the surrounding area. So far that information had availed him nothing.

"One of a wizard's primary virtues is patience." He repeated to himself the litany of old Tizzaril, one of his teachers, while limping past an attractive farm that raised pack and wool animals with long legs and necks called idrusans. "Good things take time in arriving," he quoted another of his teachers. "But I didn't think it would take this long to find a familiar. Perhaps I should return to the Schola and try another time."

A wave of stealthy movement about the farthest farm buildings caught his attention. A band of men and women, most dressed in gay colors now faded and tattered, crawled or crept from one shadow to the next.

Briastros gulped, not believing what he saw. He'd heard of the Latrons, a group of thieves who were said to live in caves in the foothills. They ranged in ones and twos throughout the country, seeking prosperous farms a larger group could return to and plunder for immediate food, staples like salt and flour, blankets, clothing, animals, and meat. Every so often the Governing Council of Illastrus sent out soldiers to find the Latrons, but few were ever captured. The rest of the thieves seemed to vanish into the rugged hill country they knew so well, only to reappear weeks or months later and begin their destruction again. They were said never to leave any of a farm's inhabitants alive.

"I must do something, but what?" The young wizard stood undecided. If he shouted, that would bring the Latrons' attention to himself. If he called a spell, it might not be enough to help all the people and animals on the farm. Both a spell and an incantation, performed one after the other, just might help—

"Caught you, spy!"

Briastros' arms were wrenched behind him, wound about tightly with rough rope. He smelled fetid breath and sweaty clothing, and heard a delighted giggle before his skull exploded and the world blackened.

Hold still. I'm trying to help.

The young wizard floated somewhere beyond his body, surprised that nothing hurt. It should. That blow he'd taken to the head should have given him a headache the size of Illastrus itself.

You want to know how you truly feel?

Pain shoved him down almost to unconsciousness before his helper confined the hurt behind a crudely constructed mental barrier.

I'm new at this. Good thing those two thought taking a wizard back to the hills would be a benefit. Otherwise you wouldn't have any pain.

Tugs pulled at Briastros' wrists. He could only feel it through his arms, or when the rope moved. That caused him to gasp with pain and made him think the Latrons had cut off his hands.

No, just squeezed off this part of your body from the rest.

"Who—what . . . ?" the wizard croaked through a dry throat.

Something warm and wet ran over his face several times. Its breath smelled sweet and fresh, like grass stippled with flowers. *I've cleaned off the worst of the blood. Open your eyes.*

Briastros did as the creature commanded. At first all he could see was sun glare, which stabbed to the back of his head almost as sharply as the pain from his head wound. He persevered. Soon he could make out the sky, the road, and a bit of whitish fence.

He lay on his stomach with his head to the left, facing away from the farm and toward the road. His hands were still fastened behind his back. As he concentrated and his eyes continued to clear, the wizard realized the fence wasn't wood at all. These uprights were fuzzy and had occasional brown spots almost the color of his hair. They grew upright from two dainty cloven feet.

A short-furred face with two large brown-black eyes lowered curiously. *Good day,* a peculiar rather high voice, the same one that had been speaking previously, said. Briastros realized with shock that the voice existed only within his mind. *I'm your—*

"My familiar!"

My name is Amosium. Call me Mosi. And we'd better do something before those cutthroats start their attack.

Briastros had forgotten the Latrons in the surprise of his familiar discovering him. "Get the rope off," he ordered.

It'll hurt.

"I know."

Squarish front teeth meant for ripping grass nibbled. The wizard sucked air between his own clenched teeth as his bound wrists moved against the fabric of his robe. Surprised that the pain wasn't as bad as last time, he followed the block to its source and found Mosi.

Briastros felt expanded, his mind stretched magnificently in all directions. An incredible tingling sensation tickled along his nerves except for where his wounds pulsed. Those pains were both blocked. The young idrusan's incredible energy fountained into him, coursing along his veins, making it possible for the wizard to consider calling three spells to mind and activating them against the Latrons almost concurrently.

If we do what you're thinking, we're both going to be really tired, Mosi stated. His mental voice had a windy quality to it, tinged with humor and a great deal of curiosity.

"It's the only combination that will take care of all the Latrons at one time. Ready?"

Of course.

Slowly Briastros levered himself to a sitting position without using his hands, and rocked to his knees. Mosi's soft body supported his shoulder when the wizard's head threatened to send him spinning into darkness again.

"I'll have to do it from here," the wizard panted. "Wanted to stand to see better, make certain I got all the thieves. If I stood up, I'd never finish."

Yes, you would, Mosi declared with certainty so thorough it startled Briastros. *I'm here. Do what you need to do.*

The young wizard levered himself upward, using an elbow propped against the idrusan's sturdy back.

When he achieved an upright stance, Mosi maneuvered in front of him.

"You don't need to protect me—"

I'm not, you thick twig. I'm steadying you. Hurry!

Briastros called the first spell to mind, mentally rehearsing it to make certain all the inflections were correct. He lifted his swollen purpled hands and held them with fingers forward except for the thumbs, which touched. Together they formed an open-ended square, encompassing all the buildings on the farm. And, the wizard hoped grimly, all the Latrons.

He launched the first voice spell. It sped along the path of the wind as Briastros readied the second. Already he could feel the drain of energy through his hands, his throat, his mind. As soon as he felt certain of the second, the wizard flung the spell farmward and sagged across Mosi's back. The idrusan struggled to bear the sudden weight.

Send the third.

"I can't," Briastros panted. "Too tired."

You can. You will.

"No, I—"

The sun of an incomprehensible fire seared his insides before the wizard harnessed the welcome raw energy and channeled it into his own near-empty cavern. Raising his hands again, Briastros checked the last spell mentally. This one shivered the air as he spoke it.

"Lastius autem mei. Tornus autem mei. Latron tilondus derond thanus cimeculam vond. Birah, birah, birah."

The wizard thought he actually saw the spell's path sparkle as it arced and dove toward the farm. In a few more moments he couldn't see anything as he and the idrusan collapsed and darkness claimed him again.

Something wasn't there that should be. Feeling oddly empty as well as exhausted, Briastros groaned and surfaced from midnight unconsciousness into glaring daylight pouring through a window across his cot. "Mosi!" he demanded in a creaky voice.

No one heard. The young wizard levered himself upright, gritting his teeth as he flexed lacerated wrists and hunched abused shoulders. "Mosi!"

Stumbling to his feet he tottered to the door, striking it hard with a forearm as he wove into the corridor. His mental agony was much worse than his new bruise and his old wounds together. Moaning, he pushed past the herdwife determined to block his way and tripped into the yard. He couldn't spot the immature white-and-auburn idrusan anywhere. Not a single animal was in sight.

Briastros thought for a moment the Latrons had murdered the animals. But no, all his spells had worked, fixing the thieves in place and binding them so they could only breathe. His mind finally surfaced a memory—he'd overheard someone say they were all in the barn awaiting the Guard's arrival.

Briastros stood still for a long moment trying to understand what had happened, then turned his feet onto the road and headed south, back toward Darynthia. He didn't notice he'd left his sandals behind. All that mattered to him was finding Amosium, and soon.

He did not notice time passing. It meant nothing to him. Someone riding north stopped when he saw the young disheveled wizard and, after taking a longer look, dismounted to walk beside him.

"Wizard Briastros, does your teacher deserve no greeting?"

The words came only faintly through Briastros' ears, but something in that commanding tone registered. He stopped, regarded his mentor with dull eyes, and finally stuttered, "M-m-mast . . . Aur . . . n."

The older man twisted to confront his student and muttered a short spell, one hand on his own familiar, the green, gold, and black snakelike Thtt, who was draped about his shoulders. "Ah," he sighed, suddenly understanding. "Familiar displacement quandary. So you did find one. For some reason, now it's gone and you're trying to find it. Perhaps if I help, I'll get to the bottom of all the mysteries and rumors I've been hearing."

The teacher mounted his lop-eared pacer. Briastros felt his sleeves rising, then pulls on his aching arms. Master Auron urged him to a seat on the animal's haunches, and nudged the beast into a walk. "Now, young wizard, tell me what happened."

For the next hour Briastros brokenly related the happenings of the last few days. When he lapsed into unhappy silence again, the older man nodded and urged their mount into an extended walk, a pace the animal could keep up for hours without tiring.

The rest of the afternoon and most of the night they traveled toward Darynthia. After sundown their road became lamped by Illastrus' two moons which chased one another in slow motion across the sky. They reached the city outskirts just as dawn streaked thin morning clouds with purple and rose.

"Briastros," Master Auron's voice jolted him from torpor. "Do you know where your familiar might be?"

The young wizard began to shake his head, then muttered "Docks," into the back of his teacher's robe.

The older man spent a short time conferring with the sentry at the gate. Checked by Auron's touch on the rein, the tired pacer turned left inside the city gates and trotted down Lynchurnas Street, the most direct way to the wharf.

The quays were already teeming with ship's laborers loading everything from pottery to fabric to vegetables, guided by the stentorian voices of Cargo Masters and their assistants. As the wizards approached, Briastros found himself awaking from lethargy and trembling with fear not entirely his own. He strained to see past his teacher's shoulder, gaze leaping from one ship to the next in search of Amosium.

"I'll stop first at the Harbor Master's office," the teacher announced. "She should have lists of what has been loaded onto each of those argosies, as well as where they came from—"

"Mosi!" Briastros slipped off the pacer before Master Auron could stop him and ran toward a merchant vessel already pulling into the Darynt's current with help from two dozen oarsmen. On its deck were several cargo nets still holding a handful of idrusans each, not yet stowed in the hold. An insistent high-pitched bleating coming from one assured the young wizard he'd found the right ship.

"Use your teeth!" Briastros howled, teetering at the edge of the wharf, uncertain of whether his familiar could hear him. "Like you did with the rope on my wrists!" He arrowed a mind picture toward the merchanter, uncertain whether it would pierce the little animal's distress.

The bleating stopped, followed by activity among the long-necked idrusans that the young wizard couldn't make out. They all became silent, most animals facing the nets that incarcerated them. Suddenly overpowering was the sound of the vessel's oars dipping with a regular beat into the Darynt, heading for the river's mouth where it could raise sail. The ship took Amosium farther and farther away with each pull.

"I explained your situation to the Harbor Master," panted his teacher, out of breath from dodging people on the quayside while trying to hurry back to Briastros. "She's not certain she can do anything to stop the ship, but she's promised to send out a boat. See, there it goes now." He pointed as a two-person skiff shot out between larger vessels toward the downriver collier. "If they can find your familiar and persuade it into the small boat, they'll bring it back."

"Why should the captain relinquish one of his valuable cargo?" asked the younger wizard, pulling each stroke with those in the skiff and urging them to more speed despite his abruptly depressed feelings. "I can't pay for Mosi."

Master Auron smiled, twisting an end of his braided mustache with one hand and stroking Thtt's dry scales with the other. "I persuaded the Harbor Master the animal is owed you for saving that farm from the Latrons, that it was loaded among the ones going to Philladras by mistake."

Briastros tore his gaze from the skiff for one incredulous look at his teacher before returning his stare to the water. "You did that for me?"

"Young wizard, it's time you learned something. Whenever a student does something as generous as you did for Wizard Zudieath in finding and buying her familiar and then giving that animal to her, or causes a stir that leaks rumors the size of cannaption eggs back to the Schola, or exhibits the power you did in capturing all but five of those Latrons set on pillaging that farm, the Masters will do all they can to alleviate a difficulty for him or her. Especially if that wizard hasn't been Ranked yet."

The skiff fought wakes that threatened to swamp it. Briastros clenched his hands as the two within the frail craft struggled on.

A triumphant cry barely reached his ears over the noise of the harbor traffic. From the deck of the outbound freighter, a white long-legged body shrugged away from the cargo net, raced across the deck, and launched itself into the sea, followed by several adult animals.

"Mosi!" Immediately Briastros shucked his robe, diving into the cold river water clad in only linen underwear. Too late, Master Auron's restraining hands closed on black fabric.

The young wizard wasn't a particularly strong swimmer, but his addled brain reasoned if he could meet his familiar halfway, they could help each other back. He felt his teacher trying to settle the rough water with only marginally effective spells. Briastros toiled on, watching for the small white head on the crest of every wake, the chill river sapping what strength remained in his already fatigued muscles.

There! He caught sight of Mosi's head, nostrils and eyes lifted just above the surface of the water, ears pointed toward his goal. The little idrusan was still paddling intently. With a new surge of energy, Briastros stroked onward to meet him.

They collided. The wizard hugged his familiar, causing them to sink. Spluttering, the two resurfaced and began swimming side by side, slowly but steadily, toward the wharf.

"Beware!" Briastros heard Master Auron's shout and looked left to see a ship, just pulled out of dock and gaining speed in the clear channel, bearing down on them. Mosi chose the angle most likely to take them out of the way and began swimming with renewed determination, towing his wizard the first few yards until the man could redirect his fear and begin an overhead stroke for himself.

The young wizard risked a look. They weren't going to make it. Already the sharp wooden keel clove the water too near them, ready to splinter their heads and toss their broken bodies beneath its hull. Briastros thought love toward his familiar, and tried to swim harder.

The Command hit the ship like a Voice from Eternity. It stopped dead, oars still sweeping through the water. It went nowhere for two instants, then creaked in every timber and crept forward. Another Command, strengthening the first, halted it again.

Briastros flailed the water now, too tired and too cold to do more. He felt Amosium failing beside him. Suddenly there were hands, warm and friendly, on his skin. Almost disbelieving their good luck, the wizard was snatched from the clutch of the Darynth by the Harbor Master's messengers. Mosi landed beside him, moaning faintly. Their rescuers sat down in the skiff and pulled hard at the oars, once, twice, and again. The merchant ship shuddered against the failing spell and surged forward, slapping the tiny overloaded boat out of its way.

It seemed to Briastros as if every wizard in the Schola stood on the docks. He and Mosi were gently handed from the skiff and wrapped in blankets. The idrusan's nose twitched in appreciation as someone served him a dish of warmed sweetened milk while others gently squeezed water from his curly coat. Mosi began sucking at the liquid as someone helped Briastros guide a quaking mug of steaming mulled cider to his lips. The wizard thought he'd never tasted anything so good as the warm spiced draught began to thaw his frozen insides.

"Is my debt paid?"

"Zudie!" Briastros' head jerked toward the familiar voice as a sable face with bright eyes peered at him from beneath another blanket. Behind the cream-and-brown ractoin smiled his beloved friend. "You stopped the ship?"

"Kuritkt and me. Helped by Master Auron and Thtt."

"Then you Ranked well."

"Better than I ever hoped. And I suspect you will, too. Drink up, you'll need it. The Masters scheduled you for tomorrow morning."

Briastros groaned. "No rest between?"

"You'll have today free." Master Auron, accompanied as always by his familiar Thtt's unnerving stare, watched Kuritkt gingerly approach Amosium. The idrusan poked a curious nose forward. Chittering, the ractoin swiped a brick-red tongue across Mosi's long cheek. Becoming friends in a matter of moments, the two settled down on opposite sides of the bowl to finish off the steaming sweetened milk.

"After the Ranking, there will be much to talk about," the teacher continued. "As the Schola's Facilitator, I'd welcome your suggestions for changes in policy regarding the choice of familiars. And, Briastros, I believe that for the rest of your life you'll have a double job: the regular duties you find as a wizard, and discoverer of familiars for others. I just heard Master Enrathal say wizards have been clamoring for your assistance ever since word about Wizard Zudieath got out."

The noise on the docks abated, as if everyone and everything awaited his answer. Briastros pondered. Both positions would require a great deal of time and energy, perhaps more than he should take on.

Zudie's hand squeezed his arm, and something nudged his mind.

I'll help.

Briastros sucked in a deep breath, watching with quiet joy while Mosi stepped near, folded his long legs,

and settled next to him with a sigh. He stroked the
soft wool at the base of the idrusan's neck as Kuritkt
happily kneaded himself a nest on his new friend's
damp back.

"I—no, we—accept."

MASTERY

by Sherwood Smith

Sherwood Smith lives in California with her husband Peter, a professor, and her children. She has published ten short stories and eleven novels. Other work by her appears in *Things that Go Bump in the Night* and *Werewolves*.

"So he held me down and said, 'What you need is a master.' "

Matir snickered. "Was he handsome?"

Next to Matir, my sister grinned. "And you said—?"

"I didn't." A vivid flash of the minstrel's drifting blond hair, sapphire-bright eyes, and long musician's hands lit my mind. Finishing my ale, I raised my cup in brief salute. "I kicked him in the teeth."

Matir gasped, and this time my sister snickered. "Must have loosened every bone in his head," I finished reminiscently.

My sister laid her dimpled cheek on her folded hands. "Was he?"

"Was he what?" I asked. "Dead? I don't think so, though he hit the hearthstone with a hefty whack."

"Good-looking." Dessra rolled her eyes. "Wake up, little sister!"

I shrugged. "I don't know. Yes. I guess. What matter, after all I just told you? He was an arrogant boor."

The corners of Dessra's shapely mouth deepened. "Most of them can be taught better habits. If they're worth teaching."

I eyed my sister without resentment. There was a certain amount of superficial resemblance between

us—curling dark hair, large gray eyes and long dark
brows, smallish hands and feet—but where she was
rosy and curving, I was compact from fifteen years of
hard riding.

The differences had been there even when we were
small and had little interest in such things; by the time
she was fourteen and I thirteen, I was still a scram-
bling monkey struggling to learn bladework, while she
could make a walk across a room an act of amorous
enticement. And since the deaths of our parents, she
had needed her particular blend of attraction, brains,
and courage to hold the inn during these times, and
keep it filled with customers.

"*You* could, perhaps," I said. "My rare bed romps
have yet to last for even a short pairing. I wouldn't
even have followed that thrice-blasted minstrel up the
stairs had I not been three parts drunk on wine, lack
of sleep, and the way he sang filthy Ywannish lyrics
to angelic Gramellkyn melodies."

"And so you left him lying there?" Matir prompted
with lively interest. A tiny redhead, she'd been with
Dessra for about eight years. First a serving maid, and
now a part owner; I'd sold my half of the inheritance
to her in order to finance my own career.

I shrugged, and leaned down to slap my canvas-
wrapped gear. "He'd been bragging about this jewel-
handled sword. In truth, it's a pretty thing—too pretty,
I thought, for a boor. Said it had magical properties.
Dire ones, supposedly. As for the rest, I robbed him
of his money, then reported him as a thief. Figured a
tour of one of those north-country Dunnain prisons
would be good for his soul, and so I continued home."

Dessra rocked with delighted laughter.

Matir sighed. "Wish you could do similar with that
rat Evand."

"Not *quite* so loud," my sister murmured, glancing
toward the darkened windows. The last customer had
left an hour ago, and those sleeping in the inn were
quiet overhead.

"Evand," I repeated. "Evand the Nightstalker? I've
heard that name several times since I hit the province,

most frequently as I neared the harbor, and none of the references were kind or loving. Has he anything to do with these gangs of roving bullies in dark woolen surcoats with an orange owl as an emblem?"

"Our latest provincial lord." Dessra's mouth twisted. "This one's a wizard as well. Booted out Grawnar, but the reprieve was short. Evand is much worse."

"We pay a lot more in bribe money now, and not just when we have a complaint against a crooked dealer and want justice, but simply to keep his thugs out of here." Matir grimaced. "It's called 'protection.' "

"In sum," Dessra's eyes gleamed with irony, "the roof *still* leaks. Welcome home, footloose little sister!"

I shook my head. "You know, it's time somebody does something about this province. Curse it, with the country! I thought it was at its worst when I finally found a way to journey off-world, but it appears I was mistaken."

Dessra eyed me warily. "He's got lots of magic, Doyel."

I grinned back at her. "I'll just nose around for a few days," I soothed. "See what I can see. You know I've always had a fine regard for the preservation of my delicate hide—"

A shriek rent the air outside. Dessra's head jerked up, and Matir snatched at the fireplace poker.

Pulling my knife, I listened at the door, eased it open. Nothing moved in the darkness.

"Best shut it—" Matir began, when the scream came again, high and childish.

"Help me! Oh, help me, please, I'm dying—"

I was out fast, running in my stockinged feet. The empty street was filthy with refuse and slime, which rendered my steps soundless as I veered obliquely toward the alley that the scream had come from.

No one to help a child, eh? I thought grimly. *Things are bad indeed—*

"NO-O-O-O!"

The girl's voice was close by now, and I heard the

thick mutter of a man's voice, followed by wild sobbing. I launched myself into the alley.

And knew a heartbeat later that I'd flung myself headlong into a trap.

Nailed a brace of them, and gave another pair some permanent souvenirs before I hit the hard ground, and something even harder hit the back of my head.

Woke up to blazing pain in my head, echoed in foursquare pattern above and below. I'd long ago taught myself to waken without movement, so, without opening my eyes, or lifting my head from the awkward angle it was dangling at, I turned my hazy attention to the rest of my body. The four subsidiary pains came from wrists and ankles; my shoulder blades, buttocks and calves ground against uneven stone. I was shackled, I realized, spread-eagled and mother-naked, to a stone wall.

Hmmm.

Lifting my eyelids a fraction, I saw a segment of empty flagstone flooring. Heard nothing, smelled nothing.

Raising my head slowly, I soon saw that I was alone in a smallish, circular room. Tower room, probably. One tiny slitted window high up on the curve of wall to my right. Opposite me was a bare, cold fireplace. Above it a glow globe gave off steady bluish light. A badly cast glow globe, I thought, narrowing my eyes against the glare. My head throbbed sharply in protest. No door was in evidence.

Straightening my spine, I was just able to brace my toes against the floor. I shifted my weight to my feet, to ease the strain on my wrists. The window was still dark. I knew I had not been there long, or my hands and feet would have felt much worse.

All right, my girl. You're obviously alone, and your body is as secure as it's ever going to be. If you're going to check, it'd better be now.

I really hate mind travel. Even at the best of times, it gives me a headache, not to mention vertigo. During my studies at the Sartoran Dyranarya Academy on the

far-off world I'd finally found after ten years of
questing, I'd envied some of my colleagues who
seemed to be able to fling souls effortlessly from bodies and fly about for miles. The best I'd been able to
manage was about thirty feet—and that was courting
danger. My strengths had never been in that direction.
But, it seemed to me now, not to know anything about
the present circumstances was a worse danger.

Breathing deeply, I let my head hang again, and
detached. Light and shadow were gone now, and objects identified themselves by density and composition
when I touched them. With a window to the right, and a
fireplace across from me, I figured if there was a door,
it had to be at my left, and I was not surprised to find
a very low-intensity illusion spell humming before a
door. The spell existed only on one side—mine.

*Didn't bother to block the door from the outside.
Either my unknown villain trusts the loyal minions, or
has to be miserly with the spells.*

A stone stairway curved downward, lit at intervals
by torches. The fires beat fitfully on my awareness,
making me dread the headache waiting for me back
in my body. . . . *Don't think about it, my girl!*

I turned my attention below, feeling already that
peculiar absence of defined place that guides us in the
material world. If I went much father, weak as I was,
I'd get lost. Staying still, trying to *hear,* I caught the
low mental murmur of two individuals below, a reference (and image-flash) to "Evand." Their primary
emotion was boredom. Guards, most likely. Sim-
mering in the air around the tower was a magic barrier. Great. The only person, then, who could summon
magic into the tower would be its master—Evand
the Nightstalker.

I sensed *purpose,* and the focused mental image of
myself on the wall. I was about to have company.

Returning, I pushed awareness rapidly through my
limbs. I missed Evand's Grand Entrance as I struggled
to keep the contents of my stomach from making their
own encore appearance. Blood under pressure whined
in my skull as I lifted my head. Before me stood a

tall man of about forty, neat black beard, long blue
velvet robe with an angry-looking owl's head embroidered in gold on the breast. A great ruby glinted smol-
deringly on his right hand.

Beside him lurked a short, ugly grayish creature,
mottled with various sizes of bruise-colored growths
and warts, who winced away from the light of the
globe. And drooled.

"Doyel the Dreamer," Evand said in a gloating
drawl. His gaze moved scornfully over my goose-
fleshed skin, then fixed on my face—probably searching for signs of fear. "Amusing, the conflicting stories
one hears about you. Mostly edifying tales of an inn-
yard brawler with a few cheap spells who races about
trying to right wrongs, like one of the long-gone
Knights of Senmereis. Pitiful—but amusing." He
smiled, watching my eyes unblinkingly. "But then, the
one who sold you out swears you've acquired, of late,
some real skills."

"Who?" My voice was a weak croak.

"Never mind. Is it true that you've mage-level
skills? Or merely the embellishments of a speculator
eager to boost the sum of the prize money?" Evand
surveyed me with fastidious distaste.

Not so the grotesque huffing with inane laughter at
his side, whose mighty and misshapen nose was only
exceeded in size by an even more repellent member
due south.

Evand's lofty repugnance intensified as he said,
"Your garments have been searched. I've dispatched
a squad to your sister's tavern, but surely, had you a
wizard's *ress,* you would not be so stupid as to leave
it behind?"

I blinked at him, trying past the persistent singing
in my head to feel for magic. The dim energies of the
globe and the door illusion were all I sensed. Was he
powerful enough to store a great deal in a *ress* and
shield it? I had to find out—fast.

"Answer me." He took a step nearer. "It would be
well to learn—should I permit you to live past this
interview—that I do not tolerate disobedience." He

slapped my face. And, as I remained silent, again, only harder.

If he's left-handed, he's clumsy, I thought hazily. His attentions weren't helping my focus any. *But what will you wager he's a rightie, and that great clunking ruby is his* ress?

I grinned.

His eyes narrowed. "What's this, bravado? How charming." Again he let his eyes travel the length of my body, with slow and deliberate insult. Then he looked down at the gray creature who crouched, squinting, near his side. *"Want human mate, Gabrial?"* he asked in a guttural form of Wenseth, while pointing at me.

So here was one of the Sleyeudi drones, far from his mountain caves and mines. No wonder the light hurt his eyes. I'd heard about them, but had never seen one: They were supposedly strong, they could see like bats in the dark, and they obeyed their kin-chieftains unquestioningly. In short, the perfect slave.

The troll wheezed and nodded violently, sending drool flying in glistening droplets to land on the velvet hem of Evand's gown. Evand hissed in revulsion, and a well-shod foot lashed out and caught the creature behind the ear. Gabrial hit the wall with a splat, and groveled, wailing.

"Stupid, filthy beast," Evand shouted. "Keep your distance!" Then, again in the Wenseth-variant, *"Get my book."* I noted with rueful pity, as the leathery-skinned troll scrambled awkwardly toward the door, that abuse seemed only to arouse him further.

Evand then turned to me, and I forestalled his next villainous threat by saying, "If you're going to teach that poor sod a taste for human females, you might give him a form that would grant him a little success now and then."

Evand laughed nastily. "He has plenty of success— when I so desire. You shall shortly experience the truth of my statement, Doyel the Dreamer, unless you surrender to me whatever serves as your *ress*. I will test for myself the strength or weakness of your claims to magical prowess. I can use additional power—and, perhaps, a quick-minded, obedient assistant—for my plans extend far beyond this province." His eyes narrowed. They were not pleasant eyes. "You appear to care little for my plans . . . and my threats. Have you, perchance, a predilection for deformed little gnomes?" He laughed richly. "We shall soon have ample time to witness your performance. And, then, if you are still obdurate . . ." His hand passed among the folds of his gown, and produced a thin-bladed knife. "I shall attempt some nonmagical form changing. Starting at your collarbones, and working downward."

I tossed my hair back, as, below, my toes clenched. I was slowly losing feeling in my feet. Better them than my hands—but if I lost the use of my feet, then my wrists would take my weight again. In which case it would not be long before I lost control over my fingers. Time was short.

My hair was still hanging in my eyes, so I tossed it again, wincing as the tender area on the back of my scalp bumped against the uncompromising granite of the wall. "I will not—" I began.

"What is this?" He interrupted with a smirk of triumph as he caught sight of the gold-and-jade earring in my left ear. "My minions appear to have overlooked this intriguing little object when they removed your garments. They shall learn better."

He sheathed his knife, smiled benignly, and with infinite care, he unfastened the catch and freed the earring. Giving me a patronizing sneer, he held the ring on his palm and, murmuring softly, passed the ruby over it. The ruby glowed with a faint inner light.

Behind, Gabrial's snuffle heralded his reappearance. I winced again, trying in vain to ease my feet as Evand flung the earring on the floor and took the book.

Writhing against my chains, I squinted at the age-mottled pages, trying to read the faded ink writing.

Evand stepped back again, smiling. "Interested? Have you ever seen a Shigellian Book of Death?" He dropped his voice with sinister meaning.

"No!" I shrieked. "Not a Shigellian Book of Death!" Did I sound horrified enough?

Gabrial snuffled, eyes gleaming like two wet fungus stones.

I writhed harder, my joints aching in protest. As Gabrial stretched one of his horny-nailed paws toward me, Evand said, "Want her, beast?" Gesturing the troll back with one of his feet, Evand smirked at me. "Not just yet. First, let's reward our honored guest with a little demonstration." When he had finished his gloating laugh, he muttered rapidly over his hand, and the ruby began to glow with a malevolent light.

Magic stirred darkly in the close air around us. As the ring released power, Evand opened the book. "Would you like a new shape, Gabrial?" he asked.

The creature looked up in mute incomprehension; the question was, of course, directed at me. "A fine new shape, just for today . . . for the pleasure of your new lover!" He began softly intoning the spell. Gabrial's grayish hide began changing to scales as the creature increased in size. At the same time, I opened my hands slowly, until the backs of my hands were flat against the rough stone, and my palms faced Evand's red-glowing power source.

To learn to gather magic, and focus it at the same time, without dependence upon the aid of a ress? *Yes, it can be done—is done by our highest adepts—but you will have to work long and hard to acquire such a skill. . . .*

My mind went back to that day five years ago, on the high, flower-tossed plateau on a distant world, when my real studies began. Closing my eyes, I sensed and gathered the magic released from Evand's *ress,* and focused.

A flash of light, which blinded poor Gabrial. As the now eight-foot-tall troll doubled over, knuckling his eyes and keening, I opened my eyes, and—*transferred!*

Evand screamed. Gabrial looked down at the naked female on the wall. He grinned, orange teeth glistening, and reached toward her with both horny paws. The prisoner's gray eyes bulged with rage and disbe-

lief. I looked down at the worn, grease-edged pages
of the book in my hand, and nodded complacently at
the dull ruby on my other hand. Inside my skull the
throbbing had grown to a roar, but as Gabrial turned
to me, I knew that the illusion of changed shapes was
holding. Gabrial barked something unintelligible.

On the wall, Evand shouted threats and insults, his
voice high with rage, while his naked body (only su-
perficially resembling mine) wrenched violently
against the iron shackles.

Gabrial's anticipatory drool was now a thick rope.
I waved a hand at the eager creature, who launched
his scaly self at his master.

Pulling off the drained ruby *ress,* I laid it meticulously on the mantel. Then I glanced at the book. As
Evand screamed at the frenzied troll, I leafed through
two or three pages. There was much destructive material there, couched in florid language and sandwiched
between crowd-awing ritual.

"A superlative example of piffle," I said over
Evand's howls and curses, "crowning the cosmic pinnacle of tosh."

I dropped the book onto the cold hearth, then, raising my palms, I used the remaining magic in the tower,
and the pages burst into flame. Evand's voice was a
continuous shriek by now. Gabrial's whuffles indicated
his own increasing enthusiasm for his sport.

Retrieving my spurned earring on the way, I passed
through the door and made my way down the circular
stairs. The sounds from the tower room echoed color-
fully below; the guards guffawed lasciviously until I
appeared. Smiling on their hastily-assumed expressions of wooden stolidity, I passed unmolested through
a Great Hall, and into a courtyard, the stones of which
were just beginning to take on color and shape in the
bleak light of another gray dawn.

No one dared to stop me as I walked through the
massive gates. I made it just beyond view of the castle
before relaxing the Evand illusion, and losing—or so
it felt—my last fortnight's accumulation of meals.

Up in the tower Evand resumed his own form. I

wished him joy of it. Then I stumbled toward the just-visible harbor.

"That's it," Dessra said, pointing to the few remaining contents of my duffel. "I'm sorry," she added apologetically. "He took me completely by surprise." Her lips curled faintly as she added: "Evand's bullies, of course, never saw even this much."

My eyes surveyed the spare dagger, three tunics, one sturdy cloak and one light one, the folded shirts and few minor bits of clothing which were the sum total of my customary traveling kit.

Next to them, gleaming quietly, were three silver coins and a scarce half-dozen platts: about what would have been left had I traveled without the money I'd stolen from the minstrel. The jeweled sword, of course, was gone, as was the fine lute I'd meant to give to Matir.

Popping my head up from the dark tunic I was hastily donning, I saw concern in my sister's face. "I wish you'd sleep a while, you look wretched," Dessra said. "I'll make you Granny's tisane."

"Something to do first," I muttered, grabbing up my spare blade.

I found him in a disreputable hostelry on the edge of the harbor. Twenty years ago, I thought as I passed silently under the worn, dripping sign, this place had probably been thriving. Before King Austaen was assassinated and his little son vanished, travelers newly arrived from the ocean had sat out on that neglected terrace, listening to gossip about crimes of love or hate, and shivered deliciously at their interesting rarity, before embarking inland on business or pleasure. Now lawlessness was a way of life that went unremarked, and the rare traveler who ventured inland on legitimate business moved with a phalanx of guards.

The company downstairs was thin, and most of those were drunk. It was close on midnight, and outside the rain continued with unabated force. Under cover of rumbling thunder I eased silently inside and up the stairs without expending too much effort. Behind the fourth door, I heard the light-toned murmur of the minstrel's voice, instantly recognizable, in between high-pitched female giggles. My anger flared hotly as I recognized in that stream of girlish laughter the same voice that had sobbed *help me!* in the alley last night.

Kicking the door open, I threw the knife. Two heads jerked up in the bed as the blade sank, vibrating, in the headboard between them. Above, on a little shelf, a candle flame flickered wildly.

The female gasped in fear and shock; with a lazy smile, the blond minstrel reached up for my knife. A second later he snatched his fingers back sharply, cursing, and the woman fell out of the bed with a thump, pulling the tangle of bedclothes with her.

"A heat spell," I offered.

"Just as well you missed," the minstrel commented pleasantly.

"I never miss." And raised my palm. The knife quivered, freed itself, and returned to my hand. "That was by way of a conversational gambit. Your attention being otherwise."

"I'm yours to command." He shrugged, grinning, in no wise discomposed at being caught sprawling naked in a rumpled bed.

With a sniff like an offended kitten, his companion picked herself up from the floor. Clutching the bedclothes about her, she fled, slamming the door behind her. He paid her no more heed than I did.

"You sold me to that worm Evand," I said through gritted teeth. "I'd say you owe me—*at least*—half the reward."

His brows went up in a mockery of outraged dignity. "You robbed me," he countered promptly. "You left me to languish in prison under a patently false charge—after you took everything I had!"

"Because you were a boor," I said. "A rude, rutting boor—"

"Wouldn't that be boar?" he murmured dulcetly. "Not, surely, a bore."

"B—shut up!" And despite my yawning guts, aching head, and exhaustion-burning eyes, I had to laugh. "Damn you!" Regathering my rapidly dissipating wrath, I added, "You were fighting to get me into that bed. I'd said 'no.' When I say no, I mean it."

"I was drunk. And wrong." He spread his hands. "You won the fight!"

"And I robbed you as a lesson in manners. I was going to give your ill-gotten gains to my sister and her partner. Times are bad enough in this hell-forsaken country—" I broke off as, beneath the crash of thunder, the creak of wood nearby warned me of danger.

Turning my head sharply, I heard just beyond the door: "She said the sword's in the cupboard. Jewels in it." Shifting a fast glance at the minstrel, I caught a look of surprise on his face. Unholy glee inspired me to crow smugly, "So she sold you out as well? Checkmate!"

Then the door slammed open. What seemed like a hundred owl-surcoated men exploded in. I just caught sight of the minstrel springing for the cupboard, and a glimpse of the polished-steel sword with its two princely sapphires, before I was too busy to notice anything beyond my immediate assailants. Their rain-sodden woolen tunics smelled absurdly of wet dog.

I fought with knife, feet, a rose-silk gown left behind by the minstrel's erstwhile friend, a chair, and a clay chamber pot. I edged steadily backward, my shoulders finally bumping up against the casement. Ripping the curtains down (and nearly choking in the resultant clouds of dust) I flung them over the heads of my foremost attackers, cracked their lunging skulls with the chamber pot, then gave a fast look back at the room as I palmed the window open and lifted one leg over the sill. Very few of Evand's bullies were left on their feet; the minstrel had backed three of them into the far corner, where they bumbled in one another's way, and he was wielding that flashing blade with joyous abandon. In the middle of the room, on a table that miraculously had not been overturned, lay the forgotten lute.

Hmmm.

My observations were interrupted by the sound of reinforcements pounding up the stairs. I looked back at the minstrel, whose head was now canted alertly, though his blade did not pause in its dance of feint, parry, and attack; much as I dislike running out on a fight, this one wasn't my battle. To stay would be frivolous . . . but I could even a few of the odds.

The candle had been overturned, and the little shelf was blazing merrily away. Snatching up the dusty curtains, I dipped one end in the flame, and as the fire caught hungrily at the rotting material, I sprang to the door and was just in time to swing my gift at the front-running foes as they neared the top of the stairs. They jumped backward, and soon a series of satisfying bumps and yelps echoed up the passage.

Tossing the curtains down the stairs after them, I dashed back into the bedroom, flung the door shut, and wedged broken crockery under it. Then, out the window. Below, I heard the innkeeper adding to the confusion by marshaling his people into a bucket brigade. I rolled down the rain-slick roof, landed on a lower roof, and jumped to the muddy courtyard below. The heavy rain masked my escape.

He caught up with me late the next morning. The wind that was driving away the clouds blew his long yellow hair back over his shoulders, and there, in his left ear, I saw a familiar green-and-gold twinkle. His horse was fresh, tossing its head nervously. My own mount—stolen from one of the thugs the night before—was also feeling mettlesome, no doubt thinking that its change in estate was an improvement.

A glance at the minstrel's speculative blue eyes. A reflection of the same shade glittered in the hilt of the sword at his side. Across his back the lute hung on its gaily colored sash.

"A minstrel," I said instructively, "might not leap first for his lute, but eventually, he might try to see that his livelihood makes it whole through the fray."

He grinned. "I'll remember."

"The sword." I nodded.. "I suppose the 'magical properties' are mythical?"

"Concocted to keep thieves at bay. The ruse, apparently, worked for my grandfather," he added reflectively.

"You told me—when we first met—you'd just won it."

His grin widened for a moment. "Won it back. You weren't listening." His fingers touched his ear. "I'd meant to ask you—before you brained me—if you'd really been inducted into the Jhorivan Brotherhood of Shadow Warriors? It being, as it were, a brotherhood."

I laughed. "I was eighteen and skinny and reckless. And very, very, far from home."

"Tell me! Was it you, then, whose much-talked-about trial concerned six Hofniriad Death-Masters, a priceless heirloom blade of obsidian, and the Emperor's nightshirt?"

"Plus four bottles of hundred-year-old fire brandy. Don't forget those." I shrugged. "I said I was reckless." Then, after another moment's thought, added suspiciously, "*Don't* tell me . . ."

"That I matched it? There was this wager, you see," he said with a spuriously apologetic air.

I snorted. Both horses sidled skittishly.

"Your sister said you'd gone inland," he went on. *So she told him, eh? With a knife at her throat, or free-willed?* "As I left the harbor, there was a great deal of talk spreading about. Concerning our friend Evand Nightstalker and a troll."

"He was a dismal magician, and a putrid lord. I thought I'd give him a chance at a third career," I said, and when he'd finished laughing, I added, "My sister wants the province cleaned up. She's tired of her leaky roof."

"My father would have considered that a laudable intention," the minstrel replied in a meditative voice. *The first fight—even old Evand. Have I been set up for some sort of test?* "I've nothing against most mercenaries—fought alongside a few, when the cause was right—but I don't sell my skills," I said.

He was stroking his horse's neck with his knuckles, slow and rhythmic. His eyes stared somewhere beyond the muddy road ahead. "I was just eight," he said presently, "when I woke up under my nurse's dead body. I had one silk suit—soon gone—and a head full of maps, historical tales, and genealogies. No money, friends, or food in my guts. The years since have been, in my mind, more in the nature of training than mere profit-seeking. Time to pick up the broom and, ah, start sweeping."

But Dessra wouldn't talk with a knife at her throat. Giving back someone's belongings is one thing; putting an enemy on my trail is quite another.

"Training," I repeated. Where were my wits? *Blue and silver, the colors of the royal house.* "Broom." I looked up, frowning. "The road?"

"The country." He leaned back, scanning the sky. He was waiting.

For a partner? The choice, I saw, was mine.

I laughed. "So where do we start?"

BIRD BONES

❖❖❖

by Jody Lynn Nye

Jody Lynn Nye lists her main career activity as "spoiling cats." She lives near Chicago with two of the above and her husband, SF author and editor Bill Fawcett. Among Jody's novels are the *Mythology 101* series, *Taylor's Ark*, *Medicine Show*, and four collaborations with Anne McCaffrey: *Crisis on Doona*, *The Death of Sleep*, *The Ship Who Won*, and *Treaty at Doona*. Upcoming works include, *The Magic Touch*, *The Ship Errant*, and an anthology, *Don't Forget Your Spacesuit, Dear!*

Zim put down the huge book, closing its brass-banded leather covers with a sigh of satisfaction. At that moment, he knew everything in the world there was to know about the nature of beetles: how they thought, what gods made them, what their names were, the uses of their parts in the Art Magical—everything! His researches had taken him the better part of five years, but it was all worthwhile. Study was never wasted. It would all be useful one day, if not to him, then to some future wizard.

Quite possibly, he thought, stretching out his arms and unkinking his back that had been too long bent over the table, *I will write a book of my own observations, and so add to the field of expertise.*

Stroking his long white beard, he stood up and looked around at his small cottage. The three-room house had maintained itself tolerably well while he had been immersed in his work. Not much was out of place, save books, which lay in piles and heaps and unsteady constructions, mainly by his bed, which he could see through the door to the left of his worktable. There were dozens of specimens, too. Live beetles in jars and boxes, dead ones mounted on cards and in shadow boxes, pictures in color and pen-and-ink stacked against the wall and on tables and shelves, making him wonder how he had negotiated the floor of this room without stumbling. How strange it was that he never noticed the accumulation of clutter while in the throes of absorbing knowledge, but once he surfaced, it was like seeing the world anew.

"I must clear my mind," he told Janel, the gray-striped cat, who lay sprawled with curled paws on his study table. She flicked her tail and squinted her eyes at him in assent. Zim had been aware of her during his researches. He remembered having fed her and opened the door for her thousands of times. Cats never put up with being ignored, yet Janel never disturbed him when he was engaged upon something *truly* important. And she kept the house free of vermin. A good creature. He scratched her head with nails unaccountably grown long. And had his skin been this wrinkled before?

"Hmm!" he said, looking at his fingers in amazement. "I'd better see about maintaining me!"

He drew hot water into the copper bath that sat beside his stone hearth, and threw in a handful of scrubbing salts. The white grains dissolved into bubbles that attacked his skin, massaging and cleansing, when he stepped into the tub. He lay looking at the high-beamed plaster ceiling with delight.

"And what shall I explore next?" he asked out loud. Sometimes he had to speak just to hear if his voice was still there. What a pleasure it was just to be able to seek out field after field of study, as he wished, when and for however long he wished. Such freedom was the product of decades of hard work and far less attractive conditions. Zim only liked to think back on those times at moments like this, when he was in the lap of comfort. Perspective was always better appreciated in sharp contrast.

When he was attired in clean robes, and his old ones were swirling about in their turn in the bath, Zim stepped outside to admire the day. The sun had risen only lately, but was already bright and clear. The sky was blue, the grass tall, the fields full of flowers and bees and a heady perfume that tickled his long nose. Birds chattered and sang overhead.

"Summer," he said, nodding. It had been winter when he'd started to read about beetles. He'd seen many, many summers and winters. That meant autumn would follow. How nice.

He lived not too near and not too far from a medium-sized market town in a deep river valley. From where Zim stood on his front doorstep on the mountainside far above the town, he could just see the common where the townsfolk grazed their beasts. But no houses. If he could see them, he reasoned, they could see him, and he liked his privacy. The townsfolk respected his wishes. They enjoyed having a prestigious wizard available to them, and Zim was, after all, a wizard of some measurable prestige. The merchants liked being able to say that he patronized their establishments—magically, of course. It was a long way down to town, and he made the trip physically as seldom as possible. His spells did that work for him.

Zim took a deep breath of fresh air and went back inside. Too much sunlight wasn't good for one. He had learned that in a previous study of the nature of light. Ah, that had been a happy twenty years, Zim thought.

"I have been looking down too long," he told Janel, as he poured milk into her porcelain bowl from a cool, tin pannikin. Fresh that morning from the dairy at the bottom of the mountain. Dairyman Melner had never failed him yet. Two clean, full cans, always placed where the fetch-and-carry spell would find them. "I think I shall devote myself to looking up. I believe that I will study the stars." Janel chirruped and bent over her bowl. Her philosophy was, why waste time in lengthy pondering? Decide, and do!

Why not? Zim thought. It was good to live with such a wise cat.

Books of general knowledge Zim had in plenty. He gathered around his deep easy chair as many as he thought might enable him to begin to ask the questions to ask the questions to ask the questions that would lead him to total enlightenment on the subject of the stars. He unrolled an ancient, illustrated scroll across his lap and bent over it, looking for the mention of comets he seemed to recall was in this text. He enjoyed this stage of study, searching out those minute threads that would take him on exciting investigations leading to the pinnacle when he could view the whole, lovely tapestry.

The trouble with stars, he thought, pausing a moment from perusing minute hand drawings and crabbed captioning beneath them, was that they were so far away. That made them difficult to see. He could use spells to enlarge one after another for his edification, but it would take centuries before he'd see them all. What he required was the correct philosophical equipment to bring them closer to him, metaphysically speaking.

He remembered that somewhere in his collection he had a back volume from the Enchanters' Smithy. Zim leaned over to look among the piles at his feet. Yes, there, in the soft, brown leather cover. He opened it at random to a page of fine, clear illuminations depicting cauldrons and alembics in every size from a palmful to a lakeful. The next page showed needles and bodkins. Zim kept turning the leaves until he saw what he wanted, and let out a huge sigh. There were measuring devices and scrutinizing devices and comparative devices, all beautifully made and guaranteed against defects.

The Smithy always had whatever one needed. The problem, Zim knew, was the price. Service, goods, or money. No spells, wishes, or promissory notes. Here were the very things he required. He had no objections to working for the Smithy to pay for his purchase—they were considerate employers, and the work was interesting—but he wanted to start his private studies without delay.

Perhaps a fellow wizard might lend him the materials he needed. Sooner or later all magical researchers delved into the same topics. Zim got up from his chair to go to his round scrying crystal, perched on a dark wooden stand beside the hearth. Peering into the stone's glowing depths, he sent his thoughts out into the ether, seeking equipment similar to that in the Smithy catalog. The mage Cairwoge had a look-far, but he was using it. The ancient sage Velmira had a few astrolabes, but they were in pieces. She had disassembled them in order to see if by combining them she could improve the design and make it capable of more complex measurements. Zim stepped away from his crystal with resignation. He'd better have new goods, then. But where to lay hands upon the necessary to pay for them?

On the corner of his table farthest from where he liked to work, there was a stack of parchments, papyri, and paper sheets. Occasionally, somebody in the village wanted to hire his services, and sent a note up to him tucked in among his purchases. Zim ignored them most of the time. The villagers had small minds. Their requests had a sameness that dismayed him. All things had their price, Zim told himself, as he pulled the pile to him. The need for earthly money was a reminder that he, too, was merely human.

The first was a request for a love philter. He threw the letter on the fire. The next asked for a bountiful harvest. *I'm already doing that for the village,* he thought. However, he put that message to one side. It was worth finding out if the writer was trying a new farming technique or a new crop, or if he was merely greedy. The former interested him; he would not involve himself with the latter.

Zim flicked through the edges of the documents, to see if any of them especially caught his eye. While he was pulling one from deep in the stack, one parchment slid heavily off the pile to the floor, where it landed with a *clank*! Zim picked it up to examine it. What

he had thought from a cursory glance was an ornate
wax seal when the letter had arrived—oh, months
ago—was a gold coin! His eyes lit up. Why, it was as
if the gods had sent him the means almost as soon as
he had made his desires known. With a coin this large
he could afford an astrolabe and a globe of the heavens! Ah, but it was a trader's trick to get his attention.
There was a task to undertake in exchange for it. He
put his wire-rimmed close-looks on his nose, and read
the clear though spidery writing.

Dear Wizard, (it read),
Mey I Conssult you on a Matter that might be of
the Greatest Interest to Both of us?
                    Mistress Vanalon
                    Goods Bot and Solld

Hmm, Zim thought, thumbing his lower lip. It didn't
say whether the coin was a token of her sincerity, or
a retainer against services rendered, or the fee itself.
Yes, those traders were good at drawing one in, then
springing the trap when they'd lured their prey to
them. No bargain was ever as good as it seemed at
the moment. But he thought of the look-far with the
brass tube and the copper eyepiece, and the bronze
astrolabe. He put his pride in his pocket and the coin
on the table, and wrote a return note.

Dear Mistress Vanalon,
You may.
                    The Wizard Zim

The one syllable always looked too short when written out, but it was best not to use more of his name,
lest he inadvertently give power over him to a malign
person. His true name, given to him when he'd received his staff from the High Council, had thirty-eight
syllables. Only he and the old grand master knew it
in its entirety, and she'd been dead for five years.

"Carrok!" he shouted. The raven who made his

home in the rafters winged lazily down and settled on Zim's shoulder.

"My friend?" he asked. Zim rolled up the scrap of parchment and offered it to the black bird, who regarded him out of one beady black eye.

"Will you take this into the village and give it to the trader's wife?" Zim asked.

"Bacon?" Carrok asked, tilting his head the other way.

Zim sighed. "Not until you return." It had been a mistake to allow the bird to get used to human food. Creatures were best when left to their own nature. But Zim had been lonely, and Carrok proved to be curious and intelligent—a good companion. The raven was bright enough to understand both sides of a bargain, however. He took the small tube in his dark claw, and winged out the window.

He and Carrok were barely finished with their breakfast when he spotted a small, cloaked figure hiking hurriedly up the sloping path below his cottage. Mistress Vanalon, Zim thought with a slight smile. He wondered what she wanted so very urgently. Perhaps if it was a wonder he *could* perform, there'd be a second gold coin in it for him. The astral rewards for his work were usually enough, but alas, the needs of the material form still troubled him.

It would be some time before she'd reach the door. Zim waved his hands in a motion to dismiss, and the table was cleared of every dish and every crumb. It had cost him the labor of a month and a week in the service of the woman wizard on the south coast to learn that spell, but it had been worth it from that moment forward. Zim made a mental note to send her another token of thanks.

Zim was deep in the Enchanters' Smithy catalog when Janel came to wind around his feet. The wizard looked up in surprise.

"Is she here already?" he asked the cat. She rubbed her head under his hand. He stood up and put the volume aside. Janel jumped up onto the stool by the

fire and sat tall, her green eyes alert. Zim reached
behind the door for his staff of office. Once he'd com-
mitted to helping a client, he had to do the thing
properly.

The woman who staggered over the threshold of the
cottage was a surprise. She pushed back the hood of
her summer cloak with thin, clawlike hands attached
to tiny, narrow wrists. She had thin brown hair pulled
back in a knot revealing the sharp lines of her face.
The deep indentations under her cheekbones were
more commonly seen in the faces of those who were
starving, but her skin was as smooth as any other
woman of forty or thereabouts, and her black, shiny
eyes were clear.

"Madam, I greet you," Zim said, magnificently bowing. The eyes of the small ivory owl on the head of
the staff glowed green with reflected magic. Mistress
Vanalon, he observed, when he straightened up, was
unimpressed by such things.

"Yes, well," she said, pursing her lips. "It took you
long enough to answer my letter, Wizard. Three
years!"

An inauspicious beginning, Zim thought, frowning.
Had it really been three years? "I was engaged upon
an important task, Madam," he said. "I could not be
interrupted. You are here now. How may I help you?"

She looked about her. The chair at his study table
was full of books, so she brushed Janel off her fireside
perch and sat down. The cat raised her tail in indignation and stalked outside.

Mistress Vanalon paid no attention to the cat.

"I am willing to pay well if I am satisfied, Wizard,"
she said, leaning forward in an engaging manner that
Zim suspected was how she began many a bargain.
She folded her hands together. "My husband and I
are well off. Well, I don't have to tell you that—you
must know it. Everyone does. I can pay for whatever
I want." She tapped her reticule with a skinny finger.

"Then what do you lack?" Zim asked, puzzled.
"Children? For I must tell you, Madam . . ."

"No, I have children. I have five strapping youngsters, though you might not think it to look at me. No," she said, shaking her head. "I want something very special. I want you to enable me to fly."

"Fly?" Zim echoed blankly. Once he had laid eyes on her, he'd been picturing magic of a much more mundane nature: stronger muscles or bones, a prettier face, the appearance of youth. Never this.

"Yes, fly!" Mistress Vanalon said, partly rising from her seat with her arms spread. "The way birds soar with their wings open on the wind and rise above the trees, almost to the heavens—oh, I would do anything to be able to do that." Her eyes opened wider and her thin face glowed avidly. "That's what I want, Master Wizard. I'll pay you well, but you must aid me."

Zim stroked his beard thoughtfully.

"I . . . do not usually alter the basic nature of a human being," he said slowly. "The strictures of magic . . ."

"Oh, but, Wizard Zim, it's my heart's desire!" she exclaimed, clasping her tiny hands to her breast.

"Well, all these things require a true sacrifice," Zim said, trying to think of ways to dissuade her. "You know as well that there will be a certain loss of mass, er, I wonder if you knew that birds have hollow bones. . . ."

"I do not mind," she said, her black eyes bright. Zim thought he saw a certain resentment of times past. "Everyone's always called me Bird Bones."

"Very well, then," the wizard said, with many misgivings. "I will grant your request."

"When? Now?" she asked excitedly.

"These things require preparation," Zim said, ushering her towards the door. "Come back on the evening of the new moon."

"Oh, I am so excited!" Mistress Vanalon said, clutching his arm with her little clawlike hands. "I shall tell everyone!"

"Come alone," Zim said, alarmed. A large audience would disrupt the ether so greatly he wouldn't be able to charm a dust mote. The small woman nodded ener-

getically and set out down the steep path toward town.
He could hear her twittering to herself as she went.

Such an undertaking required immediate research.
Zim went through the three grimoires he owned, looking for data. All three books contained flight spells,
but none of them involved a permanent transformation. He applied to his crystal ball, asking his fellow
wizards if anyone had ever made a woman fly. He
received a couple of hilarious replies from friends, plus
one lengthy and serious treatise arrived by demon-
post from an ancient wizard who lived in a university
town far to the south. Just reading the document made
Zim feel weary, but he found the fact he wanted: It
could be done. The technique in the treatise was fairly
simple. The spell would be aided by Mistress Vanalon's own physiology. She was so small and light that
the spell would work quickly.

"But pay heed," the yellowed parchment scolded
him. "Once bent, the beam of divine light changes
even more that which it illuminates."

Zim put the document to one side and assembled
the items he would need for the ritual. Then he went
to bed. The moon was to be full that night, and he
wanted to get a good look at it through his new look-
far. The Smithy promised him magical delivery by
sunset.

The day of the new moon came. Mistress Vanalon
presented herself at the moment of moonrise. As he
had asked, she wore a sleeveless shift that fell loosely
about her body to the floor. She wasn't at all nervous.
In fact, she stood in the middle of his study and twit-
tered on about where she would go and what she
would do as soon as she was freed from the slothful
pace of foot transportation. After a time, Zim no
longer heard her voice.

"Most interesting," he said, not having heard a
word. "Most interesting. Now, please stand in the blue
chalk circle. Do not touch the yellow or green lines
at all."

"These?" she asked, poking a curious finger toward

them. He seized her hand in time to avoid demonic interference, and led her to the top of the pentagram. Directing her to stretch out her arms, he drew a line on the floor where their shadow fell under the red glass ceiling lamp.

"Now, fold your arms," he said, "and be silent."

"Silent?" she asked incredulously. "Why? What's going to . . . ?"

Zim swept a finger past his own lips, and she stopped talking, shaking her head. He closed the circle behind her. It was intended to be unbreakable. Nothing living could step in or out of it. He sealed himself into his own protective pattern. Carrok flew down to stand upon his shoulder. He stared at Mistress Vanalon, who returned his regard with eyes very much like those of the raven.

"We begin," Zim intoned. With the clear diction that had been the envy of the high council of wizards during his training, he read out the words from the cracked and yellowing parchment from the university. At the appropriate moments, he pounded the floor with the foot of his staff, lit candles and incense, and directed the mystic smoke to surround Mistress Vanalon.

She coughed. Zim felt the ether before him, and decided that she was in no danger.

"Spirits and geniuses of the air, I invoke you to do my bidding!" he said, raising his voice until the rafters rang. Shapes rose out of the floor, and congregated about a cup of wine he had left in the center of the circle for them. A couple of greedy slurps, and the bowl was empty.

"Behold your task!" He pointed the ivory owl at the cocoon of smoke. "Do, and do, and do!" He brought the staff down, and thumped the floor—once, twice, thrice.

The mists changed color as the insubstantial spirits whirled around Mistress Vanalon. Zim thought that he could see the slight body drawn taller and thinner inside them, but decided it was just a trick of the light. When the smoke and colors faded away, she looked much as she had before. She looked at her hands and shoulders, and peered at him questioningly.

"Nothing happened," she said, disappointment evident.

Quickly, Zim scanned the pages in his left hand. Had he made a mistake? But, no, the spell had gone exactly as it was intended to. What was wrong?

"Come here," he said. She took a step forward, and stopped.

"I can't," she said. "I'm stuck. I'm trapped!"

Zim had forgotten. The circle was unbreakable by anything that walked the earth. But, he realized with surprise, that was the true test of the spell.

"Flutter your arms," he said. Mistress Vanalon hesitated, but then began to flap her hands. The look on her face as she rose off the floor was one of sheer surprise.

"Come here," he said again, beckoning her to him. Mistress Vanalon flapped a little harder, propelling her up to the rafters. She slowed her hands a little, and sank toward the floor. With a little backwards kick, she propelled herself at him. Zim had to catch her before she caromed into him. She was light as straw in his hands. He set her gently on the ground.

"Oh, Wizard, thank you!" she said, beaming up at him. She looked at her hands as if she couldn't believe they still belonged to her. She flapped again, and her feet left the ground. "I'm so happy!"

Zim bowed. He, too, was pleased. To have performed a spell he had never before tried absolutely correctly on the first attempt was a triumph.

"I'm pleased to have been of service," he said.

"And indeed you have," Mistress Vanalon said, instantly businesslike. She scurried to where her cloak, shoes, and reticule were sitting. With fingers trembling excitedly, she fumbled through her waist pouch, and came out with a gold coin like the first she had sent him. "Will that serve as my fee?"

"Admirably, Madam," he said. "Most generous." He accepted it graciously and placed it on the table.

She slipped on her shoes and ran to the window to

look at the moon. The silver crescent had moved about ten degrees higher above the horizon. The stars were bright and thick in the sky.

"Oh, it's still early. I must go home and show my husband! He'll be amazed!" She started to put her cloak about her shoulders. With a girlish smile at Zim, she pushed the cloth behind her so her arms were free. She buckled her belt on, and started to flap her arms.

She rose off the floor, and gave a little kick to propel herself out of the door. Once in the open air, she started to flap harder, gaining altitude as she went. She flew off down the mountain, tentatively at first, but growing more confident yard by yard, until she was chasing bats through the sky. Zim watched the white shift as she attempted a loop, her starlit arms spread out for stability. She came out of it upright, and paused, thirty feet above the ground, with a cry of triumph.

Flapping her arms vigorously, she began to sing a lively ditty that sounded like larksong in her thin voice. The sound faded quickly away in the distance. Zim went back into his cottage for the new copy of the Enchanters' Smithy catalog that had arrived with his look-far.

Several weeks followed. Zim received his second order from the Smithy, and entered seriously upon his investigation of the stars. He changed his sleeping schedule so that he was awake most nights, staring through the look-far, and making measurements with his astrolabe. He had already documented his findings on no fewer than ten thousand stars. He had found errors in some of the texts he had read, and sent corrections to the wizards who had written them. He received a demon-delivered package full of dried stink-flowers with a crank note from one wizard, but other colleagues were more gracious.

Zim went to bed at dawn after the first new moon of the autumn had set. The milk had already arrived, and with it, a clutch of new requests for his aid, more of the usual mundane pleas. Mistress Vanalon had broadcast her good news, and other villagers clearly hoped he would work magic for them, too. Zim put the letters aside on the stack that had been piling up since the morning after he had given her the power of flight. Perhaps in a year or so he would feel inclined to undertake another commission of that sort, Zim thought, settling himself down for sleep just as the morning sparrows began to sing. *Pretty melody,* he thought, drifting off into dreams of constellations and comets.

He woke up to twittering noises under the eaves of his house, interspersed with caws and mews. Someone was here. He pried open one eye with his thumb and forefinger, and immediately clamped it closed again, but Mistress Vanalon's sharp black eyes had seen.

"Ah, you're awake!" she said, patting him on the shoulder. "I brought you a gift!" She displayed a length of fine white cloth, then draped it over his chest. "Sixteen yards! Just in from the far eastern shores. I am enjoying my new life so much I had to express my gratitude once again."

"You . . . have already been very kind," Zim said, putting himself out to be polite, though he was groggy. She had sent many presents up the mountain in exchange for her spell over the last several weeks. He sat up in bed. The sun was pointing straight down at his tabletop sundial. Midday. He stifled a groan of dismay. "I ask for nothing more."

"Ah, but it gave me joy to ride up here on the wind," the little woman said, stretching out her arms. Zim peered at her face curiously. Was she developing feathers at her hairline? No, had to be a trick of the light. "Well, I must be going," she trilled cheerfully. "I am surprised that you aren't up already! Farewell!"

With that, Mistress Vanalon fluttered her arms, and rose a foot off the floor. She stroked the air as if swimming in it, then pushed herself forward and out of the door into the sun. Zim nodded his approval. She was refining her skills admirably. Janel jumped up on the bed and made a nest for herself in the silk.

"I must admit she's generous," Zim said, feeling the

fabric between his fingers. It was nice cloth, and he had to admit he was pleased by his own handiwork. The transformation had worked out well.

He was not pleased to discover that having made the trip once, Mistress Vanalon had decided that she could fly to his eyrie whenever she wished, without consulting him. She appeared on the average once a week, but never on the same day or at the same time so that he could anticipate her. He bore her intrusions three more times before he spoke out.

"Oh, but you're not busy," she said, looking about at his books and things. He had, in fact, been in the middle of a complicated calculation to find the exact center of the Universe that had taken him since the middle of the afternoon the day before. There was nothing on paper, but he did most important work in his head.

"Madam," Zim said, very patiently, trying not to forget ten to the eighteenth power, "my studies require the utmost in concentration. You must not come here unless we have made a specific engagement."

"Oh, I knew you wouldn't mind," Mistress Vanalon said, settling herself on Janel's stool with a flick of her cloak like a magpie settling its wings. She seemed more birdlike than ever. "I wanted to bring up the matter of Mistress Gennis. She sent you a query *weeks* ago about solving her problem. She's a good friend of mine, and I wanted to put her case to you myself. I don't want her to have to wait three years, as I did. The job could be most remunerative, you know."

"She wishes me to charm warts off her face," Zim said heavily. "Any hedge-wizard or herb-witch could do it. And should!"

"Yes, but you would do it so much better," Mistress Vanalon said, putting her head to one side persuasively. She looked at him out of her beady black eyes.

"No, I would not," Zim said, his voice flat. "I decline. You may tell her so."

"Oh, but I can't tell her that," the trader's wife said, looking appalled. "It means so much to her."

"That is between her and her gods," Zim said. He rose and opened the door for her. "Now you must leave, Madam."

"Oh, well," Mistress Vanalon said. "You'll change your mind. It's too good a bargain."

No bargain was good enough to trade for his peace and quiet, Zim thought, as he watched her fly away. Carrok the raven caught the edge of his mood, and let out a raucous caw.

"Rroongk!"

"Yes," Zim said, looking up at his companion. He patted his shoulder, and the raven flew down to strop his beak against the wizard's ear. "I may have made a mistake, but I can't undo what I've done without her leave. That's the law of free will. Once I meddle with that, I'm no better than a demon."

He was sorely tempted to withdraw the spell as the summer turned into autumn. He had been tracking the patterns of comets as they crossed the night sky. What with calculations and documentation, Zim was not sleeping at all, and it was telling upon his patience. He let out a low cry of frustration as he looked out of the window. Mistress Vanalon appeared on the wind over the breast of the hill with a basket strapped to her back.

"I've brought you some delicious cheese," she called out to him even before she landed. "It's from the east."

"I don't want it," Zim said, sulkily.

"Yes, you will," she said, settling to the ground on her tiptoes only three paces from his window. She leaned in and offered him the basket. "Just wait until you taste it. I've never tried anything so good."

"You must go away, Mistress Vanalon," Zim said, controlling his temper with difficulty. He didn't take the basket. She waited for a moment, then dropped it onto his papers. He pushed it away, and it rolled off the table and into the coal scuttle.

"I've got to talk to you about Mistress Gennis," she said, pulling her cloak around her shoulders and letting herself in the door. "I *know* you can do these simple things. I may be bird-boned, but I'm not bird-witted. Look what you did for the harvest, and you didn't miss a beat with your studies."

"God help me, and make me a better wizard," he said, grinding his teeth together. "The harvest spell was laid at planting-time, as it always is!"

"Great heavens, why do we pay you now if you haven't done anything for months?" she asked, surprised.

Zim stared at her. She was treating him like a common trader. He made his voice grow cold as ice, and lowered his brows until they half-covered his eyes. "Because that was the agreement between me and the village elders, for the good of all." He didn't mention money. It was time to distance himself from her and her appalling bargains.

She shrugged her thin shoulders, unconvinced and, as usual, unimpressed. "Oh, well. Then I won't ask you until you are ready again."

"Thank you," Zim said, emphatically. He felt his shoulders settle with relief. He straightened out his papers, and found the one he had been working on.

"I'll go now," Mistress Vanalon said abruptly. She rose and put her cloak behind her shoulders, freeing her arms. He glanced up. The minute hairs on her wrists had turned to true feathers now.

"Thank you," Zim said, looking down hastily. He refused to allow himself to be interested in the aftermath of his spell. Under other circumstances, he would have loved to ask her how many other changes there had been, but he did not want to encourage her to be more familiar with him than she was. He went back to his calculations. When he looked up again, she was gone.

Zim was sure he would have peace and quiet again, now that Mistress Vanalon had promised to stop asking for favors for her friends. The written requests slowed down again to a trickle, as they always did when he failed to respond. That was right and proper. It had never been his intention to involve himself in the day-to-day life of the village. Zim completed the first draft of his mystical formula and put it to one side to let his mind clear. It was always best to check calculations when they weren't fresh in his memory.

That night, he stayed up to check his observations of a pair of mating constellations in the eastern sky, and went to bed with the owls as dawn was breaking.

He woke up to the screech of loud, not particularly melodic birdsong. Without opening his eyes, he groaned. He had recognized the voice. It was Mistress Vanalon again, singing, if one could dignify the sound by that name.

Zim pulled himself out of bed, feeling every bone and muscle protest. Janel jumped down from her nest next to his pillow and stretched, yawning widely. Zim pulled on his morning robe and staggered outside.

The little woman was sitting on the lawn in front of his study on her outspread cloak, surrounded by a flock of songbirds. As he and the cat appeared at the door, the birds took to wing, rising about her like a cloud. They had been sitting with her and singing. Zim goggled as he realized what that meant. They had begun to see her as one of them. Mistress Vanalon turned to give him a cheerful smile.

"Good morning, Wizard!" she sang out, fluttering a hand. The momentum lifted her gently off the ground.

"I thought you wouldn't be coming back," Zim said, grumpily.

"Oh, I'm not here to ask for anything," she said, with a trill of friendly laughter. "I felt like singing, but everybody in town was complaining I was disturbing them. It's so nice and quiet up here. I knew you wouldn't mind. I promise you I won't come by at night. I know you're studying then. How exciting it is to have such an important wizard as yourself here," she chattered on. "I've just written a letter to my sister in the western mountains. They've only got an herb-witch in *their* town. . . ."

Zim fled inside and closed the door. His head ached from her shrill voice. Janel yowled a complaint, and Carrok added his hoarse cry from the rafters.

"I know, my friends. I can't go on like this either," he said, pacing back and forth, staying out of sight of the window, and the woman on his lawn. Why had he allowed his greed to force him to become involved with her? He felt suddenly desperate. His studies would be worthless if he couldn't concentrate. What could he do? Should he make her mute? Make her less interested in her neighbors and surroundings?

No, he told himself, driving away those thoughts with a sharp wave of his hand. Such things were black sorcery. Her voice was part of her trade, the nosiness was part of her personality, and the singing was part of the transformation he himself had imposed upon her. He couldn't change any part of her nature now. What should he do? Move away? But he didn't want to leave his pleasant home of many decades. He looked around his little house fondly. He had things arranged the way he wanted them. If he started over, it could be the next century before he was properly settled again.

Carrok hopped down from his roost and perched on the pot hook above the teakettle. Zim nodded. Yes, he needed tea. He lit the fire with a flick of his fingers, and pushed the kettle over it.

Then, what? If Zim couldn't change Mistress Vanalon, and he didn't want to change his surroundings, he was the one who must adapt.

No study is ever wasted, Zim reminded himself. He'd changed his mind before on smaller whims than this. Very deliberately, he wrapped his new look-far and astrolabe in the dry-cloths they had come from the Smithy in, and put them away in a chest. He tidied away all the books on the Universe that he had accumulated, and began to search through his bookshelves. Somewhere in his collection he had a basic text on the primal nature of music. He had always intended to study the subject. Why not now? Ah, there it was.

With the blue-bound text in one hand, he poured water from the steaming kettle over dried herbs, and lifted the cup to inhale its sweet, bitter scent. After the first cup of tea, the noise from the lawn seemed less unpleasant. Zim cocked an ear to listen critically. No, her singing wasn't really that bad, when one considered she wasn't much of a bird yet.

Zim settled down in his armchair with the music text and a blank sheet of parchment to make notes. Since he couldn't rid himself of his pest, he might as well make use of her as a resource. After all, the stars would still be there when Mistress Vanalon finally went away.

WILLY WIZARD'S MAGICLAND

❖ ❖ ❖

by Connie Hirsch

Connie Hirsch has written many excellent stories for various anthologies, including *100 Vicious Little Vampire Stories, The Shimmering Door,* and *Fantastic Alice.* She lives in Massachusetts.

Thomas chose the postcard carefully, ignoring the rest of the Magicland crapola that the giftshop carried, searching the rack until he found a picture of Stereotypical Dad and Daughter posed with Captain Yoyo. Dad and Daughter didn't look at all related, and Thomas thought Dad's hand was too friendly on the kid's shoulder.

"Dear Jen," Thomas wrote with a felt tip, in big block letters that a nine-year-old could read. "I'm having a good time and thinking about you. I wish you could be here and we could have fun again, but you ruined that, didn't you?" He held the postcard by the edges, so as not to leave any fingerprints, and left the message unsigned.

Goddamn puking kid. He should have known better, and shut her up permanently. Thomas lurched to his feet, feeling his Hawaiian shirt sweat-welded to his shoulder blades. The mailbox stood under a sign that said "MagicMail!" and was shaped like a fat, round-eyed owl: step on its foot and the beak opened. On the lower inside of the bill there was a reassuring sticker from the U.S. Postal Service that they did in-

222

deed pick up the mail from this station at ten and four o'clock. Thomas loathed it as yet one more cutesy-wutesy expression of the "genius" of Willy Wizard.

The staff here at Magicland was everything that you heard—smiling, helpful, everywhere—until Thomas wanted to vomit. And then there were Critters. You couldn't walk thirty feet down Broad Way without tripping over a foam-rubber monstrosity dancing and miming.

After three days, he sheerly and sincerely hated MagicLand, Willy Wizard, Captain Yoyo, and every other goofball merchandise Critter that Magicland possessed. They had Goons, Poltroons, even one called an Elefeatherump, each more unlikely than the last. If he never saw another puffy, short, goofy-expressioned dickweed, he would be just as glad.

But, Thomas reminded himself as he shaded his eyes from the bright Florida sun—he was cultivating an A-Number-One sunburn—he hadn't come for the Critters, or the rides, or the maintenance. You never heard about a scandal here . . . no accidents, no unhappy times, and never any unpleasantness that might happen to lost little girls.

Thomas considered himself a man of the world, and learned instinct said that this perfect record just wasn't possible. It either meant that Magicland had an unparalleled security force . . . or that management used large bribes and an attack PR department to cover up crimes and scandals.

So down to Magicland Thomas the Hunter (as he thought of himself in his secret fantasies) had come, to check out the real state of affairs. After three days of investigating the park, he'd spotted Security, all right, both the obvious guys, to keep the tourists from East Overshoe in line, and their more subtle backups. For a park this large, with this many visitors, they were definitely understaffed.

Thomas bought a lemonade slush and sat on a bench in the Welcome to Magicland Plaza, right below the white marble statue of Willy Wizard, and let his eyes linger on the happy children, on their way out of

Willy's Magic Journey through the inevitable theme gift shop, or lining up for rides on the paddle-powered Swan Boats to the strains of Muzak Wagner.

"You Put The Magic In Magicland" was the motto over his head. Thomas thought this was as apt a slogan for him as for any other visitor. He watched as one little miss, a strawberry blonde in a short light-green dress with adorable lace ruffles, wandered from bench to bench. He could see her parents talking to a vendor, oblivious to their child's whereabouts.

Casually Thomas strolled over to her, his demeanor no different than any other kindly stranger in this kindly place. She was looking at the mural of King Luddie in his Swan Castle, her eyes shining. "Hello," Thomas said. He knew better than to address her as "Little Girl"—kids hated being reminded they were kids. "My favorite's Fairy Emeraldua, who do you like?" He'd put in time researching the things that young visitors to Magicland were likely to know about.

"I like King Luddie," she smiled, " 'cause he's so funny."

Thomas took genuine pleasure in talking to children, especially girls, so uncorrupted and sweet. His interest served him well; in no time he had the girl's name, Melissa, and her trust. Yet, though he was concentrating on charming her, he kept an eye out for Security. Just because he didn't see anything . . .

His mind made up, he took Melissa by the hand . . . and led her across the plaza, right to her parents. "I believe you lost something," was all he said. "You should take better care, even in a place like this." He said good-bye to Melissa, accepted the embarrassed thanks of her parents, and strolled off with the air of a man who has done a good deed—intensely though unobtrusively alert for any official interest. Not even the vendor seemed concerned.

He permitted himself a slight smile, no more than any other happy-go-lucky tourist would wear, though his was a more sinister joy—and that increased his pleasure. Yeah, Thomas the Hunter, tweaking the nose of Security and all the other killjoys, testing the waters. And the waters *were* good; if nobody raised an alarm on a crowded plaza, well, what would happen in a deserted cul-de-sac after twilight?

The music for the Afternoon Parade was starting with a happy-wappy carillon of bells, and Thomas decided to stroll on back to his hotel room and take a siesta. There would, after all, be good hunting tonight.

Thomas found that sleep eluded him; perhaps it was the memory of that petite, sweaty hand wrapped tightly around his fingers. How it hurt to give up an opportunity so sweet! He was sweating despite the blasting air-conditioning, so he rolled over and got his maps from the bedside drawer.

The first was the standard MagicLand tourist handout. The second would have given fits to any knowledgeable Security person, because Thomas had been carefully making his own diagram. Whether by sloppiness, or design, the official map lied about distances and shortcuts. When he'd worked as a civil engineer, before the unpleasantness and publicity with little Jen, Thomas had been skilled at estimating distance. It was a knack that served him now.

In the three days he'd been at Magicland, he'd thoroughly explored the Lands, learning the traffic flows, watching the employees come and go—some alleys that looked deserted were entrances to service areas. In a professional way, Thomas could appreciate the genius of the EngiGnomes (Magicland lingo for designers); especially in the newer Lands, where there was little wasted space. The older areas had been built before the architects had it down to a science. As well, the older attractions on Pleasure Island and Treasure Island drew lesser crowds.

Thomas had highlighted two likely areas on those sections of the maps. *Will it be Treasure or Pleasure?* he wondered with evil levity. Treasure Island was more deserted, but Pleasure Island was a short walk from Willy's Magic Castle, where children were likely to get separated from their parents in the Crystal Corridors.

A grin creased Thomas' face. He hadn't truly enjoyed himself in weeks, relieved those pesky itches. Not much chance, traveling from East Overshoe to South Elbow-bone, looking for good hunting grounds, steering clear of towns with too efficient police. Once he'd gotten to Florida, he'd expected matters to improve, but he'd not been able to connect with members of Friends of Children Everywhere, a select and exclusive organization.

The directory listed no less than four members in the immediate vicinity. He'd called them from a pay phone—not willing to dial through the Magicland hotel switchboard, a precaution he probably didn't have to take. Two of the numbers had been disconnected, one had evidently been relisted as a Burger King, and on the last one, a shrill woman had wanted to know where her no-good-bum of a husband was. He'd hung up on her.

Thomas hadn't let it bother him, even if it reminded him of his last conversation back at the Nimrod Club, a bar that served as a meeting place for special interests. He'd sat down with a gentleman known as Phil A. Delfia, to trade his collection of photographs and tapes for ready cash.

"Phil" was a wizened toad of a man, strands of hair plastered atop his bald spot, with a habit of nervous darting glances, like a weasel watching out for hawks. He was legendary in certain circles for his independent wealth, his voracious appetite for certain items, and record of never being caught. Thomas hadn't meant to spill the beans about his plans for the money, but he'd had a drink or two, and he was secretly exalted at the price Phil had given him. It only took him a moment to get going about Magicland and the special trip he wanted to take there.

As he'd talked, he'd seen Phil's face change, from conspiratorial, to troubled. "Wait," the guy had said. "Hold on a minute, buddy. Magicland's not such a great idea."

Thomas had blinked, wondering if he wasn't more potted than he'd thought. A sudden attack of Puritanism in Phil seemed like a hallucination. "What?" Thomas had said at last.

"Listen," Phil said, leaning forward and lowering his voice. "I know two separate guys went down there for a little sport . . . and they never came back."

"Bullshit," said Thomas.

"I'm not kidding!" Phil whispered fiercely. "I never heard from them again—one guy, he was in the papers, big search and everything. I'm not making this up."

"You're bullshitting me," said Thomas. But Phil didn't look like he was talking trash for kicks.

"Okay," said Phil. "It's your funeral. It's just . . . there are these rumors, okay?"

"Rumors?" Thomas said sarcastically. Then he realized what really was going on. He wasn't the first guy to think of Magicland as a hunting preserve. Others had, too, and they were trying to keep it private. Phil probably went down twice a year!

Thomas had collected himself, falsely explaining that he'd had too much to drink, and said good-bye, while anger had rumbled within him.

And he was still angry, even now when he'd reached the Promised Land, and found it full of milk and honey—his special brand of milk and honey. Magicland was everything he had hoped for, and yet . . . he still wasn't entirely sure Phil had been lying.

Oh, go on. Phil is a paranoid jackass, he told himself. *He was giving candy to kids when you were in your diapers. Running you a line, to keep you away.* Thomas had been on the lookout for fellow sporting gents during his three days of research, but hadn't spotted a one. *Wouldn't it be a gas to go strolling up to Phil, sitting at a café table, and ask him if he'd like to pose with the Elefeatherump?* he thought, and grinned.

Thomas wondered if he should check his special kit again. As if the contents might have wandered off— *You're getting butterflies, Hunter,* he thought. Duct tape, gloves, blindfold, and his "toys": It was all ready and waiting.

Thomas looked over at the clock-radio with its wizard's hat decal: time to leave for the evening's hunt. A slug of adrenaline ran through his veins, leaving a warm feeling in the pit of his stomach. He never felt more alive than when he was hunting, especially if it were good hunting.

Thomas drifted in with the evening's tide of happy humanity, feeling himself a shark in fish's clothing; he wore a subdued Hawaiian shirt and a disposable camera on a cord around his neck. As he wandered, he worried about the advisability of taking pictures of his night's work, something he'd never done before; certain proof if he was caught. To keep a souvenir beyond his pleasant memories? With this debate in mind he turned down Broad Way, smiling gently at the tourists and gingerbread molding.

One moment he'd been walking, glancing onto the street where a young woman dressed in a baby-doll outfit was doing a comic dance with a puffy teddy bear, and the next he was bouncing off the spongy fingers of a purple elephant with feathery wings for ears. He recognized it as the Elefeatherump, as truly, a sickening creation of an EngiGnome's imagination as there was. "Hey," Thomas said, staggering.

Thomas' first instinct was to get angry; he'd had enough of crowds and these darned Critters, like a nightmare blend of mimes and bad cartoons—but he remembered where he was and what persona he had to maintain. Besides, the guy inside the Elefeatherump suit probably couldn't see much, or move quickly out of the way.

Thomas thought all this in a moment, before he'd even straightened up, already grinning to cover his anger, when he looked up at the Ele-Whatsis. "Sorry, I didn't see—" he started to say.

It had a huge head, no neck, a pear-shaped body, squat legs and arms. How you could get an adult in there, Magicland must hire dwarves or kids or something? For just a second, he felt a chill. The Critter was waving a thick finger in his face, like a fuzzy purple metronome.

"What?" Thomas said, more forcefully than he'd meant. The *thing* shook its head, ostrich-feather ears—in international hailing distress orange—swaying emphatically. Almost those big plastic eyes looked, what? Sad? Worried? Frustrated? "What do you want?"

People were staring, parents and kids, and one of the omnipresent vendors was coming out of his booth. Thomas felt a small thrill of danger, and it sobered him. Of course, the damn foam-rubbers couldn't talk! How would the Hunter handle this?

"I'm sorry," he said with all the false contriteness his voice could hold. "I'll watch where I'm going from now on, okay?" He hung his head and twitched his shoulders. *Yeah, put on a good show for the families—and Security.*

The Critter stared at him too long. Arms sagging down to spreading sides, it turned and waddled away. Thomas stared, collected himself, and walked on. What the hell had that been about?

His plan had been a preliminary sweep of Treasure Island, to make sure the Security routine hadn't changed, but he might have attracted too much attention just now. Thomas strolled through Luddie's Castle, took a raft across the Maroon Lagoon and got on line for The Willy Wizard Story. He'd already seen it, of course, and he didn't intend to bother with it again. Where the line snaked out of sight beneath the Pink Whale's sparkling incisors, he slipped through the ropes and continued over to Pleasure Island.

Maybe it was just his imagination, but the damn Critters were everywhere tonight. Had there been an announcement about some special event that he'd missed? Still, they were no more than an annoyance, easily avoided.

Pleasure Island was everything that he had hoped for. The Evening Parade had drawn away the crowds, and native birds sang in the trees of the little park and maze. He found a bench, partially hidden by bushes, where he could see without being seen. Thomas smoked one cigarette after another, feeling his excitement grow with the nicotine buzz, and only one family group wandered past him the whole time. *It's now or never,* the Hunter thought, and Thomas smiled. *The Magic of MagicLand is working for me. . . .*

The Crystal Corridors were magical-feeling, all right; as you moved from one reflecting room to another, your sight was befuddled, while your ears were seduced with a dissonant arrangement of the Magicland Theme. The black ceiling was high; the star-splattered floor was soft and forgiving, and the mirror walls gave you glimpses of *things* out of the corner of your eye.

Thomas could almost believe he was invisible, though his reflections everywhere belied the idea. Children ran shrieking around him, and he felt a truly Godlike power; he could pick and choose among them, focus in on one who was quiet, and compliant, and wouldn't cry out.

It was one of the tricks of the mirrors; he turned a corner and came face to face with himself. His wolfish grin scarcely looked human in a burnt-pink face, and he recoiled; his expression changing to shock, then recognition, then laughter.

It was then that a girl walked into the room, and started laughing with him, laughing at him. "Hello," he said softly. "Are you here with your parents?" She was perfect, sweet, young and beautiful: a doll for his play. He took her hand, and she looked up with such trust that he almost took her right there and then.

"Would you like to see a really special place?" he said. "We can go there, and it will be our secret—"

The girl said something in a thin piping voice. What she answered didn't matter, the sound of her acceptance was all that he listened for. He lifted her hand, a perfect movement like the start of a dance, and turned, seeing a flash of purple at the edge of his vision.

At first he stared, wondering if it wasn't some special effect that the EngiGnomes had added in the last day. It looked like a hologram of the goddamned Ele-featherump, coming toward them, liquid-metal-purple shining as it squeezed *through* the mirrors.

This was too weird for the Hunter: Thomas backed up, gripping the hand of his intended victim, ignoring her cry of dismay as he jerked her along. He bumped into a wall behind him, a mirror he would have sworn wasn't there a minute ago, but he'd obviously gotten disoriented, who wouldn't with this strangeness—

The goddamned Critter was closer. Time to make tracks, but which way? He turned to the right and saw to his dismay that a pink form was advancing down the mirrored, false corridors: Captain Yoyo, four feet tall and four feet wide, striding along like a child's block.

The kid was crying now; Thomas gave her a shake and turned toward the other direction, only to see a gang of Critters from King Luddie's Castle, including the King himself and the sparkling green glow of Fairy Emeraldua, coming through the mirror maze.

The music still played, sweet flutes and tinkling bells of the Magicland Theme. The Critters' approach was silent, save for the flat thumps of foam-rubber feet. In no time at all, they had Thomas boxed in, puffy broad *things* who incredibly filled the small room, forming an impassable circle.

Thomas tried to wet his lips with a mouth suddenly dry. "He-Hello there," he said. "Is there—something wrong?"

They were silent, their big plastic eyes unblinking, accusing.

"What do you want?" Thomas yelled. "What do you dopes think you're doing?"

The crowd moved slightly, allowing a small opening that Fairy Emeraldua flew through. Thomas stared at her in profound amazement. She was a woman the size of a Barbie doll, no more than a foot high and perfectly formed, shimmering with sparkly green light. This close, he could see that she was no special ef-fect—she was as real as the hand at the end of his arm.

Her small green eyes bored into him. Thomas was

frightened again. "You back off," he grated, dragging the girl in close. The kid whimpered, and he was glad to hear a sound that reminded him of his power.

"Get out of my way—" he said to the puffy horde, but Emeraldua pulled a tiny wand out of her belt and pointed its glowing end. Actinic green flashed through his eyes into his brain like the light of an atomic explosion, stopping him in mid-word, turning his muscles to concrete, freezing his lungs.

The Elefeatherump gently pried Thomas' nerve-dead fingers from the girl's arm, and gravely offered her its hand.

Captain Yoyo and King Luddie picked him up between them. Thomas realized he should be worried that he couldn't breathe, but his fear-glands seemed paralyzed, too. The mirrored room swayed around Thomas' fixed gaze; the last he saw of the Elefeatherump, it was leading the clinging child from the room.

The Critters carried Thomas through the mirrored wall. The world stretched and grew shiny-flat as they melted through the glass. Flashes of light and dark filled his eyes: glimpses of a cave with living swan boats, dipping their elegant necks in the sparkling waters; a sunshine-drenched flowery meadow where the sun had a smiley face and the huge flowers were *humming;* the deck of a swaying pink galleon. They either traveled thousands of miles or no distance at all: without his heartbeat, Thomas couldn't estimate time.

But time must have passed, because he had been there in the Crystal Corridors, and now he was here, in a place he vaguely recognized as Willy's Throne Room—vaguely because the one he knew was in a cartoon; this was lushly real, from the slate flagstones to the deep colors and glimmery gold threads in the wall tapestries. And real, too, was the tall, thin man who sat upon the dais, gazing into a crystal the size of a medicine ball. It was Willy Wizard himself, in the altogether real flesh.

There was little noise save for the murmur of distant bells, and the occasional scuff of a soft sole. With no

warning, the Wizard turned toward Thomas, looking
down as though there were no one else in the room:
deep, soulful dark eyes that stirred the tiny thread of
fear that was all that Thomas could feel at the
moment.

"What do you have to say for yourself?" Willy's
voice was not the cheerful goofy syrup of the cartoons,
but deep and sorrowful. He lifted something from his
lap that might have been a wand, if wands were made
of ruby and silver. He pointed it at the Hunter.

Thomas' brain and mouth and throat and lungs
woke up. So, too, did his fear wake, more fear than
when the cops had come to get him back home—but
he'd gotten out of that one, after all. "What the hell
is the meaning of this?" he said, quick to the offense.
"What the hell are you doing here?"

The Wizard did not so much as blink, but Thomas
could feel his distaste. Maybe he could see it in the
set of the old man's white eyebrows, the wrinkles at
the corners of his mouth. "I know my rights," said
Thomas. "You can't do this to me."

His bravado echoed, died an aching death in the
muffling silence, while the Wizard stared. It got to
Thomas, bad. "I didn't do anything," he said. "I never
touched the kid. You have no right to hold me."

"Mr. Hunter," said the Wizard quietly. Some quality in the man's voice silenced Thomas, made him
strain to hear. "I asked what you had to say for yourself, and your statements tell me exactly what I
feared."

"Just what do you mean by that?" demanded
Thomas, but the Wizard didn't answer. Instead he
pointed the wand again, and the animation fled out of
Thomas, leaving just enough consciousness behind to
hear and see.

"His sentence is transmogrification," said Willy
Wizard. "Perhaps he will learn the error of his ways
in a new form." He waved the wand, and well-oiled
gears rumbled in the floor. At the edge of his paralyzed field of vision, Thomas could see a trapdoor
opening in the floor like a crack of doom. It disclosed

a pool of roiling pink goo, in different hues of taffy, roses, and little girl's bows, silently boiling.

The last Thomas saw of the Wizard, as the Critters gently lowered his frozen body down into the pink, was his deep, sad eyes, already turning back to the crystal, as though Thomas the Hunter were just a minor annoyance in a life full of serious work.

Magicland opened in the morning as it did every day: The Magicland Theme played over loudspeakers, hordes of happy children and their parents entered under the festive banners and bright balloons, intent on a day spent in the special safety of Make-Believe. They walked, strolled, sauntered, and even skipped past the white marble statue of Willy Wizard, as the Critters came out to meet them from the secret entrances that no tourist ever sees. The Critters—Goons, Poltroons, Elefeathrumps and less identifiable species, waddled out into the bright Florida sun with cheerful muteness, communicating through gesture, clumsy though gentle.

Tommy Hunter was there to greet them, a green, squat block of a Critter dressed in an enormous Hawaiian shirt, who bumbled along with the rest of the pack. Somewhere deep inside the rubbery flesh, Thomas still existed, seeing with huge bright eyes, hearing with gigantic pink ears, feeling only faintly through rotund fingers, so close to his favorite prey.

And totally unable to act, even to speak. The frown on a child's face caused him pain, the cry of a child was agony. Existence was reduced to attempting to please, to atone, with the rest of the Critters. At night they rested in their rows in the Dungeon beneath King Luddie's Castle, the one no tourist ever sees, reflecting on their past misdeeds, hoping someday to be released from their punishment.

Sometimes, as proud parents stand waiting in line with their children for a photo opportunity with one of the Critters, they'll ask a park attendant where these wonderful characters come from. The answer is always the same: The Critters are characters under development by the EngiGnomes. It never seems to matter whether the Critter is old or brand new, really, for the kids always react with delight to the special magic that is Willy Wizard's.

VISIBLE BREATH

❖❖❖

by Nina Kiriki Hoffman

Nina Kiriki Hoffman has been nominated for several awards for her fiction, the most recent being for the Nebula Award for her novel *The Silent Strength of Stones*. She also has stories in *Tarot Fantastic, Enchanted Forests,* and *The UFO Files.*

Seemed like I was the only one who could see her. It was the first Saturday of Christmas break. I sat on a park bench, watching all the Christmas shoppers as they waded through slush on the sidewalks outside of Arlington's Department Store. Everyone puffed out steamy breath, as though the whole world smoked. The air smelled cold and wet. My nose was slowly freezing. My knit cap almost kept my ears warm.

I thought about what I would have bought for Christmas for my younger brother Roger if he were still alive. He was twelve and easy to shop for. He liked practically any new action figure from a Marvel comic, and they kept coming up with new Spider-Mans.

But Roger wasn't around anymore. I only had to shop for Mom and my stepdad, Bill. I had bought Mom a scarf. I didn't feel like getting Bill anything.

I knew Mom would be mad if I didn't get something for Bill. There was enough bad stuff in the air at our house already, with Roger dying just after Thanksgiving. I didn't want to upset Mom if I could help it. But I just couldn't get myself to go into a store and search out something for Bill. So I sat in the park, waiting until I was so cold I'd want to go inside just to get warm. Then I'd get the first five-dollar thing I saw that looked like a man could use it.

That was my plan, until I saw the red woman.

People were in a hurry, puffing along on the sidewalk with their arms full of shopping bags, except for two women dressed for office work, who sat on a bench not far from me, drinking steaming stuff out of Thermos cups and talking.

This woman not dressed for freezing was standing right behind their bench. She had on a dress that was scarlet red velvet from neck to wrists and on down to her toes. She wore white gloves, and she held a red velvet pouch in her right hand. Her face was white as Wonder Bread. Her hair was angely, wavy curls of streaky brown-blonde down to her waist, and she had a scarlet velvet hat on, too, one of those floppy ones that lie more on one side of your head than the other.

As the office women talked with each other, the woman in red leaned forward right between them. She watched the breaths that came out of their mouths. Every once in a while, her left hand darted out and closed around a puff of breath. Then she slipped her hand into that pouch.

I mean. There she was leaning right down between them. And they stared right through her and kept talking, even while she was grabbing their breath.

I was pretty sure they couldn't see her. And that, I thought, was weird. What were the odds on somebody like me, Tracy Kirby, C-average, fourteen-year-old girl, being able to see something other people couldn't?

The women finished their drinks and packed up and walked away. I stayed where I was, watching that woman in red, and when she drifted toward the sidewalk, I followed her.

She slipped between people on the sidewalk, or stood against windows or in doorways as others walked by, and no one turned to look at her. Weird. To me she was like a flame in the middle of ashes—

everybody else looked dull and worried and tired, and she looked like a big wildflower.

She ignored people who passed her alone, heads down, and straightened when two or more passed her, talking. Sometimes she would shadow those, reaching always for their breaths, closing her fist around white-tinted air, and then slipping her hand into her pouch.

For a while I leaned on a lamppost and watched her as she stood behind two store clerks who had stepped out for a smoke. She caught their breaths and sniffed them. Sometimes she opened her hand and let the breaths go again. From her hand, the white on the air rose like little bubbles, all round and compacted.

When the smoking clerks went back inside the store, I walked up to the woman. She didn't even look at me; I was alone and she wasn't interested in people who weren't talking.

"What are you doing?" I asked her.

She noticed me then. Her eyes were pale purple in her white, white face. Her lips were pale, too. She looked hungry.

She stared at me.

If I were smart I would have turned and walked away, pretended I hadn't talked to her. Nobody else saw her. She left alone people alone.

I didn't want to go home. I didn't want to go shopping. I didn't want to do anything to make this day like any other. I was tired of regular days.

"What are you doing?" I said again.

She cocked her head, studying me.

Maybe she couldn't talk.

"Hello?" I said. She could nod, couldn't she?

She reached out and grabbed my breath. I felt a little twinge in my throat. She slipped her hand into her red pouch. I coughed, and felt cold all over.

She smiled at me with her pale, pale lips, and turned and slipped away.

Shivering, I went into the store. The first thing for a man I saw that cost five dollars was a wide black tie with yellow happy faces all over it. I bought it, knowing Bill would hate it.

*   *   *

I couldn't get warm at home. Dinner was fish sticks and slightly burned Tater Tots. No one said anything during it. Mom and Bill didn't even talk about their days the way they used to before Roger died. If the red lady had been here, she wouldn't have found enough words to fill her pouch.

The next day was Sunday, the second day of Christmas break, and I didn't have anything to do. I didn't want to stay at home, even though Mom and Bill had gone out. No place in the house felt comfortable. I kept thinking about Roger, how he used to sit on his spot on the couch and I always had to sit in the middle—he got the arm, and Mom got the other arm; Bill had a La-Z-Boy all to himself—and even though Roger was gone, I didn't want to sit in his spot, though I had always wanted it when he was around.

I went back downtown and wandered around, looking for the red lady.

I saw her again, this time near a roast chestnut stand. It was another cold day, with steam rising from the vendor's cart, and the smell of hot chestnuts on the air. I wished I had a couple dollars to buy some, but I'd spent all my money on the two presents. So I watched other people buying chestnuts and eating them and pretended it was me.

And I saw the red lady, still hovering around people who talked. Still snatching used breath.

She wasn't so pale this time. Her cheeks had a faint pink tint, and her lips looked darker.

One conversation between a young man and a young woman kept her there a long time, grabbing. *She must like what they're saying,* I thought. And I thought about how strange and cold I had felt when she grabbed a single word from me the day before. Did they feel like that? Were they chilling as they spoke to each other? They couldn't even see her to know why they felt worse and worse, if they did.

I snuck closer.

The man and woman talked animatedly. They walked away from the vendor, sharing the newspaper cone of chestnuts they had bought. The woman in red moved along silently behind them. Seemed like they didn't feel it when she grabbed their breath.

Why was it different for me?

I followed the three of them, until the man and woman went into an apartment building and the red lady stood back. Her red velvet pouch was bulging, and she smiled wide, until she turned and saw me watching her.

I ran the other way. I didn't want her to snatch my breath as she had the day before. I ran down the sidewalk, ducking around people, and slipped into an alley when I had the chance, then hid behind a dumpster, puffing with effort. My breath rose up even though I put my mittened hands over my mouth. I felt like I was giving off smoke signals.

And it didn't matter anyway, because when I turned around, she was right there. I hadn't heard her approach. I didn't know how she had caught up with me so fast. I stood there and stared at her with the breath whistling in and out of me, and she stared back.

I didn't want to say anything. I didn't want to give her a chance to grab my breath. What was she, a breath vampire? Eww!

She waited while I caught enough breath to settle down. Just stood there, staring at me.

She had me cornered. To get away, I'd have to get her to move. She was tall and she scared me. Maybe if I waited, she would go away.

We both waited. I felt colder and colder. When I looked up into her lavender eyes, I felt like I was falling into them, so I looked away.

I checked my watch. It was only two in the afternoon. Nobody would miss me. No one would look for me. I could just freeze to death here and no one would know for hours.

"Excuse me," I said at last, walking toward her.

She let those words go without even trying for them. When I came right up to her, though, she didn't move out of the way. She touched my throat.

She had a strange look on her face, like someone

concentrating on a hard math problem. Her eyebrows were down just a little, her eyes looked out of focus, and her mouth was straight with a little frown on one side.

Her fingertips felt like freezer burn against my throat. For a second I felt like I had jumped into a pool, only to discover it was ice instead of water. It shocked and hurt, and I gasped. I tried to reach up and push her away, but I couldn't move.

Then she let go and stepped back, giving me room to escape.

I ran.

I didn't figure out what she had done to me until that night at dinner (fried corn beef hash and soggy frozen green beans). Mom said something about Christmas shopping, and I was going to say I'd finished mine, but I opened my mouth and no sound came out.

I could feel my lips move against each other and against my teeth, my tongue touch the roof of my mouth, with air moving through. No sound came out.

I tried saying other things.

I had no voice.

I panicked! I tried to shout! Nothing came out. My throat was fine for breathing, but I couldn't use my voice.

I was going to wave to get Mom's and Bill's attention. I was going to run in and get the phone message pad so I could write them a note and get them to take me to a doctor. I was going to do something about this!

Then I noticed that even though I was opening and closing my mouth and shaking my head, Mom and Bill never once turned to look at me. They just watched each other.

It was so strange. Strange I hadn't even noticed until now that my voice was gone, and strange, now, that Mom and Bill went on as if it didn't matter. They didn't notice me. When one spoke, the other answered, and as I sat there in unchosen silence, I realized I hadn't contributed a whole lot to these dinner discussions in a long time.

Even when Roger was still alive.

At dinner, Roger would talk about who was beating him up in school and what he had done in sports. Bill would give him crappy advice about standing up to bullies and congratulate him for doing stupid sports things, and I would sit and glare at my food.

I had never liked Bill. He'd been living with us for two years. Roger had learned to get along with him, but I still hated him. I never spoke to him if I could avoid it. Never paid attention to him at all. Pretty much ignored his presence as much as possible.

The same way he and Mom were ignoring me.

Well, it was going to be easy for them now.

Who needed a voice in this house?

I finished eating, cleared the table when Mom and Bill were done, and washed dishes. All the while I thought about not being able to talk. How much of a problem would it be?

In school, I usually sat right in the middle of the room, and I didn't talk much besides whispering to people near me before and after classes. I passed notes for other people when necessary, but you didn't need a voice for that. I knew there were some kids in my eighth grade classes who sat in the back of the room in every class and never talked at all. Sometimes the teachers called on them just to make sure they were awake. Then they had to talk. That might be a problem.

But I didn't have to worry about school until after New Year's Day, two weeks away. I didn't even have to think about it now.

Later that night we were watching TV. My favorite program was on channel eight, but Mom had the TV on channel seven. I tugged on her sleeve and held out my hand for the remote. "We're watching *this*,'" she said, staring at a nature program about insect communities.

I glanced at Bill, all stretched out in his La-Z-Boy. He raised his eyebrows and shrugged.

For a second I really wanted to watch my show. It was the only thing in the world I wanted. I was sure something was happening on that other channel, and if I missed it I would be stupid for the rest of my life.

I almost got up and went to the TV to change the channel manually. But then I figured, what good would that do? Mom had the remote. She would just change it back. I couldn't even try to argue her out of it.

So I slumped back and sat there a while, staring at the nature program without seeing it. Then I went upstairs, climbed into bed with all my clothes on, and fell asleep.

It was a couple of days before I went looking for the woman in red.

I tried an experiment first. How long would it take Mom and Bill to notice I wasn't talking?

Result: No one noticed. Conclusion: I could wait a long time and never get any satisfaction.

I found out I could do practically everything else I usually did without talking, too. I bought groceries for the household and smiled at the cashier when she asked me how things were going, and that seemed like enough for her. I did laundry at the Laundromat, and brought a book. Nobody even tried to talk to me. I wandered around in the streets, watching people, and realized I never talked during these wanders, either. I went down by the school and watched other kids playing on the equipment in the freezing air. I didn't need words to tell them anything. They had never noticed me when I had a voice, and they weren't going to start now.

Roger wasn't around. He was the one I had talked to about everything, and he wasn't coming back.

There were a couple of times when I really wanted to argue about something. Mom told me I was supposed to vacuum the whole house while she and Bill were at work the next morning. Normally I would have yelled, argued, and whined about this. I still would have ended up doing it, but I would have made Mom know how miserable I was.

I opened my mouth. I knew nothing was going to come out. Mom looked tired but expectant. I closed my mouth again and turned away. The next morning I sat on the couch for a while, considering whether I was going to vacuum. I hated all the dust the vacuum stirred up; it made me cough.

If I didn't vacuum, Mom would ground me.

What difference would that make?

Well . . . it wasn't like I had anything else to do.

So I vacuumed. I didn't move any furniture, or get into the corners that were sort of blocked off, but I did run the vacuum around in every room except the kitchen, which had linoleum on the floor.

The other thing I really wanted was to watch a TV movie about a little girl who made a magic wish and got the one present she really wanted for Christmas.

Mom wouldn't let me. She wouldn't give me the remote. I *did* go up and change the channel on the TV that time, but she switched it back. It wasn't even as if she was watching anything important. She just said, "Santa's going to know you're being naughty," and switched to a rerun of a show we had already seen.

With a voice, I could have argued with her, and maybe changed her mind. Sometimes that happened.

Instead I just sat there in the middle of the couch next to Roger's empty place and stared at the TV, feeling all the anger and frustration and sadness build up in me until I wanted to scream. But I couldn't. Instead, a tear ran down my face. I guess Mom saw it before I rubbed it off, because she changed the channel then. We had missed the first fifteen minutes of the movie, and that's where they put a lot of the important stuff, but I could figure it out anyway. And it made me feel good, watching that movie.

I wasn't sure I needed my voice for anything. I was getting used to working without it. But I sure missed it. Sometimes not having it made me feel so stupid. Bill said dumb things and because I didn't argue, he assumed I agreed with him. I hated that! I got so I even wanted to talk about idiot stuff, like seeing a pair of tennis shoes up in a tree while I was wandering around. How'd they get there? Why? I wouldn't even say that.

I decided to try to get my voice back.

The next morning was the day before Christmas.

It was another freezing day. I figured the red lady would be out collecting people's breath. I wondered what I could do to get her to give me back my voice. Couldn't beg and plead. No equipment.

Maybe I'd figure it out when I found her. If I ever did.

It wasn't that hard. I went to the downtown mall. Scads of people were out doing last-minute shopping. They looked fierce and frustrated, hurried and hassled. But right by the fountain, which was turned off since it was freezing, there were all these people dressed up like Christmas card people, the men in high hats and old-fashioned suits with wide-lapel jackets and pants with ribbon stripes down the sides, the women in bonnets and dresses with big skirts. They were singing carols. The lady in red was right in the middle of them, smiling wide, and collecting breaths as fast as the singers could sing.

The singers didn't get tired or stop singing, either, even though the red lady stole bunches of their breath. I couldn't figure why she hurt me and she didn't hurt other people. Just because I could see her? That didn't seem fair, or even logical.

Eventually the carolers stopped singing, and people clapped, and the singers smiled and headed somewhere else, all together, as if this was their favorite thing to do.

I watched the red lady to see if she'd follow them. Her velvet pouch was swollen like a beach ball with captured breath. She smiled and walked away from the singers down the street, and I followed her. She never looked back.

Maybe having no voice made me invisible! I had

sure felt invisible these past two days. Maybe I could use this for something.

The only idea I came up with was shoplifting. I wasn't too thrilled with that thought.

First try to get my voice back. Then, if it turned out I was invisible and there was nothing else I could do about it, *then* I would see what I could get away with.

The woman in red drifted down the sidewalk—I couldn't tell if her feet, if she had them, actually touched the ground. She was hard to keep up with, but she wasn't hard to follow, in all that red.

Eventually she ducked into a doorway. I ran, hoping the door wouldn't shut and lock itself before I reached it. It turned out to be unlocked. It had a big window in it and I peeked in. Couldn't see the lady in red, so I ducked through the door. It led right to a musty, cold stairwell that smelled like cheap stick incense. There were three mailboxes on the left wall. I stood there for a moment looking at the mailboxes, which each had doorbells under them and names handwritten onto stickers on their lids. Gaffney—Apt 1. Driscoll—Apt 2. Parole—Apt 3.

Parole was like getting out of jail. I decided to try that one. I didn't ring the bell, though, just ran right up the stairs.

At the top was a landing. The floor was wood painted black. To my left was a black door with a silver "1" on it, and straight in front of me was a green door with a silver "2" on it. To my right was a brown door with a stained-glass window in it and a gold "3" below the landscape in the window.

The landscape showed a distant castle on a green hill, and a tree to the right, all black branches and no leaves.

I went to the third door and knocked. What the heck. If someone else answered, I could just leave.

The woman in red opened the door and looked down at me. She tilted her head to the side as though asking a question and smiled faintly.

Now what? I didn't even have a pencil and a piece

of paper I could write on. I wanted to say, "Give me back my voice!" But how?

I frowned at her and put my hand over my throat.

Her eyebrows went up, and her mouth dropped open.

All my fury rose up in me then. How could she, how could *anyone,* just steal my voice? And not even recognize me later? That wasn't fair, any more than Roger dying was fair, and I had had enough of unfair things. I grabbed her arm and shook it, not even thinking about the fact that she had touched me with her hand and stolen my voice, and surely she could touch me again, anywhere she liked, and steal something else.

Her arm stiffened in my grasp. Then, even though I jerked on it with all my strength, I couldn't budge it.

She said, "Come in."

Her voice was low, and smooth as warm milk. After hearing her, all I wanted to do was come in, so I did.

Her living room was full of plants. They had vines that stretched out across the ceiling and grew across the windows. The light was stained green from their leaves against the daylight. I saw a few pieces of wicker furniture around the walls. Some of the chairs had Devil's Ivy growing over their backs. It all smelled like dirt. I wondered if she ever sat in those chairs.

I tugged on her arm and then tapped my throat.

"Perhaps," she said. Her voice was beautiful and sweet, like a ripe honeydew melon. She still wore an absentminded, faint smile, like she was humoring an idiot or a baby. I kind of wanted to slap her.

"But first you have to promise me that the first words out of your mouth are mine," she said, finally focusing on me.

How many words? What did she want me to say? Would it hurt when she took them, the way it had when she grabbed my "hello"? I wished I had been paying attention when our social studies teacher, Mrs. Winterberry, had brought a woman who taught sign language to class for an afternoon. I had a lot of questions.

"Do you promise?" asked the woman in red velvet.

I held up my free hand and wiggled my fingers at her. How many words? At least I needed to know that much. What if she got all my words for the rest of my life? Wouldn't that be the same as having no voice?

"You're free to go," she said. She slipped her arm out of my grip and turned away from me.

I could leave, without my voice, or I could stay and lose something else.

Well. I wanted my voice back. I hadn't really needed it lately, but I didn't like living without it.

I pulled on her sleeve again. The velvet was even softer than it looked.

She was so tall. She looked down at me from such a height. Angel hair, violet eyes, her face pale, not a zit in sight. Maybe she was an angel. She sure didn't act like one.

"Promise?" she asked in a thrilling voice.

I nodded.

She wrapped her pale, long-fingered hand around mine and tugged me toward a door half-hidden under tendrils of vines. The door looked old and had stuff carved on it, but I couldn't figure out what before she opened it and pulled me over the threshold into a different kind of room.

It was dark around the edges. There was a round table covered with dark velvet right in the middle of the room, with some chairs nearby. In the center of the table was a globe or a fish tank as big as a toilet, clear glass, with flowers of many-colored light blooming and fading in it. The light sent flickers dancing on the velvet and touching the shelves and shelves along the walls. I couldn't see any windows, but in the weird flickering light I saw a lot of bottles and boxes and things wrapped in paper on the shelves.

The door closed behind us. I felt like the regular world was gone now. The air in this room smelled like dust and spice. The red lady pulled me over to a chair by the round table and pressed down on my shoulder until I sat in it.

She went to a shelf and chose a bottle with a small round body and a long, thin neck. Something glowed golden through the green bottle glass, shimmering as she shook the bottle. She smiled and came back to me.

She set the bottle in my hand. The glass was cool and bumpy against my palm, not smooth like store-bought glass. There was a stopper in the mouth, with more green glass twisted into a handle. I could feel something warm through the bottle's cool skin. I lifted the bottle and stared inside at the swirling gold glitter cloud.

"When I pull the cork, you must drink quickly, or you'll never get your voice back," she said.

Drink? Drink gold glitter? What was she talking about? Did this stuff have FDA approval? Was she trying to poison me? Drug me? What was I doing in a stranger's apartment all by myself, following directions that didn't make sense?

She tugged the stopper out, and I tipped the bottle and drank down the gold glitter, wondering if I was killing myself. From invisible to dead; not a big step, anyway.

Whatever it was flowed over my tongue like warm lemonade, sizzling slightly as it went down my throat. It never reached my stomach. I coughed. "Wha—"

She had her hand out, ready. She grabbed my half a "what" before I could finish saying it.

But I *had* half-said it. I had a voice again.

With her hand still closed around whatever she had grabbed, she crossed to a different shelf and pulled down an eight-sided carved wooden box. She came back and set the box on the table, then sat in another chair right in front of me. She tilted the box lid and slipped her hand inside, then brought it back out.

"How many words?" I said, and her hands darted out, grabbing at the air in front of my mouth, even though my breath wasn't visible here. The room was cool, but not cold enough for breath to mist.

"Until I say enough," she said, shoveling something into the box and dropping the lid before it could escape.

"What do you do with them?" Wow. My own voice, moving in my throat. It felt strange and new. I had never paid attention to how it vibrated my skin, but now I touched my throat and felt the words moving through me as I said them.

This time she held out thumb and forefinger and pinched the whole question between them. I could almost see a kind of blue-green squirmy worm, its end curling up as she held it between her fingers. She slipped it into the box.

"I build things," she said.

"Like what?"

"Anything I like, once I have the right ingredients. What's your name?"

I almost answered her, the way I usually answered that question without thinking about it. But then I thought, *I say my name, she owns it. What will happen to me then?* I couldn't even imagine. So I said, "Jenny Adams," which was the name of someone I didn't like in French class.

She grabbed that one right away, held it in an open palm and stared down at it. I couldn't see anything, but it looked like she could. "A lie!" she said. She closed her hand over whatever it was and funneled it into the green bottle, then set the stopper in the neck. "Might be able to use that. Give me your name."

"No."

"Give it," she said, as she grabbed my "no."

"Nuh!" I couldn't get another "no" out. I couldn't make my mouth shape it.

She grabbed the "nuh," too. Her mouth twisted.

"What are you doing?" I whispered as she slipped my words into the box. She grabbed that question. What if I could never ask these questions again, once she got them?

Could I ever say no again?

"Your name," she said in a low, powerful voice that pushed against my cheeks.

I shook my head.

"If you could have one wish," she said, "tell me true, what would it be?"

This question was too easy, even though I was trying to be careful. "Roger," I said. My voice wasn't that loud, but in the strange stillness of the muffled, dark room, I heard my word come out of me like a big bell ringing, like a bubble blowing that just keeps getting bigger until you can't believe it doesn't pop.

She held out both her hands. She grabbed something as wide as my shoulders between them, and her eyes lit from inside with silver light.

"You can't have Roger," I said. "You can't!"

"What will you give me to get him back?" she asked.

I could almost see his shoulders between her hands, his dark head with one side shaved above them, his narrow face turning to look at me. Almost as if that car hadn't driven down our street just as Roger was running out to get his basketball. That little crooked grin shimmered in the air above her hands. Roger.

"I don't have anything," I said, and choked on a sob.

"Your name," she whispered.

I shook my head again. I didn't know what it would mean to give her my name. I didn't even know what she planned to do with Roger. If she put him in a box somewhere, would I forget I had ever known him? Would my memories of him melt? Or would I just go on the way I did now, with a big ache in my chest whenever I thought about him and how he would never come back now?

"Give me your name, and I'll give you Roger."

She couldn't give me Roger. I crushed that dream before I could start dreaming it. "Roger is dead."

"You can build him back," she said. "I'll teach you."

"Nnn," I said. She let that one go. I wondered. If she had grabbed it, would I lose my ability to say n?

"What do you want with me?" I asked. Hot fear and sorrow lodged in my throat just below my collarbone.

"I haven't decided yet."

I stared at the shadow that was almost Roger, standing quietly between her two hands. Longing rose up in me, a taste like burnt caramel against the back of my throat and a prickling behind my eyelids. "Tracy," I said.

She let go of Roger and grabbed my name. It was a gold tube about a foot long with a bend in it, and purple and pink and pale blue and green and red and gray streamers fluttered around it.

"Where's the rest of it?" she asked. Her smile lit her face. She looked happier than she had when she was grabbing carols from the singers by the fountain.

"Tracy," I said again, startled I could say something she had already grabbed, and then, "Parole."

"Ah!" A gasp whooshed out of her as she reached with her other hand, brought her palm up under a shimmering sliver bubble with iridescent streaks. It was the size of a head. Inside there was a gray, swirling cloud. "Ohhhh," she said, her eyes wide. She sat back, holding the gold tube in one hand and the bubble in the other.

Was this what a lie looked like? My "Jenny Adams" lie had been so much smaller.

After a moment when the only sound in the room was both of us breathing kind of harsh, she brought the gold tube over and touched the silver bubble with it.

Something grabbed my spine and zapped it straight, and then I was out of the chair and jerking around on the floor as if springs were spronging all through me. It hurt and it scared me, and there was nothing I could do about it. Spikes of fire and ice poked into me, burning and freezing. My teeth knocked together. I could hear and feel the thumps as I flopped against the floor. My head banged against wood. I wondered if I would die.

After a while the spasms slowed and stopped. I lay there, my mouth full of cotton, tiredness weighing me down, bruises twinging from various places. The red lady went away and came back. She helped me sit up and gave me a teacup full of something warm but not hot. I drank it. It tasted the way jasmine smelled, and it made me feel calm.

"What happened?" I asked.

She didn't grab that question. Maybe she had enough words from me. I hoped.

She stroked my hair away from my face and looked down at me tenderly. "You said a thing that might be true, so I made it true," she said. "Now you're mine."

Oh, no. Oh, no! What did *that* mean?

She kissed me on the forehead. Her lips were warm and soft. It felt good, and it made me shudder.

Gently she helped me up onto the chair. Staring at me, she touched my cheek, touched my shoulder, as if she couldn't believe I was real. Her fingers were warm. She smelled like cinnamon.

What if she wanted to do things to me like they warned us about at school? Molest me? *Never talk to a stranger.* I had thought it was just strange men I was to watch out for. I knew that whatever she wanted to do to me, she could, and I couldn't stop her. She had taken my voice and given it back. She had made me fall on the floor in fits. I belonged to her now, and there was nothing I could do about it: I had talked myself into it.

"Tracy Parole," she said in her low, thrilling voice. I felt as if there was a keyhole in my chest and those words were the key that unlocked . . . something. What? I waited, wondering if I was going to fall on the floor and start jerking again, but that didn't happen. What? What?

"I thought it might be you," she said, her warm hand tilting my chin up so that we stared into each other's eyes. "No one else has ever seen me when I was veiled." She dropped her hand and straightened. She sighed. "Now to keep my word." She took my hand. "Roger," she said.

Roger!

The shadow I had seen before stood in front of us, just his size and the outline of his shape.

Her thumb stroked over the back of my hand. "Talk about him," she said.

I described my brother.

Words came out of my mouth and shaped him right in front of us. The black hair, shaved above his right ear and long everywhere else. The crooked smile, the blue eyes, the jeans with the knees worn through and ballpoint pen graffiti all over them, the black T-shirt with a big-horned, fanged skull on it. Humor, warmth, teasing, red Converse high-tops with knots in the laces. Even his sour smell.

There he was, just the way I remembered him.

I pulled my hand free of hers and went to hug my little brother. For maybe a second he hugged me back before he dissolved into nothing.

"Hey!" I yelled, turning to glare at the red lady.

"It was your first time," she said. "You'll get better. I'll teach you."

Then she sent me home.

That night after our Christmas Eve supper of fancy TV dinners, I sat in my spot on the couch while something was on TV—this time I didn't care what—and I thought about having my arms around Roger. About him standing there in front of me. How sweet, how fast, how gone.

It wasn't really Roger.

Beside me, Mom cross-stitched a picture of a vase with flowers in it. Bill sucked on a can of beer and watched TV and yawned. Roger's empty spot was there on my other side.

"Roger," I whispered, and saw his shadow between me and the lamp on the table. He turned to watch me.

I could build him out of words. I could make him look just like he used to. If I used a photo, I could make him more real than I could just with memory. But whatever was inside—that wouldn't be Roger, would it?

I reached toward his shadow, and his shadow reached toward me. His shadow hand touched mine. He vanished.

It wasn't real, but it was something.

All those boxes and bottles the red lady had on the shelves in that room where light bloomed in a big jar.

All the words I had seen her grab. What could she build with them? Even if it was just pictures, it was something, and it seemed like something I could do now.

The day after Christmas, I knocked on the door with the stained-glass window in it. The red lady smiled and invited me in.

FAMILIAR TERRITORY

❖ ❖ ❖

by *Kristine Kathryn Rusch*

Kristine Kathryn Rusch has worked as an editor at such places as Pulphouse publishing and most recently *The Magazine of Fantasy & Science Fiction*, though she is currently a full-time writer once more. Forthcoming novels include *Hitler's Ground* and *The Fey: The Resistance*. Her short fiction appears in *Mystery Fairy Tales* and *First Contact*. A winner of the World Fantasy Award, she lives in Oregon with her husband, author and editor Dean Wesley Smith.

Every morning they went crabbing. Winston would carry the pail, and Buster would trail behind, stopping to sniff dead fish and complaining when his delicate paws sank in wet sand. Sometimes people would coo over him—they seemed drawn to a cat on the beach—but usually they would watch from a distance.

Winston knew the town thought him strange. They called him that crazy guy with the cat, and most never visited his shop. Only tourists came in, and they usually bought the mass-produced items, not his specialty items. Those he sold to select customers who never returned, although they recommended the store to their friends. He did a steady mail order business, shipping weekly all over the United States, Canada, and Europe.

He didn't care about the money. It was merely a way to maintain his warm and cozy home, built on a cliff overlooking the sea. He had worn a path from

he back door to the beach near the small town of
Seavy Village, and he and Buster tramped down the
path daily at first light, crabbing if the tides allowed,
and playing in the sand until nine A.M. Then Winston
returned home, showered, and drove to his shop on a
decrepit section of Highway 101. Buster complained
about the drive, but flirted with the customers shame-
essly while Winston studied his books behind the
counter.

It was a small life, as magic ones went, but it was
his, his and Buster's. They had shared it since Winston
fled San Francisco twenty years before and arrived in
Seavy Village to find the cliff house for sale, and a
rain-soaked kitten who spoke perfect English huddled
beside its front door.

Only this morning, Buster didn't wake up. He remained curled at the foot of the bed, eyes half open,
skin already cool. They had known the end was coming—few cats made it to twenty and remained as
healthy as Buster—but they hadn't thought it so soon.
Kind of Buster to wait until Monday, the only day the
shop was closed.

Winston put his hand on Buster's still black-and-
white side, and wished that instead of all his tiny powers, he had a single large one: the power over death.

But he didn't, and he never would. He sighed once,
cradled his best and only friend for a long time, and
then padded into his workshop to build a ship.

Buster had requested a Viking funeral.

The cat, being 90% feline and only 10% familiar,
didn't care about state regulations regarding the
ocean. He didn't care that it was against the law to
throw anything into the waves. He didn't care that
Oregon hated people tossing the *ashes* of loved ones
onto the sea, and would probably charge Winston with
a felony for tossing a dead body in.

You can cover it, boss, Buster had said. *Use a small
spell, a shield or something, to make sure nobody
sees you.*

I thought cats hate the water, Winston replied, a tad grumpily.

You observe, but you don't see, Buster said. *Cats love the water. They just hate to get wet.*

You'll get wet with a Viking funeral.

Naaaw, Buster said. *I'll be ashes by the time I hit the water.*

Why do you want a Viking funeral? Winston asked.

Buster had looked at him from his perch on top of an end table. The look implied that Winston knew nothing about cats. *Blaze of glory, my friend,* Buster had said. *Blaze of glory.*

What Winston knew about Viking funerals came from his English Lit class in high school over three decades before; half a dozen old movies; and a program he had fallen asleep to on the History Channel. Some of the Arthurian myths had Merlin give Arthur a Viking death; the proud king, wrapped in his fur robes, heading out to sea in his burning boat. Winston had made the mistake of telling Buster that story one rainy afternoon when they should have been mixing a love potion for a woman in Puget Sound.

Buster had adored the idea.

Winston didn't like the parallels. Buster was supposed to be his familiar, not his king, and while Winston had clear talents, he was no Merlin. No wizard had been that great in over a thousand years.

But in the time they had been together, Winston had only denied Buster one thing—(*Neutered, boss. Neutered. You know what that sounds like? Sounds like nullified. How would you like it if I neutered you?*)—he had done that for Buster's safety, and for the sanity of all the female cats in Seavy Village. Buster had mellowed as he got older, when he saw the effects sex had had on the wild toms. *The fights they get into,* Buster had said, *and all over a woman who'll slap 'em when she's done.* Somewhere around the age of ten, Buster realized that his sex drive would have shortened his life, and while he never admitted that Winston had made the right decision, he had stopped focusing on it.

Buster loved his life near the sea, with the storms and the fish and the adoration of the tourists who filled Winston's shop in the summer.

Buster loved all twenty years of it, and who was Winston to deny him his final request?

The ship, when finished, was two yards long, and two feet high at its lowest point. A dragon's head with oddly feline features rose from the front to guide the ship on her way. Winston had made little holes throughout which he would stuff with gas-soaked rags when the time came. He'd also lined the hollowed-out center with newspaper and kindling. Over that, he had built a box long enough and wide enough to hold Buster. He placed Buster's favorite pillow in the front of the box, and around it he put all of Buster's toys.

It had taken him twenty-four hours of concentrated work to finish. Twenty-four hours in a cold house, his fingers raw from strain. He had let the fire die and had turned down the heat so that Buster's body wouldn't decay quite as rapidly. Still, twenty-four hours wasn't enough to do this kind of work unassisted. He had to use four craft spells, one no-doze spell, and contact the restless souls of three shipbuilders to help in the process.

He was so tired his body hummed.

But it was finished, and it was as perfect as he could make it. Now all he had to do was rig the hand-sewn sail, wait till the tide was going out, and find a friendly current.

The morning dawned clear and cold with no real wind. A few fluffy white clouds dotted the sky. From his window, he saw the telltale green-gold line of a riptide, and he knew this would be his best chance to send Buster out to sea. Winston placed his friend in the ship, stretched his limbs (thankful that rigor had eased) and set his head gently on his pillow. Then

Winston stuffed a bag full of rags and tied it to his belt. He carried the ship outside.

The chill was brisk, waking him from the exhaustion that clouded his eyes. He needed enough strength to finish this, and the chill gave him some. He balanced the ship under one arm, making certain the weight was right, and picked up the half full gasoline can. And with his burden, he walked down the path to the beach.

His hair rippled in the ever-present breeze, but it wasn't strong enough to be considered a wind. The beach was a winter beach, strewn with rocks, the sand hard-packed and firm. He stopped for a moment on his favorite spot, a flat black lava rock that stood a bit back from the surf. Then he climbed beside it, set the boat and gas can down, and gazed at Buster.

Buster's sleek dark fur shone in the sunlight. He was a beautiful cat. It seemed odd for his features to be so still; even in sleep he had moved—a whisker twitch here, a kneading paw there. Winston touched him, ever so lightly, and felt the lifelessness, the lack of breath, the lack of vitalness.

"I miss you already, buddy," he whispered.

Then he sighed, and prepared to work.

The beach was empty. Even so, he took Buster's advice and made a shield spell, placing it around him, the ship, and the stretch of beach and water extending to the riptide line. He removed the rag bag from his belt, opened the gasoline can, and carefully soaked each rag in gasoline. After a rag was soaked, he shoved it into the holes he had prepared. When he finished, he capped the gasoline, and carried the ship to sea.

Even with the sail and the riptide, there was no way the ship would go into the ocean alone. It would get caught in the tide, and hug the shore. Buster had wanted what they both had imagined to be a Viking funeral; it meant disappearing on the horizon in a burning ship. Despite his exhaustion, Winston had one more thing to do.

He waded into the surf, wincing as the cold water

made goose pimples run up and down his skin. Then
he set the ship on the water's surface, and blew lightly,
mouthing a wind spell as he did so. The sail filled up,
and the ship moved forward, slicing the waves like a
ship of old.

Buster would have been proud.

Winston waited until the ship reached the riptide
line, then he snapped his fingers, reciting a simple fire
spell. Sparks touched the soaked rags, and the ship
ignited. It continued to sail forward, dragon's head
proudly leading the way as it headed to the horizon.
Plumes of smoke rose from it, and the flames licked
the sky.

A blaze of glory.

He wished he had been able to do it at twilight, as
the sun was setting. Such a magnificent sight it would
have been then, but he couldn't, since his powers often
waned at dusk.

Still, Buster would have enjoyed it. The burning
ship sailing toward eternity.

Winston stood in the surf, the water numbing his
feet and ankles, and watched as the flames consumed
the dragon's head. The air smelled of smoke and sea
salt.

Was this what Merlin smelled that twilight so long
ago? Or had he turned his back on the burning ship,
walked across the land, and gone back to his life?

The ship broke apart in a spray of sparks. Pieces
burned on the water's surface, then sank slowly, the
dragon's head disappearing last.

For a moment, the black smoke mingled with the
white clouds, and formed a black-and-white cat running toward the horizon.

Then the smoke dissipated, and Buster was gone.

Winston cleaned up his mess, broke his shield spell,
and carried the gas can back up the path. He showered, ate a small breakfast, and napped until he had
to leave to open his shop.

By the time he got up, clouds were rolling in. The
horizon looked blurred. Rain wouldn't be far behind.

He drove his ancient Gremlin the two miles down Highway 101. The rusted and battered car seemed like an affectation without Buster inside, paws on the dash, tail wagging as he watched the passing traffic. Winston had always worried that Buster would die in a slow-speed collision, something that could have been prevented if the cat had but listened and sat under the dash.

But, as Buster had always said, he was 90% feline and 10% familiar. He followed rules only when he made them.

Winston parked behind the shop and reached for the passenger side before he could stop himself. He drew back, and left the car empty-handed.

The shop was cold and damp. It smelled of incense and cat food. He turned on the lights, lit the candles, and sat behind the large counter, wondering who would flirt with the customers now. He couldn't. He had never been as social as Buster. Or as friendly.

What was a wizard without a familiar? His mouth went dry. He had gone without a familiar in the early years, as he apprenticed, and then went out on his own. He had claimed to his master, a disaffected beatnik, that he didn't like animals. His master had shrugged.

You will, he had said.

His master's familiar was a five-year-old sow that he had special permission to keep inside the city limits. She had been the opposite of Buster: grumpy, antisocial, and nasty. Winston had vowed then not to take on another soul.

And then had gone out on his own. After two months, his potions spoiled, his bottled spells rotted, and a young woman who had special-ordered an aphrodisiac had nearly died. Fortunately she hadn't yet shared it with her boyfriend, and he had gotten her to the emergency room. The cops had thought it a drug overdose, and had thought Winston the supplier. He had left San Francisco in a dead run, stopping only when he saw Seavy Village and its Gothic landscape.

Two days later, he had the house and Buster.

And he never made a mistake again.

He put his head in his hands. The nap hadn't helped. He felt lethargic. The bell tinkled, indicating the arrival of a customer, but he didn't have enough energy to look, to see who it was.

"Excuse me," a woman's voice said.

He looked up. His next door neighbor, the owner of an antique store, hovered inside his doorway. She was a pear-shaped woman whose pink polyester pants and white shirts only emphasized the flaws in her figure. She always went out of her way to be kind to him, and he was kind in return, but they'd never had more than a passing familiarity with each other.

"I—I—." She waved a hand at the door. "I was wondering. The magic and all. Did you see the burning ship this morning? It's all over town. People are calling it a ghost ship."

A shiver ran through him. He stood, then gripped the countertop, and nearly sat again. Were they coming for him so soon? Did the spells curdle without a familiar?

"Did you see it?" he asked.

She nodded. "I—ah—we—"

And then he realized that half a dozen people crowded outside his shop door.

"We thought maybe you had an explanation."

"Did you call the Coast Guard?"

"They had no record of a vessel. They scanned the waters and found nothing. No one radioed a distress call. They thought we were making it up."

He tried not to swallow hard. He was trembling. *The whole city saw you blaze, Buster,* he thought.

"Did you see it?" she asked again.

He nodded.

"Was it a ghost ship?"

How to formulate an answer that was honest and yet maintained the mystery? "I don't count something as a ghost unless it appears in the same location more than once," he said.

"If it wasn't a ghost, what was it?" she asked. "It didn't seem quite real somehow."

"It was real enough," he said. "There was a cat in the smoke."

"Yes!" she said. "A black-and-white one. He looked quite satisfied with himself."

Winston smiled. "He did, didn't he?"

She smiled in return, and then her smile faded. "What do we do if we see it again?"

Ah, the real purpose for her visit. Not just comfort, but comfort magic. "It depends," he said. His trembling hand stopped. Somehow it relieved him that someone else had seen Buster's farewell.

"Depends?"

"On whether or not you want to exorcise the ghost or use it to promote Seavy Village."

"Promotion." She rubbed a hand on her chin. "Hmm. A ghost ship. It looked rather Viking-like to me, but they didn't come up this far, did they?"

"I honestly don't know," he said.

"And it was burning. I wonder if any ships went down that way in the harbor. Do you know?"

He shook his head.

She glanced around his shop, her gaze taking in the crystals and the globes, the incense burners and the bottles of potion lining the walls. "I tell you what," she said. "If I discover anything, I'll let you know. It'd be quite a boon to your business."

He hadn't thought of that. "Thanks," he said, unable to keep the surprise out of his voice.

"Don't mention it," she said. "I'll be back when I know something."

And then she let herself out. She explained things to her friends out front, her hands moving expansively. Rain interrupted her small speech, and the crowd dispersed.

The day turned out to be one of the busiest he'd ever had. Fifteen phone orders for potions, twenty-five mail orders for specialty items, and six customers, all of whom bought. The last told him that a store like his needed a cat, and he had said softly, *I know.*

By the time he left, the rain had turned into a

squall. One of those coastal storms that Buster had so loved. Winston was glad he hadn't waited for twilight. The storm was too severe. He never would have gotten the ship afire.

The Gremlin coughed its way home. He would have to think of getting another car. Too bad the car companies no longer used magic items in their names. But he had kept the Gremlin far too long. Her usefulness had passed.

He put her in the driveway, and sighed. The day had been so busy that he hadn't had a chance to mix the new potions, let alone put up the "closed" sign for a few hours while he visited the local pound. He doubted any of the cats there would talk to him, but he had to see. He couldn't believe that Buster would leave without planning for a successor. Buster had always been too meticulous to leave any detail untended.

Winston grabbed his umbrella, opened the car door, then opened the umbrella outside, stepping into a puddle as he got out. He cursed softly—his feet had gotten wet enough this day—and then he ran the few yards to the back porch.

In his haste to get inside, he almost missed it. The tiny black cat, fur spiked by rain and wind, huddled against the woodpile. For a moment, he thought it was Buster. Not the old Buster, but the baby Buster come back. And then he realized that this kitten was all black. It had no white at all.

He crouched, letting the umbrella protect them both, and held out his hand. The kitten came forward and sniffed his fingers. Then it looked around. When it saw he was alone, it said, "You could at least offer a girl some fish."

Her voice was sultry and not childlike at all. Buster had also come kitten-sized, but with his voice and personality full grown.

"I have some inside," Winston said. He opened the door, and the kitten trotted in as if she owned the place. She went to the cool fireplace and shook the water off her fur. Winston closed the umbrella outside, and then put it in its holder. He went immediately to the refrigerator. He had some salmon he had planned to make for dinner the night Buster had died.

He took the salmon out and picked some pieces off it, putting them on a small plate. As he worked, he glanced at the fireplace. The kitten was cleaning herself, making her black coat lie flat.

Then, because he couldn't remain silent, he asked, "Did Buster send you?"

"What do you think we got—a referral service?" she asked.

Her gruffness shocked him. He wasn't ready for gruffness yet. He wasn't ready for a new personality, a new life.

A small body wrapped itself around his leg, and a purr so strong it vibrated his skin echoed up to him.

"You just want the fish," he said.

"You bet," she said.

He set the plate down and she ate quickly, without Buster's innate grace. She had been hungry for some time.

When she finished, she sat back on her haunches and glared at him.

"What's your name?" he asked.

"Ruby," she said.

"Ruby, I don't know if I'm ready for another familiar."

"You can't go without, big boy. We keep your spells fresh, and your mind from wandering."

"It took me years to find Buster," Winston said.

"He knew," she said. "And he figured you could last maybe a day alone."

"I thought you said you didn't know him."

"I never said anything like that." She stood, arched, and yawned. "We all know each other. Familiar doesn't come from your magic practices. It comes from ours. Buster had a feeling you and I'd work out. And if this fish is any indication, he was right." She tilted her head and narrowed her eyes. "But don't get any ideas about burning me at sea."

"I think we have a few years before we need to discuss your funeral."

"Good." She sauntered toward the fireplace. "Now, how about a real fire so a girl can nap?"

He snapped his fingers and a fire appeared in the grate.

"Real," she growled.

"As you wish, Your Highness," he said, hurrying toward the pile of logs beside the fireplace. She had already curled up on the rug. She was different, and, for all her big talk, she was tiny. She would never replace Buster. No one could. But she'd make the world a little less lonely.

"Do you like clams?" he asked.

"Only in the mornings," she replied.

"I go clamming with the morning tides. Should be just after dawn tomorrow."

"I'll make sure you're up," she said sleepily. Then she opened one yellow eye. "Finished that fire yet?"

"I will," he said, feeling lighter than he had all day. He built her a tiny blaze. One to keep her toasty and safe, and to let her know she was welcome in his small life. His small, magic life.

SPELLCHUCKER

❖❖❖

by John DeChancie

John DeChancie has written more than seventeen novels in the science fiction, fantasy, and horror fields, including the acclaimed Castle series, the most recent of which, *Bride of the Castle*, was published in 1994. He has also written dozens of short stories and nonfiction articles, appearing in such magazines as *The Magazine of Fantasy and Science Fiction*, *Penthouse* and many anthologies. In addition to his writing, John enjoys traveling and composing and playing classical music.

A world with a buttermilk sky. The city, Malnovia, sprawled in the warm southern climate, its spires and cupolas awash in wizardry. Malnovia, magic capital of the land, and all hopeful wizards pilgrimaged here.

The sign on the shiny black-lacquered door read:

SOLEMN UNIFIED BROTHERHOOD
OF WIZARDS

Young Zane stood regarding it. He detected a subtle spell lurking about the door, one doubtless requiring nullification in order for the door to open. A test. A test for any young aspirant who harbored any hope of joining the Brotherhood, without whose auspices one would have a difficult time finding work as a wizard in this town.

There were non-Brotherhood wizards about, Zane knew, but they tended to work at slave wages, and were in other ways shamefully exploited.

He mounted the two-stepped porch and studied the door. The spell was wizardly complex and tricky, of course, but it was of a magic thoroughly familiar. He was mildly surprised, having expected something rather more challenging. But finding only this little textbook problem barring his way buoyed hope that he could crack the Brotherhood, one of the most exclusive fraternities around.

Looking up at the milky-yellow sky, he mentally prepared himself. The counterspell he had in mind was mental only, requiring no incantation or inscribed magical device. He stepped back to the sidewalk, checking the street in both directions. No one about, no passersby to gawk or be dismayed. A good time. Might as well get right to it.

Back to the door, he furrowed his brow. Then he whirled sharply in a half-turn, throwing out his right hand, fingers spread.

With a snick and a *spung!,* the door swung back a little from the jamb and stood ajar.

"Right."

He mounted the porch, entered the building, and found a narrow hallway ending in a T with another passage. He shut the door. Echoes reverberated spookily, as in a vast cavern.

A shiver went through him. Maybe this was too easy? He stepped cautiously down the corridor, and at the T checked right and left. He chose right.

He traversed more and more corridors before finally deciding, yes, this was indeed a maze, and he had no clue how to get out. Another test, surely. But he was still confident.

No windows, but there was light. Whence—?

As if reading his thoughts, the light faded, and he found himself treading through pitch darkness. He bumped up against a wall.

"Blast."

Groping, he felt nothing but walls in every direction. Summoning his skills, he caused a small flame to gutter from the end of his right index finger, but hungry darkness around him soaked up the light. He saw not much of anything, nor any direction in which to proceed.

He did see the outline of something, though, standing not far away. Whatever it was, it had crimson eyes. These glowed. Then he saw the glint of predatory teeth.

"Charming."

He swallowed hard, though he had anticipated the test would not be a breeze.

The thing in the darkness yowled chillingly, advancing with heavy steps. He flicked his finger flame, turning it into a white-hot jet, which he directed at the target. The lurching thing summarily exploded. A shower of light debris fell on him. Chitin, shattered bits of it. He brushed himself off and proceeded down the corridor, which now came dimly into view.

Another door, this one of massive oak trimmed with wrought iron. It looked formidable, but when he tried a variation of the door-opening spell, he was pleasantly surprised to see the oak barrier slide to the right as if on bearings, revealing an anteroom filled with people sitting on comfortable leather chairs, reading journals.

People looked up. He stepped in and received a round of applause along with voiced commendations.

"Stout fellow!"

"Bravo!"

The bald, white-bearded clerk sitting at a desk on the far side of the room rose, clapping enthusiastically, smiling effusively. Zane approached him.

"Well done, young wizard! Well done indeed. And your name?"

"Zane. Zane of Hammind. I wish to join the Brotherhood."

"Of course! With such talent, the Brotherhood would be happy to have you."

"They would?" Zane was at a loss for words. Never had he expected the process to be this easy.

"You have your completed application, I suppose?"

Zane fished out a rolled paper from his side pocket, handed it over, then fished again.

The clerk took the paper and unfurled it. "Good, good. You come highly recommended. And your sample spell, written out in standard format?"

"I have it here," Zane said, finally producing another rolled paper.

"Excellent! What a pleasure to see such masterly work by one so young." The clerk glanced over the page of neatly inscribed symbols. "Daring! Very daring indeed. Trailblazing work."

"I have a number of innovations which I'm eager—"

"You have a unique style, sir!"

Zane's face lit up with expectation and greed for praise. "You really think it's good?"

The clerk eyed him levelly. "I did not know such thaumaturgy was possible."

"You flatter me."

"Not in the least."

"I suppose I should take a seat. Is the wait long?"

"Not for the likes of you, sir. This way. A special waiting room for unusual talents such as yourself. Presently you'll be ushered into the office of the Chief Steward."

"Really? I had no idea."

Envious eyes followed Zane and the clerk out of the room. Zane was led down a short passageway.

"They're mostly tyros, hopelessly amateurish," the clerk said huffily. "You don't belong with them."

"I must say, this is going more splendidly than I had ever hoped."

"Right through that door, sir. Enter and help yourself to refreshments."

"I am a bit peckish at that," Zane said, backing through the door. "Listen, thank you ever so much. This is marvelous, really—"

Suddenly, the room, the clerk, and the interior of the building vanished, and he found himself suspended in midair, outside the building. He dropped into a garbage pile in the back alley.

Unhurt, and after thrashing his way out of debris,

he looked up at the back wall of the building. Blank stone, no door visible. No window.

*   *   *

The outdoor café was just down the street.

"Yours?"

"Mulled wine, double portion."

The waiter sniffed. "Ah. Been up to the Brotherhood, I see."

"How did you know?"

The waiter daintily plucked a lemon rind from Zane's shoulder and tossed it out into the street.

Zane scowled and said dryly, "Thank you."

"We all fell for that one."

"We?"

"I wait tables for a living, but what I really want to do is wizardry."

'I confess to the same aspirations, though apparently I lack the requisite skill. I smelled the trash all right, but got not one whiff of that illusion spell."

"It's a recondite one. You fell right under it, and right out into the alley."

"Obviously."

"As I said, we've all been through it."

"Was I really in the building?"

"Perhaps. I wasn't there, so . . ."

"Wait." Zane dug into his pocket. He pulled out two rolled sheets. "Blast! I really never did give them my stuff."

The waiter guffawed. "You've been had."

Mortified, Zane repocketed them. "Thanks for your kind help."

"Sorry, friend. You'll get in eventually, but it takes some doing. Took me three years."

"You're in the Brotherhood? But—" Zane looked him up and down in puzzlement.

"Once in, the trick then is getting steady work. Most of the membership sits idle most of the time, if you didn't know."

"I didn't. And you?"

"Oh, I get a job only now and then, but I'm optimistic. I'm working on a developmental project for a new agricultural spell. I'm hoping to option it to a magic merchant."

"I wish you success. By the way, my drink?"

The waiter left Zane steeping in sour thoughts. When he returned with the wine, he had this comment. "Find a manager."

"But managers take forty percent."

"As they say, forty percent of something substantial is better than one hundred percent of nothing."

"How does one go about acquiring a manager?"

"Well, it's difficult. Most won't waste time with tyros. Now, if you had a development contract, say, with a major magic merchant, then you might be able to interest a manager in handling you."

"But you can't get a job like that without a manager. Am I right?"

"Right as reindeer. Unless you were a Brotherhood member."

"You can't get a job without Brotherhood membership, and you can't get membership without a job. You can't get a job without a manager, and you can't get a manager without first acquiring a job."

"Excellent! You are perceiving the facts of reality here."

Zane thumped a fist onto the table. "It doesn't make sense!"

The waiter shook his head slowly. "Noooo," he said, as if expressing an opinion on the chance of rain that afternoon.

"I've got to get inside that building!" Zane said, more to himself than anyone.

"Work on your magic," the waiter advised.

He worked on his magic, consulting old grimoires in dusty libraries. The city had an endless number of such facilities.

"Right," he said to himself as he approached the Brotherhood house once more. "They are going to find out they don't know who they're dealing with."

The door *spung*ed open, and he stepped in, slamming the door behind him. The echoes were deafening. He shouted above the din: "I'm back!"

The lights doused, the demon charged out of the darkness.

Whoosh!

He brushed flecks of singed chitin off his cloak as he stamped down the corridor. The people in the anteroom were the same and sat in exactly the same positions, or so he suspected, and they applauded as loudly. The clerk's smile was as effulgent as before. Zane approached him, waving off the applause.

"Well done, young wizard! Well done, indeed. And your name?"

"Same as it was two days ago. Zane of Hammind, and don't think I'm gulled by this puppet show."

"Why . . . what are you referring to?"

"The spell that weaves this simulacrum of reality even as we speak. You might as well cancel it. I'm not fooled."

The clerk's countenance fell. He shrugged narrow shoulders, then smiled sheepishly. "You've nailed us."

"You could at least have run a different variation."

"The spell trips more or less automatically. But you've penetrated the veil of illusion. And I must admit it takes some strength of character to stand there and deny the bogus reality that surrounds you."

Zane stared at him imperiously. "Well, are you going to cancel it. Or shall I?"

"Be my guest."

"Very well."

Zane made wide circles with both arms simultaneously. Once around, twice, thrice, finishing with a flourish. "Done!"

Zane turned. The anteroom was now empty.

The clerk, however, was still present, smiling with equanimity. "Very deft. You do have talent. You know . . ."

"Yes?"

Brow furrowed, the clerk stroked his hairy chin. "You *just* might qualify for our apprentice program."

"Really? That would be . . . well . . . I don't think

of myself as on the apprentice level. I've had loads of experience, out in the provinces."

"Provinces, yes. Well, you see, that's all to the good, but provincial experience isn't exactly—"

"I would be glad to sign up for the apprentice program," Zane hastened to say.

"Splendid. Now, you must make a general application to the Brotherhood."

Zane sneered. "That old ploy."

"No, you've abrogated the spell."

"Oh, very well," Zane said uncertainly as he drew out the two rolled sheets. "But I don't intend to go through this mummery a third time."

The clerk grinned. "You've shown that you are not easily warded off by magical means. Come this way. I will see if the Chief Steward can interview you now."

"That would be most amenable," Zane said with a triumphant grin. "I'm going to give him a piece of my mind about this illusion business. Young aspirants should not be treated in such fashion."

"Sir, you don't appreciate the sheer number of aspirants we get coming through the front portal. Hundreds a day, sometimes. They veritably clog the entrance. We must do something to weed out the amateurs."

"Of course, but one needs to prepare for a test of skill. One must know it is coming."

"Part of the test, the surprise."

"I suppose so," Zane said grudgingly. "Oh, I suppose it's all worked out for the best. Still, I will mention it to the Steward."

"You've pluck, too. Excellent. I wish you good fortune. We must get together for a meal sometime, if I am not being too forward."

"Love to. Doubtless you could tip me a tip or two."

"I could indeed. Let's have lunch tomorrow."

"I'd be delighted."

"And here we are. The Steward's office. Bide a moment, and I will ask if he will see you."

The clerk opened the door and walked into a huge, lavishly appointed office. Behind an immense oak desk sat the Chief Steward, dressed in traditional wizard's garb—robes and a conical hat. He rose at the sight of Zane just beyond the threshold. He smiled warmly and beckoned an invitation.

"Steward, allow me to present a very promising young man . . . uh . . . ?"

"Zane of Hammind."

"Zane of Hammind! He seeks admission to our apprentice program."

"Welcome, Zane of Hammind," the Steward said. "Enter."

"At last we meet," Zane said, taking one step. . . .

He plunged headfirst into the alley.

"Blast!"

Batting his way out of the pile of reeking refuse—he spat out an apple peeling and brushed crushed nutshells from his cloak. The best course was to remain calm. No need for a display of temper. No tantrums, please.

He viciously kicked a wooden crate to splinters. Then he threw an empty bottle against the side of the Brotherhood building. The shattered glass tinkled satisfactorily.

"I need a drink."

Remembering, he checked his pocket. The two sheets, his application and sample spell, were still snug inside.

His face turned dark. "Damn them to a hell freshly made."

"They encapsulated spells on you," the waiter opined.

"Encapsulated?"

"Yes. You abrogated their illusion spell, only to have another spell underneath you that tripped when the first fizzled. More wine?"

"Please."

"Warm today, is it not?"

"Yes. Tell me, do you know how many spells they usually have, one inside the other, like nesting dolls?"

The waiter lifted his shoulders. "No telling, really."

Zane's shoulders fell. "I shall have to read up on illusion generally."

"Yes. Something to munch on before you go back to the library?"

Zane came striding into the anteroom.

"Well done, young wiz—"

Zane cut the clerk off with a peremptory gesture. "Enough! I have pierced all your illusions. Like a needle through concentric soap bubbles."

"Really."

"Really. Here is my application." The rolled paper went into the clerk's outstretched palm with a solid thwack. "Here is my sample spell." A second thwack. "Now, let me do a quick reality check."

"A what?"

Zane snapped his fingers.

Instantaneously, he found himself back outside the building, on the sidewalk in front. He checked his side pocket. The papers were not there. He snapped his fingers again.

He was back inside, facing a puzzled clerk.

"Ah, hah! Got you! I know those are the real papers and that I've really given them to you. You must process them."

The clerk grinned. "I must. That finger-snapping business. You disappeared."

"Yes. I built a null hiatus into the spell. For a second, I was totally outside any magical influence, and could check on the facts. I checked. You have my application, I will expect you to act on it soon. And as I read the bylaws of this organization, you can't turn me down for no good reason."

The clerk threw up his hands. "We capitulate, sir! You've bested us."

Zane jabbed a warning finger. "The truth, now."

"No, no, no," the clerk said, shaking his head and laughing. "This . . ." There intervened an embarrassed giggle. "This is rock hard reality. No foolery now, sir. No. You've done it. I've never seen it done better. I think . . . oh, I should think journeyman status for you, sir."

"Journeyman wizard." Zane beamed. "That would be fine."

"Don't worry about the application," said the clerk, laying the papers carefully on his desk. "A formality. Would you care to go to the club room and meet some of your fellows? Take a drink, smoke a pipeful . . . ?"

"Certainly."

"This way."

"No tricks."

"No, I mean *really*." He grabbed the clerk's shirt-front more in a pleading gesture than a threat. "No tricks?"

"None. This way, sir."

"I never noticed this door before. Oh, my."

A room full of men and women, smoke writhing around the chandelier, a full bar, smells of good food, a fire going in the fireplace.

"Greetings!" the bartender called, waving. "What'll you have?"

"You must be good," said a man in a wide-brimmed hat, "to've been sent straight through to the club. Are you?"

"I have one or two novel techniques," Zane allowed.

"My name's Farlo. Let me introduce you to a few of your colleagues. First let me shake your hand."

Zane reached for Farlo's huge outstretched mitt . . .

. . . and fell straight into the cesspool in the vacant lot behind the Brotherhood.

He splashed out. Gingerly, he felt his pocket. The papers. Oh, yes, still there.

"Blast."

"More than an illusion. A pocket-reality spell, likely," the waiter at the café ventured, wrinkling his nose. "You were whisked into a side-pocket existence with its own set of actualities. The spell encapsulated any and all spells you could cast."

"I see," Zane said, sipping mulled wine. "Such wizardry is subtle indeed."

"Oh, yes."

"I've never cast a pocket-reality spell. Tell me, is the victim empocketed bodily?"

"Oh, yes. He disappears from workaday reality. Nifty way of abducting someone, isn't it? You never know you're bagged."

"It could be put to criminal use, if the Brotherhood's use isn't criminal in itself."

"They unbagged you quick enough. They could have kept you in there indefinitely, you know. As to the criminal aspect—uh, I wouldn't waste my time filing a complaint with the constabulary."

"I shan't," Zane said sourly. "But I shall study up on the particulars of these enchantments, and have at the buggers once again."

"There's a stalwart soul. Never say die. Mmm, but of course, they might simply have taken a dislike to you."

"Eh?"

"It happens. The Steward has been watching you, you know. As have the Board of Trustees, and the Emeritus Council. They keep an eye on everyone who tries for membership. They may have decided—sorry, old fellow, but it must be said—they may simply have decided that you haven't got what it takes to be a wizard in this town. In which case, you'll never get in."

"Nevertheless, I shall have at them again. I shall study more, and try again. And again, and again, for as long as it takes." Zane slapped down a coin, got up, and walked off.

Watching him recede, the waiter grinned. "Like his spirit. Dumb as dirt, but I do like his spirit."

He studied nights; he studied days, when he was not working odd jobs. He studied while on the job, he studied while eating; he studied lying in bed at night.

His garret room filled with books of magic. He spent most of his income on them. What lore he did not find in them he scavenged from other books, in libraries that charged reading or lending fees.

He practiced magic, and became adept at spells arcane and subtle. Once he cast a spell that gave him a gourmand's feast of a free meal in one of the city's finest restaurants. No one detected him, and he was proud of himself; though he did not risk that one again, lest he attract attention.

His aim was not to cadge free meals. His aim was to be a wizard in Malnovia, city of wizards. To do that, he had to be admitted to the Solemn Brotherhood. He remained quite fixed on that objective.

However, as he amassed expertise and acumen as well as books and manuals, wisdom settled in, along with some perspective. At length, he came to a sobering realization.

He was not as good as he had imagined. No, the truth had to be faced. He had to acknowledge the possibility that he was exactly what the Steward and the Boards likely thought him: a provincial spell-chucker who could barely manage a shoo-fly charm to clear out a pantry.

But this realization did not daunt him or deter him from striving toward his goal. He studied on, and practiced daily. He tried and succeeded at invisibility spells, teleportation spells, transformation spells, power spells, and, yes, pocket-reality spells, a mild version of which he tried on his waiter friend. Except for a moment's befuddlement after the spell was quickly canceled, the waiter never suspected.

At last Zane was ready. After three weeks' work, he came up with a spell design that had a chance of competing with the best of what the Brotherhood had to throw against him. It was a fiendishly complicated enchantment, with hidden sidebars, secret adjuncts, fall-back supports, and insurance clauses. It took no less than three devilishly difficult inscribed magical devices—for which he vandalized his apartment (part of the design had to be scorched into the wood of the floor with a bar of heated meteoritic iron that cost him a month's wages—no matter, he wouldn't be back, come what may—if this enterprise failed, he was off back to Hammind, with his tail between his legs). These pentagrams completed, checked, and rechecked, he was ready to leave for another frontal assault on the Brotherhood's headquarters.

He approached the wizards' compound cautiously, checking the sky—it was a clear yellow-white (a reflected glow caused by the excess of magic below). No bad weather brewing to upset the cosmic balance.

He assessed the magic around the premises with a practiced eye. When he'd first arrived, he had vastly and naively misjudged the place. The protective spells girding this fortress were a marvel to behold, if one had the sight to behold them. Knot after knot piled one upon the other. Concentric screens of energy. Tensions, apprehensions, and dissensions stacked and linked and staggered. Interlocking rings of power. Perimeters of death and dismay.

He took a deep breath, and mounted the porch. Not stopping to unlock the door, this time he walked like a specter right through it.

On the other side, a confusing series of images flickered in and out of existence. Light waxed and waned, and quick impressions of rooms and furnishings appeared and faded. He glided through partition after partition.

Finally, he found himself coming out of the back wall of the anteroom. Before him sat the clerk, busily scribbling on foolscap at his desk.

The clerk looked up, looked around, then bent again to this work. Finally, sensing something, he spun in his swivel chair.

"Who the devil are you?" he asked of Zane.

"You ask yet again?"

"I've never . . . oh, I see." The clerk carefully put down his quill pen.

Zane nodded. "I know full well you've never clapped eyes on me, but that is no matter. Here are my papers. Take them, please. I am eager to be shut of them once and for all."

"Papers," the clerk said. "Hmmm. How the devil

did you get in here? And what are you doing ghosting
about like that?"

"A bit of magic I worked up. Magic, my stock in
trade. Which is why I must join your venerable
organization."

"I suppose you must," the clerk said wearily.

"Now. Unless you want me to change you into a
toad—"

The clerk gave him an acerbic look. "Try for something more original."

"A slug! A gob of snot! Whatever you like . . .
unless you process that paperwork as I stand here,
and then take it in to the Chief Steward for instant
approval, you will regret the day you were born."

"I'm beginning to already. Very well, I will go
through the motions, but I must tell you something.
What you people often fail to realize is that at times
there is simply no room for even one more wizard in
this city. The Brotherhood's membership rolls have
been closed for a year. Periodically, a proscription on
new members must be put in place. This happens to
be one of those periods."

"Means nothing to me. Process those papers."

"Very well." The clerk gave Zane a look of faint,
bleak hope. "I suppose I can say nothing to deter
you?"

"Nothing."

The clerk's face fell, and he resignedly opened a
ledger book and began to write. "Don't you think that
there is a limit on the amount of work to go around?
The market's terrible right now for magic. Most of
our membership sit at home and read the trades. It's
hopeless out there!"

"Babble on," Zane said. "As long as you process
my application."

"Ye gods, all right, all right. You people give me a
royal pain in the fundament. Why you want to be
wizards is quite beyond me. You think it glamorous
work. Well, I've news for you—"

"Get on with it."

"Yes, yes."

The clerk hurriedly entered Zane's name in the ledger, glanced over the application and the sample, filled out a separate sheet, then rushed with all three papers out of the anteroom and into the Steward's office.

Zane waited, half-expecting to find himself out in the alley at any moment. He was confident, but not cocky. He had covered every last contingency he could think of, but he knew from bitter experience that there was always something to go wrong.

But this time, nothing did. The clerk came out of the office with word that Zane would at last be admitted to the Brotherhood.

"Congratulations. Now, you go home and wait for work," the clerk said. He beamed a wintry smile. "See what I meant?"

"I fully understand. But half the battle has been won."

"Take care the other half of the battle does not see you disemboweled and drawn and quartered. Good luck."

And he had good luck indeed. It was not too long a wait before he was hired as a magician to the house of the Elector of Malnovia. It was a nice little post, with light duties, leaving him plenty of time to work on his own magic. He developed powerful and wondrously wicked spells, mostly of a political nature, which guaranteed that they would see wide use. Licensing royalties began to come in. In no time, he had a comfortable second income, which he invested in various magic concerns around the land. These proved wise investments, which made him all the richer.

He finally met the real Farlo and the rest of the Brothers, who over time came to consider him one of the best of their number.

His renown as a wizard spread throughout the Empire. His name was always mentioned in discussions about the notable adepts of the age.

Fame oiled the machinery of his social life. Within a few years, he would feel aggrieved if not routinely invited to the most exclusive parties, dinners, functions, and ceremonies. Women were attracted by the power that prestige bestowed. He had his pick of the most desirable and willing women in the Empire, married and unmarried, and he tore through the lot over the space of a decade. His prowess as a lover was the talk of salons and taverns.

After dallying with scores of women, he at last found one with whom he forebore to trifle. His marriage to the young, beautiful, cultured daughter of one of the Alternate Electors brought him social status along with everything else, and he retired to the country to live in wedded bliss with his bride, where he hunted and partied with the gentry, looked after his estate, and for amusement now and then whipped a poacher or two.

Not.

It was a phantasm, yet another pocket-reality spell, this one of unusually long duration. It had been specially concocted by the Brotherhood to deal permanently with the peskiest and bothersomest country-bumpkin of a spellchucker to come along in years. Although some Brothers acknowledged that Zane had talent, it was the consensus of the Boards that he was hopelessly second-rate—and, moreover, his brashness and lack of social sophistication was not approved of. He was not liked.

So, the spell continued to be maintained for years and years (at some expense, too), and Zane was condemned to live the rest of his life inside this pleasant bubble of magical unreality.

Which was exactly how he had planned it.

PROVING GROUND

❖❖❖

by M. Turville Heitz

M. Turville Heitz is a science and environ-
ment writer/editor for the state of Wisconsin
and a part-time freelancer. Her short fiction
has been published in *Interzone* the small
press and received regional recognition. She is
now working on a fifth novel. Other fiction
by her appears in the anthology *Blood Muse*.

A hot wind swirled across asphalt road baking to
a mire, throwing the hot sticky smell into Ruperion's face. Only his nose absorbed the distraction as
he worked the chunk of driftwood he'd carried with
him these thousands of miles across this world and
across the greater void of water that led home. Beside
him crouched Denalku. The young Chieftain watched
eagerly as Ruperion's knife flicked a chunk of wood
away to form a small hollow, like the bowl on a pipe.
Ruperion tried not to let the gleam in Denalku's
dark eyes distract him, nor the way the Chieftain
grinned at nothing that Ruperion could see. The timid
youth he'd mentored had grown to a consumer of
magic, a hoarder of powers. If Ruperion had known
that the sweet boy he loved as a son would absorb
knowledge and power like the driest loam and become
a man who so ruthlessly overthrew his detractors,
Ruperion would have stabbed the child to death at
birth.
Ruperion tugged at the loose blue jeans he'd
donned on arriving in this world, freeing from a
pocket a vial of mashed manfish leaves he'd borne

across the void with him. He pressed the paste into the bowl he'd carved.

"A carriage comes," Denalku whispered.

"Car. Actually, bus. Be careful not to call attention to yourself like that."

"The dictionary you gave me said carriage is a word for such a conveyance—"

"You must remember to use the vernacular words that belong to this world." Ruperion looked up at the sound of brakes squeaking as the dark blue bus made its first stop on the other end of the dusty little town. Squat beige structures that had deceptively appeared abandoned, suddenly disgorged uniformed military staff whose chatter didn't carry over the din of wind rattling the sign the wizard crouched beside.

"No one is near to hear," Denalku muttered irritably. "How long before you're finished? The bus comes."

Ruperion handed Denalku the driftwood with its paste tamped into one end. He had hollowed out the end opposite the little bowl and tucked a thin wick running from the paste to the end of the stem.

"This is the *ilyath*. It only works this way for the Reign, not for any other caste. You may become somewhat disoriented. Just remember not to speak until I tell you it's safe." Ruperion touched a match to the wick. A curl of smoke rose toward Denalku's nose. Ruperion could tell by the way the Chieftain's gaze dimmed and his jaw sagged that Denalku had already disappeared from the view of anyone who didn't bear a wizard's seeing stone in his pocket.

The bus engine roared as the vehicle sped up the street toward them. Ruperion considered just walking away. Let the Reign Chieftain find his own way to escape the Utah desert when the *ilyath* burned out, tromping through barren hills marked only by graffiti and with nothing but the glitter of broken glass along the road to guide him toward civilization. The road threaded through the hills more than forty miles to the nearest town. Denalku likely wouldn't survive the journey.

Denalku looked up at Ruperion with a trusting gaze even as the *ilyath* burned the flesh of his palm. The wizard almost heard the young boy's mistaken call for "Father" that night when fear of a magic gone wild had cast him into his mentor's comforting arms. With an angry gesture, Ruperion, broke a sliver of shaving from the *ilyath*. Amazement crossed Denalku's dim awareness when Ruperion disappeared.

Never again. Never again would Ruperion let fondness for anyone drive him to such foolish extremes.

That moment, the bus with its bare-bones military styling pulled up beside the sign. The door opened and Ruperion led his dazed charge aboard ahead of workers who smartly paced across the dusty yards— falsely green and watered in the midst of desert—presenting their identification before settling into vinyl seats, chattering away as the bus carried them more than a dozen miles closer to the heart of Ruperion's fear.

The wizard wished he knew less about this world, wished he had never happened across the might of the military, never let Denalku leave him in this world for days, weeks, months to explore and learn the language and ways of an alien people while years passed in his own home on Metatha, where his wife, Leta, grew older than the husband who had been born before her, and Arlin swept toward his father's age. He couldn't think about it. He must honor the man who had become his ruler, even if that man had once been his pupil. He lived under the ban he, Ruperion, had made: only a Reign could wield the power of Travel, to fetch from other worlds the tools the wizards might use. It ended the era of wizards gathering ever greater arsenals and holding more power than their rulers. Ruperion had done that, a good thing.

Yet he'd made a wizard of a Reign.

Ruperion held Denalku steady as they stood near the back of the mostly full bus. Denalku's head had flopped forward, only the Reign's dark curls looking up at Ruperion for the long ride to guarded gates that warned that deadly force would hold back intruders.

Once within the installation, they slowed for herds of antelope and to drop several passengers at a concertina-wire encrusted building in the middle of open desert. The bus rumbled on through dry hills, by distant bunkers and clusters of yellow barrels collected on the sides of the road, by overgrown cement platforms and blasted zones where a sinister sense of what could be lingered.

At last, Ruperion drew Denalku off the bus to the tiny heart of Dugway Proving Ground, to the nondescript collection of buildings shedding their beige paint, to where the military claimed only defensive research occurred on chemical and biological weapons. Over black-tiled floors framed by sea-foam green walls; past defunct UV light washes and level 3 biohazard labs where negative pressure hoods that sucked contaminants out of the building hummed at the arrival of the morning shift; past the plastic-draped rooms holding quarantined rabbits, mice, and monkeys that grew antidotes in their tortured bodies and the black widow spiders whose webs captured toxin-rich dew; by clean rooms and emergency showers Ruperion led Danalku, all the way to the room with its giant red biohazard warning on what appeared to be an ordinary closet door. The black marble counters atop pine cabinets were littered with lab notes, syringes, beakers, and someone's breakfast spread out in a work space that just yesterday may have held vials of rabbit fever. Ruperion maneuvered his still-silent charge into a corner by a rust-stained sink. He waited for the morning order to come in for any of the toxins stored in that closetlike chamber of horrors. Anthrax, bubonic plague, q-fever, botulism, ills innumerable, a variety of bacteria and viruses, all waiting placidly in their tiny vials. Here in these labs, or in the vast miles of open desert, researchers would aerosolize the agent to expose it to simulated soldiers in the field.

What means would Denalku wish Ruperion to use against the saber-wielding horsemen of the Pale?

This one act, so heinous, took Ruperion but a moment. He had no need of Denalku. The Chieftain remained too addled by the smoldering *ilyath*. When the closet door opened, Ruperion merely stepped inside with the captain who filled an order for some outside research lab. While she checked the label of a container of botulism against her list, Ruperion snatched two vials of anthrax from the shelf, tucked it into his jeans pocket and scurried back to the bewildered Denalku.

So simple. Yet he knew he had sealed the fate of some poor soul who didn't have the magic of Traveling and would fear Denalku's madness for the terror it was. Would anyone even notice the missing vial in a place where lab staff ate breakfast beside botulism? Whose life would be ruined for the Metathans' scavenging?

All Ruperion needed now was water. Any pond or spring would do. The entry to this world might be tiny Potter's Flowage in west central Wisconsin—a place where Ruperion rented a hunting shack for his forays in search of magic in this world—but any body of water would take him home.

As they trudged east along the melting asphalt toward a mirage Ruperion knew would dissolve into salt flats and an alkali lake, he silently cursed himself. The whole reason he had devised a ban that would allow no wizard to Travel without the aid of a Reign— one who could monitor the balance of power among the powerful—was to prevent exactly the kind of foolishness Denalku drove him to do.

He stopped walking, listening to the silence of the desert that fell so loud on his ears. He eased Denalku down to sit beside the road in the sort-of shade of twisted sagebrush. Denalku smiled up at what he couldn't see, his eyes bleary still. When the fire at last smoldered away to nothing the Chieftain would feel only pain in his burned palm, and anger at being abandoned in the midst of a toxic desert. Ruperion walked away downhill toward the flats, leaving Denalku staring up at that spot where he thought his "father" still stood, the comforting hand that had guided him through that hellish place, the sureness of a man now no older than him for living so many of his days in a strange world. Always Denalku came back to fetch him from far worlds, welcoming him home with a friendly grin and a boyish insistence that Ruperion hear all the latest gossip from court. Lavishly Denalku honored his mentor with gifts: the finest home in the city and precious stones for magic, or merely for the pleasure of Leta and Arlin.

Ruperion stopped. Glancing back, he noted that Denalku's forehead had scrunched up a little in concern as he stared up into the sky, still silent as his mentor had begged him to remain. Denalku's power over him was too personal, too close to home. If Denalku's facility with magic didn't impress Ruperion, the Chieftain's personal guard protecting Leta and Arlin did. If Ruperion didn't return? Ruperion trudged back up the road and took up Denalku's arm, wishing he didn't need to, that he felt stronger and more cunning, and gently removed the *ilyath* from Denalku's palm so that the man stumbled into awareness with a start.

He merely muttered through Denalku's multitude of questions, trying to quell his regrets by concentrating on the surprising amount of life in this barren place, life that might not be if any of the vials in Dugway's lab were to walk away.

When at last they reached the crusty shores of the evaporating lake, with the calm of many ages of Traveling, Ruperion and Denalku took their deep breaths, expanding their lungs, filling themselves with oxygen before diving together into the brine. Ruperion inhaled again, beneath the water, knowing it would make no difference. Already the Traveling stone Denalku carried had given them the gills of a fish, turned everything they wore or carried into scales, fused their limbs to their sides, but for fingers that fanned the water as fins. Ruperion's legs snapped hard as a tail to dive in Denalku's wake. The lake they dived into might be shallow, but the void was far deeper. Soon, the briny alkali lake no longer poisoned the wizard's breath, but the mineral-rich waters of Metatha gave him the thrill of homecoming.

They surfaced just outside Denalku's palace. Almost instantly, the clean air of Metatha burned the lungs of a man, the wizard's arms and legs, deadened but a moment, responding in a flail that took him shoreward. He knew many days would pass before he felt sound and oriented again, the metamorphosis sapping from him more than strength, but his sense of time and place as well.

Denalku's manservant awaited with towels, ready to guide the Chieftain to his rest. Though deep night had settled over the valley—so deep that only a few torches lit the dark river that flowed beside the palace—Shedal had sat beside the dark river. The servant had waited for the weeks they'd been away—but days on Earth—knowing Denalku's guards also protected his family.

"Give it to me," Denalku said around a shiver.

Ruperion almost dropped the vials to remove them from his sodden pocket. Had they become a part of him during the metamorphosis? Did he now bear a bit of *bacillus anthracis*? How long before blisters formed on his skin and within his lungs? Then again, perhaps the gods had a way of protecting Travelers. Or perhaps on Metatha, this horror of Earth might be benign.

"Ruperion! You aren't listening to me!"

The wizard shook himself. He needed the security of a clear mind, not one addled with Travel sickness.

"Tomorrow, we'll take one to Shesta—"

"We can't travel so soon! Why Shesta? That world is but a simple place—"

"Do you dispute my orders? I wouldn't want to have to reprimand you, my old mentor. You must remember who is the Chieftain here, and that I will do whatever I must to protect my people from the ravages of the Pale."

Ruperion swallowed hard and bowed his head, hating the way the manservant Shedal smirked at the threat Denalku wielded before so powerful a wizard.

That would be Denalku's argument then, that they must defend the people against the ravages of the Pale's horsemen. A few raids would have what kind of reprisal? One that would show the ultimate power Denalku could wield.

The wizard sat long in the dark beside the river after Shedal led Denalku away. He dripped a pool of black water as dark as his thoughts. Tomorrow. Poor Shesta.

A lush valley opened out before them. The tiny spring they'd wriggled up through bubbled from the base of a sandstone bluff that rose red and furious from the head of the valley. Birds chattered. In the distance came the squawk of some kind of domestic fowl, and nearer at hand grazed giant shaggy beasts that somewhat resembled the bison of Earth. A gangly-legged creature, manlike, yet unclothed but for a coating of his own hair as shaggy as the Shestan bison, prodded the grazing animals with the twig end of a light tree branch, sending them toward home with a few clicks of his tongue. The man looked up and saw them, swiftly dropping to his knees.

Denalku gave Ruperion a satisfied smile, and took from the loose robe he'd donned a small, ornate box.

Denalku went forward to set a trembling hand on the head of the Shestan, who looked up at him with wide eyes, his cattle forgotten as he looked upon the gods peopling a sacred spring that had yielded many a Traveler seeking powers.

"We are pleased with Shesta's devotion," Denalku said. Both knew the Shestan couldn't understand a word of what Denalku said, if he even understood the Metathan pronunciation of the Shestan's own word for this world. "We have a gift for you, a way to honor your gods. *Na he pata.*" The last was the special greeting Metathans gave to one of their own tribe, literally, "we speak the same." And with this honored greeting Denalku gifted the furry Shestans.

Denalku flipped a small pebble from his thumb. It blazed out, then dissolved into a tiny silver leaf that

fluttered down into the grass beside the Shestan. It
was the marker they always used. Their proof of
greater power. The leaf image engraved on the box
mocked the Shestan's devotion to the Travelers.

The Shestan held out his hands, accepting the box.
Denalku pantomimed the Shestan sprinkling the vial
over a fire while his whole tribe gathered around to
see. Denalku nodded animatedly as the Shestan repeated the instructions. Slowly the Shestan backed
away from them, his head bowed in deference.

"He bears that box as if the greatest of treasures,"
Ruperion muttered to Denalku as they watched the
Shestan hurry over the hill toward his village.

"Perhaps for them it will be."

Ruperion narrowed his gaze on his one-time pupil.

"Ruperion, we don't know what afterworld his people have. Perhaps we have sent them somewhere better. Maybe they will be born to another world, a better
one. They might next become Metathan, all these
worlds are connected—"

"His luck, he'd be born in the Pale and you would
come at him again with your evil—"

"I think that's enough judgment from you."

Denalku's tone bore a little of the power Ruperion
had taught him. Ruperion felt genuine fear, low in his
gut. Had Denalku already exceeded him in skill? What
power had he unleashed on the world, worlds?

He said nothing as they waited beside the spring
become sacred since Travelers had begun to emerge
from it. The Shestans no longer ate fish, out of fear
they might catch their gods and dine upon them.
Something about that had always amused Denalku.
Ruperion wondered instead if Metathans' ability to
change the worlds they visited wasn't somehow a be-
trayal of the gods' gift of Travel.

When at last they dared crest the distant hill, they
saw a smoking fire, and beside it the sprawled figures
of the Shestans and their cattle. A child wailed somewhere, then slowly wheezed to silence. Only the fowl
continued their clatter.

"We should check to be sure they are not merely

asleep," Denalku said, taking a few steps down the hillside. He stopped, looking up at Ruperion.

"It's airborne. I'm going no closer. I think it's plenty clear from here." He couldn't take his gaze from the little village, the curl of smoke rising so pleasantly, and the tiny box beside the fire bearing the silver leaf, and death.

"Is this the way it works on Earth?"

Ruperion shrugged. "It may work differently. Just as the quartzite I bring from Baraboo means nothing to those in Baraboo, but becomes a powerful magic for Metathans, for all we know this disease is more lethal or less in another world. We don't understand traveling well enough to know what we do." That last he meant as a rebuke. Denalku brushed it aside, striding by him back to the spring, forcing Ruperion to trot like a puppy to keep up with the man who had once followed him thus. He didn't even have time to grasp a breath before Denalku had dived back through the spring, Ruperion barely following, to emerge in a small pool a short distance from the palace.

Shedal waited there.

Denalku scrubbed at himself with towels, shivering violently, his skin a mad red as if whatever madness his mind had created spread outward, invading all his cells.

"It worked," Denalku was telling Shedal. "Send my gift with a legion to the Pale." He giggled a little. "Tell them it is a Traveling magic that will take them far if they but sprinkle it over a fire."

Shedal sped away on a lone horse as Denalku and Ruperion, surrounded by the high Chieftain's guard, rode in the comfort of a carriage back to the palace city. No buses, no cars here. They were a primitive people, scavenging from other lands, like the Earth crow that stole shiny things for the mere act of collecting them. What power did those shiny things bestow upon the bird? Ruperion knew he shouldn't let his mind wander in Travel sickness. It left him vulnerable. Yet, if he didn't, the only thing he could focus upon

was what they were about to unleash in their own
world. How much time had passed on Earth? But a
few hours? Could he return to Dugway and find an
antidote in time to return, before they realized someone had walked off with two vials of anthrax? In the
days it would take Ruperion to return, months would
pass on Metatha.

"Are we certain this is a safe thing to do?" Ruperion whispered to himself, hoping Denalku would hear,
think. "What if it spreads beyond the target, is infec-
tious in a way we aren't expecting, lingers for aeons
in a place where people will encounter it again—"

Denalku glared at him. The carriage had come to a
halt in the courtyard beside the palace, the river flowing languidly by them glittered darkly with shadows
thrown by the onset of evening.

"You are becoming a liability, Rupert," Denalku
said in a tone that made Ruperion go chill, stressing
the name the wizard adopted to rent his cottage on
Earth. Denalku took him by the arm, leading him to
the edge of the river and away from the guards. "Perhaps we would be better off if you were to leave for
a while, gather magics somewhere out of the way—"

"I need to rest, Denalku. We have been to two
worlds in two days! I would see my Leta and Arlin.
Arlin is older than I am now, and I have barely been
here—"

"They're in my care now. I will retrieve you when
the time is right. Too many have seen a wizard traveling with me. We needn't raise fears. There's talk of
rebellion against me. Shedal hears it even among the
Reign! It will be safer for you if no one associates you
with what is about to happen."

Ruperion couldn't even open his mouth to protest
before he felt the splash of river water closing over
his head. Denalku had pushed him, with more than
just his hand: a hand holding the tiny Traveling stone
Ruperion had hidden in the look of white quartz,
when its true face was a dark thing of unknown origin.
Dark, like the deeds done with it. Ruperion swam
deep, knowing soon his lungs would fill with the musty

flavor of tamarack-stained Potter's Flowage and the sweet pesticides from nearby cranberry bogs.

He barely swam through the grasping snags of flooded forest to reach shore, where he collapsed into the deep sleep of the Traveler.

For two weeks Ruperion camped beside the flowage, glaring at each surfacing fish, watching each ripple from beaver or muskrat, each passing boat wake in hopes it might be Denalku returning to lead him home. Two weeks. In Metatha months, more than a year had passed . . . more than a year in which Ruperion's family continued to age while he remained the young man he had first been, long before even Denalku was born, he the wizard who discovered many of the secrets of Travel. That he could have thrown away his notes, that he could have discarded the stone, that he could have done anything to prevent what he had done. Had all of Metatha died? Would Denalku arrive demanding an antidote Ruperion had never dared seek? Would he expect greater and greater arsenals? Where would Ruperion draw the line? It should have been before Shesta. The Shestan had looked upon Denalku as god, not a god who took lives for his own gain. Perhaps this would be Ruperion's punishment for mentoring such a demon: He would forever sit here waiting for a dead man to retrieve him home.

At last, one moonlit evening when Ruperion thought certainly the worst of his fears had come true, telltale bubbles told him a Traveler rose through the twisted limbs of the dammed waters of Potter's Flowage. Ruperion waded out near the drop-off, peering at the silvery water in search of Denalku's mop of dark hair.

There— Something broke the surface, silvery like a fish, then the bright sheen of wet skin. A child's wail broke the night, silencing whippoorwill and owl.

Ruperion raised an infant from the water. The child had been wrapped in the green robe of an adult Reign, the fabric stained dark in places, as if with blood, and rent as if by the scissors of a mad seamstress. Grasped in the tiny fingers of the newborn, Ruperion found a tiny white stone.

Ruperion stumbled back to fall on his rear on the shore. The umbilical cord still trailed from the infant, who appeared nicked and bruised, his mouth still wide and wailing. Some great battle then. And Denalku in his last effort had sent the means for Ruperion's return to ruin. From whom had this child been ripped? Ruperion would still need a Reign to lead him, a Reign that knew the magic of Travel, a Reign who had reached maturity. For this infant boy, twenty-one Earth years. For Ruperion, five hundred years would pass on Metatha, Leta and Arlin long gone to dust. Perhaps by then, the soils of the Pale might have forgotten Denalku. Perhaps by then, "the gods" might return to right their wrongs on Shesta.

"Rupert" looked down on the boy cradled in his arm, the tool Denalku had sent him for finding his way home. "*Na he pata,*" he whispered in the tongue of his world, a tongue he would have to teach a boy raised in Wisconsin, words he inveighed with the power of a wizard. "We speak the same."

THE WIZARD OF THE BIRDS

❖ ❖ ❖

by Jane Yolen and
Adam Stemple

World Fantasy Award winner Jane Yolen has written well over 150 books for children and adults, and well over 200 short stories, most of them fantastical. She is a past president of the Science Fiction and Fantasy Writers of America as well as a twenty-five year veteran of the Board of Directors of the Society of Children's Book Writers & Illustrators. She lives with her husband in Hatfield, Massachusetts and St. Andrews, Scotland.

This is Adam Stemple's first collaboration, as well as his first published story. He lives with his wife, Betsy, in Minneapolis, Massachusetts.

The green heron stood one-legged in the cool water contemplating the shadows of fish. Sounds from the nearby swamp occasionally punctuated the bird's concentration, but the fish—silver flashes beneath the pond's surface—were the heron's main focus. It had scattered bits of bread, stolen from a farmyard, on the water to tempt the fish. Now there was just the matter of the wait.

Genius, the heron knew, *is simply a long patience.* An arrow-slim shape rose to the bait and . . .

"Magister Aves, there's someone come to see you."
A boy's voice, squeaking in awkward places, broke
through the heron's thoughts.

"Damnation and feathers!" the wizard said angrily,
the change coming upon him so quickly with the
speaking-aloud of his name that he found himself
knee-deep in the cold, scummy water. "And double
damnation." He waded ashore while the fish gobbled
up his leavings. "Next time wait till I've had my lunch,
Chrisos," he said petulantly.

The boy, his apprentice, nodded miserably. He
knew that his master hated to entertain visitors in wet
trousers, and the result would be a long lecture after
any business was concluded, with only sour milk and
dark crusts for dinner.

Aves stomped out of the water and waddled up the
long path toward his cottage. As a heron he was ele-
gance itself. His steps were langorous and smooth as
if timed to an abnormally slow étude. Left foot on the
down beat, right on the up, and every fourth measure
his neck extending to three times its normal length.
At the end of the piece he would strike, swift and
surprising (if not true every time), like a picardy third
at the finish of a haunting dirge. In human form, however, he more closely resembled an aardvark. He had
a nose that seemed too large to balance the face correctly, a tongue with a tendency to appear of its own
volition at inopportune moments, and a gray mustache
that waterfalled on either side of a too-tiny mouth.
It was no wonder he preferred Changing. Even the
potbellied skylark was preferable to his human form.

As he approached the back of his cottage, Aves
viewed it with growing disdain. It had been a fine
place when he was young and relatively free of work;
it didn't take much to heat and one room had been
all he could manage to keep clean. But since that successful business with the young princess and the unshaven ogre, his new-found popularity demanded
something more ostentatious. Besides, despite his
habit of getting overexcited and drooling whenever
visitors appeared, young Chrisos was showing a great

deal of promise. He deserved a small room of his own, one he wouldn't have to share with the cow. Aves nodded to himself, looking for a moment like one of those dolls at the fair, whose head and body connect with a wire causing the head to bob up and down with every passing breeze. After dinner, and after Chrisos had supped on his sour milk and crusts, he would tell the boy of his plans to add on to their home.

Rewards, the wizard knew, *taste better after punishment.*

He was smiling at his own wit, and all thought of wet trousers, lost lunches, and visitors had fled his mind when he came round the corner of his cottage and saw who waited for him. The smile died an absurdly slow and painful death as politeness warred with distaste in an attempt to hold the smile in place.

"Hell and feathers," Aves said aloud as distaste joined forces with irritation and, in a classic pincer movement, drove politeness from the field. It was Magister Fontenal, his old Master. A string of memories, most of them having to do with sour milk and dark crusts, raced through Aves' brain. It was all he could do to keep his shape and not turn into an accipiter on the moment. "Hell and feathers."

"Good to see you, too," Fontenal said, running his hand over the top of his head and the three lank gray strands of hair that covered it. "I need help, though it pains me to ask it of you. But that business with the princess and the unshriven ogre . . ."

"Unshaven," Aves corrected automatically.

". . . prompts me to come here—and here only—for aid."

The wizard's insistence on the last line, together with his false smile, confirmed Aves' suspicion that he was, in fact, the *last* wizard that Fontenal was visiting. He wondered why all the others had turned the old Master down. He guessed he would not have to wait long to find out.

He was, however, wrong.

Politeness, though defeated, was determined to get

a good settlement in the surrender proceedings. It demanded that Aves invite his old Master inside for a spare lunch of bread and butter and cheese, which he did with as little grace as possible. He thought the old man would refuse him. He *hoped* the old man would refuse him.

Fontenel accepted eagerly.

The Master then proceeded to make only small talk throughout the meal, avoiding the only subject that interested either of them: what he needed help with. He pretended to remember fondly their days together as mentor and student. He spoke of the lovely weather they had been having. He spoke of books he had read, demons he had summoned, monsters created and destroyed, enchantments cast and dispelled. Finally he stared deeply into the literally enchanting burgundy Chrisos had uncorked for the meal, sighing deeply and repeatedly.

Fearing his old Master would never leave unless something drastic was done, Aves was forced to inquire directly after the reason for the visit which, of course, immediately put the onus on him, the bonus on the Master. *The Wizard's Book of Manners* was quite specific on this point.

"You are here for . . . ?" Aves began.

"I *knew* I could count on you," Fontenal said. "Even back when you were just a young apprentice you were always there to help. I remember how you would shoe the horses and clean their stalls without me even having to ask."

"That was Miklos, not me," Aves corrected. "Lives up by Ravenscraig with the centaurs now."

Fontenal continued as if Aves had never interrupted.

"You would shine the silver every day."

"Jock of the Nell, hung for theft. I almost taught him how to turn into a magpie. Seemed a natural choice."

"Planted the crops."

"Joseph, calls himself Green Man these days. 'All your gardening needs, none of your maddening weeds.' Not much of a slogan if you ask me."

"Swept the floors."

"Helen, the hearth witch."

"Cooked the meals."

"Bibless MacDugal."

"Cared for the goat?" Fontenal asked.

"Mad Morgan, transported for bes . . ."

"What *did* you do?" cried Fontenal.

Aves could hear an edge of panic in the old wizard's voice, and wondered what it all meant. Fontenal had never been one to beg, plead, bargain, or panic. In all the time Aves had known him, Fontenal always dictated terms. This new face of the old Magister was so disconcerting, Aves was afraid to say anything. Instead, he turned into a snake-eating eagle. Not his favorite bird, but one of his most impressive and startling.

"Oh, yes," said Fontenal. "Now I remember. *Birds.*" He suddenly put his face in his hands and wept.

It was not at all what Aves expected. The sobbing, loud and sputtering, took a great deal of time. Twice Aves had to gesture to Chrisos to leave the doorway. It would not do to have an apprentice see a master magician so unmanned.

When the sobbing reached floodtide, and the floor was beginning to show signs of rising damp, Aves realized he had to take action. Either that or turn himself permanently into a teal. He reached out and patted the old wizard on the head.

"There, there," he said. "There, there." He hoped he wouldn't turn the both of them into something truly awful and unreparable. Magic had a way of sneaking up in moments of crises. *The Wizard's Book of Manners* reminded not once but seven separate times: "If your mass goes critical, you can literally go to pieces!" That's why wizards had to cultivate calm.

When there was no transformation, Aves dared another pat on the old man's head. "There, there," he said again. Except that Fontenal's hair turned a sea-green—which might have been more the damp than the magic—there was no observable change. "Tell me the problem," Aves ventured bluntly.

Fontenal looked up, his nose as red as his hair was green. "I have no memory now," he said. "Or at least I have an excellent forgettery. I've lost Names. I can't recall Spells. And my checkbook is in a horrible mess."

Aves shuddered.

"So because of your success with the princess and the unforgiven ogre . . ."

"Unshaven," Aves corrected again.

"That, too," said Fontenal. Then he sniffed one more time. "Help!" he said, his voice wavering.

Like water, Aves thought, not unkindly. *Like a stream in spate.* He shook himself all over, a duck's shake. Then he smiled. It did not improve his looks. "Magister, what do you want me to do?"

Fontenal gulped three times in succession and composed himself a little. "I'm not sure," he replied. "But my wife seems to have the utmost confidence in you. 'Get the bird wizard,' she said." Fontenal's confusion seem to lift for a moment and he said tersely, "She's quite the collector."

Aves' face brightened as he thought about a fellow enthusiast and he said, "She sounds like a wonderful woman." He wondered just when the Master had married. In all the time Aves had known him, Fontenal had been positively adverse to the female gender. He'd even had a special room built for women customers, a room he could blast with magical fire after each one had been dealt with. Sometime, somehow, he had changed. Or else some*one* had changed him. *Almost*—Aves thought suddenly—*beyond recognition.* "A truly wonderful woman." Aves meant this sincerely.

This, unexpectedly, brought on a fresh bout of tears from Fontenal, and Aves decided to quit trying to hold a conversation and return to his original strategy for calm. "There, there," he said and patted Fontenal on the head again.

The old wizard's head was now capped by a bright-green mane that moved like seaweed in a big swell. It was framed by two ears that were beginning to look suspiciously like conch shells. "That's just it," Fontenal said. "I don't *know* if she's a wonderful woman. I've just about forgotten her, too!"

With this Fontenal broke down completely and began really flooding the room. Water poured out of his eyes at such a prodigious rate that Aves turned back into the green heron and was beginning to think frantically of saving his home. The water was ankle-deep and rising; you could hear the deep boom of the ocean issuing from Fontenal's shell-like ears. The cottage that Aves had just an hour before viewed with contempt now seemed to hold nothing but beautiful memories that were about to be washed away.

For the first time since the master wizard's arrival Aves grew not just petulant and annoyed but truly angry. The thought that he had been seduced—*no, tricked!*—into offering help to the very man who had ruined his youth and was now ruining his home made the eyes on either side of his elongated heron head burn. He lost his wizardly calm—which, since he was in bird form did no particular harm to him—and gave the war cry of the green heron which is an unimpressive, low squawking. Then he launched himself at Magister Fontenal.

"Ow," said Fontenal as the first attack left a small bruise on his right shin.

"Hey!" he cried as the second attack left a similar bruise on his left shin. He stood, knocking his chair over. The attack had hurt but it did not stem the tide of his tears.

The heron watched miserably as a garish trophy for third place in a small regional competition floated toward the door. Yesterday, if he'd been asked about it, he would have said, "What trophy?" On the day he'd won it, he would have said, "I don't enjoy competitions, let alone gaudy little trinkets got through them." And even those who enjoy competition aren't

terribly fond of third place. But today the sight of
the precious memento of his hard-fought battle in the
trenches of the West Ingleshire Group III Open Spell-
ing Bee going out the door on a wave filled Aves the
heron with a fury that was terrible to behold. He drew
himself to his full height and launched himself one last
time at the object of his wrath.

His bill entered Fontenal's left buttock with surpris-
ingly little sound and came away bloody.

"Blast you, bird!" Fontenal screamed, swatting the
heron away in a swirl of feathers. He reached slowly
behind and rubbed his buttock. When he brought
his hand back and he saw the blood, his eyes began
glowing bright red. Small tendrils of smoke began
to issue from his ears. A low animal growl escaped
his throat and he raised his arms high over his head.
Bending his hands at a ninety-degree angle, he
spread his now sparking fingers stiffly in the classic
Casting Stance.

Aves remembered having no success with that particular stance as an apprentice and had never tried it
since. He did recall, however, that it was generally
used with aimed elemental spells of the lightning and
fireball class. He squawked a word, returned to human
form, and sat down heavily on the wet couch. "You
wouldn't dare!" he cried, flinging up a Counter Cover
Spell, just in case. If there was any *calm* anywhere in
the room, it would have been hard to find and so
nothing at all happened ...

... except the interchange left both wizards weak,
weary, and wet to the waist in a cottage afloat with
mementoes and crockery.

A giggle at the door recalled them both to their
senses.

"Chrisos!" Aves said, waving his hand at the boy.

"Avaunt!" Fontenal said, waving his own hand at
the boy.

The two spells met in the middle somewhere, weak
and weary and wet as their masters. But calm. They
smooged together and landed on the giggling apprentice. There was soggy smoke. There were damp flashes

of light. There was a boy's soft scream. And there was . . .

. . . a little yellow rubber duckie floating on the doorsill.

"Now look what you have done!" Aves said, frantically trying to recall anything *The Wizard's Book of Manners* said about such an enchantment.

"Not me," countered Fontenal. "Not my style. Birds R U. Besides, he's your apprentice, not mine. I couldn't really touch him. Under your wing . . . I mean, protection and all that."

Aves suddenly remembered miserably *The Wizard's Book of Manners'* caution about apprentices and damp. And about angering a senior wizard when one is wet. It was very specific. The words DO NOT had been repeated several times. "What are we to do?"

At the word *we,* Fontenal suddenly looked sly and more alert than he had all afternoon. He smiled.

Aves knew with growing certainty that he'd been seriously and horribly conned.

"We'll bring that little yellow birdie thing to my dear lady wife," said Fontenal. "She'll have an idea."

"I'm sure she will," Aves said unhappily, putting the rubber duckie in the pocket of his robe. He suddenly remembered what it was that bird collectors did. It had to do with knives and skinning and long silver pins and . . . he shivered. But really he had no choice. He had given the high ground—what there was of it in his poor, flooded cottage—to Fontenal and there was no going back. "I'm sure she will."

They walked along the mountain paths for several miles, along the seashore for several more. Aves wished with each new mile that he dared change into a bird. *A crow,* he thought. The measure would be much smaller that way for everyone knew that "as the crow flies" was the straightest route of all. But at this point, Aves felt sure, the fewer birds—real, rubber, or enchanted—served up to Mrs. Fontenal the better. So he trudged along, the soles of his feet growing sorer with each step and streaks of pain beginning to shoot up into his knees. Still he refused to show his agony by so much as a grimace.

Fontenal seemed in better shape, despite his advanced age. Or perhaps there was some sort of special magic surrounding him, easing his way. Aves kept glancing over, hoping to catch a glimpse of any such spell. But the old man's stride gave no hint of enchantment, enhancement, or knee replacement. Aves was stymied. *And* his feet and knees hurt the more for it.

"Do you want to rest a moment?" he asked the old wizard as they turned from the seashore to head inland. "I mean, if you need to stop . . ."

Fontenal shook his head. "I'm fine," he said. "No need on my account." There was not the slightest hint of fatigue in his voice.

Aves made himself think of long distance animals— reindeer and caribou who threaded their way from summer to winter and back again. Just the thought seemed to strengthen his legs. Then he remembered certain terns who flew from pole to pole, all on a spring's day. He began to feel the sun in his hair, the wind feathering his . . . No—that was *too* dangerous. In a minute he'd become a tern and then where would he be? Or young Chrisos, for that matter. He let his thoughts drift back to the deer and then to the path in front of him.

His feet hurt more than ever. But he would not give Fontenal the satisfaction of seeing him fade. "Lovely landscape," he said as they passed a midden pile on the right that was sprouting a beard of vegetable volunteers.

"Eaue de Outdoors," muttered Fontenal back at him. The return to his old surliness was surprising.

Perhaps, Aves thought suddenly, *he is less sanguine about the return home than he appears*. The thought cheered him enormously and he put a great deal of pep into his own voice and step. "Aren't we almost there?"

"Close," muttered Fontenal.

"To your dear wife," Aves reminded him.

"Women!" Fontenal said with a touch of his old disdain. "What good are they?"

"Well, there *was* that princess and the unshaven ogre," Aves reminded him. "And . . ."

But the road took a familiar turn and suddenly, there in front of them lay the road that wound up to the road that wound along to the road that wound over the mountain to Fontenal's house.

Both wizards shivered simultaneously. Aves could feel the rubber duckie in his pocket bump against his hip with each shake. The ground beneath his feet trembled resonantly.

"Perhaps we'd better control ourselves," he said to Fontenal, "before we start an avalanche."

"Avalanches take snow," muttered Fontenal. "It's full summer. What *can* you be thinking, boy?"

What Aves was thinking was that now that they were back on Fontenal's home turf, Aves was speaking just as he had when he'd been an apprentice to the old man, tongue before brain. He barely stopped himself in time from apologizing. As an apprentice he'd always been sorry. In fact, Fontenal's pet phrase for him had been, "you're a sorry excuse for a wizard." But now . . . now . . . *Now I am a wizard myself; and a fine one, too,* he told his cowering innards. He tried visualizing each gray hair on his own head. He forced himself to remember all the satisfied customers on his Solstice card list. He . . .

"FONTY!" a voice came booming down the hillside. "WHERE ARE YOU . . ." The voice had a syrupy sweetness that fought with its decibel level.

Fontenal's head snapped back, his eyes rolled up till only the whites showed. He shivered uncontrollably and with great force. Suddenly snow—great chunks of it—thundered down the heretofore flowery hillside.

Aves squawked, turned into a Snowy Owl, and lifted powerfully above the slide. He watched through yellow eyes as Fontenal tumbled head over tailbone down the hill, fetching up against a tree with a tremendous *c*r*a*s*h*!

Fluttering to the tree, Aves perched for a full moment watching the old man slowly return to consciousness. Then he sailed down on silent wings to stand at Fontenal's side. Changing back into his old self, Aves took a deep breath before attempting to aid the Master. "You know better than that!" Aves chastised him. "You certainly taught *me* better than that." He reached down to pull the wizard to his feet.

Fontenal brushed his hands away. "Tell it to the marine animals!" he said.

"I do birds," Aves replied quietly.

"Whatever." Fontenal stood, brushing off his clothes and Aves at the same moment.

"FONTY!" the voice came again.

This time neither of them shivered, but the amount of control needed was so great that they had nothing left over for conversation as they slowly trudged up the mountainside, Fontenal first and Aves a shaken second behind.

Fontenal's house appeared over the fourth major rise. Aves knew it well, was expecting it, and still was surprised by it. Mostly his surprise was at the size. Since he'd been Fontenal's apprentice, the house seemed to have almost doubled its footage, adding both a Carolina room and a glassed arboretum. There was now a widow's walk as well. Someone was standing on the widow's walk staring at them through a telescope.

She waved.

"Your lady wife," Aves remarked. It was the first thing either of them had said since the avalanche.

"I don't think I actually ever got married," muttered Fontenal. "That is, I don't remember *getting* married, only *being* married."

"Isn't it the same thing?" puzzled Aves.

"No," said Fontenal. "But if you think it is, it's best you stick with birds."

Just then the female—wife or whatever—appeared in the doorway. "Welcome home, Fonty, dear," she said.

If Aves had been surprised by the changes in the house, they were nothing to his surprise at meeting Mrs. Fontenal. To begin with, she was half the old man's age. Second she was a redhead—and a real one, Aves was sure. There was no hair dye to match that color, somewhere between pumpkin and peony. And third, she was beautiful. Not just wish-and-get beauty, but the deep-down princess kind of beauty, that no amount of exercise and deep pore washes could achieve. Aves felt every inch of his own ugly. His nose quivered with it. Something dripped from the end and with great effort he snuffled it back up.

"This must be your friend, Aves—the wizard of the birds." When Mrs. Fontenal spoke, Aves thought he heard the nightingale's voice.

That's when he knew it was all Glamour. She'd gone one step too far, trying to be sure of him, and blown her disguise. He still couldn't see through it to what she really was, and he didn't dare let her know he knew. But he knew. Oh, how he knew. He decided, though, that he'd better play Dazzled.

"You . . . you're . . ." She was really so lovely it wasn't terribly hard to fake it.

"Philomena," she said. "My name is Philomena. A bird name for a bird wizard." She laughed deliciously and added, "We are going to be wonderful friends, Aves, I know." Then she did the nightingale thing again, with a careful gurgle at the back of her throat.

Aves gurgled in return. But in fact he'd never really liked nightingales. Big birds, squawkers, were what he was fond of. Give him a loud *kreee-ahh* like one of the great hawks, and . . . He felt his right arm, beneath the sleeve of his robe, start to wing out and he had to concentrate on turning the little feathers back into dark hairs. But all the while he was thinking: *She's good. Whoever she is, she's very good.* He even began to feel sorry for Fonty.

"But you have had such a long and arduous journey on foot," Philomena said, implying that they could have come by a faster route. Or at least Aves could have. "I'll serve us a high tea, and afterward a fine dessert wine. It's a bit on the quiet side and not at all presumptuous. I am sure you will like it."

It was all Aves could do to smile innocently at her. He knew it was important not to let her know he was on to her. Though what he would do once she served him food . . . In magical wars food was always the first and often the most important battleground. There was an entire chapter on food in *The Wizard's Book of Manners,* and another just on the serving of tea. At one point in his apprenticeship he'd memorized the entire thing. Clearing his throat, he said, "I, for one, am parched" into her awaiting smile.

They followed her into the living room, now Martha-ed to a fare-thee-well with hand-dipped aromatic candles in pewter sconces, beribboned pinecone center-pieces, and doilies on every wooden surface. Aves remembered that it had been a spare and uninviting room when he'd been a student. Now it was anything but spare. Still, though, he felt its disinvitation even more keenly, and could not think why.

In all this time, Fontenal had been silent, as if Philomena's very presence precluded speech. It was this that confirmed Aves' worst fears. Philomena had to be a wizard of truly heroic dimensions to so cow her husband. But like most female wizards, her reach probably extended only to the edges of her property which was why she'd had to send a beguiled Fontenal out to collect what she needed. Or who.

The two men sat on the blue brocaded sofa, perching like demented doves so as not to knock the lace dust catchers to the floor. Philomena commandeered the rocker and commanded the tea tray.

They watched silently as she poured the tea, a splash of golden sunshine cascading into the paper-thin cups.

You could read your fortune right through the china, Aves thought, *and never have to drink the tea at all.*

"One lump or two?" Philomena asked, having already fixed Fontenal's tea without any prompting. The old wizard was noisily guzzling it without any notice-able fear.

"Black," Aves said quickly. Ordinarily he took three lumps, lots of milk. But the less additives the better. *The Wizard's Book of Manners* was quite explicit on this point. Aves suddenly remembered the mnemonic rhyme in a rush:

> *If only one*
> *It's soon undone.*

Philomena looked at him carefully, as if she were suspecting something, so Aves grinned at her, pretending he was even more Dazzled than before. Clearly his deception was working, for she handed him the cup, then turned to the tea tray and began shoveling little crustless sandwiches on to a plate.

Aves filled his mouth with the tea water, but considered the pelican, imperceptibly loosening his throat muscles to resemble the bird's large capacity beak. He swallowed a mouthful of tea, but only as far as the beak pouch, which left him still able to speak. Then he lowered his head and glanced up at Philomena out of the corner of his eyes as if struck again by her beauty. "I needed that, dear lady," he said.

She handed him the plate and he took it, wondering all the while how much the pelican beak might comfortably hold. He knew in bird form he could easily carry around a dozen fish. He wasn't sure how directly enchanted tea sandwiches corresponded to their fishy cousins, even if one of the sandwiches—here his nose twitched—was clearly made with smoked salmon.

But before he had time to worry about it, Philomena began her chanting. Fontenal sat still dazed and dazzled on the couch by his side. Aves knew that whatever was going to happen, he would have to do all by himself.

Philomena's chant took the form of an Ode, and the musicality of her voice tugged at Aves in subtle and unsubtle ways.

> *O, swan, o duck, o stilt, o dove,*
> *O avifaunas that I love,*

I call you here in function's name
That I may win the wizard game.
O...

It was excruciatingly bad, though effective in a crude way. But Aves had always prided himself on creating elegant spells and he was damned if he was going to go under to such piggery-jiggery.

"Hell and feathers!" he cried, standing and regurgitating the tea water all over himself, the carpet, and Fontenal's hand.

That roused the old man just long enough to mumble, "Remember that princess and the unshaken ogre . . ."

"Unshriven!" cried Aves loudly. But he realized now that all along Fontenal had been trying to tell him something though Philomena's spell had scrambled most of it. About that princess—he'd saved her by tricking the ogre into shapeshifting into a mouse and simultaneously Aves had turned the princess into a cat. A very quick cat.

Aves felt in his pocket for the rubber duckie. "This is going to hurt you more than me," he whispered to his apprentice. "Not many would admit such a thing." And even while Philomena continued to chant, he took out the duckie and flung it directly at her head.

Of course she tried to duck. But duck and duckie being homonymics, she couldn't avoid it. As *The Wizard's Book of Manners* took pains to point out: "Words are for wizards what tints are for a painter. They color and shade everything." The rubber duckie hit Philomena square between the eyes and she cried out, not at all calmly, which made her falter in her Ode. And *that* was a most egregious error.

The yellow duckie honked once and was still.

Aves shouted the Latin name for a frog and waved his hand in a significant manner. At the same time he thought about herons.

Philomena shrank down and down and down into a green and withered frog, splashing disconsolately in the wet carpet, her voice no longer riveting but ribbeting. The great heron above her stabbed down with his pointed beak, piercing her right through her froggy breast and what might have been the opening stanza of a Froggie Ode. The heron was never to know. Flipping the frog up into the air, the heron opened its beak, and swallowed her down.

The minute Philomena was gone, Fontenal shook himself all over, like an old dog trying to come to point and missing, but attempting the stance nonetheless. He saw the mess on his carpet, the heron, and the yellow duckie, battered and barely afloat. He looked around his spare and uninviting room. "What in Magic's name is all this?" he asked.

Reluctantly Aves returned to his human form. "A simple thank you will suffice," he said. But his plea was lost in the buzz of nearly a dozen other voices as one by one by one wizards returned from their enchanted forms: five doilies, three pinecone centerpieces, and four aromatic candles. Philomena was *quite* the collector! But it seems that it was wizards, not birds, she collected.

Of course, Aves got no thanks from his old Master. Nor did he get even sour milk and crusts for the trip home. As he made his way down the road that wound away from the house to the one that wound over the mountain to the one that wound along to the road to his own home, he took the rubber duckie out of his pocket.

"At least you'll not go hungry all the way back," he said. "That comes of being rubber. Not like me." He rubbed his hungry stomach, thinking how homonymic *rubber* and *rubbed* were and wondering idly if anything could be made of it. When he finally realized nothing could, he added to the duckie, "In a day or two, Chrisos, when I can figure it out, I'll have you back to your old self again. Then we'll have ourselves a real tea. No crusts for you, my boy. Or me. Ever again. I think crustless tea sandwiches, with smoked salmon would make a right treat."

And if the rubber duckie made a little honking

sound then, it was probably because Aves had given it a friendly squeeze before shoving it back into his pocket for the rest of the trip home. Probably. Because squeeze has no homonymic refererents that I can think of.

MIRROR, MIRROR ON THE LAM

❖ ❖ ❖

by Tanya Huff

Born in the Maritimes, Tanya Huff now lives and writes in rural Ontario. On her way there, she spent three years in the Canadian Naval Reserve and got a degree in Radio and Television Arts which the cat threw up on. Her most recent books for DAW are *Blood Debt*, the fifth Vicki/Henry/Celluci novel, and *No Quarter*, the direct sequel to *Fifth Quarter*.

T he turquoise house on the headland had stood empty for some weeks. The wind off the sea whistled forlornly through the second floor cupola, tried each of the shuttered windows in turn, and finally, in a fit of pique, tossed a piece of forgotten garden furniture into what appeared to be a halfhearted attempt at shrubbery.

The green-and-gold lizard crouched under a wilting bayberry scrambled to safety just in time. Racing counterclockwise up the nearest palm, it stopped suddenly, lifted its head, and tested the air.

Someone was coming.

Ciro had left his donkey and cart carefully hidden at the foot of the hill. Although he doubted that any of the inhabitants of the nearby fishing village would venture so far from the cove, he never took risks he could avoid. As his dear old white-haired mother had told him, right before her public and very well-attended execution, chance favors the pessimist.

He'd have preferred a faster form of transportation, but since his current employer had been somewhat vague on the size of the object he was to acquire, he'd erred on the side of caution. If he couldn't deliver, he wouldn't get paid.

For safety's sake, he avoided paths and moved, where he could, from one patch of rock to the next. As he approached the house, the vegetation grew more lush, easier to hide behind if harder to move through. At the edge of the garden, he paused and studied the structure, a little taken aback by the extraordinary color. It was smaller than he'd expected, but perhaps the most powerful wizard in the world had no need for ostentatious display.

To his surprise, the kitchen door was not only unlocked but, if the crystal his employer had given him was to be trusted, also unwarded. As he crossed the kitchen floor, Ciro sincerely hoped that the shadows dancing in the corners owed more to the way the louvered shutters filtered light than to anything the wizard may have left behind.

Stepping out into a large square hall, he found himself facing three identical doors. As he moved forward, eyes half closed against the brilliant sunshine blazing through the circular skylight, the kitchen door closed behind him.

Four identical doors.

The door on his right led to a bedroom. The bed—a huge, northern-style four-poster that overwhelmed the southern decor—had been left unmade. Ciro pulled a sandal from the closest pile of clothing and used it to block the door open before he stepped cautiously forward.

The door closed.

No need to panic, he told himself. *You can always go out the window.*

A cloak, in a particularly vibrant shade of orange, had been draped over the large oval mirror. Standing safely to one side, he tugged at the cloth and took a quick look into the glass as it fell. A man of average height, his light brown hair and beard a little darker than his skin and a little lighter than his eyes, looked back at him. He frowned and his reflection echoed the movement. Either he'd lost weight or the mirror made him look thinner.

It was the only mirror in the room.

The door proved to be unlocked. It opened when he lifted the latch and, as he stepped back into the hall, it closed behind him.

Continuing to his right, Ciro opened the next door and found himself staring into the kitchen.

This time, he closed the door on his own.

The door to his left should now lead to the bedroom but he was no longer willing to take that for granted. He checked the crystal. The wizardry moving the house about was not directed at him—a mixed blessing at best. For lack of a better plan, he continued moving to the right.

A spare room. An unmade bed and empty wardrobe. One mirror; not very large and not what he was searching for.

The kitchen again. With luck, the shadows had changed only because the light had.

A spiral staircase leading up to the cupola, a small square room containing only a pile of multicolored cushions. Peering through one of the louvered shutters that made up the bulk of the walls, Ciro found himself staring out at a view from some fifty feet above the house. Without actually lifting his feet from the floor, the thief backed up and made his way carefully down the short—the far too short—flight of stairs.

The wizard's bedroom.

A bathing room. A dolphin mosaic decorated the tiles surrounding the sunken tub. The drying cloths were large, thick, and soft. From the variety of soaps and lotions, it was obvious that the wizard was no ascetic. There was no mirror.

He hadn't found a workshop yet but figured that he would in time. He'd never known a wizard who wasn't happiest puttering about with foul smelling potions and exploding incantations.

The kitchen.

The staircase.

The bedroom.

A sitting room. Big brightly colored cushions were piled high on round bamboo chairs. A carafe, two glasses, and a pile of withered orange peels had been left on a low table. On one wall, floor-to-ceiling shelves had been messily stuffed with scrolls and books and the occasional wax tablet. There were more shelves on the opposite wall, but they were less regular. Most held a variety of ornaments ranging, in Ciro's professional opinion, from the incredibly tacky to the uniquely priceless. Out of habit, he tucked a few of the latter in his pockets.

In the exact center of the wall was an open section. In it, covered in a black cloth, was an oval object about two feet across at its widest and three feet long. Holding his breath, Ciro flipped the cloth to one side.

Even knowing what to expect, he almost jumped back.

The demon trapped in the mirror snarled in fixed impotence as it had for decades.

Ciro smiled, rewrapped the mirror in the cloth, tucked the bundle under his arm, unlatched one of the large windows, and stepped out into the garden, politely closing and relatching the window behind him.

He never noticed the watching lizard.

"Well, Emili, did you miss me?"

The tiny gray cat cradled in the Magdelene's arms hunkered down and growled.

"Because you're too old to leave by yourself, that's why. You're lucky Veelma was willing to take care of you."

The path from the beach to the top of the headland was both steep and rocky although generations of use had worn off the more treacherous edges. As the wizard climbed in breathless silence, the cat kept up a constant litany of complaint, squirming free with a final wail the moment the summit was reached and disappearing under a tangle of vegetation the moment after.

"I know exactly how you feel," Magdelene muttered, sagging against the end of the seawall and pushing a heavy fall of damp chestnut hair back off her face. "There's no place like home."

Magdelene seldom traveled. It needed far more exertion than she was usually willing to expend and experience had taught her that the easier she made it for herself, the more exertion it invariably required. This particular trip had been precipitated by an extremely attractive young man who'd come a very long way to request her assistance—and had cleverly exploited one of her weaknesses by making the request on his knees. He'd almost made it worth her while.

Reluctantly rousing herself, she crossed to the kitchen door, latched it open, and went inside. The wind followed her, only to be chased back outside where it belonged.

Sometime later, cleaned, changed, and holding a tall glass of iced fruit juice, Magdelene entered the sitting room and rolled her eyes dramatically when the opened shutters exposed a fine patina of dust.

"I've got to get another housekeeper," she muttered, dragging a finger along the edge of a shelf and frowning at the resulting cap of gray fuzz. The problem was, every time she got used to a housekeeper, they died. Antuca had been with her the longest and the fifty years they'd shared would make it even harder to replace her.

"On the other hand," Magdelene told herself philosophically, "someone has to do the cooking." Taking a long swallow of the juice, she crossed to the other side of the room. "Well, H'sak, did you . . . ?"

The section of wall was empty. Even the black cloth she'd thrown over the mirror before she'd left had been taken.

"Oh, lizard piss," said the most powerful wizard in the world.

The Five Cities were five essentially independent municipal areas set around a huge shallow lake. Reasoning they had more in common with each other than

with the countries at their backs, they'd formed a loose
alliance that had held for centuries. The Great Lake was
the areas's largest resource and the agreement allowed
them to exploit it equally. Overly ambitious city gover-
nors were traditionally replaced with more pragmatic
individuals practically before the body had cooled.

Two weeks to the day after the thief had stolen the
mirror and twenty minutes after she'd dropped the cat
back at Veelma's, Magdelene appeared in Talzabad-
har, the Third City, clutching a black velvet pillow in
both hands. Gratefully discovering that the contents
of her stomach had traveled with her, she released the
breath she'd been holding and took a quick look
around.

The picture embroidered on the pillow over the
barely legible words "A Souvenir of Scenic Talzabad-
har" had been more or less accurate. The small stone
shrine, five pillars holding apart a floor and a roof,
had been rendered admirably true to life. Unable to
anchor the transit spell in a place she'd never seen,
Magdelene had taken a huge chance using the pillow
for a reference. Fortunately, it appeared to have
paid off.

Unfortunately, the shrine was not standing in isola-
tion on a gentle green hill as portrayed but in the
center of a crowded market square and the clap of
displaced air that had heralded Magdelene's appearance had attracted the attention of almost everyone
present. Fidgeting under the weight of an expectant
silence, Magdelene looked out at half a hundred curious eyes.

Then a voice declaimed, "She has returned!" and
everyone fell to their knees, hands over their faces,
foreheads pressed against the ground.

Obviously, it was a case of mistaken identity. Magdelene, who had no time to be worshiped—although
she had nothing actually against it—ran for an alley
on the north side of the square.

Someone peeked.

"She goes!"

Experience having taught her how quickly a crowd

can become a mob, Magdelene ran faster. Ducking into the mouth of the alley, she tossed the pillow back over her shoulder.

"A relic!"

"I saw it first!"

The sounds of a fight replaced the sounds of pursuit and Magdelene used the time gained to cover the length of the alley, round a corner, and run smack into a religious procession. By the time the first of her pursuers had come into sight, she'd borrowed a tambourine and an orange veil and was dancing away down the road, indistinguishable from any other acolyte.

At the first cross street, she returned her disguise, regretfully declined an invitation to lunch, and went looking for a member of the city guard.

"Excuse me, Sergeant?" When he glanced down, dark eyes stern and uncompromising under the edge of his helm, Magdelene gave him an encouraging smile. "I was wondering, who would you consider the best thief in the Five Cities?"

"Ciro Rasvona." His dark gaze grew a little confused, as though he wasn't entirely certain why he'd answered so readily.

"And where would I find him?"

The sergeant snorted. "If I knew that, I'd find him there myself."

"Maybe later," the wizard promised. "I meant which of the Five Cities does he use as his base?"

"This one."

"This one? My, my." Magdelene was a big believer in luck—luck, coincidence and just generally having life arrange itself in her favor. It made everything much less work and she was a *really* big believer in that.

"If there's nothing else I can do for you . . ."

"Maybe later," she promised again and reluctantly let him walk on.

Ciro Rasvona had an average set of rooms in an average neighborhood under another, average name,

His neighbors, when they thought of him at all, assumed he worked for the city government, a belief he fostered by living as outwardly boring a life as possible. He met his clients in public places and he brought neither friends nor lovers home.

His own mother hadn't known where he lived. This was fortunate since, during the trial, she'd cheerfully implicated everyone she knew in the hopes of clemency.

All things considered then, Ciro was astonished when he opened his door and saw an attractive woman in foreign clothes sitting in his favorite chair absently fondling his rosewood flute. Leaving the door open in the unlikely event she turned out to be a constable and he had to make a run for it, he took a step forward, smiled pleasantly and said, "Excuse me. Do I know you?"

Behind him, the door closed.

Heart pounding, he whirled around, yanked it open, and ran back into his rooms, ending up considerably closer to the woman in the chair before he could stop.

"I've come for the mirror," Magdelene told him.

His jaw dropped. "You . . . ? You're . . . ?"

"The most powerful wizard in the world," Magdelene finished when it seemed as though he wouldn't be able to get it out.

"But you're . . . I mean . . ." He swallowed and waved one hand between them for no good reason. "You, uh, you don't look like a wizard."

"Yeah, yeah, I know. No pointy hat, no robe, no staff." Magdelene sighed. "If I had a grain of sand for every time I've heard that, I'd have a beach. But we're not here to talk about me." She leaned forward. "Let's talk about the mirror."

"I don't have it."

"You've sold it *already*?"

"Not exactly." When her gray eyes narrowed, he felt compelled to add, "I was hired to steal it."

"For who?"

"My clients don't tell me their names."

"Oh, please."

Ciro supposed he might be reading a little too much into the way the wizard's hand closed around the shaft of his flute, but it sure looked uncomfortably like a warning to him. "All right, I know who he is. But I can't give you his name," he added hurriedly. "I took an oath."

"You also took my mirror."

"It was a blood oath."

"A blood oath?" Magdelene repeated. When he nodded, she sighed and massaged the bridge of her nose. The thief had turned out to be attractive, in an unprincipled sort of a way, with good teeth, broad shoulders, and lovely strong looking hands. *And* he played the flute. In a just world, she would have found him, retrieved her mirror, and suggested a way he could begin making amends. But he didn't have the mirror and a blood oath, unbreakable by death, or even Death, put a distinct crimp in her plans.

Then, suddenly, she had an idea. "Could I hire you to steal the mirror back?"

Ciro shook his head, a little surprised that he wanted the answer to be different. "I'd never be able to get it."

"You got it from me."

"Your pardon, Lady Wizard, but your door wasn't even locked. You relied too much on your reputation to protect you, forgetting that a reputation can also attract unwanted attention."

"Like yours?" Magdelene muttered.

He bowed. "Like mine."

In the silence that followed, Magdelene considered her options and found herself a little short. Magical artifacts were essentially null and void as far as wizardry was concerned, and she couldn't force the thief to tell her where it was. Tossing the flute onto the table, she stood. "Looks like I'll have to do this the hard way."

Suddenly drenched in sweat, Ciro took a step back. "Lady Wizard, I beg you . . ."

"Relax. I haven't time to deal with you right now." She paused, one hand on the door and half turned to

ce him. "But I know you, Ciro Rasvona." Her voice
ngered over his name, sending not entirely unpleas-
nt chills up and down his spine. "When this is over,
can always find you again."

A thief had no need for a conscience, but a remark-
bly well developed sense of self-preservation made a
andy substitute. "I could *show* you where the mirror
. Actually taking you there wasn't covered by the
ath," he explained when both her brows rose. As
ey slowly began to lower again, he smiled nervously.
I, uh, guess I should've mentioned that before."

Wondering what had happened to his policy of
ever taking risks he could avoid—*She'd been about
 leave, you yutz!*—Ciro led the way down the stairs
nd out onto the street, exchanging a silent bow with
 neighbor in front of the building. When that neigh-
or raised a scandalized middle-class brow at the sight
f his companion, he took her elbow and began hur-
ying her toward one of the hub streets, aware of eyes
atching from curtained windows.

"Did you really want to spend the rest of your life
s a cockroach?" Magdelene asked conversationally.

"Sorry." Praying he was imagining the tingle in his
ngers, he released her arm. "It's just that I've worked
ery hard at remaining unnoticeable and you're at-
racting attention."

A little surprised, Magdelene tossed her hair back
ff her face and turned to stare at him. "I'm not
oing anything."

Ciro sighed. "You don't have to."

"They're not used to seeing wizards around here?"
She was wearing an orange, calf-length skirt, red
eather sandals, and a purple, sleeveless vest held
losed with bright yellow frogging. "Yeah. That's it."

"I guess you should've considered the consequences
efore you stole my mirror."

"I took every precaution. You shouldn't have been
ble to track me."

"I didn't. You're dangling a Five Cities talisman
rom your left ear, so I came directly here."

Unable to stop himself, Ciro clutched at the earring. So much for that protective crystal he'd been carrying. "You had a spell on the house to capture my image."

"No. I had a lizard."

Both sides of the hub street were lined with shops, merchandise spilling out onto the cobblestones. Magdelene shook her head as she followed the thief through the glittering displays. "This is really unfair," she muttered. "First time I make it to one of the Five Cities, and I'm here on business."

Ciro deftly snagged an exotic bloom from a hanging basket, tossing the vender a copper coin in almost the same motion. "Perhaps when you've brought your business to a close," he said, presenting the flower with a flourish, "I can show you around."

"Are you sucking up?"

"Is it working?"

"Not yet."

"Should I keep trying?"

"Couldn't hurt." He really did have a very charming smile, Magdelene decided, tucking the blossom into her hair, and she'd never been very good at holding a grudge. "Is the mirror in the city?"

"I can't tell you that, Lady Wizard."

"Call me Magdelene." Titles implied a dignity she certainly wouldn't bother living up to. Stepping over a pile of mollusk shells, their pearly interiors gleaming in the sunlight, she rearranged the question. "Are we staying in the city?"

"Yes."

"Good. I might just find H'sak in ti . . ."

"It is Her!"

"Oh, nuts." Grabbing Ciro's arm, she ducked into the nearest shop.

"What's going on?"

"I'll explain later."

"How may I help you, Gracious Lady?"

Magdelene flashed the shopkeeper a somewhat preoccupied smile. "Does this place have a back door?"

"But of course," he nodded toward a beaded cur

ain nearly hidden behind bolts of brightly colored
abric. "And on your way through, perhaps I can in-
erest you in this lovely damask? Sale priced at only
wo dramils a measure. I offer a fine exchange rate
n coin not of the Five Cities, and I deliver."

The most powerful wizard in the world hesitated,
hen sighed and shook her head. "Unfortunately,
ve're in a bit of a hurry."

"Because of the demon?" Ciro asked in an under-
one as she pushed him through the curtain.

From outside the shop came an excited babble of
oices, growing louder.

"Yeah. Him, too."

"You appeared in the Hersota's shrine?" Ciro
apped his forehead twice with the first three fingers
f his right hand—just in case. "No wonder you
aused so much excitement. Her return has been
rophesied by three separate sects."

"I didn't know it was her shrine, did I? It was just
he only reference point I had in any of the Five
Cities." She peered around the corner, then led the
vay back onto the hub street some blocks from where
hey'd left it. "So what was the Hersota like?"

"According to her believers, she was a stern and
unforgiving demiurge who preached that hard work
nd chastity were the only ways to enlightenment."

Magdelene stared at him in astonishment. "And
hey want her to come back?"

"I never said that *I* was waiting for her."

He sounded so affronted that Magdelene chuckled
nd tucked her hand into the crook of his elbow.
There was muscle under the modest sleeve of his
cream-colored shirt she noted with approval, and
vhen he shot her a questioning glance, she answered
t with her second best smile.

Her fingers were warm even through the cloth, and
or a moment her smile drove the thought of unim-
portant bodily functions, like breathing, right out of
Ciro's mind. He'd felt safer while she'd been threaten-

ing him. "I, uh, stole your mirror," he said. It seemed important that she remember that.

Magdelene waved off the reminder. "Now you're helping me find it."

"I broke into your home."

"I should've locked the door."

Wondering if he might not be better off finding a member of the city guard and turning himself in, Ciro escorted the wizard out into the Hub and around the civic fountain. "We're here."

"This is the government building."

"That's right."

'The mirror's in there?"

"I can't tell you that."

"I guess it is, then."

The government had outgrown its building a number of times, adding larger and equally unattractive structures as needed. The result looked pretty much exactly like what it was, architecture by committee—or, more precisely, a series of committees.

Shaking her head, Magdelene released Ciro's arm. "This is the ugliest pile of rock I've ever seen," she told him, walking toward it. "And I saw Yamdazador before the desert sands engulfed it."

Around the Great Lake, time had downgraded that ancient city's sudden and inexplicable disappearance from legend to parental warning; *"I swear by all the gods, if you don't stop stuffing beans up your brother's nose, I'm sending you to Yamdazador."*

Running to catch up, Ciro gasped, *"You* were at Yamdazador?"

"I don't care what you heard, it wasn't my fault."

After a moment, he decided he didn't really want to know.

"So, now you're here, what's your plan?" he asked as they reached the stairs.

"My plan?" Pausing by the entrance a more practical administration had cut into the huge, brass double doors, Magdelene turned to face the thief. "I plan on getting my mirror back before H'sak is either purposefully or inadvertently released, and then I plan on making your client very, very sorry he ever hired you."

Ciro winced. "Good plan."

"I thought so. Let's get going."

It took a moment for the words to sink in, and when they did, he actually felt the blood drain from his face. It was an unpleasant feeling. "You want me to go with you."

"I might need your help."

"But I already told you, I won't be able to get near the mirror; it'll be too well guarded."

"You can't get near it on your own, but you don't know *what* you're capable of when you're with me." She winked and led the way inside.

While his mind was still busy trying to plan an escape route, his body happily followed. *Oh, sure,* he told it, as they crossed the atrium. *One lousy double entendre and you're willing to walk into the lion's den.* "Magdelene, this is a big place and I can't lead you any closer. If you can't scan for it, you'll never find the mirror."

"Of course I will. This is a government building, isn't it?" Slipping deftly between the constant stream of robed officials crossing and recrossing the atrium, Magdelene made her way to the desk at the center of all the activity. "Excuse me, could you please tell me if any of the senior officials has recently put him or herself incommunicado? Still in the building but not to be disturbed under any circumstances?"

The clerk glanced up from the continual flow of parchment, papyrus, and wax tablets crossing his desk, pale features twisted into an impatient scowl. "Who are you?"

"If you must know, I'm the most powerful wizard in the world."

He leaned out far enough out to get a good look at her. "I find that highly unlikely," he sniffed.

"Why would he just give you that information?" Ciro demanded as they hurried through the halls.

"Successful government employees survive by recognizing power and responding to it."

"You mean kissing up to it."

"If you like."

According to the clerk, Governor Andropof had spent the day conducting research in the old library and was so insistent on not being disturbed that he'd put guards on all the entrances. *"He was in there this morning when I got to work, and he hasn't been out since. Please stop melting my wax. His assistant took him lunch, cold fish cakes and steamed dulce, but I don't know if he ate it."*

Which was a little more information than Magdelene had required but, happily, it had segued into directions. *"Go through that door, second right, past roads and public works, up the stairs, go right again, it's at the end of the long hall, and I'd be very grateful, Lady Wizard, if you could return my export documents to a recognizable language."*

"Wait a minute! You can't go in there!"

About to follow Ciro into one of the older parts of the building, Magdelene turned to see a clerk, identical but for gender to the clerk in the atrium, hurrying toward them.

"Tourists," she forced the word through stiff lips, "are only permitted in the designated areas."

"I'm on my way to see the governor."

"Have you got an appointment?"

"Have you got a desire to have a demon eat your liver?" Her tone made it clear that this was not a rhetorical question.

"Another successful government employee?" Ciro asked as they trotted up the forbidden flight of stairs.

Magdelene nodded. "I'm quite impressed by the state of your civil service, no wonder Talzabad-har runs so smoothly. I *am* a little disappointed in the governor, though."

"You're disappointed in the governor? Why?"

"Why? He hired a thief, and he's planning to use a demon for political gain."

Ciro turned to stare at her in amazement, tripped
over the top step, and would've fallen had she not
caught him. "Magdelene, he's a politician!"

"And?"

"You don't get out much, do you? This is normal
behavior for a politician. In fact," he added as she set
him back on his feet, "by Five Cities standards, he's
a bit of an underachiever."

"I've never understood this obsessive power-seeking
thing," Magdelene mused as they turned the last corner and started down a long, narrow hall, barely lit
by tiny windows up under the ceiling.

"That's because you've got as much of it as you
could ever want." Ciro waved toward the pair of city
guards standing shoulder to shoulder in front of a
square, iron bound door. "This looks like the place.
What are we going to do about them?"

"Not a problem."

"I was hoping you'd say that." Thankful that the
light was so bad, the thief kept his head down as they
approached. The last thing he needed was some bright
boy in the guards remembering his face. He needn't
have worried, they were both watching Magdelene.

"Hi. Is this where the Governor is?"

"Yes, ma'am," said the taller of the two.

"But we can't let you go in," added his companion.

She smiled sympathetically up at them. "It sure
must be boring guarding this old door. You look like
you could use a nap."

There's just something about men in uniform. Attempting to put her finger on just what that something
was, she watched the two topple over in a tangle of
tanned, muscular legs and short uniform kilts. *Oh,
yeah, now I remember. . . .*

The door wasn't warded, but it was locked. Blowing
it off its hinges in a blast of eldritch fire, announcing
her presence, as it were, with authority, had its merits,
but she didn't want to startle the governor into doing
something he'd regret. He'd only regret it for about
fifteen or twenty seconds depending on which end
H'sak started with, but since she'd then be the one

who had to deal with the demon there'd probably be less trauma all around if she merely . . .

"Magdelene?" Ciro straightened, slipped his lock pick back into the seam of his trousers, and pulled the door open a finger's width. "We can go in now."

The door opened onto a second floor balcony about eight feet long by six feet wide in one end of a large rectangular room. To both the left and the right curved stairs led down to the floor. The library shelves had been emptied of books, and any lingering odors of paper and dust had surrendered to the swirling clouds of smoke that rose from a dozen incense burners. Motioning for Ciro to be quiet, Magdelene crept forward, peered over the balcony railing, and stiffened.

In the center of the floor was a multicolored pentagram. In the center of the pentagram, suspended horizontally some four feet above ground was an unconscious, seven-foot-tall, green-scaled demon. Standing beside the demon, was a short, slight, balding man wearing what were traditionally thought of as wizard's robes.

As Magdelene's jaw dropped, he raised his arms into the air with a flourish worthy of a stage magician. In his right hand he held a dagger and in his left, an ebony bowl. Something green and moist coated the edge of the dagger blade.

"Oh, shit!"

Governor Andropof's head jerked up and around toward the balcony. "Whoever you are, you're too late!" Laughing maniacally, he bent to hold the bowl under the demon's throat, then vanished.

The chime of the dagger hitting the floor hadn't quite faded when Magdelene reached the edge of the pentagram, Ciro, fighting every instinct, close behind her.

"Where's the governor?" he panted.

"The middle of the Great Lake."

"What's he doing there?"

"Probably treading water." Circling the pentagram, Magdelene frowned down at the design.

"Why would he send himself . . . ?"

"He didn't. I did. In another minute he'd have completed the sacrifice, and we don't want that."

"We don't?"

"Trust me." Inspecting the last of the five points, she nodded in satisfaction and stepped over to H'sak's side.

"Magdelene!" Ciro spun around searching, unsuccessfully, for something to hide behind.

"Relax. This is an exact copy of one of the great pentagrams from *The Booke of Demonkind*." She had to admit that the governor had done impressive research for, as far as Magdelene knew, there were only two copies of that book still in existence, and she had one of them—it had been rather drastically overdue when the library'd burned down, so she'd kept it. "Unfortunately, the author had a tendency to choose art over craft, and all of her illustrations are completely inaccurate—but then what else can you expect from someone who spells book with an 'e'?"

"Well if the pentagram isn't holding the demon, what is?" He couldn't prevent his voice from rising rather dramatically on the last word although, when he noticed he was doing it, he did manage to stop wringing his hands.

"This."

This, was a glowing length of delicate silver chain.

"That's the Blazing Chain of Halla Hunta," the wizard explained as Ciro cautiously approached, drawn by the glint of a precious metal.

"Halla who?"

"Ancient warrior; nice buns, no manners. He had the chain forged, link by link, in volcanic fire, specifically to hold demons. It's why I didn't realize H'sak was out of the mirror; the chain's working the same way."

"Is it holding him up as well?" Ciro wondered, leaning closer.

"No. There's a Lombardi Floating Disk under his head and another under his feet, and I'd love to know how Governor Andropof's got a pair away from Vince. You didn't . . . ?"

"No."

"Then it looks like you weren't the only thief he employed." Her eyes narrowed as she bent and scooped the dagger off the floor. "This is the Fell Dagger of Connackron, also called Demonsbane. And this . . ." With her free hand, she removed a cross section of bone from a hollow between the short horns extending out of the demon's forehead. ". . . is a piece of the thighbone of Mighty Manderkew. You haven't seen the sacrificial bowl from the destroyed Temple of the Darkest Night, have you?"

"It's under . . ." Ciro waved a hand more or less up and down the length of H'sak's body. ". . . him."

"Could you get it?"

Common sense suggested he point-blank refuse to crawl under an unconscious demon confined by no more than two ounces of silver chain and held off the floor in the center of an inoperative pentagram by artifacts he couldn't see. Unfortunately, common sense got overruled by a desire not to look like a wuss in front of an attractive woman. It didn't help that green slime had dripped all over the floor from a wound in the demon's throat.

When he emerged, bowl clasped between sweaty hands, Magdelene took a quick look inside it, sighed with relief, and shook her head. "I don't know whether to be impressed or appalled. Governor Andropof must've been gathering this crap for years."

"Not quite." Recognition steadying his nerves, Ciro managed a matter-of-fact tone. "I stole this last summer from an inn in the Fourth City. They were using it as a serving bowl."

"They have much business?"

"Actually, no."

"Can't say as I'm surprised."

"Was the governor a wizard then?"

"No. Just a cheap opportunist. The power's intrinsic to the artifacts. Demon blood shed with this knife into that bowl will open the way for one of the Demon Princes to leave the Netherhells. Once he gets here, the piece of thighbone's a promissory note."

Mouth suddenly dry, Ciro stared into the bowl.

"Relax, I stopped him in time and H'sak's almost healed." Magdelene rapped the demon almost fondly on the chest with the knuckles of the hand holding the bone. "Of course, after the note's redeemed, there'd be a Demon Prince loose in the world."

"He wouldn't just go home?"

"Not likely; demons gain rank through slaughter."

"I didn't know that," he said, wishing he'd never had the opportunity to find out. "Now what?"

"Now, I think you'd better hold these for me." She held out the dagger and the bone. "H'sak seems to be waking up."

"I thought the chain was holding him?"

"It is. But he was unconscious because he'd had his throat slit." A waggle of the dagger she was still holding out toward him, directed Ciro's attention to the demon blood staining the blade. "It takes a lot to kill the demonkind and unsuccessful attempts make them cranky. Now, if you don't mind, I may need both hands free."

On cue, H'sak's lips drew back off his teeth. A shudder ran the length of his body like a small wave.

"Both hands free," Ciro repeated. "Good idea." Sacrificial bowl from the destroyed Temple of the Darkest Night in his left hand, the Fell Dagger of Connackron and the thighbone of Mighty Manderkew in his right, he backed out of the pentagram and continued moving back until his shoulder blades hit the wall.

Magdelene glanced up at the impact. "What are you doing all the way over there?"

"I'm a thief," Ciro reminded her. "I'm not good at confrontation."

"Whatever. Just hang onto that stuff until I get time to destroy it."

"Couldn't you just, you know, poof? Like the governor?"

"The governor wasn't a magical artifact. Wizardry doesn't affect them, it's why I had to come after the mirror myself."

"Then how?"

"I was thinking of using a hammer. Now, if you don't mind . . ." She turned her attention back to the demon.

Ciro watched the eight-inch claws flexing at the end of arms that no longer looked quite so limp and decided that being able to raise even one hand in his own defense was better than nothing at all. He dropped the bone and the dagger into the bowl.

A barely viscous drop of demon blood rolled off the blade.

H'sak jerked. His eyes blazed red. "The way is open!"

In the silence that followed, Ciro was pretty sure he heard his heart stop beating.

"You know," Magdelene told him, "I *had* pretty much decided that bringing me here and opening the door made up for stealing my mirror."

The demon turned toward her. "You!"

"Who else?"

"There was a man . . . Oh, wait," he snorted, "if there was a man, I should've expected you to show up."

"You're in no position to make smart-ass comments. A Prince approaches, compelled to answer a summons from the mortal world, and your blood was the instrument of his summoning. He's going to be royally pissed."

H'sak struggled impotently within the chain. "Your death will follow mine, Wizard," he growled. "And I will die happy knowing you are about to be torn limb from limb!"

"Suppose neither of us has to die?"

Ciro, who'd been watching a speck of darkness grow to the size of a dinner plate, cleared his throat as a cold wind began to blow from the center of it. "Uh, Magdelene, you'd better hurry."

"H'sak?"

"You're the most powerful wizard in the world," he sniffed, "you close the way."

"I can't close the way against the Prince's power."

"So?"

"So this is no time to sulk about being stuck in that mirror!"

The demon's lips drew back, exposing a double row of fangs. "I've been forced to endure your singing for almost two hundred years. *I* think this is a fine time to sulk."

"Suit yourself. Ciro, find the mirror, it has to be in the library." She smiled down at the demon as the thief began to search. "I'm thinking of studying opera."

H'sak cringed. "You win. What's the plan?"

"I release you from the chain so I can use it on his Highness, and you don't attack me from behind until I've finished with him."

"And what if he finishes you?"

"Then at least you're facing him on your feet."

"Deal."

Grasping one end of the chain, Magdelene began to unwind it.

With one eye on the circle of darkness, now the size of a wagon wheel, Ciro sidled toward the pentagram. "I found the mirror," he muttered, lips close to Magdelene's ear. "It's in pieces."

She leaned closer. "Don't tell H'sak."

"Hadn't planned on it." He took a deep breath and lightly gripped her shoulders. "Magdelene, in case I don't get a chance to say this later, I'm sorry I took your mirror. I'm sorry about putting the bloody dagger in the bowl."

He looked so miserable she couldn't stay angry. Her expression softened. "I'd better send you away."

"Like the governor?"

"Only drier."

"No." The rising wind from the dark gate whipped her hair into her face. He caught a strand and tucked it gently behind her ear. "I'm responsible for this, it's only fair I stay."

Eyes half lidded, Magdelene sighed. "I only regret that . . ."

"Wizard! You haven't got time!" H'sak kicked his

feet, jerking the chain still in Magdelene's hand. "And
don't raise those eyebrows at me! You *know* what you
haven't got time for! After two hundred years," he
muttered as she took a quick look at the nearly open
gate and began to frantically unwind the chain, "you'd
think that the novelty would've worn off."

Free, the demon rolled off the Lombardi Disks as
the darkness fully dilated. Hooking his claws in the
back of Ciro's shirt, he yanked the thief to the far side
of the room and dropped him. "The man is out of the
way," he hissed as a pale figure began to take shape
in the gateway. "You'll only get one chance. Don't
screw it up."

In answer, Magdelene leaned into the wind, and
snapped the chain out to its full length. Wrapped
around H'sak, the links had only gleamed but now,
they blazed. She waited, eyes locked on the materializ-
ing Prince, noting the full thick fall of golden hair,
the broad shoulders, the rippled stomach, the slender
waist, the . . .

"What are you doing?" H'sak shrieked. "Waiting
to see the whites of his eyes?"

"Not quite," Magdelene murmured and flicked the
chain forward.

The Prince howled with laughter as the delicate
links traced a spiral around him from neck to knees.
"Foolish little wizard, you cannot hold . . ." His eyes
widened, showing only onyx from lid to lid. "This is
impossible! This toy is intended to contain the lesser
demons!" He writhed in place. "I am a prince!"

Trying very hard not to be distracted by the writhing, Magdelene held out her arms at shoulder height
and brought her palms together. The gate began to
close.

He stopped struggling. The perfect lines of his face
smoothed out as he began to concentrate. The light
of the chain began to dim. "You think you have power
enough to keep me from this world?" he sneered as
link after link went dark. "You think you can defeat
m . . ."

The gate closed.

"Apparently," Magdelene said, twitching her skirt back into place.

Remembering how to use his legs, Ciro leaped to his feet and started forward. "Magdelene, you were magnificen . . ."

Magdelene turned, knowing exactly what she'd see.

"Now, we make a new bargain," H'sak announced, claws forming a cage around Ciro's head, their tips just barely into the skin of his throat.

Magdelene sighed. "You may find this hard to believe, H'sak, but I'm going to miss you."

The demon frowned. "I have the man."

Folding her arms over the purple vest, she tapped one red leather sandal against the floor.

H'sak withdrew his claws one at a time. Slowly. So that it didn't look as if he were making any sudden moves.

"Thank you."

Ciro's heels thumped back onto the floor, and he swayed in the rush of air that filled the space where the demon had been. "Where did you send him?"

"The Netherhells." She pursed her lips sympathetically at the collar of shallow punctures. "I'd have done it years ago but I didn't know the way."

"And now you do?" He glanced over to where the gate had been.

"Now I do."

Ciro managed a shaky smile. "That ought to terrify them."

"I don't see why it should," Magdelene protested. "If they don't bother me, I won't bother them. Shall we gather up the bits and pieces and get out of here?"

The guards were still asleep outside the library door. Magdelene woke them, helped them up onto their feet, and made a suggestion Ciro was rather glad he hadn't heard given the reaction of two strong men.

No one tried to stop them from leaving the building. No one paid them any attention at all until they were past the civic fountain.

"My eyes see Her!"

"Hard work and chastity," sighed the most powerful

wizard in the world. "I don't think so." She squeezed Ciro's hand, and disappeared.

A heartbroken wail went up from the crowd. A weeping woman grabbed the thief's arm. "You were with Her! Tell us, tell us, will She return?"

Gently, but firmly, he disentangled himself. And then he smiled. "You can bet on it."

It took her a week to notice.

Ciro winced at the crack of displaced air and hoped the neighbors weren't home. This was exactly the sort of thing to get a normally quiet man an undeserved reputation. "Good afternoon, Magdelene."

"Don't good afternoon me, Ciro Rasvona, you little shit! You stole the gold hieroglyph of my name!"

He got slowly to his feet and held out his hand, the small gold plaque lying across his palm. "What," he asked, "can I possibly do to make amends?"

Cut off in mid rant, Magdelene looked down at the plaque, up at the thief, and the corners of her mouth turned up into her best smile. "I'll think of something," she promised, stepping forward. "That had better be a lock pick in your trousers, 'cause you don't seem very happy to see me . . . oh, wait a minute . . . my mistake."

"I also took that big blue pearl," he murmured when he could catch his breath.

"And the crystal gryphon?"

"No, but I'm willing to go back for it. . . ."

OF TIDES AND TIME

❖❖❖

by Dennis L. McKiernan

Dennis McKiernan is the best-selling fantasy author of *The Dragonstone, The Voyage of the Fox Rider, Eye of the Hunter,* and *Caverns of Socrates.* His latest novel, *Into the Forge,* was published in September 1997. His short fantasy fiction has been collected in *Tales of Mithgar,* with other fiction of his appearing in *Weird Tales from Shakespeare* and *Dragon Fantastic.*

> *Naxianpheria is a demon with a difference;*
> *I suggest you not call out her name.*

Among demonkind, Naxianpheria was somewhat of an anomaly. Oh, not that demons themselves aren't anomalous creatures, deviating as they do from the normal or common order, form, or rule, for no two demons are alike—some being hideous, others comely, some large, others small, some amorphous, others sharply defined, some red, others green . . . they come in all colors, shapes, sizes, forms, and whatever else one can name. It's as if they deliberately go out of their way to be individuals unlike one another. And there are great demons, greater demons, lesser demons, least demons, insignificant demons, demons existing through any range of power one cares to conceive, and some entirely beyond conception—at each end of the scale. Ah, but, Naxianpheria was not only an anomaly because of being one of demonkind, she was also an anomaly because she was interested in studying things, finding out things, seeing how things work, discovering the secrets of nature and of time and space and all of creation. Being magical creatures, the other demons scratched their heads—metaphorically speaking, of course, for many had no heads, nor anything even resembling one—in deep puzzlement, for they knew of no use she could put such knowledge to that magic couldn't accomplish better. Why, any demon, or wizard for that matter, would tell anyone that everything practical that could be discovered along those nonmagical lines had already been discovered, and the cogs and wheels and levers and knobs and such that had been in use for centuries, millennia, and more, were quite adequate. *If it was good enough for our fathers, then it's good enough for us,* was a well-known truism throughout many of the Argalian realities. Oh, yes, some nonmagical things were worth studying, some nonmagical areas of progress were quite good, in fact: refinements of gears and such, that was clearly acceptable; but pure study only for study's sake, where it had no application to magic, well, that was something beyond the realm of understanding. As to Naxianpheria, certainly since she was a greater demon, she could simply draw upon the power of the realities to magically accomplish whatever she desired—within greater demon limits, that is. But she did not take this straightforward way, for she was strange: She wanted to *know.* And so she studied, and at times experimented, and discovered many things. . . .

The summons came for Naxianpheria just as she was about to enscribe a strange new rune upon the sheet of adamantium, a *mathematicus* rune, one that she would use to describe the uniting of infinitesimally small parts into a whole—the concretion of elements of virtual zero into something finite. This symbol, along with the other symbols of *mathematica* she had devised, when used in the ciphering processes she had formulated would allow the precise calculation of areas, volumes, forces, masses, velocities, distances, and who knows what else? And just as she was about to set this new rune onto a fresh page in her virtually indestructible manuscript, *that* was the moment the summons came.

She didn't even have time to bellow in fury or to fight against the spell, to try to resist and break the casting, so powerful was this summons. And she found herself in a candlelit pentagram in a circular stone chamber atop a stone tower, and she faced a young man in robes. —Nay! Not a young man, not by millennia, but a mage ancient and wise and of immense power, and of eternal youth.

He can be naught but a cursed Mastermage, and he knows my true name.

"RRRAAAAWWW!" she bellowed in fury and dashed her considerable bulk against the bounds of the pentagram, trying to break through. But the pentagram easily held; the mage who had cast it was perhaps as powerful as she . . . perhaps even of more power, for pentagrams are notoriously weak when it comes to holding greater demons, and this one most certainly held.

The ancient young mage sighed wearily, as if bored by her display of rage, and he shook his head and *tsktsked,* then said, "Naxianpheria, be silent. I *command* it!"

Wrath filled Naxianpheria's yellow eyes, yet she could do naught but obey.

"I have a task for you, Naxianpheria."

Naxianpheria did not respond but waited in silence, for so she had been commanded, but her baneful stare did not leave his face.

"I have a powerful enemy—" he gestured vaguely to the east "—one I cannot defeat, yet one who cannot defeat me. Many times we have battled, to no final resolution. I am weary of his interference in my affairs, and I would be rid of him. Yet I do not believe even you can defeat him. Instead, I have a different plan, one which requires the peculiar talents of a greater demon.

"You see, I understand that you have the power to, um, 'step' elsewhere. Is this true? You may speak."

Naxianpheria merely looked at the wizard.

"Come, come," said the mage. "I am not prying secrets from you. This thing about the demonstep, I already know."

"Then why ask?" said Naxianpheria.

"Oh, I don't know. Perhaps to enlist you as a willing ally, rather than a compelled thrall."

"Ha!" snorted Naxianpheria. "You rip me from my caldera and expect me to be a willing ally? Not likely, mage."

"Oh, well," the wizard shrugged. "It was a thought."

"Not much of one," growled Naxianpheria. Then she shifted within the pentagram. "Get on with it, mage. What task have you for me?"

"Just this: Since neither you nor I have a significant chance of slaying my enemy, I would have you seize him and, before he can counter, step through time and space and leave him in a place from which he cannot escape. You must remember, though, he is extremely powerful and ordinary prisons cannot hold him. No, this must be a place of great magic, greater than either you or I."

Naxianpheria slowly shook her head. "And you expect me to know of such a place?"

"Or to discover it," replied the wizard.

Naxianpheria sat down in the pentagram and cogitated. Finally she said, "I am anxious to get back to my studies, and it occurs to me that there may be such a prison as you describe."

The mage's eyes lit up. "Truly? Where?"

"Ha! If I told you, you would entrap him yourself, and I would yet be obligated to perform a task for you. No, wizard, you will not snare me that way. Instead, first charge me with the task, and I will then tell you."

"Oh, very well. Hear me and swear to my oath and the conditions therein: I charge you with the task of transporting my enemy to this inescapable prison you speak of, yet I would also have you show it to me so that I may judge for myself; if I truly deem it not suitable, then you yet owe me a task. But heed! You will do me no harm, nor shall you harm me afterward, nor shall you leave me in that prison; you will return here with me whenever I say or within a candlemark from now, whichever comes first."

Grumbling, Naxianpheria so swore.

"Before I release you, Naxianpheria, tell me: Is this a small prison?"

"Indeed," replied Naxianpheria.

"Good," declared the mage. "The smaller the better. I would not want him to be too comfortable."

"Oh, no," said Naxianpheria. "It is not comfortable in the least. Now release me."

"One more question, demon: Where is this prison?"

Naxianpheria pointed out one of the tower windows. "Yon. Between the stars."

"Ah, then, I will need air," said the mage, and laughed when Naxianpheria hissed in disappointment. With a simple gesture the mage cast an envelopement spell, and air gathered 'round him. At last with his foot he erased a small section of the pentagram and Naxianpheria was free.

Naxianpheria took him up in her arms and sighted on a section of space. "Are you ready?" she asked.

"Indeed," replied the mage, comfortably ensconced in his envelope of air. "Let me see this prison of yours. Take me as close as you can without actually entering."

Naxianpheria grinned widely, and she hooded her yellow gaze with her iridescent violet eyelids, and she stepped deep into outer space to the edge of a small black hole, to the very radius where entrapped light could not escape the singularity hidden within the sphere of blackness. And the wizard did not even have time to scream as the colossal tidal forces across the gravitational gradient of the mass-distorted space surrounding the black hole sucked him inward as if he were some infinitely elastic thing, stretching him into an ever-elongating, hurtling string of individual molecules sucked down like a thinning strand of mist into the blackness below. And Naxianpheria watched with her demonvision as these molecules flashed down the

gravity well of the singularity and were themselves
rent and rent again. She waited a moment, then sped
after, down and down into distorted space while gathering up the individual quarks and leptons of the sundered wizard and holding them in her grasp. That
Naxianpheria herself was not ripped apart was wholly
due to the fact that she was a greater demon, and of
course, as everyone knows, greater demons are im-
mune to such things. When she had collected all of
the fundamental particles of the disintegrated mage,
she quantum-stepped out from the black hole and
back into normal space, though hundreds of millions
of years had passed, relativitywise. She shifted backward in time and returned to the mage's tower, noting
that she was well within the interval of a candlemark,
even though the mage's death had released her from
the oath she had sworn.

She reconstituted the body of the wizard from his
billions of free-form particles—from the muons, elec-
trons, neutrinos, taus, ups, downs, charms, stranges,
bottoms, and the curiously heavy tops—and then bearing the wizard's reconstructed corpse, Naxianpheria
stepped to Ruxula, into the mists of the greater moon,
and she buried him alongside the other Mastermages
she had just as faithfully served.

When he was interred she stood and counted the
total of the graves—nine in all, which meant that now
there were but three of these science-ignorant *fools*
left who yet knew her true name.

As always, she hoped to serve them soon.

A feline lovers' fantasy come true . . .

CATFANTASTIC

☐ **CATFANTASTIC**   UE2355—$5.99
☐ **CATFANTASTIC II**   UE2461—$5.99
☐ **CATFANTASTIC III**   UE2591—$4.99
☐ **CATFANTASTIC IV**   UE2711—$5.99
   edited by Andre Norton and Martin H. Greenberg

Unique collections of fantastical cat tales, some set in the distant future
on as yet unknown worlds, some set in our own world but not quite
our dimension, some recounting what happens when beings from the
ancient past and creatures out of myth collide with modern-day felines.

☐ **OUTWORLD CATS**   UE2596—$4.99
   by Jack Lovejoy

When agents of industrial mogul Benton Ingles seize a goverment
space station, the two cats aboard are captured and brought to Earth.
But these are not Earth cats—they are fully sentient telepaths from
another planet. And these cats might just prove to be the only hope
for saving Earth from enslavement to one man's greed.

☐ **TAILCHASER'S SONG**   UE2374—$5.99
   by Tad Williams

This best-selling feline fantasy epic tells the adventures of Fritti Tailchaser, a young ginger cat who sets out, with boundless enthusiasm,
on a dangerous quest which leads him into the underground realm of
an evil cat-god—a nightmare world from which only his own resources
can deliver him.

Buy them at your local bookstore or use this convenient coupon for ordering.

PENGUIN USA P.O. Box 999—Dep. #17109, Bergenfield, New Jersey 07621

Please send me the DAW BOOKS I have checked above, for which I am enclosing
$_____ (please add $2.00 to cover postage and handling). Send check or money
order (no cash or C.O.D.'s) or charge by Mastercard or VISA (with a $15.00 minimum). Prices and
numbers are subject to change without notice.

Card #_____ Exp. Date _____
Signature_____
Name_____
Address_____
City _____ State _____ Zip Code _____

For faster service when ordering by credit card call **1-800-253-6476**

Allow a minimum of 4-6 weeks for delivery. This offer is subject to change without notice.

Science Fiction Anthologies

☐ **FIRST CONTACT**
Martin H. Greenberg and Larry Segriff, editors
UE2757—$5.99

In the tradition of the hit television show "The X-Files" comes a fascinating collection of original stories by some of the premier writers of the genre, such as Jody Lynn Nye, Kristine Kathryn Rusch, and Jack Haldeman.

☐ **RETURN OF THE DINOSAURS**
Mike Resnick and Martin H. Greenberg, editors
UE2753—$5.99

Dinosaurs walk the Earth once again in these all-new tales that dig deep into the past and blaze trails into the possible future. Join Gene Wolfe, Melanie Rawn, David Gerrold, Mike Resnick, and others as they breathe new life into ancient bones.

☐ **BLACK MIST: and Other Japanese Futures**
Orson Scott Card and Keith Ferrell, editors
UE2767—$5.99

Original novellas by Richard Lupoff, Patric Helmaan, Pat Cadigan, Paul Levinson, and Janeen Webb & Jack Dann envision how the wide-ranging influence of Japanese culture will change the world.

Buy them at your local bookstore or use this convenient coupon for ordering.

PENGUIN USA   P.O. Box 999—Dep. #17109, Bergenfield, New Jersey 07621

Please send me the DAW BOOKS I have checked above, for which I am enclosing $_____ (please add $2.00 to cover postage and handling). Send check or money order (no cash or C.O.D.'s) or charge by Mastercard or VISA (with a $15.00 minimum). Prices and numbers are subject to change without notice.

Card #_____ Exp. Date _____
Signature_____
Name_____
Address_____
City _____ State _____ Zip Code _____

For faster service when ordering by credit card call **1-800-253-6476**

Allow a minimum of 4-6 weeks for delivery. This offer is subject to change without notice.

Don't Miss These Exciting DAW Anthologies

SWORD AND SORCERESS
Marion Zimmer Bradley, editor
☐ Book XV   UE2741—$5.99

OTHER ORIGINAL ANTHOLOGIES
Mercedes Lackey, editor
☐ SWORD OF ICE: And Other Tales of Valdemar   UE2720—$5.99

Jennifer Roberson, editor
☐ HIGHWAYMEN: Robbers and Rouges   UE2732—$5.99

Martin H. Greenberg, editor
☐ ELF MAGIC   UE2761—$5.99
☐ ELF FANTASTIC   UE2736—$5.99
☐ WIZARD FANTASTIC   UE2756—$5.50
☐ WHITE HOUSE HORRORS   UE2659—$5.99

Martin H. Greenberg & Lawrence Schimel, editors
☐ TAROT FANTASTIC   UE2729—$5.99
☐ THE FORTUNE TELLER   UE2748—$5.99

Mike Resnick & Martin Greenberg, editors
☐ RETURN OF THE DINOSAURS   UE2753—$5.99
☐ SHERLOCK HOLMES IN ORBIT   UE2636—$5.50

Richard Gilliam & Martin H. Greenberg, editors
☐ PHANTOMS OF THE NIGHT   UE2696—$5.99

Norman Partridge & Martin H. Greenberg, editors
☐ IT CAME FROM THE DRIVE-IN   UE2680—$5.50

Buy them at your local bookstore or use this convenient coupon for ordering.

PENGUIN USA P.O. Box 999—Dep. #17109, Bergenfield, New Jersey 07621

Please send me the DAW BOOKS I have checked above, for which I am enclosing
$_____ (please add $2.00 to cover postage and handling). Send check or money
order (no cash or C.O.D.'s) or charge by Mastercard or VISA (with a $15.00 minimum). Prices and
numbers are subject to change without notice.

Card #_____ Exp. Date _____
Signature_____
Name_____
Address_____
City _____ State _____ Zip Code _____

For faster service when ordering by credit card call **1-800-253-6476**

Allow a minimum of 4-6 weeks for delivery. This offer is subject to change without notice.

FANTASY ANTHOLOGIES

☐ **HIGHWAYMEN**   UE2732—$5.99
   Jennifer Roberson, editor

Fantastic all-original tales of swashbucklers and scoundrels inspired by Alfred Noyes's famous poem.

☐ **ZODIAC FANTASTIC**   UE2751—$5.99
   Martin H. Greenberg, and A.R. Morlan, editors

Find your own future in these compelling stories from Mickey Zucker Reichert, Jody Lynn Nye, Mike Resnick, and Kate Elliott.

☐ **ELF FANTASTIC**   UE2736—$5.99
   Martin H. Greenberg, editor

Stories to lead the reader into the fairy hills, to emerge into a world far different from the one left behind.

☐ **ELF MAGIC**   UE2761—$5.99
   Martin H. Greenberg, editor

Fantasy's most beloved beings, in stories by Rosemary Edghill, Jane Yolen, Esther Friesner, and Michelle West.

☐ **WIZARD FANTASTIC**   UE2756—$5.99
   Martin H. Greenberg, editor

This all-original volume offers wizards to suit your every fancy, from sorcerers to geomancers to witch doctors to shamans.

☐ **THE FORTUNE TELLER**   UE2605—$4.99
   Lawrence Schimel & Martin H. Greenberg, editors

All-original tales of the mystical and malicious from authors such as Tanya Huff, Brian Stableford, Peter Crowther, and Neil Gaiman.

Buy them at your local bookstore or use this convenient coupon for ordering.

PENGUIN USA P.O. Box 999—Dep. #17109, Bergenfield, New Jersey 07621

Please send me the DAW BOOKS I have checked above, for which I am enclosing
$_____ (please add $2.00 to cover postage and handling). Send check or money order (no cash or C.O.D.'s) or charge by Mastercard or VISA (with a $15.00 minimum). Prices and numbers are subject to change without notice.

Card #_____ Exp. Date _____

Signature_____

Name_____

Address_____

City _____ State _____ Zip Code _____

For faster service when ordering by credit card call **1-800-253-6476**

Allow a minimum of 4-6 weeks for delivery. This offer is subject to change without notice.